ELIZABETH ROLLS

DEBORAH HALE

DIANE GASTON

Award-winning author **Elizabeth Rolls** lives in the Adelaide hills of South Australia in an old stone farmhouse surrounded by apple, pear and cherry orchards, with her husband, two smallish sons, three dogs and two cats. She also has four alpacas and three incredibly fat sheep, all gainfully employed as environmentally sustainable lawn mowers. The kids are convinced that writing is a perfectly normal profession, and she's working on her husband. Elizabeth has what most people would consider far too many books, and her tea and coffee habit is legendary. She enjoys reading, walking, cooking and her husband's gardening. You can contact Elizabeth at her e-mail address, elizabethrolls@alphalink.com.au.

After a decade of tracing her ancestors to their roots in Georgian England, **Deborah Hale** turned to historical romance writing as a way to blend her love of the past with her desire to spin a good love story. Deborah lives in Nova Scotia, Canada, with her four children, and calls writing her "sanity retention mechanism." On good days, she likes to think it's working. Deborah can be reached at www.deborahhale.com.

As a psychiatric social worker, **Diane Gaston** spent years helping others create real-life happy endings. Now Diane crafts fictional ones, writing the kind of historical romance she's always loved to read. The youngest of three daughters of a US Army colonel, Diane moved frequently during her childhood, even living for a year in Japan. It continues to amaze her that her own son and daughter grew up in one house in northern Virginia. Diane still lives in that house, with her husband and three very ordinary house cats. She loves to hear from readers at www.dianegaston.com.

A Regency CHRISTMAS

ELIZABETH ROLLS
DEBORAH HALE & DIANE GASTON

*M&B™ and M&B™ with the Rose Device
are trademarks of the publisher.
Harlequin Mills & Boon Limited, Eton House,
18-24 Paradise Road, Richmond, Surrey TW9 1SR*

A REGENCY CHRISTMAS © by Harlequin Books S.A. 2006
(This anthology was originally published
as *Mistletoe Kisses* in the USA.)

A Soldier's Tale © Elizabeth Rolls 2006
A Winter Night's Tale © Deborah M. Hale 2006
A Twelfth Night Tale © Diane Perkins 2006

ISBN: 978 0 263 86574 5

25-1007

*Harlequin Mills & Boon policy is to use papers that are
natural, renewable and recyclable products and made from
wood grown in sustainable forests. The logging and
manufacturing processes conform to the legal environmental
regulations of the country of origin.*

*Printed and bound in Spain
by Litografia Rosés S.A., Barcelona*

CONTENTS

A SOLDIER'S TALE

Elizabeth Rolls

Author Note

Christmas is very special, but it can be stressful when families get together. So often our nearest and dearest have bizarre ideas about how to celebrate! And often we're thinking about those we have lost. Dominic and Pippa find this in *A Soldier's Tale*.

Between shopping, cooking and end-of-year parties, it's hard to remember what we're celebrating. Why holly? Why candles? And why, if anyone still has one, a kissing bough?

For two weeks before Christmas, the houses in our nearest town are decked with lights and people come for miles. Each night the church in the main street performs a Nativity play with music and sheep, cattle and a donkey. Even a camel. There in the main street a centuries-old tradition reminds us what Christmas really means and what the greenery, candles and kissing bough symbolise: life, light and love.

I hope you enjoy Dominic and Pippa's story and that your Christmas is as joyous as theirs.

Chapter One

Miss Philippa Wintercombe sat reading in a corner of the drawing room of Alderley Hall, while her aunt, Lady Alderley, passed cups of tea to her houseguests.

'We must settle on a play!' said Miss Lancelyn-Greene with what was doubtless intended to be a fetching pout. 'Christmas is less than a week away, Lady Alderley. There must be something planned for Twelfth Night! Otherwise the gentlemen will simply play billiards all day, and sit for ever over their port and brandy after dinner.'

She cast an affronted glance at Lord Bellingham, who, deprived of masculine drinking companions, was reduced to snoring on the sofa, a neglected brandy on the wine table beside him.

'Very true, my dear,' agreed Lady Alderley, delicately *not* looking at her somnolent brother-in-law as she poured a cup of tea and passed it to Mrs Lancelyn-Greene. 'And that would never do. 'Tis inconvenient enough that Dominic is not come home yet, but to have him spending all his time in the billiard room would be very bad indeed. I am not quite sure why he has chosen to remain away so long, but it is time and more that he was home.'

Her sister, Lady Bellingham, was heard to mutter something about irresponsible young men.

'Does he know that I am here?' asked Miss Lancelyn-Greene, patting a golden curl into place.

Philippa pulled her shawl more closely about her against the sort of draught inevitable in a building built four hundred years earlier to keep out people rather than cold air, and told herself yet again that her cousin Dominic's marriage plans were no bread and butter of hers.

'I was most careful to make sure he knew that you and your mama were being kind enough to bear me company,' Lady Alderley assured Hermione.

Hermione's pout became a trifle sulky. 'Oh, I dare say he is still in a miff because I said he should not go back to war last spring. As if the war could not be won without him! If only he had admitted that he was being foolish, all would have been well.'

'Indeed,' said Mrs Lancelyn-Greene, sipping her tea daintily. 'One would have hoped that Lord Alderley might have seen the foolishness of his decision, and it *is* very sad that he has lost the sight in one eye, but I dare say there is no real harm done.'

'Quite so,' agreed Lady Bellingham.

Pippa's self-control wobbled dangerously. 'Gentlemen,' she said, 'do tend to take broken engagements personally. Selfish of them, no doubt, but there it is.' She took great pride in the dispassionate tone she achieved, when she would have liked nothing better than to fling her book at Hermione's head.

Lady Bellingham and Mrs Lancelyn-Greene favoured her with flinty stares over their tea cups, but neither deigned to reply.

Hermione, however, took the remark at face value. 'Very true, Philly,' she said. 'Why Dominic chose to break the engagement is a mystery to me!'

The suggestion that Dominic had done anything so dishonourable as break his betrothal was too much for Pippa. Abandoning irony, she opted for the direct approach. 'I was under the impression that *you* broke the engagement, Hermione,' she said bluntly, 'when you told Dominic that it was unfair to expect you to wait any longer than his period of mourning for your wedding day, and that he might be killed or even come back badly wounded. *You* asked to be released from the betrothal, and he agreed.'

The gelid look on Mrs Lancelyn-Greene's face suggested that this recollection was less than welcome.

'You forget your place, Philippa!' snapped Lady Bellingham.

Pippa bit her lip. Lady Bellingham had very definite ideas on what constituted her 'place' these days.

'Oh, well. That is all behind us now,' said Hermione dismissively. 'And if I am willing to patch up the quarrel after the *horrid* way he behaved—sneaking off at dawn, not even saying goodbye to anyone!' She swelled in indignation at the memory, and swept on, 'I am sure *he* has no need to be in a fit of the sullens!'

This time Pippa said nothing and returned to her book. She

would have to count the stars in the Milky Way to expurgate all the unladylike things she was likely to say.

'I dare say,' said Lady Alderley in placatory tones, 'that dear Dominic is as much in love as ever, but is merely being a little stubborn.' She pursed her lips. 'I cannot understand what else would have kept him away all this time now the surgeons have mended his hand. Why, there will be scarce anyone of quality in town at the moment!'

Knowing her cousin, Pippa suspected that 'dear Dominic' was amusing himself in town with company of quite inferior quality.

Hermione sniffed. 'I suppose he thinks he is teaching me a lesson,' she said. 'Anyway, the important thing now is to plan our theatricals and decide upon a play. He must come home for Christmas, after all.'

Lady Bellingham looked puzzled. 'I thought you were settled on *Cinderella* or *The Sleeping Beauty*.'

'Oh, yes,' said Hermione, 'but when I thought about it—why, 'twas silly!'

Despite herself, Pippa looked up again, her curiosity piqued.

Hermione went on. 'Why, in *The Sleeping Beauty*, she is *asleep* the whole time! They do dance at the ball in *Cinderella*, but there is so little time for them to become acquainted and fall in love! Ridiculous!'

Pippa stifled the very cynical thought that a lack of acquaintance had never proved a barrier to matrimony with an ancient title—even if the title's dibs weren't quite in tune. As an heiress, Hermione had enough dibs to tune up an entire orchestra.

'Is the lack of acquaintance such a problem?' she asked mildly. 'They are fairytales. Surely if one can believe in a fairy with a wand, or a girl sleeping for a hundred years, one need not baulk at love at first sight.'

'That is not at *all* to the point, Philippa,' said Lady Alderley. 'I am sure that it will be far more effective if Dominic and dear Hermione—ah, that is, the Prince and Princess are onstage together a great deal.' She and Mrs Lancelyn-Greene exchanged a meaningful glance.

'More believable,' elaborated Mrs Lancelyn-Greene.

'Oh,' said Pippa. 'I see.'

She did indeed see now. She was not so lost in the mists of iambic pentameter as to be totally blind to what was afoot. Everyone wanted to see the quarrel between Hermione and Dominic resolved in an advantageous marriage.

'Do you think Dominic will like playing Prince Charming, Hermione?'

Hermione stared. 'Why ever should he not?'

Pippa could think of several reasons, but it was rather like something not working in translation—if Hermione couldn't see why not for herself, then it would be useless telling her.

'Anyway, I think perhaps *La Belle et la Bête* will suit us best,' said Hermione happily.

Pippa's book fell from suddenly nerveless fingers.

'*La Belle et la Bête?*' she repeated.

Hermione stared. '*Beauty and the Beast*, Philly,' she translated in condescending tones. 'Goodness! And you are supposed to be so bookish, too!'

Stung, Pippa said, 'I know the story, Hermione.' Temptation lured. 'Rather like the story of Jephthah in the Old Testament,' she added, with malice aforethought, 'except that instead of sacrificing his virgin daughter outright, the father hands her over to the Beast.'

'Really, Philippa!' said Lady Alderley, spots of colour flaring on her cheeks. 'Must you be so *crude?*'

'I beg your pardon, Aunt,' said Pippa.

'After all,' continued Hermione, 'Beauty does live in the Beast's palace. So we, er…*they* have plenty of time to fall in love.'

Pippa felt her fingers clench into fists as she remembered Dominic's blank eyes as he rode out from Alderley to rejoin Wellington last spring, his betrothal ended. 'Yes, indeed,' she said brightly. 'And if you feel the ending is a trifle predictable, you could always revert to the biblical version and cut the girl's throat.'

'Philippa!' In unison from Lady Alderley and Lady Bellingham.

'I beg your pardon, Aunts.' Judging by their expressions, Pippa's apologies convinced neither lady.

'Oh, no! We couldn't do that!' said Hermione, her large blue eyes wide. 'It wouldn't be the least bit romantic!'

She turned to Lady Alderley. 'I do think, though, that it is just the thing. Don't you, ma'am?'

After a final quelling glare at Pippa, Lady Alderley considered the matter. 'Well, yes, dear. I do think it might answer, but it is only a story. We need a play.'

Hermione dismissed that objection with a wave of one dainty hand. 'Oh, that is a trifle. I am sure nothing could be easier than writing a play! I dare say I can toss it off in an evening!'

Pippa hid behind her book and forced her lips to utter stillness.

'Philly? Have you some paper? And a pen? I shall start immediately.'

Provided with paper, pencil, ruler, some ink and a pen, Hermione began ruling lines at the sofa table, accompanied by the occasional snore.

A moment later she put down the ruler and said crossly, 'Oh, dull stuff!'

Mrs Lancelyn-Greene said sweetly, 'Poor darling. But Miss Wintercombe is idle. Perhaps she might rule your lines while you start writing.'

Lady Alderley concurred. 'An excellent idea. Philippa will not mind at all.' She turned to Pippa. 'Will you, dear?'

'Not at all,' lied Pippa, accepting retribution for the suggestion that Hermione should have her throat cut onstage.

Collecting a supply of paper, the pencil and ruler, she settled her little writing box on her lap and began to rule lines. Mrs Lancelyn-Greene and Lady Alderley settled to a discussion of the relative merits of April weddings as opposed to May...

'One must consider the weather of course,' said Mrs Lancelyn-Greene.

'Very true,' said Lady Alderley, frowning. 'Although,' she added, 'earlier might be rather better than later.'

A horrified squeak from Hermione heralded disaster. 'Oh! I have broken a nail on this wretched pen cutter.'

Resigning herself to the inevitable, Pippa held out her hand for the offending cutter and the pen. It took five minutes and several attempts before the pen was trimmed to Hermione's exacting standards.

For a while there was silence as Hermione gazed at a blank page—except for the neatly ruled lines. Rather, Pippa thought, as though she expected the words to miraculously appear by themselves. Then Hermoine began painstakingly to write.

Pippa heaved a silent sigh of relief. Once you started, it was much easier.

A moment later Hermione said crossly, 'Really, this is dreadfully boring! And I have ink all over my fingers! You did not trim the pen properly, Philly. Come and look!'

Pippa stood up and walked over to the sofa table. She cast a glance at the current page. It already had several crossings out and numerous spelling mistakes adorned with smudges.

'*Beauty* has an *a* in it,' she observed, reaching for the pen and cutter again. 'Between the *e* and the *u*.'

Hermione glared at her.

Unperturbed, Pippa trimmed the pen and, despite her disapproval, said, 'You might find it useful to jot down a list of the characters and give them names.'

'Characters?'

'The people in the play,' explained Pippa patiently. 'Beauty's sisters, her father. I think she had a couple of brothers, too, though you could cut them. Then you would know who was meant to be speaking. And to whom. Then you need to divide the action into scenes. And acts.'

Hermione stared. 'Really? How dull. But then, I dare say you could do that, couldn't you, Philly?'

Pippa opened her mouth to refuse, but Lady Alderley chimed in, 'An excellent idea, Hermione. Philippa will not mind in the least.'

Wishing she had not succumbed to her better nature and offered any suggestion at all, Pippa sat down again and listed the main characters. Then, thinking her way through the story, she jotted down a list of suggested scenes, dividing them into three acts. Finished, she handed the pages to Hermione.

'There you are,' she said. And, unable to resist a final jab, added, 'Unless you would like me to write the play for you as well?'

Hermione looked affronted and Mrs Lancelyn-Greene gave Pippa a glare that would have chilled an iceberg. Utterly unconcerned, Pippa returned to ruling lines. Lady Alderley, Lady Bellingham and Mrs Lancelyn-Greene resumed their quiet discussion of possible wedding dates, interrupted only by snores from the sofa.

Several moments passed and a corresponding number of ruled sheets were crumpled and hurled in the general direction of the fireplace.

Then, 'Do you know…' Hermione mused '…that is quite a good notion.'

'What is, dear?' asked Lady Alderley.

'That Philly should write the play,' explained Hermione.

'But then it would not be your play, Hermione,' Pippa pointed out, cursing mentally that she had not retired to bed, or at least kept her mouth shut.

'Oh, but it was all *my* idea,' said Hermione. 'You're just writing it down. And of course I shall, you know, tidy it up a little afterwards,' she continued happily. 'It will still be *my* play. How nice my name will look on the programme—you can do those too, Philly, can you not? I dare say there will not be time to have them properly printed.' Then, in tones of great condescension, she added, 'I *suppose* you could put your own name under mine. As an assistant or something.'

'How frightfully kind of you,' said Pippa as sincerely as she could.

'A very good idea, Hermione,' said Lady Alderley. 'It will give Philippa something to do.'

'And if Dominic doesn't come home?' asked Pippa.

Lady Alderley waved that aside. 'Nonsense. I wrote to Dominic yesterday,' she said. 'Dear Cousin Alex was very happy to take it up to town for me and put Dominic in mind of his duty!'

Two mornings later, Dominic James Martindale, sixth Viscount Alderley, cracked open an eye and groaned. Even with the curtains closed, the bleak grey of a cloudy, early December day struck like a battery of nine pounders. His head ached, and he'd had more than enough brandy last night to ensure that he slept the clock round. What the hell had woken him? He groped on the other side of the bed. No. Empty now.

The noise came again. Footsteps.

Someone was moving round in the parlour of his lodgings. Briggs, his valet. He eased his aching head back to the pillow and swore. Hell and the devil. It was Briggs's day off. There shouldn't be anyone there—unless...no, Clarissa had left. His memory focused; Briggs had removed her before leaving.

Swearing, he staggered out of bed and pulled on a dressing gown. Catching sight of himself in the looking glass on the tallboy, he flinched. His appearance had not been improved by a night of wine—well, brandy; women—only one; and song—not song exactly, but Clarissa had certainly been vocal.

He needed a shave, but in this state he'd probably cut his own throat. Tugging the sash of the dressing gown tight, he stalked out of his bedchamber and along the short corridor to the parlour. Anyone possessing the infernal cheek to invade his lodgings could take him as they found them.

Chapter Two

The smell, redolent of last night's excesses, hit him squarely between the eyes as he stalked into the parlour: tobacco smoke, violet scent, stale brandy and stale sex. And—entirely unexpected—fresh coffee. But that wasn't what stopped him dead in his tracks, nor the fire that crackled merrily in the grate, making little headway against the frigid blast from the windows.

Seated in a chair by the fire, reading the *Gentleman's Magazine* with every evidence of unconcern, was his second cousin and heir, Alex Martindale—the *Reverend* Alex Martindale.

Alex looked up. Dominic tensed, but, beyond a sudden tightening of his mouth, Alex's face betrayed nothing. No shock. No surprise. Nothing.

'Ah, you're awake. I trust you will forgive me for making free with your fire. It is a trifle cold in here and I arrived just as…er…your man was leaving for his day off.'

Dominic had the grace to blush, recalling that Clarissa had left with Briggs. Not that Alex would mention that.

He cast a harried glance round the parlour, which bore all the hallmarks of dissipation: empty bottles, stubbed-out cigarillos and, most damning of all, an article of feminine underwear dangling from the corner of a print in extremely dubious taste. To his utter disgust Dominic felt his cheekbones heat.

'You could try shutting the windows,' he muttered, resisting the urge to bundle the offending item out of sight.

Alex raised a brow, and the corner of his mouth twitched. Then his eyes narrowed and his mouth flattened, as Dominic picked up the poker and adjusted a log.

'I could,' he said. 'But the cold was preferable to the smell.'

Dominic met his gaze. 'Care for a drink at this point, Alex?'

Alex indicated the coffee pot, cup and saucer on the wine table beside him. 'I made myself some coffee, but if you prefer brandy I'll join you in a glass.'

Dominic shrugged. 'Coffee, then. No doubt you've realised I had more than enough brandy last night.' He rummaged in a sideboard for another cup and saucer. 'What brings you up to town?'

'Your mother.'

'What?'

Dominic cracked his head emerging from the sideboard.

'She dispatched me to town,' said Alex. 'With this.' He dropped a letter beside the coffee pot.

'I see.' Dominic set the cup and saucer down and massaged his head. As long as his mother wasn't in town he thought he could manage.

He lifted the pot, his right hand shaking slightly at the

weight. Quickly he steadied it with his left, squinting as he poured another cup for Alex. A little slopped into the saucer and he muttered under his breath, aware of his cousin's scrutiny.

Then, his forbearance plainly at an end, Alex growled, 'Dash it, Dominic! Why the deuce haven't you said anything?'

'If you think I wanted my mother in town…' He poured his own coffee without mishap, concentrating carefully. 'The surgeons were bad enough by themselves. That's why I took this place rather than opening up Martindale House. And I did tell my mother about my…injuries.'

'Oh, very well!' Alex acknowledged the justice of this with a grimace. 'But at least you might have told me the whole truth. You must know that I would have come up to town!'

'For what?' snapped Dominic. 'So you could commiserate with me?'

Alex glared at him. 'So you'd have someone to swear at and argue with, rather than drinking yourself into oblivion and entertaining half the whores in London in the meantime!'

Dominic raised his brows. 'Preaching, old boy?' He sat down in a chair on the other side of the fire.

Alex met the cynical gaze squarely. 'If I thought it had helped, I wouldn't care if you'd entertained *all* the whores in London and drunk Berry's dry!'

Dominic choked on his coffee.

'Now, enough of this,' said Alex sternly. 'I'm under orders from Lady Alderley to ensure that you come home for Christmas, but after seeing you, I'm dashed if I'll do any such thing.'

'Not fit company for the ladies?' asked Dominic drily.

Alex bit off something vastly discreditable to his cloth. 'Gudgeon,' he went on. 'You're not fit company for anyone, least of all yourself. For goodness' sake, come home and be easy for a while. The lord knows I can understand your reluctance!' A wry grin twisted his aquiline features. 'I wouldn't fancy it myself. But the longer you put if off, the worse it will be. It's a wonder no one has written to your mother!'

Dominic grinned. 'That would be because I haven't been frequenting the sort of places my mother's bosom bows are supposed to know about, let alone enter, even if there were anyone left in town at this time of year.' He added, provacatively, 'D'you like my stays?'

Unperturbed, Alex removed his reading glasses and subjected the potentially offensive article dangling from the print to a searching appraisal. 'Hmm. Yours are they? And that stink of violet scent, too, no doubt? You've changed, old boy.'

A startled crack of laughter broke from Dominic. 'Oh, damn you to hell, Alex,' he said, chuckling. 'Doesn't anything ever shock you?'

'Not much,' admitted Alex comfortably. 'Especially not from you, old chap.' He sipped his coffee and asked, 'When do you plan to come home?'

Dominic was silent for a moment.

'Before Christmas,' he said shortly, taking another scalding sip.

'Good. They'll all be delighted.'

'All?' Dominic looked up sharply.

Alex elaborated. 'Miss Lancelyn-Greene is staying at Alderley with her mother.'

'Ah.'

Undaunted, Alex went on. 'Pippa, naturally,' he said.

Dominic frowned. His second cousin Pippa had lived at Alderley since her explorer father had left for India when she was a child. She was part of the furniture. 'Nothing further has been heard from Cousin Philip?' He felt a queer kick of pain at the thought.

Alex shook his head. 'Nothing. That makes it…' He hesitated, plainly trying to remember.

'Three years since she heard from him,' said Dominic. 'Anyone else?'

Alex's hesitation was very slight. 'Lord and Lady Bellingham at the moment, and Althea and her family are expected on the twenty-third.'

Dominic sipped his coffee. It might have been worse. He didn't mind his sister Althea and her husband Rafe. The Bellinghams were inevitable.

'I take it that everyone wishes my betrothal to Hermione to resume?'

His tone non-committal, Alex said, 'This time last year you were planning to marry Miss Lancelyn-Greene. Why should the match not go ahead?'

Why not indeed?

Dominic's cup rattled in the saucer as he set it down. 'That was before she broke our betrothal,' he pointed out. Even as Alex opened his mouth, he said, 'You needn't tell me: duty. My Uncle Bellingham's unfortunate decision to sell out of the Funds on my behalf last spring has more than halved my fortune. Marriage to Hermione will more than repair the damage.'

'That rather sums it up,' said Alex.

Dominic raised his brows. 'Quite.' Bellingham was not the only one to have panicked at rumours of Wellington's defeat and sell out his government holdings at a massive loss. He couldn't blame Bellingham entirely, if at all. Had he thought about it before sailing for Belgium, he would have given explicit instructions to Henderson, his man of business, *not* to sell. His oversight. His responsibility.

'You need to come home, old chap,' said Alex. 'Sort things out. It's your job, Dominic,' he added quietly. 'Not mine.'

Dominic said nothing. There was nothing to say. His duty, which he had been avoiding for the past five months, had risen up to claim him. Returning to war, he had known that if he fell, his title and estates would be in safe hands. Alex knew the place and its people. They knew him.

But he had not fallen.

The title and Alderley were his, along with the attendant demands and responsibilities—up to and including marriage to Hermione. He supposed he still wanted to marry her. He couldn't think of any logical reason why he shouldn't. Broken betrothals had been remade before now. Apparently, since she was staying at Alderley, Hermione was still prepared to marry him. And if his own enthusiasm for the match had lost its white-hot edge, then he supposed that was what happened to most marriages. Only in this instance the cooling had occurred before, rather than after, the wedding.

Silence lengthened between them as Dominic clumsily poured more coffee. He had very little choice as far as he could see. Hermione's fortune would more than restore his. Even with marriage settlements.

In the end Alex asked quietly, 'When were you planning to tell them?'

'Tell them what?'

Alex gave him a very straight look.

'Oh,' said Dominic. 'That.' He frowned. 'If my letter didn't make it clear, then I suppose they will know soon enough. The day after tomorrow; I'll go down then. I suppose you came up on the mail. Should you care to travel back with me?' Belatedly he offered, 'There is a spare bedchamber here if you would care for it.'

Alex grinned. 'My bag is there already, courtesy of your fellow, Briggs. Thank you. He seemed perfectly sure that you wouldn't mind.'

Dominic reached home late in the afternoon two days later. Alderley Hall reared up, limned in moonlight. The clear, bright sky promised a hard frost and a light sprinkling of snow was crisp underfoot as Dominic trod up the front steps to the huge oaken door. In summer it stood open. Now it was firmly closed. He tugged hard on the bell.

The door opened moments later to reveal the butler, *his* butler, Groves.

Smiling, he stepped across the threshold. 'Good evening, Groves. Are you well?'

The old man stepped back. 'Why, 'tis…*you*, Master Dominic!' Then, as Dominic came fully into the light, he gasped and stepped back farther.

Dominic's mouth tightened, but he said nothing beyond, 'Is her ladyship home, Groves?' He stripped off his cloak, hat and gloves, and handed them to the dazed butler.

'Her...her ladyship and her guests are...are in the drawing room, my lord.' Groves clutched his master's cloak, hat and gloves, plainly struggling to recover his well-trained façade.

'Excellent. Thank you, Groves.' Dominic strolled across the Great Hall towards the stairs, his boots clicking on the flagstones.

'My lord?'

He glanced back. 'Yes, Groves?'

'Would it not be better if...if I were to announce you, my lord? I am about to take in the tea tray. Would you...would you not prefer a brandy? In the library?'

Dominic fixed him with a chilling stare. 'I am not a guest, Groves. That will not be necessary.'

Damn it all! He'd written to his mother—warning her, telling her that there was some scarring. Hadn't she mentioned it to anyone?

'No, my lord. Of course not, my lord.'

'Good.' He started up the stairs.

Sounding desperate, Groves tried again. 'Ah, does your lordship require dinner?'

Wearily, Dominic looked down at him. 'No, Groves, my lordship does not. He dined at the Rectory when he dropped Mr Martindale off there.'

Continuing on, he reached the drawing room. He knew who would be there. His mother, Mrs Lancelyn-Greene and Hermione, Lord and Lady Bellingham. And Pippa. With his hand on the doorknob, he hesitated. Was Groves right? Should he wait and let servants' gossip break the news for him? See them all at breakfast? Perhaps send for Pippa? She had always been such a sensible little thing, for all her dreaminess—he could trust her not to have the vapours.

No. He'd put this off quite long enough.

He turned the knob and went in.

Five pairs of eyes turned to see the new arrival.

Greetings died on five pairs of lips.

And five jaws dropped in stunned disbelief.

Bellingham's shocked voice broke the silence. 'Gad! Boy looks like a demned pirate!'

Another fraught silence, broken this time by a faint moan from Lady Alderley as she clutched her throat and fainted.

Lady Bellingham stared at Dominic in shock. 'Good God!' she uttered and then surged to life. 'For goodness' sake, find Louisa's vinaigrette, Bellingham!' she snapped, rising to her feet. 'In her reticule!' she added as he dithered. She leaned over Lady Alderley, patting her hand and fanning her.

Dominic strode forward. 'Here, let me.' He took the reticule from Bellingham's fumbling hands, found the vinaigrette and opened it. Gently he waved it under his mother's nose.

Hermione Lancelyn-Greene let out a small scream and clapped the back of her hand over her mouth. 'Oh! Oh, Mama! Look!'

Dominic glanced up. Hermione's eyes were fixed on his maimed right hand, an expression of revulsion on her lovely face.

Lady Bellingham took the vinaigrette from him with a shudder. 'I'll do that, Dominic! Have the goodness to ring for your mother's maid!'

* * *

The room was cleared in five minutes and Dominic found himself sitting beside his mother on the sofa as she sniffed at her vinaigrette. Her maid was waiting outside in the corridor to help her up to bed.

'Dominic!' she said plaintively. 'That dreadful eyepatch!'

He stilled. 'Mother, I am sorry if I shocked you, but I did mention in my letter that I had lost an eye,' he said quietly.

She fanned herself. 'Well, yes. But for heaven's sake, Dominic! I thought you meant you had merely lost the sight! Not…not—' She sipped at the hartshorn. 'The…the scars will fade, will they not?'

'I suppose so.'

'And your hand!' She shuddered, averting her gaze.

His throat constricted. 'I believe I also mentioned that there was some scarring, and that my hand was damaged?' Hell! What had he needed to say?

'Oh, yes, but one never imagined anything so very distas—' She broke off. 'Dearest, perhaps a glove in company? Such a sight must be very distressing, especially to any female of sensibility.'

'I'm sorry, Mother.' A glove would make him even clumsier.

'I wonder that you did not think of it yourself,' she said reproachfully.

He had. Only he had hoped that here at Alderley there would be no such need. Optimism was an inconvenience he could probably do without.

'Well, I am sure it is very nice to have you home,' said Lady Alderley, not at all as if she were sure. 'But…'

Dominic came to her rescue. 'You look tired, ma'am. Perhaps your maid should put you to bed. I will see you in the morning.'

She looked relieved. 'Yes. Yes, that will be best. A good night's sleep—although I dare say I shall not sleep a wink! I did not imagine—' She broke off, and began to rise.

Dominic manufactured a smile, then helped her to her feet, using only his left hand, and escorted her to the door, which he opened.

'Goodnight, then, Mother.'

'Goodnight,' she returned in frail accents as she tottered off in the care of her solicitous maid who was all agog.

Repressing the urge to swear, Dominic went back downstairs. He was home. And he definitely needed that drink Groves had suggested.

Reaching the hall, he stopped and gazed round. Home— grey stone hung with tapestries that seemed alive in the draughts that rippled their edges. The light from the oil lamps at either end of the refectory table—pillaged from a local monastery, according to family tradition—glinted on ancient weapons and cast flickering, dancing shadows in the darkness of the raftered roof, and on oil paintings of assorted Martindales depicted in various military endeavours.

All younger sons, of course. Including himself at nineteen, his dog at his side, just after his commission had been purchased. Everything familiar, yet something felt different. Perhaps himself. As a younger son, he had been dispatched to seek his way in the world. To be master here had been Richard's destiny.

Ironic. *He* had survived years of campaigning in the Peninsula, culminating in the bloodbath of Waterloo. Richard, the heir, had remained at home to manage the estates and succeed to their father's room. Perfectly right and proper; Richard had been as suited to the care of Alderley as he had been to the army.

Yet here he was, Viscount Alderley, while Richard had been buried these eighteen months.

When last he had been here he had half-expected never to return. He had expected to die and he hadn't really cared. He had never wanted Alderley—certainly not at the price of his brother's death.

His expectations and desires had not been consulted. Instead of the expected military career, he had Alderley.

He stared up at the shadowy portrait of Richard over the fireplace. 'I'll do my best, old chap,' he said quietly. 'Sorry about the delay.'

He went into the warmth of the library. Firelight played over the richness of leather bindings, shimmered on the Persian rugs that covered the floor...and the occupant of the wingchair drawn up to the fireside. Startled, he went closer. An oil lamp glowed on a sofa table beside the chair...what the devil?

A few more soft steps; the occupant of the chair was obviously sound asleep. He knew who it was now. Firelight gleamed on tawny brown curls escaping a prim chignon to frame a pale face.

His cousin, Philippa Wintercombe—who *hadn't* been in the drawing room—fast asleep, her writing box about to slip off her lap. He smiled. It wouldn't be the first time Pippa had fallen asleep over...over what? A letter to her father?

Carefully he lifted the writing box from her lap and set it on the sofa table before it could fall and disturb her. It was the writing box he'd given her for her tenth birthday.

Ever since she had come to live with them Pippa had written a weekly letter to her father, even when she hadn't had the least idea where he might be. Even when the letters from Philip Wintercombe stopped coming three years ago she had continued to write. *Did* she still write to Cousin Philip? Did he even need to ask?

Gently he took the quill from her slackened grasp and put it on the table.

Her fingers were cold. Cold and ink-stained. He'd never known Pippa *not* to have ink-stained fingers. A large shawl was slipping from her shoulders. He bent to tuck it about her more securely and the fragrance of lavender wreathed round him, tugging at his senses.

A loose curl lay partially over her face. He stroked the curl back with fingers that trembled. Lord, she was soft, and the curl had wound itself round his finger, as though it were alive…as though it invited his caresses. Involuntarily his fingers feathered over the curve of her cheek. The lashes flickered and he froze… For an instant the lashes lifted fully, revealing sleepy hazel eyes, and his breath jerked in. Surely Pippa would not react, not be revolted?

'Oh. Is it you?'

'Yes, it's me.' He held his breath. Then with a little sigh and wriggle she settled again, snuggling into the folds of the shawl.

So quiet and peaceful. Relief breathed out of him and he turned to rebuild the fire.

* * *

Pippa's dreams drifted and parted. The Beast stood by the fire, tall and shaggy in the gorgeously embroidered old coat she had found in the attics…no, he wasn't…he had changed already, and he wore a dark coat and buckskin breeches. Vaguely she was aware of gentle hands removing a weight from her, someone bending over her and the same hands tucking her in. Papa? He had always tucked her in at night when he was home. Papa returned. She forced her eyes open to see him.

It was not Papa. It was Dominic, the Beast.

She drifted again.

A log falling drew her back. The figure in the other wing-chair leaned forward and pushed the log back into position…a familiar figure, tousled dark hair falling over his brow, warm brown eyes…no, something was different…

At her startled gasp he turned and she cried out in shock. She was still dreaming…where the left eye should have been was a black hole laced with livid scars.

She shut her eyes. No. It must be one of her nightmares. But she could feel the heat of the fire. 'Dominic?' She opened her eyes again, and gasped in horror.

He stiffened, turning away.

'Dominic?' She couldn't help the wobble in her voice. Slowly he turned and she braced herself not to recoil. No, it was not so very bad after all. Yes, the scarring on his left cheek was bad, but no doubt it would fade with time. And the black velvet eyepatch was a dreadful shock, but one…one would grow accustomed. At least he was back. Safe. Probably much the same as ever.

Or was he? Something about the hard lines bracketing his mouth told her that he was not quite the same.

'Good evening, Cousin.'

She did recoil at that. At the chill bite in his voice. And his face hardened even more. Closing her out. He'd never called her *Cousin* in that icy way before. But then she'd never cried out at the sight of him before.

She had to say something. Anything! 'I…it is lovely to see you, Dominic. I…that is…we have all missed you.'

Dominic's jaw clenched. She was still staring at him, shocked. Damn it! Did she have to look like that? Clarissa hadn't seemed to mind… A small, cynical voice reminded him that he'd been paying Clarissa. Generously.

'Why are you here?' he asked roughly.

She kept her chin up and met his gaze. 'The fire in here was lit,' she said steadily. 'I wasn't expecting you.' With which she rose to her feet and picked up her belongings. 'Please don't get up, Cousin. Goodnight.'

He could have bitten his tongue out at the look on her face. It was as though he had slapped her. 'Pippa, I didn't mean—' Oh, yes, he had. Only now he regretted it. Bitterly. But she was already walking towards the door.

Without thinking he was out of his chair. Three swift strides after her and he caught her wrist.

'Pippa, I'm—'

Her horrified cry silenced him. His stomach congealed as he followed her gaze to the hand gripping her wrist. His maimed right hand, minus the middle finger, scarred and, despite the surgeons' best efforts, slightly twisted. It looked as though some brute beast from a fairytale had captured the slender wrist, ready to drag the maiden off to its lair to devour... He dropped her wrist as though it had scorched him.

'I beg your pardon, Cousin,' he said politely, unable to keep the hard edge out of his voice. She just stared at him, her eyes dark in her pale face, biting her lip as though to keep from crying out again.

He continued. 'I did not intend to disturb you. Goodnight.' He bowed and left her.

Chapter Three

The door shut behind him and the tears Pippa had held back spilt over helplessly. Why hadn't he *told* them? Yes, they had known that he had lost the sight in one eye, and that his right hand had been injured, but not that… Not what? That he was scarred and had lost his left eye? That his hand was maimed? Was that any reason to cry out in horror? Shame at what she had done scorched her—such a stupid, missish reaction. But if only she had *known!*

The thought of his pain, of what he must have gone through, sickened her. And he hadn't told them. No. Dominic wouldn't, he hated anyone fussing over him. Had she known, Lady Alderley would have gone up to London in the grandest of grand fusses.

Her blurred gaze fell on the writing box and she shuddered. The play. It would never be performed now. She opened the box and drew out the manuscript, fumbling through the closely written pages.

Dominic. Oh, Dominic. More tears fell. This must be

burnt. Immediately. She would give her own right hand to spare Dominic the sort of pain and embarrassment this could cause him. The lines describing the Beast's costume and appearance leapt out at her…

The dancing shadows coalesced, until it seemed that he stood before her as he had in her dream, firelight glinting on his gold embroidered eighteenth-century coat and waistcoat. The shaggy horsehair mask she had imagined for him had vanished, replaced by a dishevelled and dirty wig. His face remained shadowed, one eye patched, and his right hand stuck defiantly in his pocket. Slowly the hand came out, reaching for her, crippled… For the first time she wondered how the Beast might have felt about his transformation…always wondering whether the spell *could* be undone, if anyone would ever see past the ruins and love him. How much worse *knowing* that it could never be undone, no matter how much he was loved.

She shook her head, dispelling the vision. Her stupid imagination! There was nothing there, only her foolish fancy. Gathering up the manuscript, she took two steps towards the fireplace and stopped, biting her lip. Poor Beast, he didn't deserve to be consigned to the flames, did he?

She hesitated, staring at her untidy writing. Her pen and ink pot stood on the table beside the writing box. She sat down again. Madness. She should burn it, but…

Five minutes later she was hard at work, crossing lines out, scribbling in the margins, her mind working furiously. It would be more *real* this way. Of course, it could never be performed, she was wasting her time—but the Beast was real to her now, as he had not been before, and she could not leave him stranded in limbo. Blinking hard, she pulled a fresh page towards her and started to write. Even if it were only on paper, she would give her Beast his happy ending. And make sure that no one else ever saw it.

Breakfast the following morning was one of the most awkward meals Dominic had ever endured. He was moved to wonder just how long everyone would manage to avoid looking at him. No, that was a little unfair. They looked when they thought he wouldn't notice, for which he didn't really blame them. But it was wearing, attempting to converse with people whose gaze kept sliding past your left ear, as though looking at you might somehow transfer the livid scarring to their own faces.

Pippa, he noted bitterly, had her eyes fixed firmly on her plate and had scarcely spoken to anyone. She wasn't eating much either. No doubt the horrid sight of him had destroyed her appetite! He reached for the coffee pot with his gloved right hand, not looking, and knocked over the marmalade.

'Oh, poor Dominic!' cooed Hermione. 'Does your hand hurt dreadfully? Shall I pour the coffee for you?' Without awaiting a reply, she did so, adding several lumps of sugar and a liberal dash of cream.

'Thank you, Hermione,' he said. And repressed a shudder as he sipped the syrupy brew.

She beamed at him, lashes a-flutter. 'I am sure it is not the least trouble in the world to help you, Dominic.'

He forced a polite smile. At least she was looking at him.

He took another sip of the coffee and smiled at his mother.

'What have you arranged for Christmas, Mother?' he asked. 'The usual dance and supper for the tenants on Twelfth Night? And the Yule log on Christmas Eve?'

Lady Alderley's tea cup rattled into its saucer.

Lady Bellingham stared. 'Really, Dominic! Surely it would be better to cancel all that! You will hardly wish to expose yourself in such antiquated and ill-judged—'

'I beg your pardon?' He didn't bother to sheathe the naked anger.

Everyone looked up.

He continued in biting tones, 'There is not the least reason to cancel anything on my account. I am not ill. Nor incapable. The usual entertainments are to go ahead.'

He stood up and pushed back his chair. 'Perhaps you will excuse me for the morning. I have the estate books to check.'

'Really!' Lady Bellingham pursed her lips as her afflicted sister sank into a chair in the morning room after breakfast.

Lady Alderley pressed a hand to her heart and said faintly, 'Such a shock, dear Gussie! That eyepatch! And his hand! It is entirely too much! Philippa!'

'Yes, Aunt Louisa?'

'You must oversee the arrangements,' said Lady Alderley in frail tones. 'I cannot possibly do so—you will have to hire the musicians. I had thought a supper—perhaps bread and cheese and some ale—would be enough for the tenants, but if Dominic means to insist upon a dance—' She shuddered. 'And remind Mrs Higgs that Althea and Sir Rafe arrive today. With their children.'

Flipping through a copy of *La Belle Assemblée*, Hermione

said happily, 'A dance on Twelfth Night will be just the thing to top off our theatricals, don't you think?'

Pippa's stomach turned over. Surely Hermione didn't still think to—?

'Hermione…' she began.

'Hermione, dear,' said Lady Alderley, in failing accents, 'you have not quite understood—' Pippa breathed a sigh of relief. Much better if Aunt Louisa pointed out the obvious. 'We are not talking about a proper dance, dear, but a *tenants'* dance,' went on Lady Alderley. 'For the farmers and their wives, and the villagers.' She shuddered. 'Not at all the same thing. Naturally one attends, but one sits on the dais and does not mingle.'

'Oh!' Hermione looked horrified. 'But we can still have our play?'

'No,' said Pippa grimly. 'You can't.' Like irony, tact was wasted. 'You *can't* ask him to do it, Hermione! Only think how exposed he must feel!'

'Oh, pish!' said Hermione, pouting. 'Why, it will be just the thing to amuse him and if he is happy to have this tenants' dance on Twelfth Night, then he cannot be too worried about people seeing him!'

'That is not quite the same thing as standing up onstage dressed as a Beast!' said Pippa. 'He won't do it! And he ought not to be asked.'

'Very true, dear,' said Lady Alderley comfortably. 'I think it will be better not to mention the *title* of the play to Dominic quite yet.'

Pippa's jaw dropped.

'Exactly so, Louisa,' said Lady Bellingham. 'Once everyone is gathered, he will see the impropriety of refusing to do his duty. I am sure no one can be more distressed than I to see him so disfigured, but—'

'Ma'am, cannot you see that it will be the worst thing for him, to draw everyone's attention to him in such a way!' said Pippa furiously. 'The very title of the piece—'

'Oh, but that makes it so much more appropriate!' cried Hermione.

Mrs Lancelyn-Greene tittered. 'My dear Miss Winter-combe! Surely you don't have a *tendre* for his lordship?' she said maliciously.

Pippa blushed to the roots of her hair, and suspicion flared in Lady Alderley's eyes.

'You forget your place, Philippa,' said Lady Bellingham coldly. 'Dominic's well-being is not your concern. Are you not going to the village this morning? Yes? I suggest that you go then. Now.'

Dismissed, Pippa choked back her fury and distress as she left the room. There was only one way to ensure that the play could not go ahead and that Dominic never knew anything about it. One way to make up for her foolishness the previous night.

There was no time now. She did have to go to the village— and before that she must see Mrs Higgs, the housekeeper. And she had better find out where to hire musicians. The days were so short! It would be dark by half past three. When she came back—her fists clenched—she would take enormous pleasure in telling Miss Lancelyn-Greene that the manuscript was burned.

An hour after breakfast Dominic was still going through the estate books. Things had fallen behind while he was away, and the lack of ready funds didn't help. There were jobs that ought to have been done this last summer that had been let slide.

Frowning, he picked up the book and a pencil, and strolled over to the fire. It was a damned chilly morning for sitting at a desk, so he made himself comfortable in the wingchair with his back to the door. With luck, anyone seeking him would think he wasn't here and leave again.

He looked again at the entries for the previous month. After ten years in the army he recognised his duty when confronted with it. But this particular duty flummoxed him. He was a soldier. Nothing in his experience would help him in the intricate task of running the estate. He had a good steward; he would learn.

Another thing—he'd better speak to Mrs Lancelyn-Greene in the next day or so and renew his betrothal to Hermione. Then the wedding date could be announced on Twelfth Night. Although, if she continued to fuss over him in that ghastly way...

The door opened and shut.

'In here, dearest. Just a private word.'

Mrs Lancelyn-Greene's cooing tones floated to him.

'Yes, Mama?'

''Tis about his lordship. *Poor* Alderley.'

About to declare himself, Dominic froze.

'I simply wished to make perfectly certain that you are quite happy for the betrothal to go ahead before Alderley speaks to me—which I am sure he will do as soon as may be. Are you—?'

'Mama!' broke in Hermione. 'Why should this make the least difference?'

Despite every dictum of good manners demanding that a gentleman should declare himself immediately, Dominic sank back into his chair.

'I don't deny it was a horrid shock,' continued Hermione, 'but after all, what difference does it make?'

Dominic closed his eye.

'He is still a viscount…'

His eye snapped open.

'…even if he *is* horridly disfigured. And I dare say once he has his heirs, he will prefer to spend most of his time down here at Alderley, and I can be in town or visiting friends. There will be no need to see much of him. It will be vastly convenient.'

His stomach churned.

'There is that, dearest. Of course, these things *are* quite different once one is married, you know.'

Dominic found that his fists had balled.

'Yes, Mama. Poor, dear Dominic. It would be very unkind in me to repudiate him now, especially with the estate beggared.'

This last in tones of glowing virtue. A wonder, thought Dominic, that the reek of burning martyr didn't fill the room. Along with the more-than-a-whiff of hypocrisy.

'Quite so, dear. And he *was* disposed to be very generous with the marriage settlements,' mused Mrs Lancelyn-Greene. 'Yes, on reflection it will do very well still. As you say, Alderley will likely prefer to remain here with his rustic amusements and you will be free to pursue other entertainment.'

She would indeed, thought Dominic savagely as the door closed behind them. He wouldn't dream of interfering with Hermione's future.

Half an hour later, he was striding along the woodland path towards the village, his breath smoking. A memory floated by—dragon's breath, they had called it as children. He dismissed the fancy. Cold fury burnt in him.

He'd been a blasted, damned fool. He'd ignored every sign, every hint that Miss Lancelyn-Greene's loveliness might not be more than skin deep. Her occasional tantrums he had put down to wilfulness; the inevitable consequence of being the spoilt only child of extreme wealth. Until she broke their betrothal. Even then he had not wanted to believe the truth: that her beauty had been the hook to land a very willing fish.

She had one thing right—he had far rather be here for most of the year, seeing to his acres, than indulging in the social round. Oh, he'd have to go up to town for Parliament, he couldn't ignore that responsibility, but for the most part he'd be here, taking up his new command.

He swore fluently and lengthened his stride, the frost crunching under his boots. Unfortunately he still needed a bride, which meant braving London for the Season to find one. His mouth hardened. He had no illusions. Many débutantes, sweet young things one and all, would have exactly the same reaction to him as Hermione.

He grimaced. One couldn't blame them; he wasn't a pretty sight. An older woman, perhaps, with sufficient maturity to see past his maimed hand and ruined face. Not a young girl. Even Pippa had recoiled from him last night, had cried out at his touch. He dragged in a deep breath. Pippa—of all his family, he had thought…

No. He had to be rational about this. Logical. It was the only way to avoid making a complete and utter fool of himself. Some good-humoured, intelligent female in her mid, or even late twenties, past hoping for a husband. He would be doing her a favour, and she would be helping him do his duty. A no-nonsense, honest bargain in which both parties would know exactly where they stood. That was the marriage for him.

It might be colder than the chilly blue sky above, but it would be safest. He was still racking his brain to think of any likely candidates for the vacant post, when he came out of the woods and saw the spire of the village church three fields away, beyond the dip that marked the course of the river. And, much closer, a small, cloaked figure scrambling over the stile into the next field. He narrowed his eyes. Was it…? Yes, it was Pippa, who, from her reaction the previous night, would probably prefer that he didn't hail her. At which moment Pippa turned. She waved.

Pippa waited on the lowest step of the stile, her heart pounding as Dominic's long strides brought him near. The pale sun glinted on his dark unruly hair. He looked thin, tired, his mouth set hard. Her heart ached, wondering if his hand pained him. Knowing better than to ask.

She waited, watching as the half-grown setter she had brought with her frisked up to him, tail wagging furiously. Dominic stooped and petted the dog. Spoke to him. Did he realise that it was Ben, the puppy he had chosen last spring?

Determined not to shame herself again, she said, 'Good morning, Dominic. Are you going to the village?'

'Cousin—' his nod was dismissive '—yes. I thought to ask Alex to dinner tomorrow.'

'Oh.' She managed a smile. 'I'm going to the Rectory, too. Do you wish—?'

'Thank you, no,' he said with brutal chill. 'I prefer to walk alone, Philippa.'

Philippa. She fought not to let him see how much his rebuff hurt. 'Yes. Of…of course.'

'Is that Ben?' he asked.

She eyed him warily. 'Yes. I've been walking him, and…and training him.' He had asked Barling, his head gamekeeper, to train Ben as a gundog, but Ben had turned out to be gun shy, so she had taken over.

He glared at her. 'If you wanted a lapdog, it might have been better if you had not plumped for one of my hunting dogs! No doubt you've spoilt him for work!'

Red flared on Pippa's cheeks and she stepped back down off the stile.

'*Ben! Come!*'

The dog bounded up.

'*Sit.*'

Ben sat, tongue lolling out.

She bent, clipped a leash to his collar, and straightened up, eyes blazing.

'*Stay.*' The next moment the leash was thrust into Dominic's hand.

She stopped on the lowest step of the stile.

'Why didn't you *tell* us?' she hurled at him. 'Did you ever think what a shock it might be? That we might be hurt? That we might actually *care* about you?'

She turned away quickly, forcing back the heat behind her eyes. Her foot slipped on the worn wood and, with a cry of fright, she lost her balance, stumbling.

'Pippa!' Dropping the leash, he leapt forward to break her fall, catching her awkwardly, his right hand trapped between them as she fell against him. Pain sheared in to him, stabbing bolts through his hand and up his arm. Somehow he hung on to her, steadying her until she had her footing, clenching his jaw against the dizzying pain.

She struggled free and turned to him, her eyes wide.

'Dominic?'

He didn't trust his voice to answer, but tried to breathe deeply as he sat down abruptly on the stile, willing the pain away. Carefully he cradled his gloved hand, massaging it, trying to ease the spasms.

'Dominic! Your hand!'

Before he could react she was kneeling beside him, stripping off her gloves, taking his maimed hand in both of hers. Small, shaking hands pulled off his heavy glove and he watched, dazed, as she massaged his hand, slender fingers kneading, pressing, her thumb circling his palm. The pain ebbed to a dull ache, faded completely. Yet he could not bring himself to pull his hand away. It lay a willing captive.

'Is it…does it still hurt?' Her voice sounded strained.

He shook his head. 'No. It's fine. Thank you.' It felt exactly right just where it was.

Her eyes lifted to his face. 'I'm sorry,' she whispered. 'I'm so sorry I hurt you.'

He stared down at her. She was still kneeling on the damp ground, hazel eyes sheened with pain. In that searing moment, he saw the truth; she wasn't talking about jarring his hand. And she hadn't hurt him anywhere near as deeply as he had hurt her.

Without thinking, he reached out and touched her face clumsily. She didn't flinch, didn't look away. So soft. A single tear spilt over. It was like a blow to the stomach. In his bitterness he had seen rejection where none existed, and dealt it out where it was not deserved. Very carefully, he brushed the tear away.

'Last night—' she began; he stopped her by the simple expedient of putting his hand over her mouth. Warm, soft lips.

'No,' he said quietly. 'You don't need to say it. I understand.'

He did, too. He remembered a young girl crying her eyes out as she helped him release a pet dog caught in a trap, horrified by the creature's suffering, as though it somehow hurt her… Juno's pain had sickened her, not the mangled leg itself…a simple human response to another's pain.

He pulled her up on to the bottom step of the stile beside him and slipped his arm round her. Soft curves nestled against him. Soft, womanly curves—and a very different sort of ache banished any lingering pain in his hand. Shock slammed into him. 'It wasn't your fault. None of it,' he managed to say, standing up. Good God! This was Pippa, whom he'd known from a child! Still reeling from his body's unbidden response, he tried for humour. 'I've been going over the estate books,' he said, helping her up.

She responded gallantly, 'Oh. Well, I suppose that's enough to have anyone feeling like a bear with a sore head.'

'Not exactly the career I envisaged,' he said wryly, tucking her hand through his arm.

'No. But it is still an important job,' she said thoughtfully. 'Something to do with your life. A different duty?' The smile became mischievous. 'Without the inconvenience of being shot at.'

He laughed. 'Occasionally it was more than inconvenient,' he pointed out.

And wished he hadn't as he felt her shudder.

She took a deep breath. 'Is…is that how it happened?'

'My hand? Yes. A musket ball. The face and eye were the result of a sabre cut that became infected.'

He felt a shiver rack her and stopped. 'Are you cold?' He began to shrug off his cloak, and to his utter shock she reached up to touch him. He stiffened, but held still. Careful fingers, a gentle tracery on the seamed, scarred skin around his eyepatch.

Not curiosity. Certainly not pity. Just simple acceptance.

'We were lucky,' she said shakily.

And thankfulness.

It shook him to the core.

She drew back. 'That is why you knocked the marmalade over at breakfast, is it not? Judging distances is difficult?' Her voice was very neutral.

No. Not pity. Just trying to understand.

He forced himself to answer as they walked on. 'Partially. And my hand is not perhaps as strong, or as controlled, as it was before.' He managed a smile. 'I've knocked over quite a few jars of marmalade, not to mention dropping things.'

Were those tears glistening in her eyes?

He didn't dare ask and at last they crossed the old stone bridge into the village, Ben trotting ahead.

Chapter Four

She stopped at the Rectory gate and opened it. 'I will leave you here. I have promised to read to Mr Rutherbridge this morning.'

Dominic frowned. Rutherbridge was the widowed Rector.

'Is he unwell?' He liked Rutherbridge, who had been tending the souls of Alderford for the past forty years. He had baptised every child in the village, and married most of their parents—including his own. In the last year he had slowed down and appointed Alex Martindale as his curate, in the expectation that Alex would one day take over the living.

'A bad cold that has gone to his chest,' said Pippa. 'But the main problem is that his eyesight is failing. So I come down two or three times a week to read to him.'

'Surely Alex—'

'Alex has enough to do looking after the parish,' said Pippa. 'And I like to do it. Mr Rutherbridge has always been so kind to me, and now that Mrs Rutherbridge has gone, I think he is a little lonely.'

Dominic smiled. Yes, that was Pippa. She liked doing things for people.

'So I will come back for you—when? An hour? Two?'

She shook her head. 'You need not.'

He opened the gate for her. 'Are you refusing to keep me company?'

'You could take Ben,' she pointed out.

He ignored that. 'Two hours,' he informed her. 'Tell Mr Rutherbridge to expect me.'

The hazel eyes narrowed. Then... 'Yes, *sir!*' And she snapped to attention, saluting smartly as she clicked her heels together. Then she swept through the gate and up the path. Dominic watched, smiling, as the door was opened for her by the housekeeper, Mrs Judd, who stared at him in undisguised curiosity. Pippa's soft greeting floated back to him, followed by Mrs Judd's clarion accents.

'Well, and indeed. We was wondering where you might have got to, miss. And is that his lordship with you? Well, I never...' The door shut, sparing Dominic whatever it was that Mrs Judd had never.

Two hours. He had two hours in which to amuse himself in Alderford.

In the end two hours was not long enough. He strolled round the village, greeting acquaintances, oddly untouched by the commiserating glances as the villagers took in his eyepatch and scarred visage. The scars would fade. No one seemed particularly bothered by shaking his maimed hand, although he noted that they clasped it carefully, but more as if they feared to hurt him than as if it repulsed them. People would become accustomed. It was more important to think about what Pippa had said.

How had she understood the very thing he had been groping towards? That he was still called to do his duty. Only the form of the duty had changed. Not the call. Nor the necessity to obey.

His thoughts were interrupted by Barling, his gamekeeper, who came up to greet him. After discussing the coverts and the best places for Dominic's guests to amuse themselves, he said, 'Now, that pup you asked me to train, my lord—Ben.' He shook his head. 'Gun shy.'

'Gun shy?'

Barling nodded. 'Aye. Good-natured dog and Miss Pippa's taken him in hand, training him up and all. Make a nice pet, but no use for hunting.'

Humble pie had a very unappealing taste and texture, he reflected after leaving Barling.

He met Alex coming out of a cottage, just as he was thinking it must be about time to head back towards the Rectory.

'Ah, Alderley!' said Alex. 'Just the fellow we wanted. You remember Obadiah?' He indicated the old man stumping unevenly down the garden path behind him.

Dominic grinned and held out his hand. 'I do indeed. How are you going on, Obadiah?' Obadiah Battersby was a rascally, one-legged ex-poacher who had enthralled several generations of village children with apocryphal tales about the fate of his missing leg.

The old man nodded. 'Middling, me lord, fair to middling.'

'Obadiah has a problem with his roof,' said Alex.

Dominic looked up at the roof in question—which just

happened to belong to him. He frowned. Several tiles were missing outright, and the whole roof looked as though it could do with some attention. Annoyance flared. Why the hell hadn't this been seen to before winter set in? A few more good frosts and it would have been impossible to send workmen up there safely.

He looked at the old chap, who watched him uneasily, twisting his cap in his hands.

'I did tell the Reverend and Miss Pippa it weren't nothin' ter bother yer lordship about, m'lord, but—'

'Miss Pippa?' Alex, yes—but, Pippa?

Obadiah looked very self-conscious. 'Miss Pippa tried to get Mr Hopkins to have it fixed, but he said as how it would have to wait.'

Dominic's jaw hardened. Hopkins was his agent. He should have seen to this. With or without Pippa's directions.

All he said was, 'Obadiah, your roof needs mending. I'll have a chap up there by tomorrow.'

The old fellow's mouth opened and closed. 'Well, I'm sure I'm very obliged to yer lordship. An' it's good ter see yer lordship back safe an' sound.' Then, perhaps thinking this sounded rather after the fact, he added, 'Roof or no roof.'

They chatted a few moments longer; then, after extracting a promise that Obadiah would be along for Twelfth Night, Dominic strolled off with Alex.

'There. Not so difficult after all,' murmured Alex. 'Just slightly different orders.'

Dominic stared. 'Have you been talking to Pippa?'

'Pippa? Not this morning. Why?'

Dominic told him what Pippa had said.

Alex smiled gently. 'Pippa is a woman of rare perception and intelligence.'

He didn't deny the intelligence, but—'Woman?'

Alex blinked. 'Well, she was when last I looked.'

Smiling and nodding a greeting to the miller, Dominic mulled that one over. 'She was a little girl the last time I looked,' he said. He wasn't entirely sure when he had last looked. Really looked.

An amused brow lifted. 'Ah, yes. You were looking at Miss Lancelyn-Greene last time you were home.'

Dominic reminded himself that Alex was in holy orders. Planting him a facer was out of the question. Instead he said, 'I've recovered.'

Both brows lifted. 'Good. I hope the medicine wasn't too unpalatable.'

He let that one pass. Looking rationally at his infatuation, he could see that the marriage would have been a disaster, even if he had come back whole. He tried to imagine Hermione walking to the village to read to old Mr Rutherbridge or worrying about Obadiah's roof. His imagination ran aground. Hermione saw Alderley as no more than a setting for her beauty and social triumphs. She would never have fitted into its life, understood the people, or seen it as a home.

'And where are you off to now?' enquired Alex.

Dominic pulled his watch from his waistcoat pocket and consulted it. 'The Rectory. To meet Pippa. She is reading to Rutherbridge.'

They found Pippa in the book-lined parlour of the Rectory. A small pile of books was stacked beside Pippa's chair, and she was still reading in a low, melodious voice, while the white-haired old gentleman leaned forward to catch every word.

Ben looked up and thumped his tail as they entered the room, but did not otherwise shift from his position by the fire. Dominic smiled to see that Rutherbridge's slippered foot was rubbing the dog's back.

Pippa glanced up, but did not stop reading. Dominic listened, watching her. She had removed her bonnet and several tawny curls had escaped their bonds. He swallowed. Alex was right. She had grown up. Sitting before him was not the young girl he remembered, but a young woman. A very appealing young woman… How had he missed seeing that?

She reached the end of the passage and stopped.

The old man eased back in his chair, eyes closed. 'Mmm. Thank you, my dear. That will do for today. Very kind of you to come again.'

'It is a pleasure, sir. You know that,' said Pippa. 'And here are—'

Rutherbridge chuckled. 'You'd come even if it weren't a pleasure,' he said. 'And as for this business of his lordship's eye—' he went on, sublimely unaware of any other presence '—well, that's sad. No denying it.' He shook his head. 'But better he went back to do his duty and face out Boney, than ate his heart out, believing himself a shirker. Losing an eye is bad enough. Self-respect is worse.'

Helplessly, Pippa looked at the two men in the doorway. The perils of being blind and more than slightly deaf were legion.

'I'm glad to hear you say so, sir,' said Dominic simply. 'I'm afraid I've come to steal Pippa.'

His swift smile tipped her completely off balance.

Mr Rutherbridge slewed round in his chair. 'Alderley? Goodness me. This is very pleasant.' He squinted. 'Eyes not what they were, you know. But I have blessings.' He smiled at Pippa. 'Miss Pippa for one. And this hearthrug she brings with her.' He gave Ben a poke with his foot. The tail thumped.

'I'm here, too, sir,' said Alex.

Rutherbridge beamed. 'Excellent. We'll have time for a little game of chess before dinner, eh?'

Pippa rose. 'When should you like me to come again, sir?'

'Now, you're not to put yourself out, young lady,' said Rutherbridge. 'I know how her ladyship depends on you. And with guests, it's a busy time up at the Hall—'

'Nonsense,' said Pippa. 'I'll come when I can.'

Rutherbridge snorted. 'You mean when her ladyship doesn't have enough for you to do! I may be stuck in this house now, but I still hear things! Take her away, Alderley.'

'There's Obadiah Battersby,' said Pippa, waving to the old man now sitting outside the inn. 'Dominic, Obadiah's roof—'

'Alex told me. It should be mended tomorrow,' said Dominic, noting that Obadiah had raised his cap to Pippa in a positively courtly fashion. A group of children were clustered about him.

'Telling them all about the pirates who fed his leg to the sharks, do you think?' murmured Dominic. 'That's what he told me as a lad! Good God! The old rascal is pointing at me! What does he mean by it?'

Pippa gave an enchanting choke of laughter. 'That you are one of the pirates, perhaps? A descendant at least!'

He saw the moment she realised what she had said. The pain in her eyes—and something else—as she forced herself to meet his gaze.

'I'm sorry, Dominic,' she whispered. 'I'm such a fool! Forgive me.'

He smiled. 'There's nothing to forgive, goose. The eyepatch does after all lend a certain *cachet!*'

She managed a smile.

'Better than Obadiah's wooden leg?' he wheedled. 'Even with the sharks?'

A reluctant giggle escaped. 'He told *me* his leg was bitten off by a crocodile.'

Dominic roared with laughter. 'And did you believe him?'

She blushed. 'I was eight. Of course I believed him!'

That brought him up short. 'Eight?'

She nodded. 'About that.'

She was…nineteen now? Which meant… 'Pippa—you've been with us eleven years?'

The blush ebbed. 'Yes.' All the glow and laughter faded from her eyes and face, as though a candle had been extinguished.

Dominic could have kicked himself. What the devil was he doing, reminding her how long it was since she had seen her father? And three years since she had heard from him. Had hope faded now?

Instinctively he caught her hand and drew it through his arm, anchoring it on his elbow. The thought of her always waiting, never knowing, never quite sure, tore at him.

They walked on in companionable silence for perhaps half a mile before Pippa spoke again.

She spoke quietly, as if his thoughts had somehow echoed in her heart. 'He must be dead, I think. My head tells me that it must be so. And yet—'

'You still write, though.'

She flushed. 'Yes. I know it's foolish. He's gone…but just to *know*, even that he was dead. It's the not knowing. The never being able to grieve and then let go.'

'Not foolish at all,' he said gently. Of course she still wrote. Without proof she would always wonder…how and why…and when. Should she have written just once more? And again after that? Which letter was the last one he had ever read? Had he received any of them?

There was not one single damn thing he could do about it.

She changed the subject. 'What will you do with Ben? He's…he's gun shy, you know.'

'You've done a good job training him,' said Dominic, accepting her reticence. 'And, yes, I knew. I ran into Barling. He told me why you took over Ben's training. Thank you.'

Pippa flushed. 'Oh, nonsense! How difficult is it to train a puppy?'

Not hard at all. For Pippa. He frowned. She loved animals, but never had her own, always riding someone else's horse, petting someone else's dog. Her residence at Alderley had been considered temporary. But—eleven years…

'Should you like him for your own, Pippa?' The offer was out before he knew it was there. And for one split second, the unshadowed delight in her eyes told him he had said the right thing. Something in his chest squeezed tight. 'A New Year's gift,' he added.

The blazing delight dimmed and she bit her lip. 'Thank

you, but it would be better not,' she said. 'That wasn't why I looked after him.'

He frowned. 'I know that, you goose! But look at him; he's your dog. I wasn't here. I can choose another pup.' He grinned. 'A bitch. Then we can fight over the pups.'

The light in her eyes dimmed further.

'Sweetheart—what is it?'

Abruptly she pulled her hand free and walked on. 'I don't want to become too fond of him,' she said shortly, when he caught up. 'Giving him back would hurt too much.'

Dominic stared. 'Give him back? Why the dev—er, I mean, why the deuce would you do that?'

'When...when I leave,' she said in a very matter-of-fact sort of way.

The whole world tilted crazily. Leaving? Why—?

Understanding slammed into him. And with it an emotion he could scarcely identify. At least he assumed it was an emotion. More like some savage beast inside him, clawing its way out, roaring a protest. Alex had given him the clue; Pippa was no longer a little girl. She was a woman. Even if he had been blind, other men weren't.

Other men would have seen what he was seeing now: the soft, full lips; the delicate line of her jaw. Not to mention a set of very womanly curves hiding under her shapeless old cloak. And those soft hazel eyes that seemed to see straight through one. And Pippa herself, quiet, dreamy, oddly practical Pippa.

In tones approaching civility, he managed to ask, 'Then...then some sensible fellow has offered for you?' He could imagine no other reason for Pippa to leave. Alderley was her home. And damned if he'd give his consent if the fellow wasn't good enough for her!

She flushed. 'Goodness, no! Don't be silly, Dominic. Why would anyone offer for me? I don't even have a dowry!'

The green-eyed beast subsided into muted rumblings.

In any other woman, Dominic would have treated this question with the cynicism it deserved. But not with Pippa. He wanted to protest the mercenary attitude of society that unless some fellow fell head over ears in love with Pippa, without connections and a dowry… His mind tripped over that. Not just the bit about some undeserving scoundrel making free with Pippa's heart, but the bit about the dowry…

'Hold hard there,' he said. 'You do have a dowry. In the funds. Cousin Philip adds—added—to it from time to time. There must be several thousand pounds there. My father used to administer it for you.'

Her eyes fell. 'Oh, that. Well, it's…it's not very much, after all. I don't regard it. Do you think we ought to hurry a little? Your sister will be arriving this afternoon. And I promised Aunt Louisa that I would supervise the arrangements in the nursery.'

Dominic ignored that. 'So, if no one has offered for you—*yet,*' he said with emphasis, 'why do you think you will be leaving Alderley?'

Her chin lifted a little. 'Because you were right; it is time I accepted that Papa is not coming home. And…and that if I have to make my own way in the world, it is time I started doing it.'

'What the devil put that maggot into your head?' he growled, not bothering to temper his language.

'It is not a maggot,' said Pippa crossly. 'It is common sense! I can hardly remain here, sponging off your family for the rest of my life!'

Sponging? Who had—? Furiously Dominic realised that Pippa was perfectly capable of putting things into her own head.

He gave her to understand in no uncertain terms that if she dared refer to her residence in his home as *sponging* ever again, she would eat her dinner off the chimney piece for a week.

Pippa accepted this with every appearance of meekness, silently thanking a merciful providence that she had diverted him from the subject of her non-existent dowry. She dare not discuss it with Dominic. She knew his code of honour. If he found out what had happened to her dowry, he would insist on replacing it. And he would have trouble enough salvaging the wreck of the Martindale fortunes.

They walked on briskly until they came to the stile leading from the woods into the park. Ben bounded over it and then wriggled back under it, his tail wagging furiously.

'Idiot dog,' said Dominic with a laugh. Pippa's heart leapt to hear it. Perhaps he was much the same as ever. Only... No. Somehow he *was* different. She didn't know quite what it was about him that was different. He stepped up on to the stile and glanced down at her with a smile—his old smile that had always made her heart lift—and held out his hand to help her up. She took it, almost hesitantly. Perhaps it was her—*she* was different—because she didn't remember that Dominic's smile had ever left her breathless before, or the touch of his hand had ever caused her to shiver. It must be the cold or something. Only...only he had never called her *sweetheart* before…and she was a silly little peagoose even to let herself dream that he might mean anything by it beyond cousinly affection!

Dominic leapt down as easily as Ben. Pippa started to step down, and found herself suddenly swung into the air, his hands at her waist lifting her effortlessly. Shock rippled through her and she stumbled as he set her down. Instantly his arms hardened round her, steadying her against him so that she could smell sandalwood and the faintly musky scent that must be him, himself. Spicy…exciting.

Exciting?

The world spun like a child's top, and settled back to rest somehow slightly altered, as though her view had changed. Shaken, she wriggled and stepped back. For an instant she thought his arms, his whole body, tightened. Then he had released her.

Despite her burning cheeks, she looked up. For an instant their gazes locked, his fierce, heated. Then it was gone, and the easy, friendly smile was back, teasing her.

She tried for dignity, determined to hide the shock, and the sheer melting sensation in her knees. 'I can get down by myself, you know.'

'Of course you can,' he agreed, a wicked twinkle in his eye. 'I was being self-indulgent.'

Chapter Five

Her heart skipped a beat and her stomach turned over at the thought of Dominic being self-indulgent with her. Warmth shimmered through her, lighting all the corners of her heart that she never dared to look into.

No. Madness. She dare not indulge herself with that particular dream. It was not for her. He was only teasing her, as he had always done. Never with any malice, but simply as a dear friend. Almost a brother. He did not care for her in *that* way. As well that he did not. It would be an appalling misalliance for him.

She stepped back, lifting her chin, ignoring her flushed cheeks. It was just the raw wind.

'I must hurry, Dominic. I…I promised Aunt Louisa and—'

Dominic, still queerly shaken by the thoroughly *un*brotherly response of his body to Pippa's slender waist under his hands and her sweet weight in his arms, consigned his mother's errands to hell and beyond in a few caustic words.

'Mother has enough servants to call upon,' he finished. And then, for good measure, caught her hand and tucked it into his arm to forestall the escape he could see coming in the independent tilt of her chin.

'You're mine for the day,' he informed her. It sounded right. And her small, gloved hand felt very right exactly where it was. He anchored it there with his free hand and strolled on. 'We're going to walk round the park.'

'Should you not take Ben back to the kennels?' she asked when they reached the house at last.

His brows rose. 'Why would I do that?' he asked mildly.

'Because,' she said, in tones of reproof, 'your mama does not like dogs in her house.'

'It's my house,' he informed her. 'And I do like dogs in the house. Besides which, I've no intention of taking your dog to the kennels for you.'

He took considerable satisfaction in the dropped jaw and wide eyes.

'But I *told* you—'

'Ben is yours,' he said. 'As for this nonsense about your leaving—I forbid it. This is your home and will remain so.'

He caught her hand again and towed her into the house, whistling for Ben.

'Dominic! How lovely!'

At the delighted voice Pippa flushed and whisked her hand free of his.

Dominic looked up. Hurrying down the stairs with a delighted smile on her face was his sister, Althea, Lady Fanshawe.

Halfway down she faltered, staring. Then, 'Oh, Dominic!

You look positively piratical! You do realise that you are going to give your nephews nightmares?'

'They can compare notes with their grandmama,' he said drily. Trust Althea to say something outrageous.

Althea winced. 'Quite.' She reached the bottom of the stairs and came towards them. Unhesitatingly she hugged Dominic hard and kissed him soundly. 'Silly clunch. Why on earth didn't you say something in your letters?'

He shrugged. 'Because there wasn't a great deal *to* say, beyond that I'd lost an eye and my hand was a bit of a mess. And I said that.'

Althea fixed him with a glare. 'Perhaps "I look like a pirate king and was lucky not to lose the whole hand" might have given us a slight clue?' She shook her head. 'Try to remember that we are rather fond of you, and don't appreciate being kept in the dark! Anyway, you're safe and well, and that is all that matters. Apart from the boys' nightmares.' She turned to Pippa. 'And you! What is this I hear about you taking a position as a governess?'

'No,' said Dominic baldly, 'she isn't.'

Pippa glared at him. 'Yes, I am.'

'Not without my permission you aren't,' said Dominic calmly.

'What a fascinating discussion,' said Althea, suppressing a grin. 'Pippa, I suggest, before you embark on governessing as a career, that you spend some time with my sons. It may change your mind!'

Another voice joined in. 'Philippa, what is that animal doing in the house? Kindly return it to the stables at once. You quite forget your place in bringing it in.'

Dominic turned towards his mother's voice. Lady Alderley was descending the stairs, her expression one of extreme disapproval.

'Dominic?' He glanced at Althea, who looked utterly shocked.

'I heard,' he said grimly. And he fully intended to get to the bottom of Pippa's change in status from member of the family to dependant. His brain whirled. Pippa had always been treated very much as a daughter of the house, but apparently that had changed—why? Did it have to do with her dowry?

He spoke in accents as frosty as his mother's. 'It's all right, Mother. I've told Pippa that her dog is welcome in my house.'

Let's see what that *flushes from cover.*

The inference was subtle, but Lady Alderley took the point immediately.

'*Her* dog?' She reached the hall. 'But Philippa will be leav—'

Dominic's jaw turned to solid granite, and he spoke through clenched teeth. 'No. She won't. And while we are on that subject, there is a small matter that I wish to discuss with you, Mother. Perhaps in the library?'

He shot a glance at Pippa and caught her look of sudden consternation. Damn. He'd been right, then. Something was wrong. Badly wrong.

He turned to Althea. 'I'll find you in the—?'

'Long Gallery,' she said cheerfully. 'Miss Lancelyn-Greene has something organised for all of us. Rafe is still in the billiard room, I should think. Come and see the boys first,

Pippa. They have been asking all the way if they will be old
enough this year to play Snapdragons with you. Bring your
dog and leave him there. They will love him. And what is all
this I hear about having a proper kissing bough? Miss
Lancelyn-Greene was full of it. Luckily Rafe and I brought
some mistletoe up from Herefordshire, so…'

Making a mental note to keep an eye out for stray mistletoe
and associated ambushes, Dominic ushered his mother into the
library and closed the door on the rest of Althea's discourse.

There was nothing to gain from beating round the bush. His
mother could do enough of that for both of them. Having
seated her comfortably by the fire, he went straight to the
point.

'What has befallen Pippa's money?' he asked bluntly. 'She
had a dowry. Not a big one, but enough to guarantee her inde-
pendence and secure her a respectable marriage.' The idea of
Pippa's marriage still irked him. She was far too young, no
matter what those sweet curves suggested to the contrary.
Barely nineteen. And as for the ridiculous notion of her making
her own way in the world! He shuddered at the thought.

'*Philippa*'s dowry?' said his mother with a convincing
display of surprise. 'Oh, well. I wouldn't call it a *dowry*, precisely. I believe it is not more than a few hundred pounds at
most.'

Dominic's blood congealed. 'At the time my father died,
there was a sum of several thousand pounds set aside for
Pippa by Cousin Philip. What has become of it?'

His mother gave an airy wave. 'Oh, as to that, I don't
understand these things. Only that it was all that monster

Napoleon's fault! As you know, poor Bellingham thought it best last June—after all, *everyone* thought that Wellington had been beaten!'

Then he understood and closed his eyes in despair. Acting in his stead, Bellingham had apparently sold Pippa's holdings as well as the Martindale investments.

'I am sure no one regrets Philippa's misfortune more than I,' said Lady Alderley in sorrowful tones, 'but as my sister Bellingham says, we must accept that her situation is sadly altered, and—'

'And that I have an obligation to rectify it,' he finished for her.

'And that—you have *what?*' Lady Alderley sank back in her chair, clutching her throat.

Clearly, thought Dominic grimly, that had not occurred to his mother. Nor, for that matter, to Pippa. But although he could shake Pippa for not telling him, he wasn't really annoyed. Pride he understood. But his mother's attitude— Lord! Judging by the panic in her face, you'd have thought he'd suggested turning over all his remaining fortune to Pippa.

'You must see that, Mother,' he said quietly. 'Pippa's fortune was in our care, and Bellingham was to a great degree acting in my name. I cannot replace the full amount at this time, but I can certainly provide enough for her to make a decent marriage.'

Some of the panic left Lady Alderley's eyes, although she still looked as though she had bitten into a lemon. 'Oh. Well, if that is all…but I do think you might take more thought for those more nearly connected to you than—'

'You were well provided for at my father's death,' he pointed out. *All?* What the devil did she mean...*if that is all?* What did she think he had meant to do? He brushed the question aside. 'It will hardly beggar me, and even if it did—' He left the sentence unfinished. Even if it did, he could not leave Pippa in such dire straits. The potential for disaster chilled him. She might be safe immured in a girls' school, but—no! He wouldn't permit it. If he hadn't come home now—his spine iced over—she would have been gone before he knew about it.

Lady Alderley fiddled with the strings of her cap. 'I dare say you think me quite heartless, Dominic,' she said defensively.

'I should not have put it in those terms, Mother,' he said. 'But even if I could not replace part of her dowry, I still would not consent to her leaving. It would betray the trust Cousin Philip placed in us when he left her here.' And it would leave a very big hole at Alderley, he suddenly realised.

'Well, I must say,' said Lady Alderley with asperity, 'one did not expect she would be here always! And she says herself that she wishes to find an eligible situation.'

'That is nothing to the point, ma'am,' he said shortly. 'Pippa will remain and that is the end of the subject.' If Pippa wanted to leave, it was probably because she now felt herself to be a burden.

'Be that as it may, Dominic,' said Lady Alderley crossly. 'I believe that you are expected in the Long Gallery. Some entertainment that dear Hermione has planned.' She stood up and stalked out, skirts swishing.

Dominic swore under his breath as the door closed. An entertainment arranged by Hermione? He sat back in his chair. What the hell was he going to do about that situation?

Not marry her. That was what. Damn everyone's expectations to hell. Hermione had broken the engagement herself. And the only reason she was willing to take him back was because it would make her Viscountess Alderley.

His jaw clenched. Not damned likely. Being married for his title was one thing; being expected to be grateful for stale crumbs doled out in cold charity by a heartless little baggage was quite another.

The Martindale fortunes might be at the low watermark for now, but a few years of economy and careful management would see an improvement. He would survive.

And if the Lancelyn-Greenes, not to mention his fond mama, tried to hold him to the betrothal—what then? The last thing he needed was a suit for breach of promise. He drummed his fingers on the desk, glaring at an inoffensive bust of Socrates. No. Not hemlock. Things weren't that bad. Hermione was an heiress. Her mother and trustees would be determined to secure a generous settlement for her—if he were stubborn about that… Yes, the settlements would do his business for him, if it came to that. In the meantime, if he dropped enough hints that with the estate in such a mess he was unwilling to waste money on frivolity in London…that not only would he be remaining largely at Alderley, but that his wife would remain there as well… His mouth twisted into a smile that would have sent a basilisk to grass. By the time he had named his terms, Hermione would be only too happy to have the betrothal remain broken.

In the meantime he'd better go and find out just exactly what blasted entertainment Hermione, no—*Miss Lancelyn-Greene*—had arranged. Hopefully it wouldn't involve mistletoe.

After greeting the Fanshawe boys and leaving Ben with them and their extremely tolerant nurse, Pippa ran along the gallery towards her bedchamber. She must do what she should have done the previous night and burn the play. Hermione would be furious, but in the end it would be for the best. Dominic would be unutterably hurt if he ever found out just what had been planned.

Philippa saw Lord Bellingham at the far end of a corridor and her eyes widened. Drat! If he saw her, she would be held up for at least fifteen minutes, breathing as shallowly as possible because of his overuse of rosewater. The thought of his eyes slithering all over her and the supposedly avuncular way he patted her hand every time he apologised for the loss of her dowry were enough to have her diving under a tapestry to hide in the servants' stairwell until he had passed.

Ten minutes later she was in her room, leaning against the door, regaining her breath. She pondered the likelihood of Hermione throwing a tantrum when told the play was burnt. Surely by now she would see how inappropriate the play was? Pippa's common sense informed her that she was deluding herself, and she went to light the fire. She needed it burning brightly before she put the manuscript on.

A few moments later the fire was crackling merrily. Pippa stared at the dancing flames. Hermione was lovely, of course. And charming—when she wished to be. She was an heiress.

In Dominic's world she was the perfect bride. Love matches were dreams for young ladies who had nothing else to offer. And anyway, Dominic did love Hermione. That had been quite plain last spring. He'd had eyes for no one else.

But did Hermione love Dominic?

Of course she does! How could she not?

She shied away from what that told her about the state of her own heart.

What was important now was to burn the manuscript. She knew how the story ended. She had got all the changes down last night. Her Beast had his happy ending, it would not affect him if the manuscript were destroyed. He was perfectly safe in her imagination. Anyway, it didn't matter any more. Not beside the need to protect Dominic.

And your heart? She crushed the thought mercilessly, and went over to the dressing table where her writing box sat.

She frowned. Odd. She always left the key in the lock, but it sat beside the box. The maid who dusted this room must have knocked it. Inserting the key in the lock, she turned it. The key wouldn't turn. Puzzled, she tried again. Still it wouldn't turn. Automatically she tried the lid, which lifted immediately.

Then she stared. In utter horror.

She closed the writing box with trembling hands. Empty. Yet she remembered, positively, putting the manuscript in there last night. *And* locking the box. Yet it had been unlocked just now. And she *had* left the key in the lock. Why ever would she remove it? There was nothing of value in there. Only the manuscript. And who would take…? Her stomach turned to ice.

Who would take it? Of all the foolish questions! She knew, beyond all possible doubt.

Chapter Six

***

Dominic found the entire party assembled in the Long Gallery with the exception of Pippa. His gaze raked the group gathered by the fireplace—dammit, even his mother was there, sitting by the fire with Mrs Lancelyn-Greene.

Hermione came forward, her bright smile firmly in place. 'Here you are, sir! We are all waiting for you. We cannot possibly proceed without you!'

She held out her hand, the smile brighter than ever, but he had the distinct impression that she was not really seeing him at all, that she was focused on some point beyond his ruined face. Beyond as in the next county.

Reluctantly he extended his hand. His right hand. Gloveless. Watching closely, he saw the stiffening of her face, the tiny flicker as her smile slipped slightly. Then her hand was in his. Small, delicate. Lifeless.

''Tis all arranged. You have but to speak your part.'

'My part?'

'In our theatricals, my lord.' Hermione fluttered her lashes at his left ear as she led him forward. 'Everyone is to take a role. 'Tis part of your welcome home.'

Every nerve sizzled a warning. Whenever someone had suggested Christmas theatricals during his boyhood, he'd always taken good care to play least in sight, lest some idiot aunt dress him up as a pageboy, or worse.

His brother-in-law, Sir Rafe Fanshawe, hailed him with what sounded uncommonly like relief. 'Hurry up, Dominic. Only one copy of the script is bad enough, but without the hero it's a lost cause.' The expression on Rafe's face said, quite clearly, *Save me!*

Dominic stared at Rafe in disbelief. 'I beg your pardon? *Who* did you say is supposed to play the hero?'

Rafe said, 'Ah, well, *you* are, old chap. It was all in Lady Alderley's invitation, y'know.'

Dominic forbore to point out that, as the unsuspecting host, he had not been privy to an invitation.

Rafe, apparently taking his silence for approval, continued. 'Miss Lancelyn-Greene has the whole thing organised,' he said. 'She even wrote it. Can't disappoint a lady,' he added with a wicked grin.

Oh, couldn't he? Fury surged. He knew damn well why he had not been told. He'd have made his position plain immediately; to wit, he had not the least intention of standing up mouthing fairytale nonsense about happily ever after with… His brain stopped. With whom?

'Do come on, Dominic,' urged Althea. 'What have you been *doing?* Mama said you were coming up directly. We have found a costume for you.' She held up an ornately embroidered coat that Dominic was willing to swear their great-grandfather had worn at the court of Versailles. Birds and flowers rioted all over it in unbridled enthusiasm. He gulped. The damn thing looked as though it would fit, too.

He rallied his wits. 'And the heroine of this piece?' he enquired, already sure of the answer.

At his icy tones, Althea appeared to realise that something was not quite right. She cast a querying glance at Hermione. 'Well, Miss Lancelyn-Greene, of course. After all, you and she...' Dominic's brows rose and her voice trailed off.

'She and I? You fascinate me, Althea.' Althea's eyes widened in sudden comprehension. Satisfied that she understood, he turned to Hermione with a slight inclination of the head, keeping a death grip on his self-control.

'And this play, Miss Lancelyn-Greene? Something from your own pen, did Rafe say?' It was news to him if Hermione was capable of writing anything more taxing than a brief letter.

At this inopportune moment the door at the other end of the gallery burst open and Pippa rushed in. 'Hermione! Did you take—?' She saw Dominic and gasped. 'Oh! Oh, dear God!'

He frowned. 'Pippa? What's—?'

His mother intervened quickly. 'I am sure nothing could be more pleasant for you young people than to have some theatricals to amuse you over the holiday. There is nothing the least improper in such things.'

'Did I say that there was?' asked Dominic mildly.

The temperature in the gallery, already distinctly chilly despite the fires blazing at either end, seemed to drop several degrees. Dominic strolled over to the sofa table and picked up the pile of paper. The temptation to see what Hermione's pen had produced before he dropped it in one of the fires was irresistible.

Glancing at it, he frowned. It was not Hermione's hand, and yet the untidy writing was familiar. Very familiar.

Icy bands contracted round his heart.

He looked up at Pippa's blanched face. 'This is your writing, my dear,' he said softly, conscious of a queer pang that felt oddly like betrayal. He focused on the title. *'Beauty and the—'* He glanced up again at Pippa, saw her swallow. 'Ah, I do see why you cast me in the role,' he said, replacing the pages on the table. 'Well. That does change things, does it not?'

Lady Alderley looked at him dubiously. 'You'll do it, then?'

'But could you doubt it, ma'am?' he asked silkily. Despite his fury he could recognise a heaven-sent opportunity when it hit him in the face.

The triumphant look Hermione shot at Pippa puzzled him, but he said, 'Naturally I am prepared to take my part. So apposite, too.' His gaze speared Pippa. He was savagely pleased to see that she bit her lip, that her cheeks were now scarlet. Dammit! How could she have let him in for this nonsense? He'd trusted her. Yet not a word had she said this morning! She'd even written the damn play apparently! By God, he'd teach her a lesson while he made his position with regard to Hermione abundantly plain.

He went on smoothly. 'My only concern is the possible impropriety of the piece.'

'Impropriety?' his mother protested. 'Why, 'tis no such thing. Indeed, I was very clear with Hermione—'

'Oh, for heaven's sake, Dominic!' grumbled Althea.

'Hermione?' queried Dominic in the deadliest of voices. 'I was under the impression that Pippa had penned this opus.'

Lady Alderley flushed. 'Oh, very well! Of course Philippa wrote the play down for Hermione, but it was all Hermione's idea, so…' She faltered, then rallied. 'I was most insistent with both girls—there must be nothing at all *warm*. And Philippa assured me that there was to be only one kiss at the very end—you know, when Beauty has agreed to marry the…that is, the, er—' She caught Rafe's eye and ground to a halt.

'Beast,' said Dominic, helping her out in a spirit of pure devilry. 'But one must look a little more closely at the scenario—does not Beauty live in the Beast's palace with him? Alone?'

'Chap does have servants,' said Rafe, plainly bent on being unhelpful.

'Invisible ones, I believe,' said Dominic, glaring at his brother-in-law. 'No. I could not possibly countenance something that might lead to all manner of conjecture and perhaps damage Miss Lancelyn-Greene's reputation. After all, one never knows when a Beast might take it into his head to do something, er, beastly. Does one?'

Judging by the strange noise emanating from him, Rafe Fanshawe was choking on something. Probably Dominic's uncharacteristic concern for propriety.

Lady Alderley demurred. 'But, Dominic—'

'No, ma'am,' he said, striving for a virtuous expression. 'It would be most improper to place a young lady so wholly unconnected with the family in such an invidious position. One must always consider the proprieties.'

Rafe's choking fit became alarming and Althea, losing patience, thumped him on the back.

'Nonsense, m'boy! Fiddle faddle!' put in Lord Bellingham. 'Why, in my day—'

'And Hermione is not *quite* unconnected!' protested Mrs Lancelyn-Greene. 'I am sure that if I see no objection there is no reason for anyone else to object!'

Lady Bellingham joined in. 'Yes, under the circumstances—' Her voice died away under Dominic's suddenly intent look.

'And what circumstances would those be, Aunt?'

She quailed. 'Well, naturally, Dominic, one has assumed that you and dear Hermione—an unfortunate misunderstanding last spring, but now, of course—'

He cut her off. 'Let me be quite clear—there are no circumstances, or anything else, between Miss Lancelyn-Greene and myself that could make it anything but improper for it to be suggested that she had lived unchaperoned in my castle without benefit of clergy!'

Hermione's protest was drowned by Lady Alderley's saying crossly, 'Then unless we invite some other young lady to come and play the part, that leaves no one except Althea!'

His gaze narrowed on Pippa. 'Not quite, Mama. Pippa is, after all, my cousin and has lived here as a member of the family for years.'

Right on cue, Pippa's eyes snapped from the floor to his face, a look of sheer horror in them.

'Almost like a sister,' he continued. 'No such consideration would apply any more than if she were my sister. And without the other unfortunate interpretation that would apply if she *were* really my sister and I kissed her onstage.'

He ignored Althea's splutter of indignation. He was safe.

Writing the play was one thing, but Pippa was far too shy to agree to take part. She would refuse point blank and the whole thing would be off. Except, of course, that Hermione—being Hermione—would probably inveigle Bellingham into prancing round the stage pretending to woo her, in the vain hope that *he* would succumb to a fit of jealousy and relent. Hell would freeze over first! And when he got Pippa alone, he was going to give her a piece of his mind that she would never forget.

Pippa felt the floor heave under her. He had agreed? With the stipulation that *she* played the part of Beauty? No. He couldn't have. Surely he didn't want…?

She stared at Dominic and knew perfectly well that his suggestion did not spring from an ardent desire to play her lover onstage, or anywhere else for that matter. He was just trying to avoid an awkward situation. If only Hermione and Aunt Louisa had listened to her! Of course Dominic didn't want half the county looking on while he renewed his courtship with Hermione.

And of course he didn't want some other girl in the part. Especially when the Beast, transformed into the Prince, kissed the girl at the very end. Her heart sped up. She met Dominic's confident smile. No. He'd suggested her because he needed someone who wouldn't set Hermione's back up. Someone Hermione couldn't possibly view as a rival. Someone it wouldn't matter if he kissed onstage.

No. She couldn't do it. Writing the play and imagining…imagining… She slammed an internal door shut on that particular daydream. Writing the play was one thing. Standing up in front of everyone being kissed by Dominic was quite another. Especially when she would know perfectly well that he would far rather be somewhere else kissing Hermione. She couldn't do it. She took several deep breaths and tried to steady her pounding heart.

A voice she scarcely recognised as hers spoke. 'Very well.'

An instant later she knew that she had made an appalling mistake. Dominic's dropped jaw radiated disbelief.

'Oh, really!' said Mrs Lancelyn-Greene with an arch titter. 'Miss *Wintercombe* to play Beauty? It seems a trifle unlikely, does it not?' She cast a glance round the rest of the party, as if inviting their agreement.

Rafe's voice sliced coldly. 'Not a bit of it. Pippa will look quite different in a pretty gown and her hair dressed properly. She's not some sort of antidote precisely!'

Pippa flushed. No, not precisely, but she certainly wasn't any sort of beauty. With or without a capital *B*.

Dominic's gaze was on her, she realised, and it was like being looked at by a stalking wolf.

'Perhaps, Cousin Philippa, you might grant me the favour of a few words in the library?' suggested Dominic, holding out his arm. His voice cut like a whip; she'd be lucky if she had any hide left by the time he'd finished with her.

'Well?'

His cold voice speared her. Not a word had been spoken between the Long Gallery and the library. The silence had practically bounced off the stonework in frozen echoes. Standing before the library fire, Pippa braced herself to be flayed.

'What have you to say for yourself?'

Nothing. Absolutely nothing. She had not the least idea how to explain. She tried anyway.

'I…didn't mean…that is…you were never meant to see it!' She shut her eyes in despair—as an explanation it left a great deal to be desired.

His brows rose. 'A little difficult to learn my part, then.' He placed the manuscript squarely in the middle of his desk.

Why did she always start in the wrong place? 'It was written before you came home! Before I'd seen you!' Honesty forced her to add, 'Mostly.'

He laughed. A harsh sound without any vestige of amusement. 'And it didn't occur to you *afterwards* that perhaps your choice of entertainment might be inappropriate?'

Numb with pain, she nodded. Of course it had. But what could she say without causing more trouble between Dominic and Hermione? He was just as furious as she had expected.

If she were tactful…skated round the truth… Swallowing hard, she said, 'Dominic, I knew you would not wish to take part in any play. Even before I saw you—'

'Merci du compliment!' he said savagely.

She flinched, but floundered on. 'Last night—I should have burnt the play, but I didn't. I…I did say to Hermione this morning that it was not a good idea, but she…well, she seemed to feel that you…that you—' her voice faltered at the set look on his face '—That…that I was being over-sensitive, and that you—'

'So she took the play, and it did not occur to *you*,' he said in freezing accents, 'to mention the circumstance to me this morning?'

'No.' It hadn't occurred to her because, not knowing that Hermione had already taken it, she had intended to burn the wretched thing the moment she reached home. But telling him all that was pointless, and much of this was her own fault—she should have burnt the play last night. Not sat up until all hours redeeming the Beast.

'Confound it, Pippa!' he exploded. 'Why the hell did you give it to her? Why did you even write it?'

Her temper flared. 'Because your mother told me to write it, of course!' She bit her lip. She had not meant to allude to her now dependant position.

His jaw solidified. 'You still could have warned me.'

There was no answer that could squeeze past the choking lump in her throat. Willing back the hot pressure behind her eyes, she forced her breathing to steady and went to him, holding out her hands. 'Please may I have it?'

Frowning, he noticed that her hands were shaking. That her soft mouth was set hard, as though she steeled herself to an unpleasant task. He swallowed. *Was* being near him that unbearable?

'Please. Give me the play.'

Automatically he handed the manuscript over. Then, furious with himself, he said, 'Back to the rehearsal now, my dear?'

What Pippa said about the rehearsal rocked him back on his heels and left a faint blue tinge in the air. Too shocked to remonstrate, he could only watch mutely as she went over to the blazing fire… What in Hades—?

'*No!*'

The shout left his throat without him even being conscious

that it was there, and he had leapt across the room to snatch the manuscript from her hands before she could feed it to the flames.

Why the hell should he care?

He swallowed, remembering a little girl who hardly ever spoke, whose poem had inadvertently been used to light a fire. A little girl who had fled from the room and cried her eyes out in private over the loss. Even then he had known that in some odd way, Pippa's writing was important to her... His breath jerked in; was that why she hadn't been able to burn the play last night?

'Give it to me, Dominic.' Her chin was up, her voice quite calm, as though she planned to burn a month-old newspaper.

'No. You are not to burn it.' He couldn't let her do that. Very well, she could have warned him, but...how? He'd been like a bear with a sore head the previous night at her reaction to his injuries. Small blame to her if she had hesitated to raise the subject even indirectly. Especially after this morning.

'I'm sorry,' he said simply. 'If I hadn't been such an idiot last night, you might have found it easier to tell me.'

Some of the tension eased from her face. 'I should still burn it,' she said miserably.

He shook his head ruefully. 'Too late. Everyone heard me agree to do it. From what I can gather, this is the main entertainment contrived to amuse everyone.' *If not me,* he added mentally. Although it would serve to indicate his complete indifference to Hermione. He added, 'And it might keep my uncle from pawing at too many of the maidservants!'

She looked unconvinced. 'Then surely you wish Hermione to play Beauty, and—'

'No!'

She jumped.

Realising that he had practically bellowed, he said in more moderate tones, 'That would not be at all a good idea.'

She looked puzzled. 'Then I'd better alter the stage directions at the end.'

He hadn't looked at the end. 'Why?'

Her cheeks pinkened. 'Because,' she said in the tones of one on the scaffold, 'you can't possibly desire to kiss *me!*'

His brows rose at that. Couldn't he? He considered the matter: the lips in question were just now set mutinously, but usually—his stomach contracted—usually they were soft and full, slightly kicked up at the corners as though a smile hovered, waiting. Her mouth was a little too wide for beauty, but such a luscious pink...

Good lord! When had he noticed all that? And why was he imagining those soft lips trembling under his, parting in surrender...

Realising that he had actually stopped breathing, he dragged in a breath and reality crashed into him with it. In her tactful way Pippa was indicating that she had no desire to kiss him. Or to be kissed by him. The disillusionment was startling.

'I assure you,' he said coldly, 'I intend no more than a stage kiss!' He hoped.

Comprehension, swiftly followed by—hurt?—flared in her eyes. Then her face went blank; her voice was very still as she said, 'I never thought it would be anything else. Will you excuse me now?'

He knew that expression. He'd seen it often enough when he returned from the war after Toulouse. At every post that had brought no letter from her father. He'd hurt her. Pippa. Who had always been like a little sister. Pippa, whom he ought to protect, rather than lusting after her one second and snubbing her the next as though his unruly thoughts were her fault. Not that he could tell her that.

'No.' He managed a smile. 'I'm an idiot. Come. Give me a hug and forgive me.'

She came, hesitantly, to stand before him, her eyes still shuttered, wary. It shamed him. This was Pippa—one of his dearest friends. She had done nothing to earn his anger.

He drew her to him gently, meaning only to offer comfort, an apology. The shock of contact slammed through him in slow waves of heat. He hadn't expected her slender body to fit against his as though completing it. Nor had he counted on the instantaneous reaction of his body. Hell's teeth. He ought to be used to holding women by now. But none of them had been Pippa. None of them had made his blood leap at the simple pleasure of just holding them.

He continued to hold her. Gently. His hands stroking her back. Clumsy, fumbling fingers burying themselves in the soft, tawny curls at her nape. He breathed deeply, inhaling the sweetness of lavender and rosewater. And the soft, underlying fragrance of woman. Pippa.

It was an appalling mistake.

Chapter Seven

Dominic's body informed him unmistakably that brotherly had nothing to do with what he was feeling. Reeling with shock, he whispered her name.

She looked up, her eyes wide, lips soft, rosy—parted. Temptation incarnate.

'Dominic!'

The outraged voice ripped the spell to shreds. Pippa pulled herself away with a gasp as though a bucket of icy water had landed on her. Shaken to the core, Dominic released her and turned to glare at his mother.

Who was doing a fair bit of glaring on her own account as she shut the door behind her swiftly.

'Philippa, it will be as well if you return to the Gallery.' Icicles hung from her voice. 'I wish to speak with Alderley.'

Dominic frowned at the formal use of his title. Every instinct told him not to let Pippa go, but she was already moving. The door shut firmly behind her.

For once Lady Alderley did not mince words.

'Dominic, you must reconsider this foolish decision to have Philippa play the part of Beauty. If the scene I just interrupted is anything to judge by, she has every intention—'

'*What?*' Fury scalded him.

She broke off. 'Well, as to that, I am sure I wish Philippa only good, but you must see that it is unfair to put her in such a position. It must raise hopes that you have no intention of fulfilling.'

'Which hopes would those be, Mother?'

She bridled. 'You know very well what I mean!'

He did. Her earlier relief over his intent to replace Pippa's dowry, that that was *all* he felt obliged to do…she had feared he meant marriage… His brain tripped over that. Marriage—marriage to *Pippa?*

'Yet you had no such qualms about raising these hopes in Miss Lancelyn-Greene's breast,' he remarked calmly as a stunning idea revolved in his mind.

'Dear Hermione,' said Lady Alderley warmly, 'would not *dream* of taking advantage! All I am trying to say is that you do not wish to find yourself in a situation where you must disappoint Philippa. It would be most unkind in you!'

Dominic's fists clenched.

Lady Alderley went on, 'And I should not have to point out that if anyone but myself had caught you with her in your arms just then, you might well have found yourself honour bound to offer for her! And we don't want *that!*'

On this pronouncement she stalked out, leaving Dominic to his thoughts. Which were not, he conceded, quite what his mother would have wished. Far from raising hopes that he would be unprepared to fulfil, Dominic thought that he might be only too happy to fulfil them. Now that he thought about it, Pippa had every qualification to fit her as his viscountess. In the meantime, he'd better remove himself to the Long Gallery for the rehearsal. All in all, as a way of wooing a bride, theatricals had a great deal to recommend them, up to and including kisses.

As for Hermione… A wicked thought came to him. A quick side trip to the nursery would pay dividends.

Pippa fled up the stairs. Her mind whirling and her legs thoroughly wobbly, she battled to reduce her thoughts to order. He hadn't been going to kiss her. It wasn't possible. Or if he had, then it was just to reassure her about kissing her onstage. Surely she had imagined the heat in his gaze!

But it was not Dominic's intentions that bothered her. She had *wanted* him to kiss her! Her body had felt as though it were melting into his. Shameless! Wanton! If Aunt Louisa had not walked in at that moment… She pressed her hands to her burning cheeks. Aunt Louisa would be furious. Somehow she must remove that kiss from the stage directions. Or, if that proved impossible, at least it need not be rehearsed. Would that work?

She smiled vaguely at a maid who dipped a curtsy.

She shivered. If just being in his arms affected her like that, a kiss would have her melting into the floor.

You might become immune to it if he did kiss you. Like only getting the measles once… As if to contradict the idea, that strange, aching heat flooded her again. What if, when he kissed her onstage, everyone saw how she responded? Her stomach churned. Dominic would certainly notice—and draw one of two possible conclusions: either that she was a wanton, or worse…he might realise the truth…

No! Better if she could think of something to replace the kiss. Such as…such as…a waltz! That was it! Pondering that, she came to the Long Gallery and hesitated as she reached for the door. She had danced with Dominic often enough and it had never bothered her at all. It was only the way he had held her, as though he were about to kiss her, that had affected her, so they could dance instead of kissing. It would last a little longer and provide some closing music, since Althea played the harp very prettily. Yes, it would work beautifully.

And… Her thoughts faltered here; if he changed his mind and Hermione took the role, the kiss could be reinstated.

Drawing a deep breath, she went in and found every eye trained on her.

'Has he come to his senses?' asked Hermione at once.

'We are agreed that I should play the part,' she said.

'Oh.' Hermione looked furious.

Mrs Lancelyn-Greene eyed Pippa as one might a particularly wartsome toad. 'Well, I must say—'

'We had better get on with it,' said Althea cheerfully, cutting off whatever Mrs Lancelyn-Greene had felt she must say. 'It will be best if the performance is just before the tenants' supper and the dancing in the Great Hall on Twelfth Night, but we haven't much time, you know. Tomorrow we must decorate the Hall, and we ought not to rehearse on Christmas Day, and we are all invited to dine at Bransteade House on New Year's Day. So we have only a clear week, really. Where is the script?'

'Dominic has it,' said Pippa. 'I suppose he will be up soon.' After Lady Alderley had reminded him of his duty.

Althea sniffed and said, 'Very well. We shall arrange the costumes while we wait. And this evening we shall all make copies of the script for ourselves!'

Dominic arrived in the Gallery with Ben at his heels, to find a scene of industry sorting out costumes. Althea pounced on him, snatched the script and made him remove his coat so that she could bundle him into the embroidered one she had threatened him with earlier.

'And here.' She thrust a very old, shabby wig at him. 'Put this on.' A few deft tugs left his cravat in complete disarray.

She stood back to survey the effect. 'Excellent. You look just the part. A veritable monster of wealthy slovenliness.'

'Thank you,' said Dominic meekly. 'Is there something I should do?'

'Yes. Sit down and listen. I'm going to read out the play so we all have an idea of it. Tonight we shall all make copies for ourselves, and—'

'But we can't all copy the same script,' protested Hermione. 'Oh, go *away,* you horrid thing!' She pushed hard at Ben, who wagged his tail at her. 'Call him off, Philly! He'll dirty my gown!'

Althea gave her a disgusted look. 'It's just a dog, Hermione. I dare say, with Dominic home, that he will be inside a great deal.'

Hermione looked absolutely revolted at the prospect.

Dominic smiled. 'I gave him to Pippa, but, yes—he will.'

Flushed, Pippa clicked her fingers and Ben went to her at once, collapsing at her feet.

'As for the script,' went on Althea, with a speculative

glance at Dominic, 'no one can copy more than one page at a time, Hermione. It will work. Then we can start in earnest learning our lines. We all have our parts. Uncle Bellingham is to be the merchant, Aunt Bellingham is to be the merchant's housekeeper, you and I, Hermione, are to be the horrid sisters, and Rafe is to be a brother. And we shall all be invisible servants in the Beast's castle. Agreed?'

In the face of this merciless organisation, no one raised a murmur.

The only change Althea made to her reading was to hand the script to Dominic and Pippa for the second act, saying innocently, 'Since only the two of you have speaking roles, you might as well read your own lines.'

Pippa gulped. She had never envisaged acting the part herself. Nor had she envisaged Dominic's large frame leaning to read over her shoulder. In a flowery coat and wig, no less. She stumbled over her lines, wishing that she had refused the part, or that Dominic had never suggested it.

He didn't seem to mind. Indeed, judging by the expression he was putting into his speeches, the wretch was enjoying himself hugely.

The reading over, Dominic sat back and cast a bemused glance at Pippa, whose gaze seemed to have glued itself to the floor. She had really written that? A play. A whole play with characters that sounded...*alive*, damn it. He couldn't think of a single word to say.

'Oh, it's lovely!' said Althea. 'Well done, Pippa! Don't you think so, everyone?'

'I suppose it's all very well,' said Mrs Lancelyn-Greene

with a superior sort of smile. 'I am sure Miss Wintercombe did her best.'

Dominic stiffened, and a noise suspiciously like a growl escaped him.

'Jolly good show, what?' said Lord Bellingham, rubbing his hands. 'Jolly affecting when the father has to say goodbye to her, eh?'

Another growl escaped. If Bellingham thought this gave him licence to paw at Pippa... The green-eyed beast snarled in agreement.

'Something in your throat, Dominic?' murmured Rafe.

Dominic skewered him with a glare and didn't answer.

'But the Beast is so rude to Beauty at first!' said Hermione. 'He's supposed to be in love with her.'

Pippa spoke up, her voice diffident. 'Not then. He's only just met her.'

Hermione's eyes widened. 'Silly! She is supposed to be beautiful—he falls in love with her at first sight, of course. You really aren't romantic at all, Philly! Still, we can change it. Just a few tweaks.'

'And where did you envisage these "tweaks"?' enquired Dominic silkily, reining in anger.

'Well, in the middle,' said Hermione. 'It doesn't make sense! What was all that about his paw feeling more like a hand to Beauty, even though it still looked like a paw? How could it *feel* human, if it still looked like a paw? And the spell isn't broken at the end at all. You...er, I mean, the Beast doesn't really *change*. He...he just looks tidier! And he's nicer to Beauty.'

She glared at Pippa, and said outright, 'It's silly. Not at all how *I* imagined it!'

'Then perhaps you should have written it yourself,' suggested Dominic. He could only dimly imagine how Pippa must feel. Probably wishing she had been quicker getting the manuscript on to the fire. Then it would still be safe in her imagination, not exposed for idiots to sneer at.

Pippa spoke again. 'I…I suppose that we could—'

'Rubbish!' interrupted Rafe, before Dominic could draw breath. 'It works very well. Miss Lancelyn-Greene—all the Beast's changes are in his character. Which is surely far more important than what he looks like! Once he *behaves* like a human being, then Beauty can see, and feel, past the exterior and fall in love with him. Perhaps there are some minor alterations that might be made to strengthen this, but the basic idea should stand.'

Dominic's world shook. Was that how Pippa had meant it? She was nineteen, for God's sake! How could she possibly understand?

Rafe had turned to Pippa. 'Good girl,' he said.

Pippa's confidence recovered somewhat. Perhaps it wasn't so dreadful. Maybe it was even a good thing Dominic had stopped her burning it, if only… 'There is one change I should like to make.' Not daring to look properly, she flicked a glance at the embroidered coat sitting beside her. 'Just in the stage directions at the end, where…where it says "He kisses her"?'

Hermione sniffed.

Lord Bellingham guffawed, slapping his knees, then subsided at Lady Bellingham's baleful stare.

'Just a crumb in my throat, don'cha know?' he excused himself.

Rafe nodded helpfully. 'Go on, Pippa.'

'Well, I don't think the Beast really needs to kiss her,' said Pippa hurriedly. 'At least—'

'This Beast does,' came a barely audible murmur from the embroidered coat. 'At the *very* least!'

Her cheeks flaming, Pippa said, 'I thought they could waltz instead.'

'Excellent idea,' said the coat aloud.

Pippa beamed.

'Only make it "as well" not "instead,"' said the coat. 'Don't you agree, Rafe?'

'Oh, absolutely,' said Rafe.

Pippa's jaw dropped at this perfidy.

'Wonderful,' said Althea. 'So that's settled. Thank you, everyone.'

Dominic spent the following morning in the library virtuously learning his lines. That Pippa, little, quiet Pippa, could have written this, still amazed him. How could Pippa, untouched, nineteen, possibly understand how the Beast felt? His frustration every time he knocked something over with a clumsy paw? His consciousness of people staring at him? The urge to yell that there was still a human inside?

The same way she understood you yesterday?

He stared unseeing at the pages before him. Pippa. Who would have thought it? Alex was right. She was no longer a little girl. She was a woman. He let out a breath. And thank God for it, or he'd be calling himself out for some of his imaginings.

He stared at the sealed letter he'd written to Henderson. His instructions. He'd send a groom up to town with it on the twenty-seventh. No point any earlier. Henderson could do nothing until after the holiday.

Slowly he became aware of gales of laughter in the Great Hall. What the devil—? Oh, yes. Althea had said they would be decorating the Hall. Pleasure bubbled up as he remembered how much he'd enjoyed helping with that as a child. Without quite knowing how it happened, he was on his feet and heading for the door.

Chapter Eight

❦

He discovered a scene of near bedlam. What looked like every indoor servant and a fair sprinkling of gardeners and grooms were crowded into the Hall, laughing and joking as they hung greenery everywhere. With a queer pang he saw that Richard's portrait was garlanded with rosemary. His own sported a complete frame of holly and all the old weapons over the fireplace dripped with bay leaves. The rather tatty boar's head by the stairs was well and truly bedecked with bays *and* rosemary, he saw with a smile, and ivy trailed everywhere, great swathes hanging in festoons from every available projection.

In the midst of all this Pippa was perched at the top of a ladder steadied by his valet, Briggs, carefully affixing the kissing bough to the chandelier in the middle of the hall. He noted that the usual candles in the chandelier had been changed for red ones.

He looked up at Pippa. Her tawny curls framed her face in soft tendrils, one tumbling over her brow, so that his fingers itched to push it back. Her face was flushed, and her eyes sparkled with laughter at something Briggs was saying.

'Oh, nonsense, Briggs!'

Briggs grinned up at her. 'Aye. 'Tis tradition, Miss Pippa. Her that puts the kissing bough up has to be kissed when she comes down. Just to make sure it works!'

Pippa blushed. 'Briggs! You old scoundrel! You just made that up!'

'I've not the least doubt of that,' said Dominic, strolling forward to stand by the ladder. He suppressed a smile at the startled squeak and wide-eyed stare she gave him. 'Are you coming down from there?' he asked in a deliberately neutral voice. Aside to Briggs he murmured, 'My privilege, I think?' He felt distinctly feudal. *Droit de seigneur* and all.

Briggs grinned. 'Always happy to defer to an expert, my lord.'

Dominic choked, but held up his hand to Pippa, who placed hers in it. His fingers closed in gentle possession. In this way, he thought, his intentions would be signalled to everyone. Unmistakably. He reached up and plucked a berry.

Hesitantly, Pippa came down, aware that her treacherous heart was pounding. Despite plucking that berry, which supposedly meant he could claim kisses as long as it lasted, he wouldn't really kiss her. Not…not a proper kiss. Just a peck on the cheek. Or maybe very quickly on the lips.

Simply, easily, he swung her off the second-bottom rung of the ladder and Pippa's feet touched ground, only, for the second time in two days, to find herself in Dominic's arms. This time with a full and delighted audience.

Her breath hitched at the look on his face. Heated.

Intent. 'I'm...I'm sure it works beautifully!' she said hurriedly.

'I don't doubt it,' he murmured, with a smile that ought to have been illegal. Her lungs seized as he drew her into his heat and strength. Closer until her breasts touched him, and he bent his head slowly. Possessively.

His mouth brushed over hers lightly. Again and again. Wonder held her captive. She trembled, waves of heat and longing washing through her at the caress of his lips. So this was a kiss...

His lips settled over hers and firmed, their gentle movement weaving sensuous enchantment, a beguilement she had never dreamed of.

This was a kiss.

She had never known that a kiss could melt every bone in a girl's body to warm honey until all she could do was cling. Never known that a man's arms could both protect and imprison—nor that she could feel ravished and yet utterly safe.

She had known nothing—

'Goodness me, Dominic!' came an amused voice. 'Are you testing the kissing bough or something?'

Dominic broke the kiss to a volley of applause, unsure whether to murder his sister or thank her. Given the audience and the smoking state of his own control, he suspected the latter was in order. Althea stood in the entrance to the hall with her sons and husband, their arms full of greenery. Her eyes glinted with laughter.

Rafe's brows had practically disappeared into his hat and he was regarding Dominic with mingled understanding and disapproval.

Dominic stood, shaken at the violence of his response. As kisses went, that had to be the most chaste he had ever given, or received. And yet his body had hardened to iron, his blood hammering. He dragged in a breath. Physical desire. No more. Surely. He knew about desire, wanting a woman. But this—this was shatteringly different. He didn't simply want *a woman;* he wanted Pippa. Just Pippa.

He stared down at her. The greeny-brown eyes were dazed, her lips rosy soft and—desire kicked sharply—moist from his kisses.

Their eyes locked and Pippa's face flamed as she pulled herself free.

'I…I think the kissing bough is quite…adequate,' she said.

Adequate? Dominic shot a glance upward at the wreathed greenery. The damn thing was lethal!

He was still shaken and dazed that evening when they brought in the Yule log and lit it from a scrap of the last one, with laughter and cheering for a joyous year of peace ahead. Pippa, he noticed, kept well in the background, as far from the kissing bough as possible.

Even the following morning in church, on Christmas Day itself, his mind drifted to that kiss. So sweet, so full of… He shied away from the forming thought and forced his mind back to Alex's sermon…on the subject of love.

'Most of us cannot understand God's love directly. Not here. Not now. We perceive it only dimly through others. God's love could not fit into our world, so he became man, that we might see love in action…in every act of human love, God is there…'

Was that it? The thought shocked him. For heaven's sake! He had known Pippa for years…but love? How could he miss that? He glanced down the pew towards Pippa, sitting between Althea's boys, her face hidden by the poke of her bonnet. Her gloved hands lay quietly in her lap. He could not see *Pippa,* yet he knew she was there. Small Tom wriggled beside her, and immediately her arm slipped around him in a quick hug. Tom settled and snuggled closer.

Something shifted inside him…opening…

She was a child. You've always loved her. Perhaps God knew precisely what he was about in hiding this part of it from you…

This. This aching need to possess and be possessed. To give a gift that he had never offered before. Himself, without reservation. Nothing held back.

Was that love?

At Christmas dinner Pippa sat at the far end of the table, next to Rafe, laughing at his quips, her cheeks flushed, eyes sparkling. At the end of it, he knew only one thing. He was going to marry Pippa. He would use this Christmastide to woo her, then after it was all over and their guests had gone, he would propose. Beg her if necessary. He didn't care if it took him longer to bring the estates back into order and rebuild what had been lost. With Pippa, it would be a labour of love and joy.

The tidied-up Beast, a fresh and very neat wig on his head, bent for the promised kiss that was supposed to follow his heartfelt declaration of love. To his chagrin the slender Beauty in his arms backed away, in complete disregard of her own stage directions. Exactly as she had for the past several days.

'Very well,' she said hurriedly. 'We don't need to rehearse the kiss. We…we can take that as read.'

Dominic's brows lifted. 'Oh? I don't usually read kisses. I take them!' He added, *sotto voce,* 'And not just kisses.' Four days into the New Year and his control was smouldering at the edges.

Pippa's eyes widened and her breath caught at the wicked smile that suggested all manner of things that the Beast might take. Such as Beauty herself. He was teasing her. He must be. Not to mention infuriating Hermione, whose blue eyes resembled twin daggers.

'As you wish,' he said, the smile deepening. 'Just our waltz, then.'

She gulped. This waltz was among the worst ideas she had ever had. But before she could protest Dominic had swept her into his arms and Althea had struck up on the harp. She must have a word with Althea; she rather thought, had she been capable of coherent thought, whirling in Dominic's embrace, that the waltz became longer each time they rehearsed it.

How she had imagined she would be able to waltz with Dominic without coming apart at the seams, she didn't know. The moment she was in his arms her skin heated and her heart pounded. Worst of all, her bones turned to warm honey and all she wanted to do was to melt against him.

She tried desperately to keep a proper distance between them, but Dominic was having none of it. Heated strength held her scandalously close; lost in the circle of his arms, sensuous enchantment held her, her heart whirling in time with the music. So close that his powerful thighs brushed past her skirts, so close that he filled her vision, and she could believe his smile was just for her. That having her in his arms was everything he could ever desire. Except, of course, for that wretched kiss!

It would be so easy, so foolishly easy to pretend just for now, and believe that the intimacy of this dance and his smile really were for her. And so dangerous. Her breasts brushed against him, the slow, deep ache spreading through her inexorably.

She missed a step and lost rhythm, only to be swept back into it by Dominic. A titter from Hermione gouged at her and she missed another step. She couldn't do this. She couldn't.

It wasn't just the dance and the kiss. With every rehearsal her speeches grew more wooden, so that she stumbled through them. And Dominic waited. Prompted her gently, as though he knew her lines better than she did.

She knew her lines. They were engraved on her heart, but she couldn't pretend, she simply couldn't. Because she wouldn't be pretending.

'Look at me, sweetheart.'

Heat stabbed through her at the husky endearment, a nameless longing, as his hand slid from her waist to her hip and flexed. Fire shot through her.

She stumbled and pulled back, breaking the rhythm.

'Really, Philly!' said Hermione. 'If you can't do better than that—'

'It was my fault,' said Dominic. 'I trod on her toes.'

Pippa blushed scarlet at the brazen lie, avoiding his heated gaze. He knew, then. Knew the effect he was having on her!

Why then, was he doing it?

'I…I am sorry for being so clumsy,' she said.

'Nonsense,' said Althea, with a suspicious glance at

Dominic. 'I think we've all had enough for today. Pippa dear, you will be fine. Just try to relax a little.'

Relax? She felt as though she were about to shatter.

Bellingham yawned. 'Jolly good, then. I'll be off. Billiards, Fanshawe? Just need to go along to my room and I'll join you.'

'Very well,' said Rafe. 'Are you coming, Dominic?'

'I've some work to do,' he said. 'I'll join you later.'

He went down to the library to continue his study of the fascinating subject of manures. His mind kept wandering to Pippa's flushed face. He'd miscalculated. He knew she was shy. Of course she didn't want to kiss him in front of an audience. Come to think of it, he'd rather kiss her privately, too. Very privately. Somewhere no one would disturb them. Like his bedchamber.

The opening door banished this delightful fantasy. He slewed round in his chair and every instinct of self-preservation leapt to full battle alert.

Hermione.

Her sweetest smile curved her lips as she glided towards him. 'Poor Dominic,' she said, in a breathless little voice. 'Are you finding all this a sad trial? I dare say poor Philly has never been asked to dance the waltz before, so one cannot expect her to feel quite comfortable…and, of course, she is quite unused to this sort of thing! She cannot be enjoying it.'

Dominic stood up and stepped round the desk, keeping it between them. 'Is that so?' he said coolly.

She ran a dainty forefinger up and down the edge of the desk, peeping up at him under her lashes. He considered the performance dispassionately. Contrived, to say the least. He took several strategic steps to the chimneypiece.

'Don't you think, dear Dominic,' she murmured, 'that you might cease your play-acting? After all, we both know the truth, do we not?'

The truth was going to shock Hermione right out of her kid slippers. In the meantime, he reached for the bell pull.

Hermione frowned. 'What are you doing?'

His smile verged on the dangerous. 'Summoning a chaperon. This won't work, Miss Lancelyn-Greene. I'm far too hardened a rake. You will only ruin your reputation.' He didn't elaborate further, but the shot had gone home. Hermione blushed, and for an instant her eyes narrowed.

Then, with a tinkling laugh, she said, 'How chivalrous! I shall be off then.'

The door closed behind her, and Dominic heaved a sigh of relief. That had been too close. From now on he would take damn good care to give the chit no chance to corner him. Waiting for the party to break up before declaring himself to Pippa suddenly seemed madness. A public betrothal to Pippa would put paid to Hermione's machinations.

And once they were betrothed—he dragged in a breath— he would be able to kiss her. Really kiss her. In fact, he'd go and find her now.

'Now, now! Naughty Puss. Sheathe those claws!' chuckled Lord Bellingham, grabbing Pippa's wrists again and pulling her to him. 'You don't bamboozle me, my pretty! Just what you want, a bit more kissing under the mistletoe!'

'There isn't any mistletoe up here!' she gasped, turning her face away from his hot breath. A strong odour of brandy hit her. Which probably explained Uncle Bellingham's shift from leering to lechery, but didn't make it any more pleasant.

'Come along, now. Just a bit of fun. I've got the mistletoe in my pocket,' he assured her, grabbing at a breast.

Far from encouraged by this assurance, Pippa kicked out, catching him hard on the shin. One wrist came free and she swung hard, her small fist landing squarely on his pudgy jaw with a loud crack. He dropped the other wrist with a yelp of pain.

'I suggest you find something else to do, Bellingham,' came a steely voice. 'Preferably at the other end of the house.'

Pippa whirled. Dominic stood a few yards away, his gaze a naked sword, both fists clenched. He started towards them, lethal intent in every stride.

Bellingham spluttered. 'Oh, come now, Dominic! No harm. Just a bit of sport, don'cha know?'

'No,' snarled Dominic. 'I don't. Not with an unwilling girl anyway.' His jaw resembled solid granite. His voice spat contempt. 'Keep your hands off Philippa in future, Uncle. And the same goes for all the maidservants. One murmur from any of them, and you're out.'

'Now, see here!' blustered Bellingham.

His control gone, Dominic took one threatening step and Bellingham decamped as fast as his portly frame would allow.

He turned back to Pippa. 'Are you all right?'

She nodded. 'He…he doesn't really mean anything, you know. It's just…not very pleasant.' In a rush she said, 'He smells dreadful! Like an old goat!'

A sound, half-groan, half-laugh, tore from him. Yet his jaw

clenched at the thought of Pippa subjected to lecherous pawings. 'I'm sorry,' he said harshly. 'It won't happen again.' Not if Bellingham wanted a whole skin. 'Look, Pippa—can we talk? Somewhere private?'

Her gaze wary, she nodded.

He looked around. Somewhere no one would bother going. But not somewhere that would raise any censure... He knew just the place.

Chapter Nine

'Dominic, where are we going?' asked Pippa. They had reached the corridor above the Great Hall.

Footsteps and voices sounded round the corner.

Before she could protest, he urged her through the door on to the musicians' gallery above the Great Hall.

Pippa stared around wildly. As a child she had often hidden here. It was quiet. Within the house, yet somehow apart. A small child could peep over the balcony at the dancers below without being seen. Watching her older cousins enviously, longing to be down there, part of it…

She realised Dominic was watching her, an odd, intent expression on his face. Determined. Tender?

Her mind whirled as what he meant to do crashed in upon her. 'Dominic,' she whispered, backing away.

'You'll have to kiss me eventually,' he pointed out, with a wicked smile. 'Wouldn't it be—'

'No!'

He went very still. Just as in her dream, his maimed hand

reached out, then it fell back to his side and his mouth twisted. 'Am I so loathsome, then? As bad as Bellingham?'

Horror slashed at her. 'No! Oh, no! It's not that. Never that. Just...' Her voice faltered.

'Just?' His smile nearly broke her heart.

Just that I love you? She slammed a door shut.

Inspiration struck. 'Just,' she said, without pausing for further thought, 'that I don't want to kiss you, knowing that you would rather be kissing Hermione!'

His jaw sagged. 'Hermione?' He sounded as though he might be strangling. Then words exploded. 'Dammit, Pippa! I'd liefer kiss a viper! It's you I want to kiss! Why do you think I kissed you the other day? Why do you think I won't let you take it out of the stage directions?'

Her certainty rocked on its foundations. 'You want to kiss me? *Me?*'

'You,' he affirmed. 'Let me show you.'

Shock slammed into her. Every maidenly precept shrieked at her to run.

She stayed.

At last. Dominic's blood roared with triumph over a frantic voice attempting to remind him there was something he'd meant to say first. Something he'd meant to ask her. He brushed the voice aside. Want to kiss her? He wanted it more than his next breath. And this, after all, was far better than a chaste brushing of lips with an audience. He gathered her to him, his scarred hand capturing both of hers and bringing them to rest against his heart.

He could hear every trembling breath, feel her shaking as he slid his free hand into the silken tawny tresses. They caressed his fingers, burning him. The line of her cheek, soft, like peach silk. She was lovely. Sweet. So damned yielding. Slowly he bent his head and covered her lips with his.

Pippa's mind fractured in the dizzying delight of his mouth open on hers. She clung, helpless, with no idea of what to do. His tongue traced her lips, teasing, licking. All she could think of was to get closer. As close as possible. To press her suddenly aching breasts against him. Uncertainly, she parted her lips to his wordless urging.

With a low sound he surged deep into her mouth, claiming it as he plundered the yielding sweetness. And then, with a shock of joy, he felt her first tentative response. Her slender body melting into his embrace, moulding to him in absolute rightness. The shy, untutored touch of her tongue dancing, mating with his. Already aching, his body hardened savagely.

Not here. Not now. Just a little further. A little more.

She was so sweet, her trusting innocence burnt at his control. He groaned into her mouth, shuddering in pleasure as clumsy fingers slid into his hair, pulling him even closer. God! If she knew how close he wanted to be… He shook at the very thought. His hands roamed delectable, soft curves in aching need.

His mouth took the startled gasp as he cupped one small, rounded breast, stroking gently over the nipple. He felt her tremble, felt the shock turn to pleasure as her body quivered in delight and her mouth softened further under his in complete surrender.

The buttons of her bodice fell to his swift fingers and he eased it aside to tease the swell of her breast through her chemise. Beautiful. His mind reeled as the peak hardened, stabbing into his palm.

His. All his. His blood exulted.

'Good God! What is this?' Mrs Lancelyn-Greene's outraged voice fell like a hammer blow.

Shocked, Dominic broke the kiss and whirled, sheltering Pippa with his body. Too late. Hermione, Mrs Lancelyn-Greene, his mother and Bellingham stood below in the Hall, staring up, with Rafe and Althea close behind them. Pippa's face was utterly blanched, leached of all colour. She fumbled uselessly with her buttons.

'Let me,' he murmured, brushing her trembling fingers aside. What the hell had he been thinking to put her in this position? Pippa's bodice restored to decency, he turned to face the others, and the appalling silence that spread from them.

A silence broken at last by his sister.

'Really, Dominic!' said Althea crossly. 'This is the outside of enough!'

'I'm sure,' said Rafe ominously, 'that Dominic has something to tell us.' His expression defined challenge.

'Nonsense!' broke in Lady Alderley. 'I do not deny that Dominic has been very thoughtless, but I dare say…that, well—' she floundered briefly '—it is nearly Twelfth Night and I suppose with the kissing bough, and this foolish play! I knew how it would—'

'Mama,' said Althea, 'the kissing bough is down here! There isn't any mistletoe up there! Only ivy!'

Rafe snorted. 'Even if there were, there wouldn't be any berries left after that effort!'

Pippa's white face told Dominic that this was not the right moment to announce a betrothal. Hell's teeth! He'd meant to ask her before kissing her witless.

'Oh, come now!' said Bellingham jovially. 'No need for high drama.' He dug Rafe in the ribs. 'Philly knows better than to take Dominic seriously. Just a bit of fun and gig. Dare say he forgot that the kissin' bough is down there in the hall!' He eyed Pippa lasciviously. 'Why, I'd forget m'self, such a pretty piece as she is now. Eh, Dominic, m'boy?' he added, an edge to his voice. 'Just a bit of sport. Nothing to get into the fidgets over.'

Only the distance between their respective positions saved Bellingham from instant death. Instead Dominic said, with a calm he was nowhere near feeling, 'Excuse us. Pippa and I have something important to discuss.'

She followed him blindly downstairs, not caring where they went. He was going to offer for her. Because he had to. She had been caught with her bodice half-undone and her arms round his neck—it could not be passed off as a mere cousinly kiss.

Heat pricked at her eyes, threatening to spill over as he opened the library door and gestured her in. He was bound in honour to offer her marriage. And no matter how little he might desire the match, he would try to insist that she accept. Somehow she must hold firm and make him accept her refusal.

Dominic could feel the tension in her body as he pushed her gently into a chair by the fire. 'I'm sorry, Pippa,' he said quietly. 'I didn't mean it to happen quite like that.'

'It's…it's quite all right, Dominic,' she said shakily. 'I…I shan't regard it. I dare say it is quite my own fault anyway, and—'

'Your fault?' he growled. 'How the devil was it your fault?'

She blushed. 'Never mind. The point is, none of your family will gossip, so—'

He said something highly improper about gossip. 'That's not why I'm offering for you,' he added.

She blinked. 'But truly, you do not need to offer for me—'

'Oh, yes, I do,' he said grimly.

There was a silence, then they spoke almost simultaneously;

'Only I'd planned to ask you without everyone knowing about it!'

'Please, I…I would rather you did not!'

His heart slammed to a halt. She would rather…? Dear God, he had thought she loved him. But if she didn't…he still wanted her. On any terms. Her eyes met his, dazed, questioning—a blaze of some fierce emotion. His heart contracted. No—not on any terms. If she knew how much he loved her, wanted her…would she accept out of pity?

Shock drove the breath from Pippa's body. For one searing moment hope flared, incandescent. He was watching her, a queer, almost desperate look on his face. He wanted her then. Her. He loved her. And he was asking her to marry him, not because he had been caught kissing her, but because he wanted her, cared for her. That was why he had been kissing her, so—her throat swelled with emotion, choking the words of acceptance, of love.

He spoke, diffidently. 'It would be the sensible thing, sweetheart.'

Her heart shuddered.

She hesitated, her gaze fixed and intent on his scarred

visage. He had called her sweetheart. Again. She wanted so much to believe him, but—

A word struggled past the aching lump. 'Sensible?' Her voice was quite steady.

He nodded. 'For both of us. We're…fond of each other. And I need a wife, you need a home.' He added the final clincher. 'It would be a convenient match.'

She dragged in a breath. 'I…no, Dominic. Thank you, but it would be better not.' She didn't feel in the least sensible. She hadn't even known what she was about to say until the words were out. But they were said.

As the dreadful, aching silence froze hope, Dominic felt the universe grind to a halt. Along with his heart.

'Pippa, I am not offering because I was caught kissing you,' he said very carefully. 'I kissed you because I intend to marry you. Not the other way around.' He smiled ruefully. 'I got it out of order, though. It should have been propose first, then kisses.'

Her face was leached of all colour, and even as he watched a tear spilt over, sliding down her cheek in silent grief. It tore him apart.

'I am sorry, my lord,' she whispered. 'I cannot return your sentiments.'

The door closed behind her, leaving Dominic staring at it, shaken to the depths of his soul. She had refused. He swallowed hard. Had he been mistaken, thinking that she had responded to him? Had she simply been too shocked to resist and he had mistaken it for response?

When the door opened a few moments later, he was staring

at the fire, wondering what next he should do. He turned round, ready to snap.

It was his mother, her face set in tragic lines. 'My poor boy! I knew how it would be! But you wouldn't listen. My sister Bellingham is quite of my mind; there was not the least need for you to—but it is all too late now. When is the wedding?' This last in tones of martyred resignation.

'She refused me,' he said quietly.

Lady Alderley had continued talking. 'I hope I know my duty, but—I beg your pardon? She—?' Her face cleared. 'Oh, my dear boy! What a lucky escape! Although I dare say she did not mean it for a moment, so we must immediately make it quite plain that your magnanimous offer has been rejected! And it will be as well if she goes away with my sister. Just to be *quite* safe. Even Rafe must see that there is no further obligation, and—'

'Mother!' he cut in.

She quailed at the steely tone.

'Pippa remains here,' he stated softly. 'My offer remains open. Unless—' The thought sickened him, but he forced himself to voice it. 'Unless she accepts some other man in marriage.'

He scarcely noticed his mother's departure. He sat down at the desk and stared unseeingly at the book-lined walls. All the wisdom of the ages there, or at least a fair sampling of it. Yet it maintained a mocking silence on what he should do now. How to salvage the wreck.

A discreet knock came at the door.

'Yes?'

Groves came in. 'The post, my lord.'

Dominic nodded. 'Thank you. Put it on the desk.'

He picked up the bag as Groves left. Letters from various friends, three for his mother, a packet from— He frowned, and opened it quickly; Henderson—his man of business—no doubt acknowledging his instructions.

'My Lord,' it ran, 'I have made a note of the amount of the money you wish to set aside to the use of Miss Wintercombe, and shall put that in motion as soon in the New Year as may be. As for your other request, I was able, through a fortuitous family connection, to conclude that today. I therefore enclose—'

Dominic dropped the letter and stared at the enclosed document in disbelief. How on earth had Henderson managed *that* in the time? It simply wasn't possible. Let alone at this time of year! The irony of Henderson's efficiency was not lost on him. He sighed, opened a drawer in his desk and tucked the document away safely.

By the following morning Pippa was tired of reiterating that she and Dominic were not to be married. Rafe had taken her aside and told her very seriously that she was making a great mistake. Althea still wished to know when the marriage was to take place. Bellingham had called her a sly little puss, with a very knowing wink. As for Lady Bellingham and Lady Alderley, it wasn't what they said aloud, it was the exchanged whispers, the darkling glances in her direction. Not to mention the Lancelyn-Greenes, who looked as though they would cheerfully tip powdered glass into her tea cup.

She had not seen Dominic. To Lady Alderley's ire, he had shut himself up in the library.

Dodging everyone, she found her cloak and a bonnet and

slipped out of the house by a side door. She needed to think, and she could not do that with her aunts on the one hand viewing her as a designing little hussy, and Althea on the other in transports of delight.

The bitter wind whipped about her and her pattens crunched on the frosty grass. Once across the park and into the shelter of the woods, she took the path to the village. Mr Rutherbridge would be happy to see her, and reading to him might ease her aching heart.

Her eyes were tired and scratchy after a sleepless night. Why hadn't she said yes? Would he mind if he realised how much she cared?

But why choose her? Plenty of other females would be convenient. Indeed, a well-connected, *wealthy* bride would be sensible. She was neither of those things. Was it because he pitied her? Worried about her?

And that was the crux of it; the fear that his offer sprang from obligation, or pity. With Dominic of all men, she could not bear to think that he had offered marriage because he viewed her as some sort of pitiful stray. Worse, if he realised how much she loved him, and she doubted that she could hide it if she accepted him, he might even pity her for that.

Alex greeted her with pleasure when she reached the Rectory.

'Pippa! What brings you here?' He smiled. 'News has travelled. I understand we've to wish you happy, my dear.'

Somehow she lifted her chin and stiffened her spine. 'No, Alex. I...I have refused Lord Alderley's obliging offer.'

'Refused—?' His jaw dropped.

Chapter Ten

A̲n hour later Alex bade her farewell, an odd smile twisting his mouth. He'd have to do something about this. Not that Pippa had said very much to them, but for the life of him, he couldn't imagine why she would be so upset about refusing Dominic's offer if she had not wanted to accept it. And she was upset. No tears. No wobbly voice. Just her usual cheerful smile, but with a shadow in the hazel eyes…and they looked red, sore—as if she hadn't slept much.

Which meant… He considered the situation carefully. Interfering between a couple, playing cupid, came high on his list of objectionable behaviour… She turned and waved from the gate, her chin high and a cheery smile on her lips.

He raised his hand, and she shut the gate behind her and started off along the lane, her step determined.

Tomorrow was Twelfth Night. Another Christmas over. The message of Christmas was one of unfailing, unswerving love. God's love for man, reflected in human love. He had preached on the subject on Christmas Day. And, as a man of

God, surely his task was to foster love in the world that it might be offered back to God? One Old Testament writer had said quite a bit about the nature of love between man and woman in the Song of Solomon…of course, it represented the love between God and his people, but surely in using such images it also suggested that human love, properly directed, was holy even in all its physicality…that it was part of God's plan? He sighed. Sometimes people could be very blind to things that were staring them in the face. They needed a friend to point it out. Tactfully.

His jaw set. If a little judicious interfering meant he was doing God's work and helping two people he dearly loved to find their happiness, then interfere he would! Although, he cast an apologetic glance heavenwards, he would not care to swear on the bible for the tactfulness of his dealings with Dominic!

He looked into the library. 'Sir?'

'Yes, lad?'

'I'm going out. A pastoral visit.'

Rutherbridge snorted. 'Suggest you club him over the head with the nearest heavy object! Marriage of convenience indeed!'

Alex chuckled as he closed the door.

'The Reverend Mr Martindale, my lord.'

Dominic looked up from his desk as Alex strolled in. Ben bounced from the hearth and leapt to greet him.

'Congratulations,' said Alex calmly.

Tensing, Dominic said, 'Obviously *all* the news hasn't reached you.' A surprise in itself. In her undisguised relief, his mother had been doing her best to spread it far and wide.

'Which news would that be?' asked Alex, fending off Ben. 'Get down, Ben. You were better behaved when Pippa had charge of you.'

Even hearing her name sent a shaft of pain through Dominic.

I am sorry, my lord, I cannot return your sentiments... Damn it all to hell, had she just been too kind and polite to repulse his advances?

Meeting Alex's enquiring gaze, he said flatly, 'Pippa refused my offer of marriage.'

Alex raised one brow—an ability that had always made Dominic long to hit him. 'Yes. I knew that. She told me when I wished her happy.'

Dominic's hackles rose. 'Then why in Hades—?'

'It's a first,' said Alex. 'You have the dubious distinction of being the only man I know who has ever offered marriage to a girl head over heels in love with him, and been refused.'

About to recommend that Alex mind his own misbegotten business, Dominic's power of speech deserted him. He couldn't have heard correctly...

Alex eyed him dispassionately. 'Without even having the excuse of being totally ineligible. Amazing. I can't begin to imagine how you did it.'

Abruptly, Dominic regained the use of his tongue. 'If you are suggesting that I deliberately offered in such a way as to force her to refuse—!' he snarled. 'Damn it! I intended to ask her anyway! What sort of scoundrel do you take me for, to be kissing Pippa like that unless I wanted to marry her?'

That blasted brow lifted in what could only be viewed as scepticism. 'Why?'

'*Why?*' Dominic could barely believe his ears. 'Why what?' Then his brain caught up with the question he really wanted answered. 'What gives you to think Pippa is in love with me?'

Alex's jaw hardened. 'Because that was pretty much the reason she gave me when I asked her why she refused you.'

'*What?*'

Grimly, Alex continued. 'Now. Back to my question. Why did you offer for Pippa?' His mouth thinned. 'Leaving aside the fact that, according to Althea, you were caught kissing her in a most *un*cousinly fashion, without a kissing bough within spitting distance!'

Goaded, Dominic consigned the kissing bough to a highly improper fate, and added, 'I offered for her because I damn well love her, you idiot! Why else?'

'Why indeed?' said Alex sarcastically. 'You left that bit out, you gudgeon! The part where you tell *her* that you love her, that you want her because she's Pippa—not because she's convenient and you want to look after her to salve your conscience! For God's sake, Dominic! You've told *me* easily enough! Why didn't you tell her? What on earth were you thinking?'

Put like that… He wasn't quite sure what he'd been thinking, but he knew precisely what he was thinking now— that he was a thrice-damned fool.

'She…she loves me?'

Alex nodded. 'Yes.'

Dominic swung round and strode over to the window, to stand staring out at the snowy landscape. If she wanted him, cared for him, why then had she refused? He cast his memory back…

'Think, Dominic,' came Alex's quiet voice.

He had asked her to marry him…and for a moment he had thought she was about to accept—there had been that flare of emotion in her face. Then…and then she had hesitated. He swore. Instead of waiting, he'd opened his big mouth…thinking to encourage her…protecting himself.

It would be the sensible thing, sweetheart…for both of us. We're…fond of each other… I need a wife, you need a home.

At that point every scrap of colour had drained from her face.

He shut his eyes. Oh, yes. If she loved him, he could understand why she had refused. Easily. For the same reason she had not mentioned her dowry to him. She had not wanted charity. Exactly the same reason he had hesitated to tell her what blazed in his heart—he had not wanted her to accept him out of pity.

If he had been reluctant to admit to his love, how must she have felt after hearing his oh-so-sensible proposal? If he had waited, would she have told him that she loved him? Remembering the flaring emotion, he rather thought she might have… Or if he had kissed her again at that point… He suppressed a groan. Instead, he'd told her that their marriage would be convenient, sensible—because he'd been too cowardly to risk telling her that he loved her.

He swore vigorously. And then remembered his company and turned round to find an amused look on Alex's face.

'I've made a complete fool of myself, haven't I?' he said ruefully.

Alex nodded. 'You have. But at least you learn fast. Now, how quickly do you mean to apply your lesson?'

* * *

Dominic swiftly discovered that a wall of feminine propriety surrounded Pippa. It was impossible to come near her all afternoon. She was seated at the far end of the table during dinner, and in the drawing room afterwards it transpired that she was now to sleep on a truckle bed in Hermione's chamber.

This last came out as he was settling down to a rubber of whist with Bellingham, Rafe and Alex, who had stayed for dinner.

Inwardly Dominic's hackles rose. Damn it! Did they think he was so lost to all honour, that he'd actually—

'Dominic! Your lead!'

He blinked. Rafe was glaring at him from the other side of the card table.

'Oh. Sorry.'

Bellingham gave him such a lewd wink that he barely refrained from snarling, and played quite the wrong card.

Rafe rolled his eyes at Dominic as Bellingham smirked and trumped it.

Visiting Pippa in her chamber *had* occurred to him. He gritted his teeth as a delightful vision of Pippa in a nightgown rose before him. Only to be followed by an even more delightful vision of Pippa *not* in a nightgown…

He forced himself to notice that Rafe had played a small diamond.

Involuntarily he glanced across at her, seated by the fire talking to Althea. Firelight gleamed on the soft tresses, flushing the pale cheeks. Her kerseymere gown was shapeless, but under it… His body tightened, remembering soft, rounded breasts and a mouth of honeyed delight yielding to his. He strangled the thought before his trousers strangled him.

To his right a throat cleared violently.

Alex caught his eye, and with a rueful grin he eased himself to a less uncomfortable position, reflecting that Hermione's bedchamber might well be the safest place for Pippa right now. Apart from which, Alex and Rafe would draw straws to see who called him out if he didn't behave. But somehow he had to get Pippa alone.

'Leave it to me,' murmured Alex, playing a spade.

'Leave what to you?' muttered Dominic, as Bellingham took the trick.

'Arranging for her to be alone. You concentrate on your cards.'

Dominic reflected that if Alex's parishioners ever realised that their curate numbered mind-reading among his skills, they'd all flock to the Methodist Chapel at the other end of the village.

The following morning Pippa was summoned to Lady Alderley's bedchamber and found the atmosphere distinctly frigid. Lady Alderley—surprise, surprise—had a scheme for keeping her out of Dominic's way.

'Dear Alex tells me that poor Mr Rutherbridge is very much confined to bed again,' she said, sipping a cup of weak tea. 'This cold weather goes to his chest, you know, and he is over eighty now. I thought we should send him a little hamper—perhaps a bottle of port wine and some brandy.'

Pippa blinked. Mr Rutherbridge had looked much improved yesterday. Out of bed, enjoying a roaring fire in his library.

'You might take them, Philippa,' continued Lady Alderley. 'Alex mentioned that Mr Rutherbridge is always very cheered by your reading. You will have plenty of time before you need to be back here to prepare for the play.' Her lips thinned.

Pippa knew exactly what she was thinking—that it was a pity Dominic still would not hear of her being replaced as Beauty.

As she was leaving, Lady Alderley said, 'My sister Bellingham will be leaving in a very few days. She has asked that you go on a visit to them. Naturally I have given my consent.'

It was another brilliant winter morning when every twig was edged in frost and the pale, clear sky swung limitless overhead. Pippa took the path through the woods to the village again. Most of the trees reached up with bare, pleading branches, but here and there holly berries blazed scarlet against their dark green leaves. There was even a single hopeful primrose in a sheltered spot.

Winter would not last for ever, she reminded herself firmly. The world continued to turn, and the seasons. Spring would come, and then summer. Only she would not see them here. She shivered. Perhaps it was wise to go to Hampshire with the Bellinghams. Away from Alderley her bruised heart would recover. At least in part. She did not think that she would ever stop loving Dominic, but away from here she might learn acceptance.

One day at a time. One did not always get what one wanted, let alone one's heart's desire. She could still be happy. Eventually. She blinked back heat.

A shout from behind brought her spinning round. All her carefully constructed detachment and self-discipline came crashing down round her, as she realised that Lady Alderley's neat scheme to keep her out of Dominic's way had backfired with a vengeance. Plainly intent on catching up, Dominic's raking stride devoured the distance between them.

She waited. There was no point in anything else, and she had nothing to fear from Dominic. Except that he might crumble her resolve not to accept his offer.

'I needed to speak with you,' he said simply, as he came up with her. And smiled.

Her world turned upside down at that heart-stopping smile that wrinkled the corners of his eyes—even the one that wasn't there. The smile that looked as though it had never been given to anyone but her. The smile that, if she weren't careful, would tear her heart from her breast and lay it at his feet.

'If you are going to repeat your offer of marriage—' she began.

He cut her off. 'No. I'm not. Perish the thought!'

'Oh. Well…good.' It was good. It really was. Temptation still licked at her. It would be so dreadfully easy to say yes, if he repeated his offer. She was relieved. Truly.

Could lead freeze? Her heart felt as though it might be possible.

He captured her gloved hand and drew it through his arm, anchoring it safely, and her foolish heart leapt back to painful life.

His warmth enveloped her and she was violently aware of everything about him. His gloved hand resting on hers, the curve of his body leaning towards her. The faint shadow beard on his jaw. The elusive mingling of shaving soap, leather and musky male. Her resolve quaked.

They walked in silence at first. Then he spoke.

'I wasn't entirely honest with you the other day,' he said. 'All those logical reasons I gave why we should marry...wonderful reasons, but—'

'They weren't true?' She tried to keep her voice steady, but it wobbled dangerously.

He didn't seem to notice. 'Oh, they were valid enough,' he said. 'But they weren't the whole truth.'

'The whole truth?' she faltered.

He stopped and turned to her, gathering her into his arms, shutting out the bitter chill of the wind. 'Nowhere near it,' he said huskily. 'There was something else, too. Something I was too damn stupid to admit.' His smile was tenderness itself as he drew her closer, his arms hardening possessively. 'There was this, too,' he whispered.

She knew what he was going to do. He was going to kiss her. She could—*should*—push him away, tell him that she didn't want his kisses. It would be a lie, a dreadful, shameless lie. She wanted his kisses and his love more than her own next breath—she would be more than happy to settle for his, but she should be noble, selfless—there was no guarantee that she wouldn't blurt out something foolish if she were unwise enough to permit him to kiss her again. Such as...

I love you.

His smile deepened, and a sigh of what sounded very much like relief breathed from him.

'Thank God for that, my darling.'

As though she had spoken aloud.

And with a shock, she realised that she *had* said it. Aloud. And that his answer blazed in his face, alive with joy and delight.

Slowly, so slowly, he bent his head and kissed her. Softly, gently, with infinite tenderness—yet his mouth was a fire of possession, his tongue surging deep. She yielded her lips, her mouth, straining against him, caring nothing for who might come along the path if only she could get closer to him. And she was crying—crying, for heaven's sake! As though she had not just been given the world, the moon and the stars wrapped in sunshine.

At last he broke the kiss and whispered against her lips, 'You're mine, Pippa.' He brushed a kiss over her damp cheeks. 'I'll never let you go,' he said fiercely, and kissed her again.

Eventually they walked on towards the village, hand in hand. He hadn't actually said the words, not aloud. He hadn't, she realised, even renewed his offer of marriage. Not in words. But she had no doubts. The words were there, shimmering between them in the pale sunlight, in the brisk wind buffeting them. Perhaps all the more powerful for being as yet unspoken.

She understood now why he had said that he was not renewing his offer. This was a different offer.

'I'm supposed to be on my way to the Rectory,' she said shakily. 'To…to read to Mr Rutherbridge again.'

'Are you indeed? What an excellent idea.' Dominic sounded completely unsurprised. 'I need to speak to him myself.'

She looked up shyly. 'Are you going to ask him about a marriage licence?'

His grin was positively wicked. 'Oh, I think I might mention it.'

Twelfth Night. The Great Hall at Alderley glowed, firelight and candlelight spilling over the stone walls and tapestries, and shining on red-scrubbed faces as all the tenants watched the crimson-draped stage under the gallery. Paper roses trailed everywhere. On the stage were Beauty, gorgeously dressed in a gold-embroidered hooped gown, and her Beast, in his richly embroidered coat, his wig shabby, his expression remote.

'Will you not let me see your paw, Beast?'

Beauty's clear tones reached everyone in the Great Hall. Alex, standing beside Dominic's valet, Briggs, found himself holding his breath for the reply as Beauty held out her hand to the Beast.

''Tis naught. A thorn. One of the servants will remove it.'

An icy wall of indifference.

'Please, Beast?'

The maimed hand was thrust into a pocket as the Beast turned away.

'You cannot wish to touch the filthy paw of a Beast!'

It was a snarl, low, dangerous, yet she went to him, laying her hand without hesitation on his arm.

'Can I not wish to help a dear friend?'

Alex thought of Dominic as he had found him in London a few short weeks ago—tired, bitter and deeply unsure of himself...ready to snap...

But slowly, oh, so slowly, the Beast turned back to her, his shadowed face wary.

'Am I that?' His voice still rough, cold.

Yes, you fool! How can you doubt her? For an appalling moment Alex wondered if he had actually shouted it.

Beauty's smile tore at Alex's heart.

'Most dear.'

Go on, then! Trust her!

Hardly daring to breathe, he watched as the Beast slowly laid his paw in Beauty's hand for her to remove the thorn. Watched as she cradled the paw in both hands, saw the dawning puzzlement on her face.

'What is it, *ma Belle?*'

'Your…your hand.'

And the Beast flinched, pulling his paw away and shoving it back in his pocket. Remembering a man fumbling with his coffee cup, Alex could feel the Beast's pain.

''Tis no hand. Just a paw. Clumsy and ugly like the rest of me.'

'No, Beast. That's just it. There was no paw. I felt the hand of a man. Strong, gentle.'

'You need not mock me!'

Alex shut his eyes for a second.

'Do you call me a liar then, sir?'

Beauty held out her hand to him again, and hesitantly he took his paw from his pocket and laid it in her hand. Her fingers closed over it.

Suddenly Alex wondered if for Dominic and Pippa there had been a moment like this—a moment where a risk had been taken, a hand held out even in the face of rejection, and finally accepted.

From beside Alex came a satisfied mutter: 'About bloody time, too!'

Amused, he looked round at Briggs.

The valet gave him a slow wink. 'No need for any more worry, sir. He'll do now that he's got her.'

Alex's brows rose.

Briggs grinned and turned back to the stage.

Beauty had redeemed her Beast and been swept into the waltz to thunderous applause that almost drowned Althea's harp. Alex's throat closed at the sight of Dominic whirling Pippa round, alight with their joy—just as he had seen them this morning at the Rectory. Could anyone else see it? Pippa had recoiled from the idea of an announcement this evening and Dominic had felt that tomorrow was soon enough to break the news to his family. But surely no one could see this dance and not realise? Not see the love that blazed between them?

The dance ended at last and Dominic swung Pippa to a halt facing the guests, his arm still about her waist, triumph and pride ablaze on his face. He met Alex's gaze and grinned, lifting Pippa's hand to his lips to another roar of applause.

Pippa's hand still in his, Dominic came down from the stage followed by the rest of the players to mingle with his guests. His people, he realised with a queer pang. People who depended on his doing a good job. He still had a place. A damn good place.

As he and Pippa greeted the guests, servants began setting out food and drink on the trestle tables round the sides of the hall, and a small band of musicians tuned up in the gallery with squeaks and plunks. Rafe and Althea's boys chased, laughing, in and out of the crowd with the other children. The din was phenomenal.

'A boon, my lord!'

Obadiah Battersby stood before him, cap in hand, his lined

old face split from ear to ear with a grin. Miraculously the roar died away as people turned and craned to see.

Dominic grinned back. 'Name it.' Tonight of all nights, there wasn't much he wouldn't grant.

Obadiah spoke loudly. 'There's them here will remember back when I were a little lad—'

'Damn few!' came an interjection from the crowd.

Obadiah waved this away. 'When I were a little chap— which would be in yer lordship's grandsire's day—'twas the tradition on Twelfth Night to name a king. My Lord Misrule, we called 'im. We've not done that these twenty-five years, my lord. Useter pull his name out of a hat, an' I did hear from *my* grandfer, as they useter elect him with a bean hid in a cake!' He paused for breath. 'Well, that won't do at all. We've talked it over, some of us, my lord, and yeh're invited to be our Lord of Misrule for the evening!'

Dominic shouted with laughter. He could see Althea and Rafe grinning away. And his mother and Lady Bellingham, positively stiff with disapproval.

'Of course,' went on the old man, 'there was another tradition—the Lord of Misrule must have a Queen for the night, so—' He held out his cap. 'In here, my Lord Misrule, are slips of paper with names writ on them. Take yer chance, my lord—be she young and fair, or be she old and grey!'

Hell! Dominic stared at the proffered cap, at the tightly twisted scraps of paper. He'd forgotten that part of it. His mother, of course, had stopped the tradition after his grandfather's death, on grounds of vulgarity. Apparently on one occasion she had been elected as Twelfth Night Queen to raucous applause and soundly kissed beneath the mistletoe by one of the grooms. Under any other circumstances he'd be only too happy to revive the tradition…but tonight, of all nights! If Hermione's name came out of the cap—! He glanced down at Pippa.

She smiled back. 'A boon, my lord,' she said softly.

Trapped, he looked back at Obadiah, who winked. 'Come now, young master. Take your chance—and your Queen.'

Understanding hit Dominic—why, the old devil! He'd rigged it!

He reached into the cap, grabbed a twist at random and unravelled it. The expected name leapt up at him—and his jaw collapsed.

His voice ragged, he read out, 'Miss Pippa—' and stopped right there. Good God!

A great roar of approval went up.

Battersby stood grinning at them. 'Ah, well. And here be yer first duty, my Lord Misrule. To make her yer Queen, yeh have to kiss her under the kissin' bough. That's how we do it in these parts. Then she's yours.' He added, 'If so be she don't slap your face!'

Dominic turned to Pippa and captured her hands. 'Well, my Queen?' he whispered. 'Will you take me as your Lord of Misrule?' Her trembling smile was all the answer he required.

Laughing, he led her to the central chandelier, ablaze with its red candles. Just above his head the kissing bough glowed in the candlelight, dark gleams on the holly leaves, shining on their scarlet berries and the white berries of the mistletoe.

He reached up and plucked a berry from the mistletoe. With a wicked grin he tucked it into the pocket of his coat.

'According to tradition,' he said, 'I can claim kisses as long as the berry lasts. I might,' he added softly, 'have it preserved in wax!' With that he swept her into his arms and kissed her soundly to a deafening round of applause.

Eventually he broke the kiss, and, still keeping her within his arms, looked up at the musicians in the gallery.

'Hi! You, up there! Where's the music?'

Chapter Eleven

Briggs was laying out a nightshirt when Dominic reached his bedchamber after farewelling his tenants. Odd. Briggs had still been in the Great Hall having a quiet word with Groves when Domini had left it. He must have raced up the servants' stairs like lightning.

'Wonderful night, sir,' said Briggs. 'Everyone's enjoyed themselves a treat.'

Hmm. Yes. He sounded rather breathless. Dominic nodded, glancing round the room. 'Thank you, Briggs. Are you done? I won't keep you from your bed.'

A queer look crossed Briggs's face. Almost a grin. 'Oh, aye, sir. Will that be all?'

'Yes, thank you. I'll bid you goodnight.'

'You'll ring in the morning then, sir?'

Dominic stared. 'Ring? What the devil for? Just wake me at my normal time.' He'd likely be awake anyway. Frustrated. Contemplating the joys of abstinence, whatever they were.

'Ah. As you say, sir.' Briggs cleared his throat. 'Was in

the village this morning, sir. Happened to speak to Ellie Judd.'

Dominic's gaze narrowed suspiciously. Ellie Judd—the Rectory housekeeper.

'Briggs?'

'Yessir?'

'That will be all.'

'Yessir.'

The door shut behind Briggs and the unholy grin on his face, and Dominic finished getting ready for bed. He informed himself that he was doing the right thing—that he had, through no fault of his own, his heart's desire: Pippa loved him. She was his, and he could wait for the rest.

So what, demanded his unruly body, *about the desires of the flesh?* Why wasn't he doing something about them? Apparently his body was completely unconvinced, not to say unimpressed, by his unprecedented attack of chivalry.

Not that he had been given a great deal of choice. That damned feminine conspiracy had sprung up around Pippa as the evening drew to a close. She had been swept off to her confounded truckle bed and that was that.

He swore. It was just as well. How big a scoundrel could he possibly be? He'd taken her by surprise this morning. The least he could do now was let things take their proper course. The fire crackled, echoing the consuming fire in his body. Behind him the bed, his huge, empty bed, waited.

Setting a candle down on the bedside table, he climbed in. And stared in shock at the seasonal additions. No wonder Briggs had sounded breathless! With a groan, he slid between the sheets, blew out the candle, and shut his eyes. He was in for an appalling night in a cold—he kicked a flannel-wrapped hot brick out of the way as he rolled over—empty bed. He punched the pillow. Damn Briggs. Did the wretched fellow have to rub it in?

All he could think of was Pippa in his arms under the kissing bough—soft, pliant, her body a miracle of sweetness in his embrace, her parted lips a taste of heaven. Surely he could have come up with some way to circumvent the others… No! Only a thoughtless, selfish rake would have taken advantage of her situation and persuaded her to his bed in these circumstances.

His bedchamber door opened. And shut again. Very quietly. He froze.

'Briggs?'

No answer.

Suspicion prickled as he sat up. Hermione would not be the first young lady to force this sort of situation…which would be more than embarrassing.

And then she was there, a slender, ghostly figure in the glow of the fire. Her curls hung over one shoulder and the shyest smile trembled on her lips.

'It's…it's me,' she whispered.

His mouth dried as the world tilted. 'Pippa—' His voice cracked and he tried again. 'Pippa, why are you here?' His body, aroused to the point of insanity, suggested that he should stop asking stupid questions.

'Well, it's not very comfortable on that truckle bed,' she said. He was sure she was blushing. 'And…and I couldn't sleep last night.'

He raised his brows.

'Hermione snores!' she added desperately.

He smothered a laugh. Every nerve, every instinct he possessed was howling at him to get on with it. His conscience, however, albeit under heavy fire, made one last, heroic stand.

'Pippa, do you…do you have the least idea what you are doing?' he managed, shocked at the hoarseness of his own voice. He had to be utterly sure that she wanted this. Not otherwise would he take her.

'N-no. Not really,' came the whisper. 'But I…I thought that you…that is, if you wanted me…' Her voice trailed off.

His mind fractured, along with his breath. If he wanted her? *If?*

'Yes?' he prompted.

She hung her head. 'That you wouldn't mind showing me.'

His heart shook in his chest. 'Pippa…' It was all that came out. A sort of strangled groan.

'You asked me to be your Queen for the night,' she said. 'And then, when you kissed me…I thought—' She stopped, uncertainty choking her. It had seemed easy enough on that wretchedly uncomfortable truckle bed. So easy to go to him and say…and say…

'If you were thinking while I was kissing you,' said Dominic conversationally as he pushed back the covers, 'then I obviously wasn't doing a very good job.'

Her disagreement died on her lips as he hauled his nightshirt off over his head and dropped it beside the bed. Her eyes widened at the expanse of lightly furred chest exposed to her helpless gaze. Firelight gleamed on hard curves and planes, sliding across all the textures of that magnificent male body exposed to the waist.

'If you'd like to come here,' he said softly, 'I'm very willing to try again.'

She gulped. She hadn't thought about this bit. Actually, she hadn't thought at all; she hadn't dared in case she lost her nerve. What now should she do? Did he expect her to disrobe and climb into bed with him? She took a deep breath; she had been this shameless…

Her fingers shaking, she untied the sash of her dressing gown and let it slide from her shoulders to the floor. That left her nightgown—heavy, sensible linen buttoned to the neck.

'Leave that,' came a husky whisper from the bed, as her fingers went to the first button. 'For now,' he added. 'Come to me, my Queen.' A wicked smile played about his lips. 'Gladly will I be your Lord of Misrule.'

Dominic shuddered with need, heat surging through his veins as she came to him. That demure, buttoned-to-the-neck nightgown was the most erotic thing he'd ever seen. God help him if she removed it at this point; his self-control would last about ten seconds. Maybe.

He held out his right hand, palm up. Slowly, slowly she laid her hand in his.

'You are sure, Pippa? Quite sure?'

'I love you,' she whispered, and lifted the maimed hand to her lips.

His heart shattered. Such a simple gesture, and three such little words to contain his entire world and set it ablaze. Her lips traced the scar on his palm; briefly she rested her cheek against it and he felt the warmth of her tears. Then she leaned forward and kissed his scarred face.

The last of his resistance, vague thoughts of chivalry, honourable restraint, were incinerated and he swept her into his arms and his bed. She came willingly, soft breasts pressing against him as, with a groan of pleasure, he slid his fingers into the fragrant silk of her hair, spilling it over the pillow, holding her still for his kiss. Hotly, urgently, he traced the seam of her lips with his tongue, probing, licking.

Her mouth trembled, opening sweetly to his sensual demand, her gasp of shock muffled as he took her mouth. Instantly he gentled, cradling her against his aching body, still kissing her deeply. Intimately. He willed himself to restraint. He had all night to love her as she deserved to be loved. Slowly. Tenderly. For ever.

He couldn't speak. Words didn't exist for what he felt. He could only show her.

His tongue surged deep in her mouth. Rhythmic. Insistent with need. Every soft gasp, every burning shift of her body against his seared him. With shaking, clumsy fingers he fumbled at the tiny buttons of her nightgown. Small, trembling hands caught his, stilling them. He froze, lifted from her. Oh, God—had he frightened—?

She sat up, her eyes on his. 'L-let me,' she whispered.

Sheer lust roared through him as one by one those tiny buttons yielded to her fingers. At last the nightgown hung open to her waist, revealing creamy, rounded breasts. His mouth dry, he pushed the gown off her shoulders, so that it fell to her waist.

She shivered.

He fought for control. 'Pippa—you are sure you want this?' Shocked at the hoarseness of his voice, he tried for humour. 'According to Althea, I look like a damned pirate.'

Her smile glimmered, banishing self-doubt. 'Didn't she tell you?'

'Tell me what?'

'What maidens dream about, of course.'

He choked. 'I haven't known that many maidens,' he murmured, leaning forward to cup a breast, stroking a thumb over the taut nipple. 'Just one,' he added, as her gasp burnt him, and she arched, giving herself helplessly to his caress. 'But I am very ready to fulfil her every dream.'

He drew her closer. 'So tell me, little one—' he nipped gently at her lower lip '—what *do* maidens dream about?'

She blushed enchantingly. 'Pirates, of course.'

His mouth twitched. 'Pirates?'

She wriggled against him. A provocative little wriggle that heated his blood to boiling point. 'And Beasts. The…the ravishing sort.'

A low chuckle escaped him. 'Well, let me assure you, this particular piratical Beast is definitely the ravishing sort!'

He lowered his head and pressed a hot, open-mouthed kiss to the flying pulse in her throat.

Pippa shuddered and cried out at the fierce caress, her body arching again, helpless as his lips trailed fire to her breast. He drew the aching peak deep into the heat and wetness of his mouth. Her mind fractured into blinding pleasure. She had not known. Not known that desire was an ache that burned from within; his hands and mouth a sweet fire on her body, consuming her. And somehow her nightgown was gone, swept away as she clung to him, completely abandoned to his loving.

His weight, hot and hard, came over her. Tender, demanding. One thigh slid between hers, opening her. Wicked fingers that teased and possessed, that knew every secret fold, traced the soft melting of her flesh until she sobbed, arching with need. Liquid heat burst through her, spilling over his fingers.

'You're so wet,' he whispered, and slid a long, strong finger into the soft entrance. Shock splintered through her at the soul-shaking intimacy. At the emptiness crying out within. Crying out for him. More hot silk burst between them, startling her.

'Dominic—'

He held her close. 'Shh,' he whispered. 'You're beautiful. This—' he stroked gently as his thumb found a spot that laced her body with sensual lightning '—this is your body's welcome to me.' His voice shook. 'Soft. Wet. Ready.'

Exquisitely ready for his possession. He stroked intimately, savouring the cries that rippled from her and seared him soul deep. He wanted her. Now. Ten minutes ago. For ever.

Gently he pressed her thighs wide and settled between, taking most of his weight on his elbows. Desire hammered in his blood. His whole body had hardened to the point of insanity. He fought for control, not to sink into her at once. Dear God, she was soft, hot and wet...so damned sweet... He eased in a little way, his mouth plundering hers, distracting her from the steely invasion at her core. Every muscle locked as she sobbed and her hips lifted, caressing him with hot, liquid silk.

He clamped a hand to her hip, holding her still, and lifted his head. He needed to see her, to know. Her head was flung back over his arm, her eyes closed, her lips slightly parted, moist and swollen from his possession. Shuddering with restraint, he pressed deeper, finding the taut veil of innocence. He stopped, shaking. 'Pippa—' He scarcely recognised his own voice, ragged with urgency.

Her eyes opened, dazed, dilated to leave only a burning rim round the black. Her hips moved, lifting against him, offering herself in sweetest abandon.

'Please…Dominic—'

Her voice broke on his name, and he rocked carefully, shuddering with restraint.

'Oh, God,' he groaned. 'I don't want to hurt you, little one.'

'I don't care!' she gasped. 'Please. I want you.'

She shifted again, pleading, burning beneath him. The hot, silken caress raked him with fire. With a groan he eased his iron control and took her. Feeling, seeing the shattering instant when her body yielded and she became wholly his.

Her soft cry tore at him, and he mastered his need, forcing his loins to utter stillness, while he feathered kisses over her eyes, her brow, her trembling lips.

'Sweetheart—' his voice shook '—I've hurt you.'

She shook her head. 'No. Not really.' A smile quivered. 'And I am yours now. Am I not?' One small hand traced his jaw, the corner of his mouth. Clumsy, shaking fingers caressing him.

'You were always mine,' he whispered, turning his head to kiss her fingers. 'Lord knows why it took me so long to realise.' Gently he touched her lips, her mouth, kissing her with deepening intimacy until her body relaxed again, melting sweetly round him. Her arms enclosed him, drawing him down.

And then he moved, the rhythm deep and sure, the melody ageless, yet for ever new. It had never been like this; an infinity of love welling up endlessly from within, to temper passion with tenderness. He loved her as he had never loved another woman, in a burning of desire beyond his imagining.

Her body, soft and yielding, flamed beneath him until she cried out, shaking with the force of her release. He felt it, the sweet convulsions of her body stripping his control, pulse by searing pulse. He surrendered in aching joy, pouring himself deep within her in sated possession.

Pippa awoke to the sound of quiet voices and then a door opening and closing. Still half-asleep, she rolled over and became conscious of several aches and twinges. She felt utterly relaxed, steeped in soul-deep contentment…except that she was apparently alone in the bed… No sooner had she realised this, than a large weight depressed the mattress and abruptly she found herself enveloped in a warm embrace. Heat pressed all along her body.

'Dominic?'

A chuckle greeted this. 'I hope you didn't think it could be anyone else!'

She opened her eyes and found him leaning over her, smiling tenderly. His lips brushed lightly over hers, gentle fingers pushed a lock of her from her face.

'Who were you talking to?' She reached up and twined her arms round him.

An odd smile curved his lips. 'Briggs,' he said. The smile deepened as she drew him down. 'He had a message for me.'

'Oh.' She kissed him.

He broke the kiss with a ragged groan. 'We have to stop,' he said regretfully.

'We do?'

'We do,' he said firmly, removing himself from the bed. 'Much as I would like to spend the rest of the day here, ravishing you like any self-respecting pirate—' he grinned at her blush '—I'm afraid we'd better get dressed and go down to the breakfast parlour.'

An appalling pit opened in her stomach. She hadn't even thought of getting dressed last night!

'But I've only my nightgown—'

'It's all right,' he said, with a slightly harried look. 'I've, er, got one of your gowns for you.'

She looked her question.

He gave her a rueful grin. 'Briggs fetched it for me.'

Speech failed her. At least she wouldn't have to try sneaking back to her chamber to dress, but still—!

Dominic laughed. 'He came to warn me that the house is in uproar—searching for you, it seems.'

'What?' Sitting up and clutching the bedclothes to her naked breasts, Pippa asked, 'Why? It can't be that late!' Then uncertainly, 'Can it?' Her gaze flew to the clock on the chimneypiece. And she realised that it could.

Half an hour later she stood outside the door to the breakfast parlour, trembling, her cheeks hot with anticipated embarrassment. Dominic, on the other hand, seemed to be brimming with suppressed delight, an odd, secretive smile playing about his lips.

He reached to open the door for her.

She hesitated. 'Dominic—if they've been looking for me—what on earth am I to say? Are we going to—?'

'I think you'll find it sorts itself out,' he said, opening the door with a wicked look. 'Go on, sweetheart,' he urged, and gave her a gentle push over the threshold.

'But—*ohhhh!*'

The protest died on her lips and she stood staring, as if gripped by a spell—unable, not *daring,* to believe. There, sitting at the breakfast table with Althea and Rafe, was—

'Well, my girl? Well?'

The familiar, half-forgotten voice shattered the spell into shards of piercing joy.

'Papa! Oh, Papa!' And she fled across the room to the thin, grey-haired man smiling at her. He held out his arms and she flung herself into them, sobbing as though her heart might break. The arms closed about her.

Dominic watched, his vision blurring slightly, as he swallowed the lump in his throat. He'd thought this morning when he woke that he couldn't be happier, but if anything had been wanting to complete his own joy, it was this. Her words came back to him: ...*just to know, even that he was dead. It's the not knowing. The never being able to grieve and then let go.*

She had her resolution. Everything he could have ever wished for her. When Briggs had come to tell him—well! Shakily he met Althea's gaze. She smiled mistily and Rafe handed her a large handkerchief.

At last Philip Wintercombe looked at Dominic over his daughter's head. Unashamed tears stood in his eyes, spilling over the weatherbeaten cheeks, and he freed one hand to hold it out to Dominic.

'Thank you, my boy, for your family's care of her—God!

If you could only know how I've worried in the last two and half years!' His face worked.

'What happened, sir?' asked Dominic, shaking his hand.

The older man grimaced. 'A mudslide high in the mountains. Remote place. My leg was too badly smashed for me to walk for months, let alone to try to get out before the snows came.' He hugged Pippa again. 'The tribe that took me in—they were kind enough, but I didn't speak their dialect, and all my bearers had been killed, so I couldn't get a message out. And when I did finally start to make my way out, I came down with some fever and was caught for another winter.'

'Cousin Philip, I am afraid that she is nowhere to be—oh!' Closely followed by Hermione, Mrs Lancelyn-Greene and the Bellinghams, Lady Alderley sailed into the parlour. She looked crossly at Pippa, still enfolded in her father's embrace. 'You've found her,' she said, rather unnecessarily.

Wintercombe smiled. 'Alderley found her for me.'

'Well, I'm sure that's very odd,' said Hermione sweetly. 'I have just been telling Lady Alderley that Philly left our room last night to fetch a book and when I awakened this morning her bed hadn't been slept in at all! I was dreadfully worried!' She added, in tones of spurious innocence, 'Then, if you please, I went up to my chamber a little while ago and saw Alderley's valet leaving with some of Philly's clothes. So heaven only knows where she has been!'

Dominic's eyes widened. Not quite how he had planned to make the announcement, but needs must and the Devil seemed to have the whip hand right now.

'Oh, not just heaven, Hermione,' he said, with a perfectly straight face.

Lady Bellingham glared at him. 'This is no time for shameless levity, Alderley!'

'Shockin'! Quite shockin'!' pronounced Bellingham, with ill-concealed glee.

Ignoring them, Dominic met Philip Wintercombe's suddenly hostile gaze squarely.

'Do we have something to discuss, Alderley?' Every line in the older man's face had hardened as his arm tightened round his blushing daughter.

'No, Papa!' said Pippa. 'You don't understand! We're—'

'We do indeed, Cousin Philip,' said Dominic smoothly. 'Marriage settlements, for one thing.' That might ease the poor chap's mind. It wasn't every day a fellow arrived home after years away, only to be met with snide suggestions that his daughter had been bedded by an impecunious scoundrel.

'Perhaps,' came the icy rejoinder, 'we might discuss my permission first?'

Dominic considered that. It was a trifle late, but… 'If you wish, sir,' he said in placatory tones. Best get it over with. 'May I have your retrospective permission to marry your daughter?'

Dead silence followed this request. The sort of silence that precedes a storm of apocalyptic proportions. It positively shrieked, broken only by a moan from Lady Alderley.

'Retrospective, Alderley?' Suspicion edged Cousin Philip's voice, as well it might. Then, with dawning comprehension, 'Does that mean—?'

'Dominic!' broke in Althea. 'Have you—?'

'Pippa and I were married by special licence at the

Rectory yesterday morning,' said Dominic, over Althea's squeal of delight.

Hermione's jaw collapsed. 'But you *can't* have!'

'Really?' asked Dominic politely. 'I assure you, I have.'

Rafe leaned back in his chair and roared with delighted laughter.

'*Married?*' gasped Lady Alderley. 'But, Dominic, *why?*' It was a wail of despair. 'There was no *real* need…at least…' Her voice trailed off. Dominic could almost hear her mind ticking—wondering if there had been a need.

In minatory accents Lady Bellingham demanded, 'Who witnessed this marriage?'

'Rutherbridge's housekeeper, Mrs Judd, and Alex were the witnesses,' said Dominic calmly. 'Cousin Philip, I beg your pardon in not waiting for your permission, but—' he searched for a way to put it delicately, and settled for honesty '—we weren't expecting you, sir!'

'No, I dare say not, Alderley. Married, eh?' Philip Wintercombe sounded somewhat mollified. 'Well, I dare say it's all as it should be.' He turned to his daughter. 'Eh, Pippa?'

'Y-yes, Papa.' Pippa sounded as though she might expire with embarrassment.

He smiled at her and took her hand. 'Since I didn't have the privilege of doing this yesterday…' He turned to Dominic. 'Come here, Alderley.'

His throat tight, Dominic went to them. Pippa smiled up at him through her tears. Clumsily he reached out and brushed a tear away.

'Hold out your hand, lad.'

Unhesitatingly Dominic held out his maimed hand.

With simple pride Philip Wintercombe laid his daughter's hand in it. 'There you are, m'boy. She's yours. God bless you both.'

Dominic's fingers closed tightly on the precious gift. 'He already has, sir. Thank you.'

Smiling at Pippa, he reached into his pocket and drew out a ring. 'You had better wear this again, love,' he said and slid it on to her finger.

Althea let out a satisfied sigh and sniffed loudly. 'Oh, how simply beautiful!' she said, wiping her eyes. 'And you won't have to call him out after all, Rafe!'

The day passed in a whirl of joy. Even Dominic's confession about the fate of Pippa's dowry failed to worry Philip Wintercombe.

They had retired to the library after dinner to discuss the settlements, and Wintercombe's hazel eyes, so like his daughter's, narrowed as he set down his brandy. 'Are you telling me that you took her with only a few hundred pounds, Alderley?' he asked with a very odd expression on his face. 'And your own fortune in ruins?'

Dominic flinched. 'It's not as bad as that, sir. I dare say it's not what you wanted for her, but I assure you—'

Wintercombe's chuckle silenced him. 'I wouldn't ask better for her, lad,' he said. 'Quite apart from the money I had set aside for Pippa in the Funds, I've a tidy little fortune tucked away in gems and the like.' He smiled. 'But you took her believing her practically penniless.' He shook his head. 'And there I was, thinking I'd be beating off fortune hunters!'

'*Fortune hunters?*'

'Fortune hunters,' confirmed his father-in-law. 'You know—scoundrels who make up to a girl for her money. As opposed to those who fall head over heels in love.' And he lifted his glass in salute.

With the departure of her father and Dominic to the library, Pippa retired to bed. At her announcement that she was tired and would go up, Lady Alderley had panicked, pointing out that the chamber designated for the lady of the house was still occupied by herself and that, really, it would be better if—

'For heaven's sake, Mama!' said Althea. 'If Dominic chooses to get married in such a havey-cavey way, he deserves to have his bride quartered in his own chamber!' She cast Pippa a very naughty glance. 'Although I dare say he'll find it perfectly convenient.' She turned to her husband. 'Don't you think so, Rafe?'

Rafe grinned. 'I think we can safely assume that. Goodnight, Pippa.' He stood up and went to open the door for her.

She left, wondering if she would ever manage to stop blushing.

By the time Dominic appeared she was clad in a nightgown, brushing her hair. She doubted that the nightgown would last long, but, at the thought of waiting for him stark naked, her nerve failed.

As it was, when he came in and locked the door behind him, she felt as though she might as well be naked the way he looked at her.

Hot. Intent.

Desperately she resumed brushing.

She was wildly aware of his every action as his coat, waist-coat and shirt were swiftly consigned to a corner of the floor. Firelight slid and glowed on hard male curves, etching muscles in dusky shadow and golden gleam. Clad only in his drawers, he came to stand behind her, reaching round to pluck the brush from her suddenly trembling fingers and to lay it on the dressing table.

'No regrets, little one?' He turned her to face him, cradling her against his body.

She shook her head. 'Of course not. Only, I was thinking—'

'Mmm?' He feathered kisses along her jaw and her breathing shattered.

'If we'd waited a day, then—'

He snorted. 'Just as well we didn't!' Her eyes widened—one by one the buttons of her nightgown were falling victim to his fingers. 'Judging by the look on your father's face when Hermione dropped her bombshell, he'd have shot me if I'd taken you *without* the benefit of clergy!' He slid the nightgown down over her shoulders and let it drop.

'But…you wouldn't… I wouldn't have come if we hadn't been—'

Encountering his raised brows, she blushed scarlet, violently conscious that she was, after all, stark naked. And he, the perfidious pirate, still had his drawers.

'No?' Swinging her into his arms, he walked to the bed and laid her on it. An instant later his drawers sailed to join the rest of his clothes and he slid in beside her. '*You* might not have been shameless enough to come to me last night under those circumstances, but I wouldn't have wagered a groat against the likelihood of me coming for you!'

Her eyes widened. 'You wouldn't have!' Then she gasped as his body shifted suggestively against her.

'I'm a pirate, remember? And a beast to boot. The ravishing sort.'

'Oh, I remember that,' she whispered, and nestled closer.

He grinned. 'I thought you might. Besides, look up. But don't blame me. Blame Briggs. He wasn't taking any chances! I understand half the staff helped him.'

Puzzled, Pippa followed his gaze. Her jaw dropped. The inside of the bed canopy was festooned with greenery, and hanging from the middle of it all was the kissing bough. A helpless giggle escaped her. 'But surely—that wasn't there last night, was it?'

Dominic chuckled in very male self-satisfaction. 'Are you telling me you didn't notice? I'm flattered.'

She blushed again.

'I understand,' murmured Dominic against her breast, 'that the greenery is supposed to have something to do with fertility.' He suckled gently and she arched in helpless response.

'But, how…how did he know? Ohhh!' She gasped as a powerful thigh slid between hers. Plainly Dominic was taking this fertility business seriously.

He kissed her collar-bone. Trailed fire over her throat as he caressed her softness. 'Briggs is a sly old fox,' he said, nipping gently at her lower lip. 'He was in the village when we went to the Rectory, and Mrs Judd is the biggest gossip in the parish. I'll wager the news was all over Alderford before we left Mr Rutherbridge!'

'It was? H-how do you know?' Her voice broke as he stroked wickedly and pleasure speared her.

'Because,' said Dominic, 'of that scrap of paper I pulled out of Obadiah's cap last night. Do you know what was written on it?'

'N-no.'

'It said "Miss Pippa."' He eased her thighs wide and moved over her. '"Miss Pippa—My Lady Alderley!"'

* * * * *

A WINTER
NIGHT'S TALE

Deborah Hale

Author Note

From my youngest years, books have been a special part of my Christmas. The one picture book I still have from my childhood is a lovely story about three children and a snowman. When my own children came along, I started a collection of Christmas books for them, which has grown to many cherished volumes. On dark December nights we often snuggle on the sofa to read our favourites.

I am delighted to have this opportunity to share a romantic Christmas story of my own with you. Ever since I sold my first book, I have wanted to participate in a Christmas anthology. As a reader, I have received so much enjoyment from them over the years. Novellas are just the right length to give me a little break during a busy time of year, and reading them always puts me in the Christmas spirit.

I usually buy several copies, because they make perfect gifts for so many special people on my list – affordable, compact, easy to wrap and certain to provide hours of enjoyment! I hope my story about Christmas magic and a second chance at love will bring a warm holiday glow to your heart.

Thank you for making it part of your Christmas!

I dedicate this story with admiration to all the care-givers of this world. The true Spirit of Christmas lives in you every day of the year!

Chapter One

December 11, 1816
Bishopscote, England

'Mama!' Young Nicholas Wilton shook his mother's arm. 'There's a man at the door. May he come in? He might have brought me a present!'

Come to *present* her with some overdue bill, more likely. Christabel pulled the swathe of shawls tighter around her slight shoulders. Though the weather outside was not especially cold for St Nicholas Day, the very marrow of her bones felt frozen.

'I gave you your gift this morning, dearest.' She forced her lips into a reassuring smile and willed her teeth not to chatter as she spoke. 'And we are not expecting any company.'

She should just get up and answer the door herself, but a dull ache gnawed at her flesh until she could not bear the thought of stirring from her chair by the fire. If she rested here another hour or two, she might be able to summon the strength to make Colly his supper and put him to bed. Christabel had no intention of squandering that energy to confront some abusive creditor.

'T-tell the man to come back another day, dearest.' Even as the words left her mouth, she knew she had spoken too late.

The door hinges creaked and firm, deliberate footsteps approached.

'Pardon my intrusion, ma'am,' said the intruder, his courteous tone quite at odds with his presumption of crossing her threshold uninvited. 'Mrs Wilton, isn't it? Formerly Miss Hastings of Lollingham in Somerset?'

Christabel dragged herself to her feet to bid him be gone. But his questions knocked her back on to her seat with the force of a hard gust of winter wind. Like a strong wind, they snatched her breath away, too.

Her caller seemed to find the answer he sought in her silence. If he had any doubts, Colly dispelled them by declaring, 'I am Nicholas Wilton and this is my mama. Do you know her?'

'Once upon a time, I did,' the man replied in a tone of grave courtesy that Christabel recalled from her past. 'Though perhaps she does not remember me. Mr Jonathan Frost, at your service.' He bowed to Christabel and her son.

Perhaps there were women in the world so unfeeling that they could conveniently forget men they had jilted. Christabel was not among their number. Jonathan Frost's name and likeness were indelibly etched upon her conscience.

Though perhaps that image no longer quite matched the gentleman who stood before her. She did not recall him being so tall, nor half so handsome. The intervening years had pared away any trace of boyish roundness from his face, making him look more severe…and more attractive.

'Of course I remember you, Mr Frost.' Christabel struggled to catch her breath. 'It is a great surprise to see you again after such a long time. Whatever are you doing in this part of the country?'

One of the few charms Derbyshire held for her was the unlikelihood of meeting with any of her old acquaintances. But this was the second to cross her path in a fortnight. Cross her path? Nay, Mr Frost had clearly sought her out, though she wished he had not.

What did he mean by coming here today? Had he wanted to see her reduced circumstances first-hand so he could gloat? Or to remind her of the life that might have been hers if only her reckless heart had not got the better of her good sense? If either of those was his design, then she'd done well to escape a union with the man, no matter what the privations of her present life.

But when the gentleman spoke again, no edge of contempt sharpened his tone. 'For the past year, I have made my home not ten miles away—a small estate just this side of Gosslyn.' Nothing in his manner suggested that Christabel's small, draughty cottage was vastly inferior to his usual surroundings. 'Our mutual friend, Miss Jessup, has recently come to the vicarage there, to keep house for her brother. When she told me of meeting you in the market… I say, are you ill?'

Before she could summon a convincing denial, he strode towards her and pressed the backs of his fingers to her brow. Their touch was so gentle and so pleasantly cool, Christabel could not bring herself to protest the liberty he had taken.

'Good Lord, woman!' He wrenched his hand away almost as soon as it made contact with her forehead and his voice took on the tone of brusque authority she remembered from their brief courtship. 'You are burning hotter than the miserable fire in that hearth! How long have you been like this? And why are you not in bed where you belong?'

She would say one thing for the man—at least he made her forget how miserable she felt. Also, his manner eased the worst of her shame over the way she had once treated him. Why would any woman have wed such a high-handed, officious creature except for his fortune?

'You may have noticed, sir, I have a child to care for.' Christabel channelled some of the chill from her bones into her voice and glare. 'I cannot take to my bed at the slightest indisposition. But as you see, I am not well enough to entertain callers.'

Mr Frost refused to take her blatant hint. In fact, he hardly seemed to have heeded a word she'd said. 'Have you summoned a doctor, at least? When did you eat last?'

What presumption, to barge into her house after all these years and demand answers to such questions!

Before Christabel could sputter her outrage, Colly spoke up. 'Mama never eats very much. She says she has no appetite.'

'Thank you, young man.' Jonathan Frost turned his attention back to Christabel. 'Then you have been ill for some time?'

Not ill—poor. And with a growing child who needed his nourishment more than she did.

'I refuse to have a physician.' Not that she could have afforded such a luxury. 'Most of them do more harm than good, especially for passing ailments like mine. A little rest and quiet will soon see me well again.'

Gathering her strength, Christabel heaved herself to her feet. 'Now, if you will be so kind as to leave us in—'

The whole tiny parlour of the cottage began to spin around her. The only thing that held steady was the face of Jonathan Frost. His wide mouth was compressed in a stubborn line. The dark curls that tumbled over his brow could not disguise the furrows of worry that creased it. The steely resolve that glinted in his blue eyes was tempered by warm concern.

She would not swoon! Christabel clung to the slippery rope of consciousness. She would remain on her feet until Mr Frost had the courtesy to quit her house. She did not want his meddlesome pity.

'I'm sorry, Mrs Wilton, but this will not do.' He moved towards her, throwing his face out of focus so the room spun more violently than before. 'I cannot leave you here in such a state. You and the child had better come with me.'

Come where? He didn't mean to cart them off to a workhouse, did he? As Christabel struggled to keep her wits about her, Jonathan Frost swept her into his arms.

He held her in a firm, steady embrace that made her feel strangely safe. Some part of his face bushed her brow with a whisper of tender reassurance. Hard as she tried to resist it, she could not help herself.

Chapter Two

Only the presence of the child kept Frost from cursing.

This was *not* how he'd meant his interview with Christabel Wilton to unfold. He'd never wanted to come in the first place. But that meddlesome Miss Jessup had prattled on and on until he'd agreed to pay a call. He'd hoped to find her account of Mrs Wilton's straitened circumstances exaggerated. Instead, they were worse than he'd expected and he'd had no honourable choice but to involve himself in her affairs.

He hoisted her into his arms, before she could fall to the floor and compound her illness with an injury. When *had* the woman eaten last? She weighed almost nothing. Her head lolled against his shoulder, her eyes closed. Except for the feverish flush in her cheeks and the dark smudges beneath her eyes, her face was pale.

Frost felt a vigorous tug on his coat-tails. He glanced down to find the boy staring up at him. 'What is the matter with Mama? What have you done to her?'

'Nothing!' Why did he feel so responsible, then? 'I am only trying to help her. You want her to get well, don't you?'

The child considered for a moment, then nodded. 'I want her to play with me and not be so tired always.'

Frost glanced around the tiny parlour, almost bare of furniture, but scrupulously clean. No wonder the poor creature was tired if she could not afford to keep a servant.

'Then I must take you both to a place where you will be well looked after while she recovers her strength.'

The child looked doubtful. Perhaps he remembered how his mother had bidden Frost away before she collapsed. Two years ago Frost would have had no idea how to reason with a child, but since then he'd gained some insights into the workings of a young mind.

'You seem like a smart fellow, Master Wilton. I could use your help.'

The boy pointed to himself with an amazed look on his small face. 'You need *my* help?'

Frost nodded. 'Indeed I do, if you will oblige me. Could you open the front door? I have a carriage waiting outside where I can settle your mama.'

Almost before he had finished asking, the boy scurried off and Frost heard the creek of door hinges. It came as no surprise to him that Christabel Wilton had raised a helpful child. No doubt she'd been forced to rely on hers more than most mothers.

'Well done,' said Frost as he carried the boy's mother through the open doorway. 'Now, could I trouble you to fetch some blankets? We must keep your mama warm on the journey.'

When the coachman saw his master coming, he made haste to throw open the carriage door.

'Thank you, Samuel.' Frost nodded toward the cottage. 'Will you go help the little fellow round up some blankets?'

'Aye, sir.'

'And don't say anything to alarm him about his mother's condition.'

'Indeed I won't, sir.'

By the time Frost got Christabel propped up in one corner of the carriage, Samuel and the child had returned, bearing blankets.

'Got these off the wee lad's bed,' the coachman muttered as he handed them to Frost. 'The ones on hers were thin as muslin.'

That information did not surprise Frost. It was clear to him that Christabel Wilton had been going without far too many common necessities in order to provide for her son, which was well-meant folly if it had led to her present illness. The child needed a healthy mother more than he needed the extra food and warmth she'd furnished him at her own expense.

As he tucked the blankets around Christabel, Frost motioned for the boy to climb into the carriage. 'I shall be sure to tell your mama what a great help you were to me, lad. What's that you've brought with you?'

'A hobbyhorse, sir.' The boy straddled his plaything and rode it into the carriage. 'Mama gave him to me as a St. Nicholas present.'

Made with her own hands, no doubt, and cleverly, too. The thing had a grey wool head with twists of coarse yarn for a mane. With two bright brass buttons for eyes, it boasted a genuine leather bridle and harness contrived from an old belt.

The mop-handle shaft had been sanded smooth to prevent the chance of small fingers picking up splinters. Frost wondered how many hours of secret, loving work Mrs Wilton had lavished on this gift for her son.

'A fine-looking hunter, indeed. Have you named it yet?'

The boy shook his head. 'I was too busy riding.' He passed his hand over his horse's mane in a fond caress. 'Can you help me think of one, Mr Frost? I say, are you Jack Frost who paints our windows all white?'

The twinkle in the child's hazel eyes told Frost he was teasing. Clearly he'd inherited his late father's winning manner.

He shook his head in answer to the boy's question. 'No indeed, though some boys at school used to rag me with that name.'

While they were busy discussing a proper name for the horse, Frost's carriage pulled away from the Wiltons' tiny cottage.

The slight lurch roused Christabel. 'Where are we?' She stared around her in alarm, but calmed a little when she spied her son nearby. 'Where are you taking us?'

She tried to pull away from Frost, but he held her in a firm grip. 'Do not fret. This is my carriage and I am taking you and your son back to my house for a few days until you recover. Master Nicholas is anxious for a visit, aren't you?'

The child gave a vigorous nod. 'Oh, yes, Mama! May we go, please? We never go anywhere.'

Christabel looked too sick and weary to argue. 'Very well, but only for a short while. We must not impose upon Mr Frost.' Her words trailed off in a whisper as her slender body relaxed in Frost's arms and her eyes shut again.

'Hurrah!' cried the child.

Frost wished he could work up as much enthusiasm for their visit. It was imperative Mrs Wilton receive good care if she was to recover. Though that duty had fallen to him by default, he would not shirk it. But neither did he relish it. The past was better left to the past and Christabel Wilton represented a painful chapter of his history that he would rather forget.

'Look, Mr Frost!' The boy pointed out the carriage window. 'It's snowing. Perhaps I should give my horse a Christmas name.' He thought for a moment. 'Holly?'

'Or Yule,' Frost suggested.

By the time they reached Candlewood, the name Mistletoe had been agreed upon and a gossamer blanket of snow had settled over the grounds and forecourt.

Frost gathered Christabel up in his arms and carried her into the house while a small parade of servants followed in his wake, along with Master Nicholas riding his hobbyhorse.

'Lay a good fire in the main guest room,' Frost ordered as he strode towards it. 'And fetch a warming pan for the bed.'

Before long, Christabel was installed in the great bed, swathed in covers a good deal thicker than muslin. Frost put her son in the care of a rosy little housemaid who looked almost young enough to enjoy a romp down the gallery on the hobbyhorse. 'Jane, take Master Nicholas down to the kitchen for a good tea. Then amuse him as best you can.'

The child looked eager at the prospect of 'a good tea,' but his small brow furrowed. 'Perhaps I ought to sit with Mama. She did with me when I was ill.'

Frost suppressed a smile. 'I'm certain your mother will rest easier if she knows you are being well looked after. Besides, she is sleeping now, and there are plenty of people who can watch over her in case she needs anything.'

'But they are strangers. She might be frightened if she wakes, like she did in your carriage.' The child's small features creased in a worried frown, then suddenly brightened. '*You* are not a stranger, Mr Frost! Will you sit with Mama until I come back?'

'I would, but…other matters need my attention.' Matters that would take him to the farthest corner of the house and keep him there until Mrs Wilton was well enough to leave. Seeing her again had brought back too many regrets—too many memories that were best forgotten. 'My servants are all very capable and kind. She will be well tended, I promise you.'

The child shook his head. 'If you cannot stay, then I must.' He marched towards a chair near his mother's bed.

Stifling a vexed growl, Frost stepped into the boy's path. 'Go along with Jane and get your tea.' He lowered himself on to the chair. 'I suppose I can sit with your mother for a while.'

What would it matter? She'd probably be asleep the whole time. And once the boy became acquainted with Frost's servants, he would not be so stubbornly opposed to leaving his mother in their charge.

Frost started when a pair of stout little arms were flung around his neck in a hearty embrace. 'Thank you, Mr Frost! You're very kind!'

I am an indulgent fool! Frost kept the words to himself for fear of injuring the child's feelings. Not that he could have forced them past the lump he found unaccountably lodged in his throat.

He recovered his voice as the boy raced off, hand-in-hand with Jane. 'Be sure to clean your plate, now. And give that horse of yours a good workout.'

Once the boy had gone, Frost rose from the chair and busied himself with one thing and another. He sent a footman for the doctor. Then he ordered a pot of piping hot beef tea in case Mrs Wilton woke up hungry. Privately he vowed to make certain she left his house several pounds heavier than she had entered it.

At last there was nothing more to do and no more servants left to order. Frost sat down in the chair for a while, but found his gaze continually drawn to Christabel's face. He told himself he was only watching for any change in her condition. In truth, he found himself picturing her as she'd been six years ago, when her face had a youthful plumpness and her cheeks a healthy glow.

She had not been the most beautiful woman of his acquaintance, but her cheerful disposition had seemed to brighten every room she entered. In her company, every sound took on a musical quality, colours appeared more vibrant, smells and tastes seemed sweeter.

This would never do! Frost jumped up and began to pace the room. Christabel Wilton had not been two hours in his house and already she was making him yearn for a past that was lost and a present that had never come to be! By stubborn dint of will, he succeeded in turning his thoughts to other channels. But when Christabel stirred and murmured in her sleep, he flew to her side.

'The doctor should be here soon.' He smoothed back a stray lock of hair from her hot, moist brow. 'Try to rest. You and your son are welcome to stay here until you are quite well again.' His conscience smote him at the thought of ever sending her back to that small, bare cottage.

Her eyelids fluttered and her lips moved, but Frost could not make out her words. He leaned closer.

Christabel opened her eyes fully and stared up at him, her gaze warm with recognition and…affection?

Frost glanced in horror at his fingers, which still held a lock of her hair, fondling it. He let go with a guilty start.

'Monty?' Her lips caressed the name of her late husband— the man for whom she had jilted him.

'I'm afraid not, ma'am. It's Jonathan Frost. I brought you to my house to recover from your illness.'

Though her gaze never left his face, she seemed not to hear him. Frost had the unsettling sensation that she did not truly *see* him either.

'Dearest Monty.' She raised one thin, work-roughened hand to caress his cheek.

Frost tried to pull away, but he could not. Once again he tried to deny that he was Montague Wilton. But the words got stuck in his throat.

Christabel's flushed face blossomed into a smile of un-earthly radiance. 'You have come home to me at last, my darling!'

Her hand slipped around Frost's neck and drew him towards her as she canted her head and parted her lips to kiss him.

Chapter Three

Christabel's lips were soft and warm beneath Frost's. He remembered kissing her once or twice during their engagement, but those stiff, awkward exchanges had been nothing like this. Now, the subtle movement of her lips beguiled and invited him.

But he could not accept her invitation! The woman was gravely ill and out of her head with fever. Besides, her kiss was meant for a dead man and Frost had no right in the world to claim it. Still, it took every ounce of resolution he could summon to disengage her arms from around his neck.

'Lie still, my dear.' Frost humoured her feverish delusion. He knew from experience that trying to reason with her would be futile and only agitate her when she needed rest. 'I am here and will stay for as long as you need me.'

He wrapped one hand around both of Christabel's to keep her from entangling him in another embrace. He was by no means certain he could behave in a rational, honourable manner if she kissed him again with such tender passion. His other hand caressed her cheek to reassure and calm her—or so he told himself.

One of the housemaids entered with a tray, which she set down on the nightstand beside the bed. 'There's the beef tea you ordered, sir. The doctor's been sent for. Is there anything else the lady needs?'

Frost shook his head. 'The little boy? How is he? Getting enough to eat?'

'I should say, sir.' The girl's rosy face lapsed into a motherly smile. 'For such a wee fellow, he has an appetite to satisfy even Cook. From the quantity of her ginger biscuits he ate, you'd think he'd never tasted such a thing in his life.'

Perhaps he hadn't. Though the child's sturdy build suggested he'd seldom gone hungry, Frost doubted his mother had been able to afford many sweets. 'I'm glad to hear he's settling in well. Show Dr Bradstreet up as soon as he arrives.'

Once the maid had curtsied and departed, Frost poured a cup of the beef tea and managed to coax a little into Christabel before she drifted back to sleep again. Then he wet his handkerchief in some cool water from the nightstand ewer and mopped her fiery brow.

He remembered the night he had first laid eyes on her at the modest assembly hall in rural Somerset. Come to think of it, his *ears* had first drawn him to the merry music of Christabel Hastings's laughter. He'd been a stranger, visiting the area and uncertain of his welcome. But once he had begged an introduction and asked for the honour of a dance, she'd immediately put him at his ease. How much ease or laughter had she enjoyed since then, poor creature?

Brisk footsteps heralded the arrival of the doctor, whose

old-fashioned wig was further powdered with snow and his broad face nipped red by the cold. 'This is not the patient I expected, Mr Frost. Another relation of yours, is she?'

'An old friend.' Frost moved from Christabel's bedside to make way for the doctor. 'When I heard she was living nearby, I paid a call and found her ill.'

'Why in heaven's name did you bring her here?' Doctor Bradstreet pulled out his pocket watch, then pressed the fingertips of his other hand to Christabel's delicate wrist. 'In my experience, patients recover more quickly in familiar surroundings.'

'I assure you, she is better off here.'

'I see.' The doctor continued his examination. 'Not much of her, is there? Small wonder she fell ill.'

'Her late husband was a cavalry officer.' Frost stared out the window at the swirling snow. It had been during the Christmas season six years ago when Christabel had broken their engagement by eloping with Montague Wilton. In some ways it felt like a lifetime ago. In others, it seemed like only yesterday.

The doctor gave a grunt of vexation. 'It's a perfect scandal how this country rewards the men who gave their lives fighting against tyranny—letting their families languish in poverty. Any children?'

'A little boy. It is as much for his sake as hers that I brought them back to Candlewood.'

'Is he ill, too?'

Frost shook his head. 'A fine, strong lad as far as I can tell. I'd be obliged if you would have a look at him before you go, just the same.'

Bradstreet had just finished his examination when the child came galloping into the room. 'Is Mama better yet?'

'A little, I believe.' Frost dropped to his haunches to bring him eye-to-eye with the boy. 'But she will need plenty of rest and nourishment yet. You won't mind staying here a while, will you?'

The boy shook his head. 'I like this place. The food is splendid and Samuel promised he would let me ride on a real horse tomorrow if you say I might.'

'We have a bargain.' Frost held out his hand to the child. 'Plenty of horse rides and ginger biscuits for you, rest and beef tea for your mama.'

Nicholas Wilton shook Frost's hand with a solemn air. 'But what do *you* get out of the bargain, sir?'

The question caught Frost off guard, but he quickly rallied. 'Why, the enjoyment of your company, of course.' And perhaps the relief of a lingering guilt?

Once the boy went off with Jane to get ready for bed, Frost turned back to the doctor. 'So, how long do you think it will take Mrs Wilton to recover her health with warmth, rest and proper food? Two weeks? A month?'

'I believe she could rally very quickly. Her underlying constitution seems strong, considering how she has abused it.' Bradstreet looked strangely grim for a physician delivering such encouraging news. 'That is, *if* she survives this devilish fever. Of that I am by no means certain. I shall bleed her, of course, though I'm not sure how much good it will do. Her resolve to live is more likely to decide matters.'

'If you doubt it will help, then do not bother,' said Frost gruffly. He did not believe Christabel's fever was caused by an excess of blood. The poor woman did not look as though she'd enjoyed an excess of *anything* in a long time.

When Bradstreet had gone off to examine the boy, Frost shovelled a bit more coal on the fire, then stood at the foot of the bed, staring at Christabel. She bore very little resemblance to the young woman who had conquered his heart six years ago—a woman he had not allowed himself to think about for quite some time. Yet, as he faced the possibility of her dying, a frigid chill gripped his chest.

Christabel stirred in her fevered, dream-troubled sleep. The chill still gnawed at her bones, but the great pile of bed-clothes over her and the nearby crackle of a good fire offered a reassuring promise of warmth.

Monty? She pried her eyes open and made a feeble effort to lift her head. Finding herself already propped up on several thick pillows, she managed to sweep a glance around the large, comfortable-looking room. She saw no sign of Monty, but of course he would not be here. She had been a fool to yearn for him, even in her dreams. Why, then, did the aching sweetness of his kiss still linger on her lips?

A soft buzz of snoring lured her gaze to a large armchair drawn up beside the bed. A man slouched in it, his head sunk to his breast, fast asleep. Christabel sensed she should know him and that his identity was somehow linked to this place where she found herself.

Jonathan Frost—that's who he was! He'd paid a most un-expected visit to her cottage and… Christabel could not recall him leaving. A fleeting wisp of memory caught in her mind of being held secure and told that Mr Frost was fetching her and Colly back to his house.

Colly! Her first thought should have been for her son, not his charming, irresponsible father.

Christabel rallied the dregs of her strength and fought against the paralysing ache in her flesh to sit up. A soft whimper of pain and frustration escaped her lips, bringing Mr Frost instantly awake.

'For pity's sake, woman, lie still!' He restrained her with gentle strength. 'Whatever it is you want, just ask and I will fetch it for you.'

'Colly?' she demanded in a harsh whisper. 'What have you done with my son?'

Frost pointed towards a shadowy corner of the room. 'He refused to be parted from you, so I had a cot brought in for him. A stubborn little fellow for one otherwise so agreeable. I congratulate you upon him. He has my entire household doting upon him after a few hours' acquaintance.'

His matter-of-fact tone calmed her. Christabel sank back on the pillows.

Frost let go of her and rubbed his eyes. 'Now that you have roused me, is there anything I can get for you? The beef tea has gone cold, I fear, but Cook sent up a cup of eggnog, which she swears has amazing restorative powers.'

Before Christabel could reply, her stomach answered for her with a hollow rumble.

A ghost of a smile flickered on Mr Frost's solemn countenance…or perhaps it was only a trick of the firelight. 'Eggnog it is, then.'

He balanced the cup with a delicate touch in one hand,

while sliding the other beneath her shoulders and lifting her to a more convenient posture for drinking.

That eggnog—why, it might have been heavenly ambrosia! Christabel could not recall the last time she'd tasted anything so smooth, rich and sweet. Frost tipped it to her lips at the proper shallow angle so she might drink as much as she wished without forcing more upon her than she wanted.

At last she gave a little nod to indicate she'd had enough.

Frost eased her back down on to the pillows, then returned the cup to a small table that appeared well laden with anything she might require during the night.

Glancing at the quantity of liquid remaining in the cup, he gave an approving nod. 'It is good for you to take nourishment.'

He reached his hand towards her forehead, then hesitated before making contact. 'May I?'

When she nodded, he pressed the backs of his fingers to her brow. They felt so cool, Christabel wished he would glide them over the rest of her face.

'Still burning up.' He looked very severe, almost… haunted.

'A doctor?' whispered Christabel. 'Was he here or did I dream him?'

Frost nodded. 'Bradstreet examined you. He is a good man.'

'What did he say? How soon will I be well enough to take my son home? I do not wish to trespass long upon your hospitality.'

Her questions made Frost scowl.

'Is it serious?' she asked doubtfully. 'Am I in danger?'

His frown deepened. She sensed he was torn between telling her a comforting falsehood and impressing upon her the true gravity of her situation.

The chill in her bones intensified tenfold, but her fear was not for her own welfare. A dizzy, foggy sensation began to steal over her again. Christabel refused to surrender to it until she had settled one vital matter.

'I have no right to ask anything of you, Mr Frost, and for my own sake I would not. If anything happens to me, will you look after my child? I have no other friends. My father disowned me. You are the one person who has shown me any kindness in a very long time.'

Perhaps this was all she could do for her son. Colly would be far better off in the care of a man of property than a penniless mother, no matter how much she loved him. 'Please, will you promise me?'

Frost's silver-blue glare pierced Christabel's misty vision of her son's future. He jumped from the bed as if her fever had reached out to scorch him. The noise made Colly stir in his sleep, but he did not wake. Jonathan Frost ploughed his fingers through his dark hair as he strode to the foot of the bed.

'No!' he declared in a hoarse, angry whisper. 'I will not let you abdicate responsibility for him!' He stabbed his finger in the direction of Colly's cot. 'I will not make it easy for you to give up. Fight, damn you! Fight for your life and for your child. If you die, I promise you his situation up until now will seem like paradise by comparison.'

Unfeeling brute! What folly had ever made her believe he had an ounce of compassion in him? She'd been right not marry him, no matter how comfortable a position it might have afforded her. She did not dispute his right to treat her with all the contempt he wished, but her son was an innocent child who'd done him no harm.

A heavy, cold weariness threatened to envelop her, but Christabel fought against it with grim resolve. Even if Jonathan Frost should grudgingly relent once she was dead, she could not abandon her dearest child to the cold mercies of such a man!

It made Frost quite bilious to speak such cruel lies, especially to a woman he had once loved and hoped would bear him children. But he refused to flinch before her look of wounded outrage. Let her think him a monster, if it gave her a better reason to live.

Besides, some of what he'd said was true. All the horses and ginger biscuits in the world would not compensate Nicholas Wilton for the loss of his mother. Frost had bitter reason to know. Would he have grown into a different man if his mother had lived? More affable—able to inspire affection and give it without reserve?

Now he channelled his deep-buried anger over his mother's early death to bully Christabel Wilton into living. Even if she only did it to spite him. Even if she ended up despising him more than ever.

When she drifted into a fitful doze, he added more coal to the fire, then returned to his chair by her bed. There he bathed her face with his damp handkerchief and prayed with fierce desperation that her life be spared.

He did not mean to sleep, himself. In fact, he feared to shut his eyes again, in case she should slip away during the deepest, deadest hours of the night. But the warmth of the room, and perhaps the exertions of the previous day, overcame him at last.

He woke with a jolt when the first feeble rays of dawn gilded the frosted window panes. Christabel lay so still and pale, the sight of her wrung a sob from deep in Frost's chest. Then she heaved a soft sigh in her sleep. He touched his trembling fingers to her forehead—it no longer burned with fever, but neither was it cold in death.

Frost lowered his head to rest against the edge of the bed and allowed relief to shudder through him. But that relief was tainted with a fresh fear—that when she woke, she would despise him for what he had done.

Chapter Four

Christabel woke to find Jonathan Frost slumped in a chair beside her bed, fast asleep. His face was drawn with exhaustion and sported a raffish shadow of dark stubble. The man looked as if he had been through a night of hell.

But then, so must she!

The desperate desire for five minutes' use of a comb and mirror was Christabel's first clue that she might be on the mend. Not that she cared what Mr Frost thought of her looks, now or ever, but she did have a little pride left. She could not stand the thought of him regarding her with pity.

Her head no longer felt as if it were encased in an iron cap two sizes too small. Her limbs, though weak, felt truly warm for the first time in days. And she was hungry.

Events of the past day and night were hazy and jumbled in her mind, mixed with such vivid snatches of a dream that it was hard to sort out what had been real and what a product of her fevered fancy. She had a strong recollection of angry words traded with Mr Frost in the middle of the night. What *could* they have been arguing about?

Before she had managed to remember, Frost stirred from his doze with a guilty start. 'Blast it all! I only meant to close my eyes a moment after I sent your son off to get his breakfast. Have you been awake long?'

Did he expect her to chide him? 'Only a moment or two. And do not reproach yourself for resting your eyes. I should beg your pardon for robbing you of a good night's sleep.'

Frost dismissed the notion with a shake of his head. 'I should not have been able to sleep until I was satisfied that your fever had broken. When I checked a while ago, it seemed to have abated. How do you feel?'

'Much improved from yesterday.' Christabel managed a weak smile. 'Then, I suspect, I was too ill to know how ill I truly was.' She cringed to recall the rude welcome with which she'd greeted his call and her ingratitude for his well-meant interference in her affairs. 'I shudder to think what might have befallen us if you had not intervened.'

'I should have come to see you sooner!' He muttered the words like a curse upon himself. 'I might have prevented you from falling ill in the first place, but I feared it would be awkward between us. As if awkwardness mattered at such a time.'

'Perhaps not,' said Christabel. 'But I can understand your desire to avoid it. I should have felt the same if our positions had been reversed.'

She wished she could have avoided the awkwardness of *this* moment, but it was no more than she deserved after her ungrateful behaviour. 'I cannot begin to thank you for your extraordinary kindness to me and my son.'

'About the boy—' Frost rose abruptly and strode to the window. 'If you recall the harsh things I said last night, I hope you can understand—'

'That you were trying to make me fight for my life?' Though she had only been awake a short time, Christabel already felt tired again. 'It was clever of you. Most men in that situation would have promised anything to pacify the patient, even if they never meant to keep their word.'

Her late husband had been a genius at placating her with such false promises.

'I was sorry to distress you.' Frost's glance strayed towards her as if he doubted her forbearance. 'I wish I could have thought of a better way.'

Christabel directed a rueful, weary smile at him. 'For what you were trying to do, there *was* no better way. Do not reproach yourself.'

She was the one who should reproach herself for all the horrible things she had thought about him. And her illness was no excuse for it. Perhaps part of her had needed to think badly of him, to justify her past conduct. 'You have been more than generous to do so much for us, especially after the infamous manner in which I once treated you. I deserve your censure and resentment, not such kindness.'

Indeed, she could hardly believe Jonathan Frost was the same proud, severe young man her father had once pressured her to wed, then disowned her when she had not. If she had made an effort to become better acquainted with him back then, might she have discovered his finer qualities?

Frost turned to face her, his hands clasped behind his back, his attractive features tightened in a harsh expression. 'That is all in the past, madam. Besides, in such matters it is always a lady's prerogative to change her mind once she has undergone a change of heart.'

Christabel marvelled that he could say those words with a straight face. He must know she had undergone no change of heart. Perhaps she was begging his pardon for the wrong action. Her worst offence had been to accept the proposal of a man she had not loved.

'I would take comfort from your words, sir, but I fear you pardon me too easily.' How prim and stilted her long-overdue apology sounded! 'I cannot excuse my thoughtless conduct, no matter how long past. Whatever my feelings, I might have spared you injury and embarrassment if I had behaved with greater propriety.'

He stood silent for a moment. Then, just when he appeared about to speak, an odd little voice called from out in the corridor, 'Papa! Papa, where are you?'

Frost gave a visible start, then made a hasty bow to Christabel. 'I pray you will excuse me, Mrs Wilton. You need plenty of rest to regain your strength and I have kept you from it too long already.'

He dashed from the room, leaving Christabel bewildered and strangely dismayed.

Papa? Did Mr Frost have a wife and family, then? He had never said so, but then he had never said not, either. Events had moved with such speed, he'd had little opportunity to tell her anything about his present life, such as why he had come to live in Derbyshire. Did this estate belong to his wife, perhaps?

It should not surprise her to discover such an attractive, agreeable man of property was married. Quite the contrary.

Just because she had once spurned him did not mean some wiser woman could not have recognised and appreciated his many fine qualities. And surely she was not so selfish as to begrudge the man whatever domestic happiness he had found?

Could his marriage be the reason Mr Frost was able to speak of their past connection with such cool detachment? Perhaps Christabel had done him a service all those years ago, by freeing him to find a loving wife whose influence had mellowed his character. His kindness to her and Colly might have been an unspoken acknowledgement of that debt.

Suddenly the symptoms of her illness—chills and aches—returned to plague Christabel. Only this time, they were concentrated in her heart.

She did her best to ignore them, just as she strove to disregard her dizzy head and the weakness of her limbs. With stiff, feeble movements driven by a resolute will, she crawled from her sickbed in search of her clothes. Now that her fever had broken and she was out of danger, she and Colly must leave here at once.

Difficult as it had been to accept help from Mr Frost, Christabel could not bear to trespass another moment on the charity of *Mrs* Frost.

For a moment she clung to the bedpost and looked around the room. A large decorative screen hid the far corner of the room beside the hearth. Christabel guessed she would find her gown, shawls and undergarments behind it. She staggered toward the dressing screen, her legs growing weaker with each step.

She had not got more than halfway there when the guest

room door swung open and Mr Frost strode in. 'Pardon the intrusion, ma'am. I just remembered—'

Something about his sudden appearance gave Christabel's memory a powerful nudge. Dear heaven, she had kissed Jonathan Frost last night! And not a chaste, fond peck, either, but the lush, wanton kiss of a woman eager to be bedded.

She'd been confused, believing Monty had come back to her, charmingly repentant, as always, and eager to seduce his way back into her favour. But it was not Monty who had returned her kiss. His mouth had not tasted of spirits, for one thing. And there had been a gentle restraint in his manner that she'd found curiously stirring.

Now Christabel knew what must have happened. Something in the gaze Frost fixed upon her confirmed it.

'Good Lord, woman,' he cried, striding towards her, 'what are you doing out of bed?'

Overwhelmed by embarrassment over her vivid recollection, Christabel swayed on her feet. Before she had a chance to recover her balance, Frost scooped her into his arms and carried her back to the bed.

'Only last night your life was in danger.' He spoke in a stern tone that Christabel might have resented had she not sensed an air of sincere concern beneath the rebuke. 'Just because you feel a little better now, does not mean you are recovered enough to be up and about.'

The protective strength of his hold gave Christabel a feeling of warmth and security she had not felt for a very long time. When he eased her back on to the bed, she found herself wishing she could linger in his arms another moment or two. Immediately she caught herself—she had no business entertaining such improper thoughts about another woman's husband!

'I beg your pardon, sir.' Christabel struggled to sit up, but Mr Frost hovered over her. If she raised herself much higher, her face would come in contact with his. 'But now that I am out of danger, I must insist upon returning home with my son.'

His brooding nearness frightened her with the threat it posed to her fragile self-control.

Before he could protest, she continued, 'I can never repay the generosity you have shown us already. I will not be so un-grateful as to trespass longer on the hospitality of you and your good wife. Especially during this festive season.'

Mr. Frost stared at her, his brow furrowed in a look of intense perplexity as if she were addressing him in a foreign language. Really, had it never occurred to the man that his wife might resent the presence of his former betrothed in her house?

'You may be expecting guests for the holidays.' She lifted her hand to his chest and tried to push him back, but she did not have the strength to budge him. 'Or perhaps you are invited to join friends and family in another part of the country. Either way, the last thing you need is an invalid house guest and her child spoiling your plans.'

The puzzled look on Mr Frost's face did not ease. He remained poised on the edge of the bed, leaning over her. Slowly he raised his hand to her face.

Christabel's breath quickened. He was not about to caress her cheek, was he? And how might she respond if he did?

But Frost's hand bypassed her cheek, pressing instead to her forehead. 'Has your fever come back and made you de-lirious again? I have no wife!'

Chapter Five

Wife?

Christabel Wilton's brow felt cool to Frost's touch, but she was babbling nonsense. Or was she so eager to escape his company that she had to think up any kind of daft excuse to leave Candlewood?

Suddenly he became aware of the provocative posture in which he hovered over her as she lay upon the bed. Did she suspect he had dishonourable motives for bringing her here?

'I assure you, madam, I am not married.' He struggled to subdue his ragged breath and backed away to a less intimate distance. 'Nor have I ever been.'

He'd never come closer to it than with her. Frost could not suppress an arousing image of him and Christabel in this bed together the way they might have been if she had honoured her promise to wed him.

'I don't understand.' She glanced towards the door. 'Just a moment ago, I heard a child call for her father, and you answered.'

'Oh, that.' Frost felt as if she'd doused him with a bucket of cold water. 'Do you recollect my aunt, Lady Havergill?'

'The one who raised you and bequeathed you her fortune?' Christabel gave a feeble nod. The strength that had carried her out of her sickbed seemed to have deserted her. 'I met her once, before…you asked me to marry you. You needed her approval that I would make a suitable wife.'

Even after so many years and all that had happened, Christabel's voice still rasped with an undercurrent of bitterness.

'Did you think I was wrong to seek my aunt's approval of my choice?' It had long since ceased to matter, yet Frost felt compelled to know. 'Without it, I would have had nothing to offer you—no means of gaining your father's permission.'

Christabel shook her head as she tried to smother a deep yawn. 'It was altogether sensible of you. I can see that now.'

'But *then?*' Frost persisted. 'Would you rather I had asked you to run away with me and the devil take both our families?'

'What did you expect?' The wistful irony of her smile could have broken Frost's heart all over again. 'I was a foolish chit of eighteen with a head full of silly romantic fancies. Of course I wanted sentimental speeches and grand, impractical gestures. I thought that was…love.'

Did it follow, then, that his prudent, proper courtship had signified a lack of feeling? Frost longed to assure her otherwise, but the time for that was past and gone.

Mrs Wilton seemed no more eager than he to dwell on that sore subject. With some effort, she raised her hand and gave a listless wave as if to dismiss such talk. 'Tell me, pray, what all this has to do with the child?'

'That was no child you heard calling.' Part of Frost shrank from telling her, fearing she would find the whole situation distasteful. Another part yearned for a sympathetic friend in whom to confide. Was he mistaken to hope Christabel Wilton might prove such a friend? 'My aunt's mind has been failing for some time. It is as if it grows younger as her body ages. She believes she is a child again, and grows quite agitated if we try to convince her otherwise. Because I bear a strong re-semblance to my grandfather, she thinks of me and addresses me as her father.'

'How sad!' murmured Christabel, her words followed by a deep sigh.

Frost would have scorned a look of such obvious pity from anyone else. But her soft features gave it an air of touching beauty he could not help but treasure.

'I suppose it is.' He turned away, unable to sustain the lingering gaze that shimmered between them. 'But I console myself that it could be far worse for my aunt. At least she is well cared for and happy enough in her way. I brought her to Candlewood because it was her childhood home. Once we came here, she grew more settled and content.'

'I wondered what had brought you here.' Christabel spoke the words more to herself than to him.

'Often I question whether I have done the right thing by indulging this fancy of hers,' continued Frost. Perhaps some assurance from Christabel might put his misgivings at rest. 'When Aunt Fanny first began to act strangely and become confused about the past, a doctor told me I should commit her to a madhouse. Can you imagine? I would not consign a dog to one of those places!'

'I *can* imagine,' Christabel replied in a rueful whisper. 'Too many people think only of their own interests and comfort and care nothing for responsibilities that might inconvenience them. Duty is sadly out of fashion at present.'

No doubt that was how she had regarded him when they were younger—dutiful but dull. Seen through her eyes, was his present life a pointless waste?

'I do not wish to excite either your admiration or your pity, Mrs Wilton.' Frost headed for the door. 'I only wanted to make you aware of my peculiar domestic arrangements so you would not be alarmed by things you might see or hear during your stay at Candlewood.'

'Alarmed?' Christabel struggled to sit up. 'Should I be alarmed? Does your aunt pose any threat to my son?'

'Not in the least.' The notion was so absurd it made Frost chuckle. He motioned for Christabel to lie still. 'Aunt Fanny is very good natured—far better than when she had all her wits about her, poor thing. And I make certain she is supervised as carefully as any young child who might come to harm or get into mischief. Your son has nothing to fear from her.'

His reassurances sparked an idea in Frost's mind. 'Would you permit them to play together—if he is willing? Fanny is always after me to find her a playmate.'

Seeing the strange look Christabel gave him, he hesitated, flustered. 'Listen to me. I talk as if she truly is a child. In fact, I often find myself thinking of her as if she were. Perhaps I am the one who belongs in a madhouse.'

He pulled the door open with a savage tug. But before he could rush away, Christabel called out, 'Mr Frost, wait! You have not heard my answer.'

With some reluctance, he glanced back, his brows raised in a mute question.

'If Colly is willing and if your aunt might enjoy his company, I see no reason why they should not play together. It is the least we can do to repay your hospitality.'

Her response elated Frost far more than he wished it would. Since he'd first set eyes on her again, Christabel had provoked his normally temperate emotions to unwanted extremes.

'Good, then let us have no more talk about *repayment*. Your presence at Candlewood is no inconvenience to anyone. And no more insistence on leaving before you are thoroughly recovered. I assure you, Aunt Fanny and I have no special plans for Christmas that you would spoil.'

That thought haunted Frost as he hurried away. Was it possible they might *make* some special plans for Christmas at Candlewood? Plans involving Christabel Wilton and her son?

A furtive rattling of her bedchamber door handle brought Christabel awake with a start. She opened her eyes to see a small person open the door and scurry inside. Christable recognised Mr Frost's aunt from the bygone days of their engagement.

Lady Havergill had large blue eyes and delicate features, including a tiny mouth that might have been compared to a rosebud in her youth. Her hair was covered with a cap such as little girls often wore. She had on a simple gown of sprigged muslin with a high neck and elbow sleeves. From a distance, or at a quick glance, she might easily have been mistaken for a child.

When her ladyship spied Christabel sitting up in bed, she gave a squeal of surprise, then clapped a hand over her mouth to stifle a giggle. 'Pardon me! I didn't know there was anyone in here. Who are you?'

Christabel could scarcely reconcile her memories of a haughty dowager with this elfin little creature. 'I am Mrs Wilton, an old friend of Mr Frost's. He found me ill and brought me to Candlewood to recover.'

Lady Havergill nodded over the information as she sidled closer to the bed. 'He does that sort of thing all the time. He's a very charitable man, you know.'

'I am most grateful to him.' It galled Christabel to think of herself as an object of charity, but it was no use trying to hide from that humiliating truth.

Fortunately, her visitor did not dwell on the matter. Instead she bobbed a quick curtsy. 'I'm Miss Frances Frost, but most everybody calls me Fanny.'

'A pleasure to meet you, Miss Fanny.' Christabel smiled. She could see now what Frost meant about thinking of his aunt as a child.

The wrinkles on Miss Fanny's brow deepened, then her eyes suddenly widened. 'You're the little boy's mother, aren't you? Now, what was his name?'

'Nicholas,' said Christabel. 'Though most everyone calls *him* Colly. He's been keeping you company, has he?'

Miss Fanny nodded. 'He has.' Then, with the air of a child aping her elders, she added, 'He does you great credit.'

'Why, thank you. I'm pleased to hear he has been behaving himself.'

'He let me ride his hobbyhorse.' Miss Fanny's small face

lit up. 'It was great fun! I wish Papa would get me a hobby-horse—a white one, like in the rhyme: "To see a white lady upon a white horse."'

Christabel chuckled. 'Will you wear rings on your fingers and bells on your toes?'

A soft tap on the door interrupted their conversation.

'Come in,' Christabel called.

A tall, middle-aged woman bustled in. 'There ye are, Miss Fanny. Ye shouldn't have disturbed the lady, and ye shouldn't have run off! Ye know how upset the master gets when ye go hiding on me like that.'

'She didn't disturb me,' said Christabel, though it was not strictly true. 'We were having a very nice chat.'

'*May* I come and visit you again?' Fanny asked politely.

Christabel could not resist her air of sincere eagerness. 'Please do. I would enjoy the company.'

The servant woman looked relieved that Christabel was not vexed at Miss Fanny's barging in on her without warning. Her sharp tone softened. 'Come along, then. It's almost time for yer tea and Cook made yer favourite, jam tarts.'

'Jam tarts!' The old lady took a skipping step towards the door, then paused and turned back towards Christabel. 'Goodbye, Mrs… Oh dear, I've forgotten your name already!'

'Mrs Wilton.'

'Yes, that's right. I remember now.' Miss Fanny waved. 'Goodbye. I'll come and visit you again.'

'How are ye feeling this morning, Mrs Wilton?' asked the housemaid a few mornings later as she set a breakfast tray before Christabel. 'Pardon me for saying, but ye look a great deal better than ye did a week ago when the master brought ye here.'

'I *feel* a great deal better, thank you, Violet.' Christabel's mouth watered at the savoury aromas wafting from the tray. 'So much so, that I cannot continue to impose upon your master's hospitality.'

In truth, she had been well enough to go yesterday, perhaps even the day before. But with the weather so cold, she had not the heart to take Colly away from the warmth and abundance of Candlewood back to their tiny, cold cottage. But there was a limit to how long her conscience would allow her to malinger on Jonathan Frost's charity.

This morning, she had reached that limit. 'Will you ask Mr Frost if I might have a word with him later about our departure?'

'As ye wish, ma'am.' The girl crossed to the hearth and began to stir up the fire. 'Though it will be a shame to see ye and Master Colly go. Candlewood's been a different place altogether since you came. Miss Fanny will take on dreadful over losing her playmate, I'm sure. I don't envy poor Mr Frost the managing of her.'

Christabel paused with a spoonful of buttered egg halfway to her mouth. 'He's very good with her, isn't he?'

'Aye, he is, ma'am.' The maid turned from her fire-tending duties. 'He's that patient with her when she gets in one of her tempers, wanting to visit some friend who's been dead for thirty years. Shall I come back and help ye dress, ma'am, after ye've eaten your breakfast?'

'I believe I can manage on my own, thank you, Violet, but perhaps you could dress my hair for me. I felt ever so much better after you helped me wash it yesterday.'

* * *

Like all Mr Frost's servants, Violet proved most obliging. By the time Christabel descended the stairs to his study, she felt more like the lady he had once known, and less like some pitiful charity case.

She found him standing by the window, gazing at the snow-mantled garden. The wistful ghost of a smile softened his crisp features as he turned towards her. There was more she would miss about Candlewood than its warm fires, thick blankets and plentiful food.

His expression grew solemn again when he turned to greet her. 'So, you are recovered enough to be up and about.'

'Even you cannot dispute that I am finally well enough to return home.' She shot him a teasing glance.

He made no effort to contradict her, which left Christabel vaguely disappointed. Instead he replied with gentle gravity, 'I think you look very well, indeed.'

Perhaps it was the faint glow of admiration she fancied in his eyes that made her blush for the first time in years. 'I have you to thank for it, and I do with all my heart. But I must get my son back home and make our preparations for Christmas.'

A bit of greenery to decorate the mantel cost nothing. Nor did sitting by the fire and singing her little one to sleep with Christmas carols. Somehow she would contrive a better meal than usual for Christmas dinner. Though the most lavish spread she could afford would be nothing to their regular bill of fare at Candlewood.

'Ah, yes, Christmas.' Mr Frost's expression turned positively grim as he stared her with his hands clasped behind his back. 'I know I said you must not think of repaying me in any way for the small service I have rendered you.'

'Small service?' The words burst out of Christabel in a mixture of amusement and exasperation. 'It may have been a trifle to you, sir, but I am convinced I owe you my life. I only wish there were some way I could begin to—'

Frost raised his hand for silence. 'Would you think me quite mercenary if I now suggest there is a great favour you could do for me in return? But…no, I must not impose upon you.'

As she had imposed upon him for the past week?

'Please tell me what it is!' Christabel cried. 'You have only to name your request and I will be delighted to grant it.'

His stern, anxious expression relaxed and the briefest flicker of merriment twinkled in his eyes. 'I see the years have not curbed your impulsiveness, my dear. You must be careful about making such reckless promises before you discover what may be asked of you.'

'Time *has* curbed my impulsiveness.' Christabel struggled to keep a note of bitterness from her voice. 'But I trust you would not ask anything of me that I would not readily give.'

The moment the words left her mouth, she wished she could unspeak them. Jonathan Frost had once asked for something she'd been loath to grant—her hand in marriage. And though she had promised it to him, she had later broken her word. No wonder he was hesitant to ask anything of her now.

Frost gave no sign that thought had occurred to him. 'I wondered if you and your son might consider remaining at Candlewood through Twelfth Night as my Christmas guests?'

Christabel gathered her breath to refuse. It did not take a bluestocking to realise this 'invitation' was a thinly veiled pretext for offering her more charity.

Perhaps sensing her opposition, he pressed on, not allowing her an opportunity to refuse right away. 'I would like to give Aunt Fanny the kind of old-fashioned family Christmas she knew as a child. That is difficult to accomplish with just the two of us. "The more the merrier," as they say. You were always a great promoter of merriment in our youth. Can I prevail upon you to help me make this a merry Christmas at Candlewood?'

Christabel could think of many reasons to say yes, not least of which was the sincere impression that Mr Frost needed her help. She hated the thought of him and his aunt spending Christmas alone, especially if it was within her power to keep them company. Besides, she had long wanted to give her son the kind of Christmas she had never been able to afford.

Set against all those was the uneasy conviction that every day they spent in the comfort of Candlewood and the congenial company of Jonathan Frost, the harder it would be for her and her son to leave.

Chapter Six

Was he making the second biggest mistake of his life? Frost wondered as he waited for Christabel's answer to his invitation. Fie, he hadn't been this anxious when he'd proposed marriage to the woman six years ago! Of course, back then, he'd been too inexperienced to fear her refusal. Having experienced the cruel sting of rejection, he was warier now.

What had compelled him to extend the invitation? When he'd gone to pay his call upon her, he had been resolved to do as little as courtesy demanded, then make a speedy escape. Then, when circumstances had forced him to bring her into his home, he'd resolved to keep his distance until she was well enough to leave. That had proved impossible, though, and every moment he spent in her company further eroded his prudent resolutions. If it continued, how would he bear to part from her after Twelfth Night?

Don't be such a coward, man! he chided himself. If Aunt Fanny continued to regress, this might be the last Christmas she would be aware of the festivities and able to take pleasure in them. And what a bleak Christmas the Wiltons would have back in that bare little cottage. Those considerations signified far more than any foolish apprehensions of his. Besides, he was no longer a calf-eyed boy. He was a man who had mastered his feelings and got on with his life. He could do it again if he had to.

Mrs Wilton inhaled a deep breath, squared her shoulders and raised her gaze to meet his. 'Very well, Mr Frost. For the sake of your aunt and my son, I accept your kind invitation. I will do everything in my power to make this a truly merry Christmas for them.'

Her countenance and tone left Frost with no illusions that she expected to enjoy the holidays in his company. She clearly regarded the whole affair as an obligation, just as she had accepted his marriage offer out of obligation to her father.

'Very good.' Frost struggled to hide a traitorous pang of disappointment over her lack of enthusiasm. Mrs Wilton had no need to fear—he would not continue to impose his odious company upon her once Christmas was over.

He glanced towards the window again, wary of holding a gaze that had often seemed to divine more of his thoughts than he wished to disclose. 'Aunt Fanny and your son asked if I might take them for a sleigh ride this afternoon. Would you care to join us, or would you prefer to rest?'

'I should like to come, if you have room for me.' Her voice betrayed a tantalising hint of eagerness. 'I have done little but rest and eat since you brought us to Candlewood. A ride in the fresh air would be most welcome.'

'I had hoped as much.' The promising beginnings of a

smile tugged at the corner of Frost's mouth. 'If I may prevail upon you to round up the rest of our party and see that they are warmly dressed, I shall have the sleigh harnessed and meet you all in the courtyard.'

When Frost drove the sleigh into the courtyard a quarter of an hour later, he found that Christabel had followed all his instructions, save the one about dressing warmly. The boy was wearing a coat far too large for him.

'One of the footmen lent it to us,' Christabel informed him in a tone of mild defiance. 'The long sleeves will keep his hands warm.'

'My apologies,' muttered Frost as he helped her into the sleigh. 'I never thought to bundle him up properly the day I brought you to Candlewood. Now that you'll be staying, I must send someone to fetch your clothes.'

'Thank you. That would be very kind.'

Christabel's subdued reply made Frost wonder if the boy owned a decent coat. At least Colly looked warmer than his mother, bundled in her miscellany of shawls.

Frost picked up the boy and set him in beside his mother. 'I think we can all fit if we squeeze up.'

As he lifted Aunt Fanny into the sleigh, she leaned close and whispered a suggestion in his ear. Frost chided himself for not thinking of it.

'Clever girl,' he whispered back. 'But let's keep it a surprise. Christmas is a time for surprises.'

She gave a vigorous nod and stifled a giggle.

As long as she didn't let an incautious word slip in the next few minutes, Frost knew his aunt would forget all about her suggestion and be every bit as surprised as the Wiltons when it came to fruition.

He tucked thick blankets around them, for the day was clear and brisk. Then he sent a young footman to fetch warm bricks on which to rest their feet.

At last he climbed in beside Aunt Fanny. 'We'll just go for a short drive today.' He picked up the reins and gave them a twitch, coaxing the team of matched bays into a leisurely jog. Seeing Colly's lower lip thrust out, he added, 'If you enjoy it, and if the snow stays, we can go for a longer one tomorrow.'

Christabel could not recall when she had last been for a sleigh ridse. She has almost forgotten how it felt—a carriage drive did not begin to compare. Even the swift, perilous phaeton called the High Flier did not give the same sensation of flight as skimming over the snow in a crisp winter breeze.

Colly and Miss Fanny laughed and squealed with childish glee when Frost urged the horses to a brisk trot over the snow-covered fields. It was such an infectious sound, Christabel soon found herself joining in. After lying so many days in a sickbed, the cold winter air smelled clean and invigorating. The jingle of bells on the horses' harness played rollicking, merry music in time to the crunch of their great hooves on the snow.

How long had it been since she'd laughed more than a pallid chuckle? True, she'd had little cause for laughter in the year and a half since Waterloo…and even before that. But what cause did she have now? Yet gale after gale of gleeful laughter gushed out of her from some secret spring that had been too long dammed up with regret and bitterness and self-blame. How good it felt to let it flow again!

Perhaps she needed to find more simple ways to enjoy life in spite of its present misfortunes—for Colly's sake. There was so much else she could not afford to give him. He deserved a happy childhood. This Christmas visit at Candlewood would be the perfect opportunity to change her outlook on life and revive a crumb or two of her old dauntless optimism.

Mr Frost glanced over at his passengers as they shrieked with mirth. 'Are you frightened?' he inquired with mock-concern. 'Should I slow down?'

'No!' they cried, laughing harder and gasping to catch their breaths. 'Go faster!'

'You're sure?' Frost pulled on the reins to bring the sleigh in a wide arc heading back towards Candlewood. Then he gave them a sudden, vigorous skip against the steaming rumps of the bays and cried, 'Get up!'

The horses broke into a swift gallop for home, sending Christabel, Colly and Miss Fanny into fresh gusts of wild laughter. By the time the sleigh slid to a stop in front of the house, Christabel's sides ached and she could scarcely catch her breath. But she felt as if something long caged inside her had been unexpectedly set free.

'That was such fun!' cried Miss Fanny. 'You must take us again tomorrow. Promise you will?'

As Frost lifted her from the sleigh, he swung her around, prompting another volley of high-pitched laughter.

He set her on her feet, careful not to let go until she had regained her balance. 'Perhaps if you eat a good dinner and behave yourself for Mrs Penny, you may get your wish.'

Glancing over the top of his aunt's bonnet, he winked at Christabel.

Colly jumped down from the sleigh without waiting to be helped. 'Thank you, Mr Frost! Miss Fanny is right—that was even better fun than riding Mistletoe!'

'High praise, indeed.' Frost chuckled, and, when he glanced up from looking at Colly, his eyes held the same soft glow of fondness Christabel had seen in them when he'd spoken to his aunt. Only this look was not muted by a shadow of wistful sadness.

One long stride brought him back to the sleigh. 'What is your opinion, Mrs Wilton? Do you make it unanimous?' His voice rang with forced heartiness as he lifted her to the ground.

'I do indeed.' Christabel found herself wishing he would twirl her around, as he had Miss Fanny. 'I enjoyed the ride very much. This winter air is a marvellous tonic. My appetite is already sharp-set for tea.'

'I'm delighted to hear it!' This time the hearty note in Frost's voice rang with perfect sincerity.

Did he hold her a moment or two longer than necessary when he set her on the ground? Or did she cling to his warmth and strength?

He looked down into her eyes, and Christabel felt suddenly weak and dizzy—though in a curiously pleasant way. 'It was good to hear you laugh again.'

'Thank you for reminding me how.' A bubble of laughter—or perhaps it was something else—rose in Christabel's throat. 'I was in danger of forgetting.'

'We cannot have that, can we?'

The front entrance opened and Miss Fanny's servant beckoned her. 'Don't stand about in the cold. Come in and get yer tea.'

A delectable aroma of spices wafted out into the courtyard.

Frost inhaled a deep breath. 'It smells as if Cook has prepared something tasty to satisfy your well-whetted appetite.'

'So she has, sir,' said Mrs Penny as she ushered Colly and Miss Fanny into the house. 'Hot mulled cider. Just the thing to warm ye all up.'

The awkward intimacy of the moment shattered like a shiny icicle fallen from the eaves of Candlewood. Christabel could not decide whether she was relieved or disappointed. A sudden gust of cold wind pierced her layers of old shawls and made her shiver. She hastened into the fragrant warmth of the house.

Miss Fanny gave an appreciative sniff as she untied her bonnet. 'It smells like Christmas.'

Colly peeled off the footman's oversized coat. His small cheeks glowed like a pair of plump, ripe apples. 'It is Christmas—very nearly.'

'Is it?' Miss Fanny cast Frost a questioning glance, her face a-quiver with suppressed excitement.

He nodded, looking pleased to confirm happy news. 'And what is even better, the Wiltons have agreed to stay for the holiday as our guests.'

For an instant Miss Fanny looked uncertain. 'The…who?'

Frost nodded towards Christabel. 'Colly and his mother. Isn't that splendid?'

Her confusion gently allayed yet again, Miss Fanny was once more wreathed in smiles. 'The Wiltons, of course! That is splendid!'

After they had removed their wraps, Frost led Miss Fanny and their guests towards the drawing room. 'And Mrs Wilton is planning all manner of diversions to amuse us, aren't you, my dear?'

'That sounds exciting!' Miss Fanny nearly danced with eagerness. 'What sorts of diversions?'

'I haven't quite decided.' Christabel took a seat on the chaise-longue in front of a bountifully spread tea table and drew Colly down beside her. 'Tell me some things you enjoy doing at Christmas time.'

Miss Fanny nibbled on a muffin, her features clenched in concentration. 'Well…I like nice things to eat—roast goose and Christmas pudding and such. And I do like presents.'

Colly endorsed both suggestions with eager nods.

Frost ladled the hot cider into cups for all of them. Christabel wrapped her chilled fingers around the warm cup and inhaled the spicy aroma.

Miss Fanny took a sip of her cider, then exclaimed, 'It's always great fun to deck the halls on Christmas Eve…and play games…and roast nuts over the fire…and play Christmas hymns on the pianoforte!'

'Good heavens.' Frost chuckled. 'At this rate we'll be celebrating Christmas until Ash Wednesday!'

He did not seem greatly bothered by the prospect.

And neither, in her heart of hearts, was Christabel. For too long she had endured an Ash Wednesday existence of penitence and regret. Now it was time to light a candle, deck the halls and celebrate life's gifts.

Chapter Seven

'My goodness, whatever can this be?' exclaimed Christabel several days later when Frost set a large parcel on the chaise-longue beside her. 'It is not Christmas yet.'

'It was Miss Fanny's idea.' Frost glanced towards his aunt, who sat watching the Wiltons with an expectant little grin.

A feeling of anxious anticipation quivered within him, too. He hoped the gifts would please Christabel, but she appeared more dismayed than elated at the moment.

'See what it is, Mama!' Colly looked eager enough for both of them.

'Very well.' Christabel's fingers fumbled as she untied the string and peeled back the thick brown paper. 'Oh, my!' The soft gasp of her words assured Frost that she liked what she found.

'Is this for me?' Colly swooped down and grabbed a dark blue coat with brass buttons.

'I doubt it would fit your mama,' said Frost, 'so it must be for you.' He pulled a matching cap from the parcel and set it on the boy's head with a flourish.

'Put on the coat, too!' cried Miss Fanny. 'See how handsome it looks on you.'

'May I, Mama?'

After an instant's thoughtful hesitation, his mother nodded.

While Colly and Miss Fanny were occupied with getting his new coat properly buttoned, Christabel looked through the rest of the clothes in the parcel with an air of bemusement.

'However did you get all these things made up so quickly?' She caressed the thick, warm fabric of one of the gowns between her thumb and fingers.

By paying a generous premium to every seamstress within miles. But Frost sensed that was not what Christabel wanted to hear. 'Let us say it was a little Christmas magic at work.'

She shook her head. 'I cannot accept all this. Not after everything else you have done for us.'

Frost dropped to one knee beside her. Guessing she did not want Colly to overhear her refusing the gifts, Frost lowered his voice, too. 'They are made and paid for. What would you have me do—give them away to someone who may need them less? I know we are always told it is more blessed to give than to receive. But sometimes it can be a blessing to receive a well-meant gift with grace and gratitude.'

'Practicality before pride?' Her lips twisted in a self-deprecating grin. 'You are an altogether sensible man, Mr Frost. I must endeavour to learn from your example.'

A spark of merriment twinkled in her eyes—a twinkle Frost had never forgotten. Now it smote him a powerful blow.

'Is that a tactful way of saying I am a tiresome bore?'

Christabel let out an exasperated sigh as she unfolded a

thick woollen cloak and draped it around her shoulders 'You are a fine one to talk of receiving gifts with good grace, when you will not even accept a few sincere words of praise without turning them into an insult.'

She had him. Frost acknowledged it with a rueful chuckle.

Before he could ask if they were both beyond redemption, Christabel continued. 'Good sense is far less tiresome than foolishness. Seasoned with generosity and spiced with a dash of humour, it is a most agreeable virtue indeed.'

Frost resisted the urge to disparage her compliment. 'If these garments warm you as your words have warmed my heart, I shall be most gratified.'

His hand fairly trembled with the suppressed urge to reach up and caress her cheek. Frost knew his heart was slipping into danger, but that did not trouble him as it once had. Christabel was no longer in a position to pick and choose among a bevy of suitors. And she had learned the harsh consequences of letting romantic impulses overrule her good sense. Might she be prepared to secure her son's future with a prudent match to a man she did not love, but could respect and trust?

Colly had been swaggering about in his new coat and cap for Aunt Fanny's amusement. Now the two of them descended upon Frost and Christabel. 'Can we go for a sleigh ride? Please!'

Half-grateful for the distraction, Frost stood up. 'A capital idea. We can drive over to the bit of woodland on the edge of the estate and look for greenery to deck the halls on Christmas Eve.'

A few hours later they returned, nostrils tingling with the festive tang of fresh-cut evergreen boughs, cheeks aglow with cold and sides cramped with the mild, pleasant ache of laughter.

'I think we gathered enough greenery to deck the whole of Derbyshire!' Christabel declared as she untied the ribbons of her new bonnet and let Mr Frost help her out of her matching cloak.

She could not recall the last time she had felt the sense of joyous anticipation bubbling inside her. For too long she had faced each new day with a faint, secret dread of what it would bring—bad news from some distant battlefield, another creditor looking for money, the nagging sense of failure.

Plenty of worries lurked in the shadows of the New Year, ready to pounce upon her once this sweet holiday idyll was over. But she refused to let them taint her present happiness. Instead she would draw strength from it, preparing herself to better meet whatever challenges might lie ahead.

Their appetites sharpened once again by the crisp December air, they ate heartily of all the special dainties Cook had prepared for tea, washing them down with more hot, spicy cider.

'I want to play a game,' announced Miss Fanny when they had eaten the last crumb of seed cake. She turned to Colly. 'Have you ever played Hoodman Blind?'

The little boy shook his head. 'Is it fun?'

'Oh, yes.' Miss Fanny grabbed Frost by the hand. 'Let's show him how to play. You can be the first to go.'

Frost glanced at Christabel, one brow raised. 'What do you say? Are we too sober and responsible for such frivolity?'

Was he trying to ask her about something more than a children's game? Christabel wondered. 'A little frivolity now and then is not a bad thing, is it?'

The flirtatious note she heard in her voice shocked her. She had no business flirting with Jonathan Frost, even if she wanted to. Did she want to? The answer to that question surprised her.

'Not a bad thing at all.' Frost rose from his seat and extended his hand to help Christabel up from hers. 'During this festive season, especially.'

One of the housemaids produced a suitable length of dark cloth, which Mr Frost volunteered to have tied over his eyes. A merry chase ensued as the others called teases to him, scurrying out of the way when he tried to grab them. At last, he caught his aunt, whose uncontrollable giggles had given her away. Mr Frost had no difficulty guessing her identity, the other part of the game.

Miss Fanny took her turn and chased the others about with great glee for several minutes. When Christabel sensed the old lady becoming confused and agitated, she quickly allowed herself to be caught, then whispered her name for Miss Fanny to *guess*.

Next the blindfold went around her eyes and she had to blunder about the drawing room, following elusive voices and scampering footsteps. She was laughing and gasping for breath by the time her hand closed around a bit of fabric.

At first she thought it might belong to Colly's jacket. Then she caught a faint whiff of Mr Frost's shaving soap. His name sprang to her tongue, but instead she found herself running her fingertips over his strong, regular features. The game provided a polite excuse for taking such liberties, though more often it was the gentlemen who took advantage of the opportunity.

'Is that you, Colly?' she asked with mock-gravity. The

touch of his smooth-shaven chin and the unexpected softness of his lips beneath her roving fingertips provoked a warm, ticklish flutter deep in her belly.

'Guess again,' Frost replied in a crackling falsetto which was followed by a sputter of laughter.

Was it only her fancy, Christabel wondered, or was the moist warmth of his breath coming faster? Hers raced to match it.

'M-Miss Fanny?' Somehow she could not bear for the silly ruse to end a moment sooner than it must.

Colly and the real Miss Fanny chortled and cried, 'No, no!'

Then Frost's arm slipped around Christabel's waist. With his other hand he raised the blindfold, hesitating an instant so his fingers rested on her hair. When the darkness lifted from her vision, she found herself staring deep into his steadfast blue gaze…and thinking she had never beheld a more excellent man.

Had her heart played its own game of Hoodman Blind? Grasping after the elusive mocking lure of love, when all the time it had been near enough to touch…if only she had slowed down long enough to recognise it?

'Can it be my turn now, please, Mr Frost?' asked Colly. 'You've had one already, remember? But I haven't.'

Her son's words fairly pushed Christabel and Frost apart.

'Of course you must have the next turn.' Frost knelt to tie the blindfold around Colly's eyes.

Christabel used the moment to gather her shaken composure. Her cheeks stung as if she had just come in from a long, brisk stroll around the grounds of Candlewood. She knew if she tried to speak she would sound tongue-tied and breathless.

When Colly took his turn at the game, Christabel could scarcely keep her wits enough about her to stay out of his way.

Her gaze kept straying towards Mr Frost, anticipating his next turn to don the blindfold. Did she dare let herself wander into his reach and risk the pleasure of his touch?

Christabel never got the chance to find out. No sooner had Colly caught and identified Miss Fanny than she declared herself tired of the game.

'My knees feel stiff and I'm all out of breath. Let's play something without so much running.' She pondered for a moment. 'I know! The Twelve Days of Christmas game.'

Frost and Christabel exchanged an uncertain look. The contest Miss Fanny had suggested was apt to tax the memory.

'What if we play as teams?' Christabel suggested. 'The ladies against the gentleman.'

'I don't know that game.' Colly looked quite prepared to play Hoodman Blind all evening. 'How do you play it?'

Frost settled himself in an armchair opposite the chaise-lounge and beckoned the boy to sit in the one beside him. 'It isn't hard to pick up. Just listen and see.'

'I'll start.' Miss Fanny sank on to the chaise-longue. 'On the first day of Christmas, my true love gave to me…a white horse with a golden bridle.'

'A rich fellow, your true love,' quipped Frost as Christabel seated herself beside his aunt. 'On the second day of Christmas, my true love gave to me a brace of hunting hounds and a white horse with a golden bridle.'

Miss Fanny rattled off the first two and added three velvet gowns to her bounty.

'I see how it goes now.' Colly turned to his partner. 'May I take a turn?'

Frost nodded. 'I told you it was easy.'

'Wait till we get to the eleventh and twelfth days,' Christabel warned him. 'See if you think it's so easy then.'

'On the fourth day of Christmas,' said Colly, 'my true love gave to me four wooden soldiers...'

Christabel was quite proud of her son's cleverness when he recited the rest of the list without a mistake.

Miss Fanny got a bit mixed up on her turn, but Christabel came to her rescue. A few minutes later, when it was their turn to add the seventh day's gift, Miss Fanny said, 'You do it this time.'

'On the seventh day of Christmas—' Christabel found her gaze drawn to Frost '—my true love gave to me...' She wanted to say 'a parcel of lovely new clothes.'

This time Miss Fanny came to *her* rescue, whispering a suggestion in her ear.

'Seven ivory fans,' said Christabel, then she recited back the rest.

As the game progressed and the list of gifts grew longer, Colly and Miss Fanny relied increasingly on their partners. Christabel's mouth went dry every time she had to say the words 'my true love gave to me.' And every time Frost said them, her heart gave a curious flutter.

She tried to ignore both sensations by concentrating on the game, but to no avail. At last, while reciting the list of gifts for the twelfth day of Christmas, she got mixed up and made a hopeless muddle of them.

'We win!' Colly cheered and clapped his hands.

Though Miss Fanny looked a bit disappointed, she endeavoured to console Christabel. 'It is very hard to remember so many things.'

Christabel's throat tightened. She gathered her partner in a comforting embrace. 'Don't worry. We shall best them next time.'

Frost rose from his chair. 'I believe, as the winners, we are entitled to a forfeit.'

'Indeed?' Christabel smiled up at him. This might be a good distraction for his aunt. 'What sort of forfeit did you have in mind?'

Frost nodded towards the pianoforte. 'I was hoping you ladies might favour us with some music. As I recall, you play and sing very well.'

'Never *very* well.' Christabel cast a longing glance at the fine instrument. 'Except to the most partial audience. And I have not put my fingers to a keyboard since…well…in a very long time.'

'I assure you, we are a most partial audience.' Something in Frost's expression suggested he would be disappointed if she did not oblige him with an attempt, at least. 'And readily forgiving of any mistakes.'

'I'll go first.' Miss Fanny scrambled up from the chaise-longue and tottered to the pianoforte. 'Then you shall see that you cannot do worse, for I do not practise half so often as I should.'

She stumbled through a simple but pretty melody Christabel did not recognise, then hopped up and bobbed a little curtsy to acknowledge the applause of the others.

'I shall be ashamed to follow you,' said Christabel as she slid on to the bench. 'But since you have borne your part in paying our forfeit, I must not shirk mine. I was the one who lost us the game, after all.'

She plundered her memory for a little sonata or minuet that might do. But another kind of music rippled through her thoughts instead—snatches of popular love songs she had played so often during her younger years. After dithering in embarrassment for a moment or two, she placed her fingers on the keys and let them wander where they wished. What came out was a simple version of 'Silent Worship,' played with surprisingly few mistakes.

Mr Frost led the applause when the piece concluded. 'You were too modest about your skill, Mrs Wilton. As I recall, you have a fine voice, too. Perhaps another evening we can persuade you to sing that piece for us.'

His request flustered Christabel. 'I should make an awful muddle of it, I fear. Even when I practised faithfully, I was never good enough to accompany myself.'

It was quite true, but not the whole reason. The thought of singing a love song to him filled her with dismay.

But later that night, while she prepared for bed, Christabel could not resist singing the lyrics under her breath. 'Though I am nothing to her, though she may rarely look at me, though I could never woo her, I love her till I die.'

Blowing out her candle, she burrowed under the bedclothes as if she were a child again, trying to hide from imagined creatures that lurked in the dark. But she could not hide from the worry that dogged her.

'Fool!' she chided herself in a harsh whisper. 'Are you finally falling in love with Jonathan Frost…six years too late?'

Chapter Eight

F rost fairly bounded out of bed on the morning of Christmas Eve, looking forward to the day with an eagerness he had not felt in years. The pretty tune Christabel had played the night before hummed in the back of his mind. How he wished he could have persuaded her to sing it for him in her sweet, clear voice.

But for that one tiny regret, the day had been everything he'd hoped for when he invited the Wiltons to spend Christmas—music, merriment and lively company. He could not recall when he had enjoyed himself more. Back when he'd first courted Christabel, perhaps? Even then, the certainty that she did not return his feelings had cast a shadow over the merriest times.

Did he truly have reason to hope now? The good sense for which Christabel had praised him told Frost not to. If he had not been able to make her care for him when they were both young and eligible, surely there could be no chance of it now. Besides, the woman had only lost her husband eighteen months ago—no doubt she still grieved and yearned for him.

The passionate kiss she had given Frost in her husband's stead should be proof of that, and yet… In the midst of overwhelming doubt there flickered a tantalising spark of hope, like a Christmas candle lighting the darkest days of the year.

Frost closed his eyes and conjured up the memory of Christabel's fingertips caressing his face. For all her feigned confusion, she had known it was him. But she had touched him in a manner almost as intimate as a kiss. In that touch he had sensed curiosity, fondness…and desire? Or had he only fancied what he wanted to be true?

Christabel had praised his good sense. Frost pondered the fact as his valet shaved him for the day. Afterwards he grimaced at his reflection in the looking glass. Christmas was not a season for good sense, was it? he asked the fellow in the mirror. It was a time to celebrate wondrous reversals, such as the birth of a king in a rustic stable. It was a time for believing spring would return, in the very teeth of winter's dark, cold despair.

Frost took far more than usual care choosing his clothes for the day, including a waistcoat the colour of well-aged burgundy shot with gold threads. Once dressed, he headed for the breakfast room with a brisk stride, humming a Christmas carol.

Mrs Wilton and her son were already seated at the table, though they had not yet been served.

'A very good morning to you both!' On an impulse, Frost seized Christabel's hand and raised it to his lips. 'I hope you slept well. We have a busy day ahead.'

His unexpected gesture seemed to ruffle her composure, but in a pleasant way. Her dark eyes sparkled when she glanced up at him through her lashes and a mysterious little smile played on her lips.

'You must have enjoyed sweet dreams, Mr Frost. I have never seen you in such high spirits.'

A dish of buttered eggs was served, from which Frost took a liberal helping. 'I hope you approve.'

'Very much so. The other day when you said it was good to hear me laugh *again*, I was going to observe that it was good to hear you laugh *at all*.'

'Impudence!' Frost feigned an unconvincing frown and the menace of his growl was quite ruined by a chuckle.

But one person at the table was fooled. 'Please, Mr Frost, don't be angry with Mama! I'm sure she didn't mean to vex you.'

'Nor did she, sir!' Frost felt a trifle ashamed of himself to laugh at the poor little fellow's dismay, but he could not help it. Besides, it might help convince the child he was not truly angry. 'I was only teasing your mama back for teasing me. That sort of thing is permitted among old friends. And she was quite right—I do not laugh often enough. It is a fault you are helping me correct this very moment.'

As Christabel spooned some eggs on to her son's plate, her gaze caught and held Frost's. She mouthed the words, 'Thank you.'

Was she grateful to him for reassuring the boy, Frost wondered, or for calling her a friend? Whatever he had done to merit that luminous smile and glowing gaze, he must be sure to repeat it—soon and often.

'Will Miss Fanny be joining us?' asked Christabel.

Frost shook his head, his good cheer dampened a little. 'She takes breakfast in her rooms. Mornings are often difficult for her. Once we get busy decorating, no doubt she will be eager to join in the merry-making.'

Christabel seemed to sense his mood, and was quick to distract him with talk of their plans.

By the time Aunt Fanny joined them, they were tacking swags of holly and bay to the walls with bows of scarlet silk. After that they decked the great sideboard in the dining room with ivy and gold paper stars and fashioned a matching centrepiece for the table. At her insistence, they hung sprigs of mistletoe over several of the doorways.

Later, with the help of Cook, Frost compounded a wassail mixture of ale, roasted crab-apples and nutmeg, which Christabel sampled and pronounced altogether delicious. It was ready none to soon, either, for parties of men and boys began to arrive from the village. Before long, the great entry hall of Candlewood rang with rustic carols, laughter and applause. To Frost, it all sounded as sweet and joyful as any chorus of angels.

Christabel could not recall ever spending a more congenial Christmas Eve, not even during her affluent, carefree girlhood back in Somerset. As she watched her son cut a little caper to one of the rollicking Christmas tunes, then fetch wassail cups for the thirsty carollers, she reckoned she must have caught some of his infectious enjoyment of the holiday. Or perhaps the deprivations of recent years made her savour the comforts and pleasures of Christmas at Candlewood.

With all the company that afternoon, they had missed their tea altogether, but enjoyed an early dinner of Cook's succulent game pies, followed by poached pears in custard. Then they sat around a roaring fire in the drawing-room hearth in which Mr Frost helped Colly and Miss Fanny roast nuts. Meanwhile Christabel read to them from a book of poetry.

She had just concluded a passage from Spenser's *Faerie Queen* when Mr Frost announced, 'We have two sleepyheads here, who had better get off to bed soon if they hope to enjoy the festivities tomorrow.'

'Oh, please!' Miss Fanny caught his hand. 'Can we not stay up another quarter-hour on account of Christmas Eve?'

'Very well.' Frost fished out his pocket watch. '*If* you can both go the next two minutes without yawning, I will allow that you are not tired enough to go to bed yet.'

Though they made a determined effort, neither Miss Fanny nor Colly were able to go a single minute without yawning, much less two. Frost summoned Mrs Penny and Jane to take them off to bed.

After they had gone, Christabel closed her book and laid it on the small table beside her chair. 'It has been a most enjoyable day. Thank you.' She rose to follow her son.

'Must you go as well?' Frost called after her. 'I did not catch you yawning with the others.'

She turned and took a few tentative steps towards him. Her pulse quickened to the brisk, lively tempo of a wassailer's carol. 'That was a fine parenting trick, just now. I must remember it for future use with my son.'

Frost closed his pocket watch with a decisive click. 'It hardly ever fails. Nothing makes a person want to yawn so badly as trying to keep from doing it.'

'I expect that is true of a good many things.'

Such as yearning for her host in a way she had no business doing? Such as constantly finding something new to admire about him? Such as wondering again and again what her life might be like now if only she'd had the good sense to marry him when she had the chance? To linger here with him after the others had retired would only encourage her fruitless preoccupation.

But she owed him so much. If her company would help him while away a lonely hour or two, how could she be so ungrateful as to refuse? 'Do you wish me to stay?'

'I do. But not if you truly prefer to retire. I do not want to overtax your strength.'

'You seem to think me quite frail.' Christabel resumed her seat. 'I assure you I am perfectly recovered. Shall I read some more?'

'I fear it might strain your eyes.' Mr Frost settled back on a low stool by the fire.

He had earlier removed his coat. Now the white sleeves of his shirt billowed out from his richly coloured waistcoat and his cravat fell in loose folds from his neck. Christabel's fingers tingled to untie it, and to graze over the springy softness of his side whiskers.

'There you go again!' Her flustered feelings vented in a nervous bubble of laughter. 'I promise you, I am not apt to collapse at the slightest exertion.'

'Could we not just talk?' He gave a rueful shrug. 'Or would you find that too tiresome? Since you arrived at Candlewood we have not had many opportunities to catch up with one another.'

'We have not,' agreed Christabel, 'and I would find your

conversation anything but tiresome.' There was much she wanted to know about him. 'Tell me, has your aunt long been as she is now?'

'The condition of her mind seems to have settled somewhat since I brought her to Derbyshire. Before that—' a mild shudder went through Frost '—there were times I feared for my own sanity, especially before it became clear there *was* something wrong.'

And he'd had no one with whom to share that burden. No one to distract him from his worries. No one to reassure him he was doing the best he could in a most difficult situation. Now Christabel urged him to confide in her, though she knew it was too little, too late.

'We have neither of us had an easy time of it, have we?' said Frost at last. 'You have made a brave show for your son these past few days, but I imagine you must feel the loss of your husband more keenly than usual at this time of year.'

It was on the tip of her tongue to profess the conventional sentiments when something made her reply instead, 'I cannot deceive you, sir. My son is the greatest joy of my life, but he is one of the few my marriage afforded me.'

Her frankness clearly took Frost aback. 'Forgive me for asking. I did not mean…that is…I'm sorry.'

'I do not deserve your compassion.' Christabel stared down at her hands as they moved in restless agitation upon her lap. 'It was my own fault, I know. I should never have been so wilful and foolish as to elope with Monty before getting to know him better and learning his character.'

'Did he mistreat you?' Frost's tone was sharp and urgent as he rose abruptly from his seat by the fire.

'No, never!' Even to secure his sympathy, Christabel would not malign her son's father that way. 'He was not a bad man, but we were ill suited and our slender means did not help matters. I believe that was why he gambled—in a desperate effort to secure our fortune. But it only encumbered us with debts that I am still struggling to repay.'

'By going cold and hungry to honour the long-forgotten turn of a card? That is infamous! You must let me help you!'

Help her? She had taken far too much from him already. That debt of the heart would cripple her worse than the shillings her late husband had wagered at cards. 'I do not think Monty believed my father would disown me for wedding against his wishes. To the end, he was convinced Papa would eventually relent and help us.'

'I believe he would have if his final illness had not come upon him so suddenly.' Frost knelt by Christabel's chair and took her hands. 'And I feel certain he would have been as distressed as I am had he known of your situation. You must believe I never wished you anything but the most sincere happiness in life.'

'I do believe it.' She could not bring herself to meet his gaze. 'For that is the kind of good man you are. It is I who have never been able to forgive myself. For humiliating you, for encumbering Monty with a penniless bride, for never reconciling with my father…for dooming my son to a life with such limited prospects. You must admit, it is a great deal to answer for.'

Even with all the allowances he had so far made for her, surely he would have to agree. Any deprivations she had suffered were just deserts for her folly.

He raised one hand to tilt her chin gently with the knuckle of his forefinger. 'You take too much upon yourself. I doubt it was ever your intention to cause anyone harm. You made a mistake in judgement at an age that is prone to such errors. Forgive that impulsive girl who fancied herself in love. You have punished her far too long.'

It made such compassionate good sense, especially coming from him. Part of Christabel wanted very much to heed him. But it was difficult to look back on everything that had happened to her since she'd eloped with Major Wilton and not see the stern hand of divine punishment at work.

Her one comfort came from the certainty that Jonathan Frost had not loved her any more than she'd loved him at the time she jilted him. To have injured his heart as well as his pride would have been too great a regret to bear.

Chapter Nine

$\mathscr{O}\!\!\mathscr{D}\!\!\mathscr{D}\!\!\mathscr{D}\!\!\mathscr{D}\!\!\mathscr{D}$

Once upon a time, Frost had knelt beside Christabel and held her hand. Then he had stammered out what must have been the baldest, least romantic proposal in the history of matrimony. The wonder was not that she had run away to marry another man, but that she had accepted his offer and stuck with their engagement for as long as she had.

Was it love that had prompted her to elope with Major Wilton? Frost wondered. Or had her growing aversion to the prospect of marrying him pushed her into an unwise decision made in haste? If that had been the case, then he was the one with much to answer for.

But he must heed his own advice to her and not torment himself with blame. He had never meant to injure her, after all. If she had approached him then, seeking an end to their engagement, he would have released her from it. Not happily, perhaps, but without reproach or bitterness.

Since they were alone and he was already on his knees, Frost flirted with the notion of proposing to Christabel again.

But the capricious magic of Christmas had not overturned his natural restraint to that great a degree.

They had only been reacquainted for a few days—not nearly long enough to show her the small but significant changes he had undergone in the past several years that might recommend him to her. Having endured the pain of one unhappy marriage, Christabel might be justly wary of contracting another. Then there was the whole matter of his aunt. Christabel must know her condition could not improve and her decline would surely place a greater strain upon his household. Could any financial advantages of their union compensate for that?

If he asked her now and she refused, as he was convinced she must, he could not hope for a third chance to win her. This second one was a rare and precious gift enough. He must not squander it with undue haste.

Before the urge could overwhelm him, he released her hands and scrambled to his feet. 'You must forgive me. I have kept you from your…bed for far too long.'

This time Christabel did not protest the strength of her constitution as she rose from the chair. 'I should not have burdened you with my troubles.'

Nothing she shared with him could possibly be a burden. Frost yearned to tell her so. But would such a declaration betray his feelings and intentions towards her—both of which she might not yet welcome?

As he stood there mute and awkward, struggling to decide what he should say, Christabel Wilton suddenly seized his hand and lifted it to her lips. 'I fear your broad shoulders invite confidences whether you wish them or not.'

Before he could stammer a coherent reply, she released his fingers and hurried away, leaving him gaping after her. In a daze, he raised his hand to his cheek as if he might effect a transfer of Christabel's kiss. It was, without doubt, the most treasured Christmas gift he had ever received.

Neither time nor misfortune had altogether tempered her impetuous spirit. A wave of embarrassment overwhelmed Christabel when she remembered the hasty but ardent kiss she had pressed to Frost's fingers, and the look of shock it had provoked from him. At least she'd cultivated enough self-control to kiss his hand, rather than his lips as she'd so badly wanted to.

When he had knelt beside her, fixed her with his earnest gaze and entreated her to forgive herself, she'd longed to throw her arms around his neck and kiss him breathless!

At breakfast the next morning she was too embarrassed by the whole incident to meet his gaze or mutter more than a word or two of conversation. Fortunately, Colly had enough to say for both of them and Mr Frost, with his accustomed courtesy, gave no sign that anything untoward had taken place.

Though Christabel knew she should appreciate his forbearance, she feared such cordial indifference could only mean he felt no more for her than he ever had. She must not be so foolish as to mistake his generosity for any fonder attachment. She no longer had any advantages to attract a man in his position, least of all one she had used so ill when she'd had the opportunity of securing him.

After breakfast the three of them drove to church in Mr

Frost's carriage. Throughout the Nativity service, Frost's words from the previous night kept repeating themselves in Christabel's thoughts. *Forgive that impulsive girl who fancied herself in love. You have punished her far too long.* The familiar prayers, lessons and Christmas hymns all seemed to echo his appeal with their assurance of divine mercy.

Was it possible the hardships of recent years had not been intended as punishment, but rather a necessary lesson to cultivate her better virtues and help her appreciate the simpler gifts of life?

Out in the churchyard after the service, Christabel sensed many curious gazes upon her. When the colonel of the local regiment stopped Mr Frost for a word, she was grateful to spy the vicar's sister approaching her, wreathed in smiles.

'What a pleasant surprise to see you here this morning, Mrs Wilton, with your charming little boy! Did Mr Frost fetch you all the way from Bishopscote?'

'Merry Christmas, Miss Jessup. As it happens, Colly and I are spending the holidays at Candlewood as guests of Mr Frost and his aunt.'

'How lovely, I declare!' cried Miss Jessup. 'And to think neither of you might ever have had any idea of the other residing so nearby if it had not been for me. Why, I feel quite an instrument of good fortune!'

'So you were.' Christabel did not grudge the lady a particle of her obvious satisfaction. 'I thank you with all my heart for your intervention. I do not deserve such kind friends as you and Mr Frost have proven yourselves, but I am truly grateful for you both.'

For too long she had kept to herself, refusing help of which she felt undeserving, yet conversely was too proud to accept. Seeing Miss Jessup's keen pleasure at having been of service, Christabel vowed that from now on she would not deny people the satisfaction of helping her if they wished.

On the drive back to Candlewood, Mr Frost announced, 'Colonel MacLean tells me he means to host a ball at the local assembly on New Year's Eve. He says his people in Scotland make quite a celebration of the New Year. I never was much of a dancer...and have not kept up whatever small skill I might once have had. But I wondered...if you might do me the honour...'

Christabel hated to see him so flustered on her account. 'Why, Mr Frost, are you asking if you may escort me to Colonel MacLean's ball?'

'Would you allow me the honour?' He looked strangely anxious as to her reply.

'You are generous to call it such, considering the disparity in our positions, but *I* would be honoured and pleased to accompany you if you wish.' Perhaps her trunk at home might still hold an old ballgown, gloves and slippers that could be pressed into service for the occasion.

'Splendid.' Mr Frost's solemn tone and countenance belied the fervour of that word.

'Can Miss Fanny and I go too?' asked Colly.

The boy's question coaxed the fleeting hint of a smile from Mr Frost, but he shook his head with a convincing pretence of regret. 'I fear Colonel MacLean's ball will carry on long past your bedtime and hers. However, I promise to contrive some sort of New Year's treat for you both instead. What do you say to that?'

Colly bounced on the seat and cheered.

Christabel put her arms around her son to quiet him. 'Really, Mr Frost, I fear you will spoil him.'

'This young gentleman is too well reared to spoil easily.' Frost winked at Colly. 'And a little spoiling on holidays is not such a bad thing in my opinion.'

'You will make some lucky child a wonderful father, one day.' The words were out of Christabel's mouth before she could stop herself.

Fortunately Mr Frost seemed more amused than offended at her presumption. 'You flatter me. There was a time when I might have disagreed with you, but one small blessing of my recent situation has been discovering a greater capacity for affection than I ever thought to possess.'

Lucky the woman to inspire and receive such bounty! Christabel managed to curb her tongue, though she feared the longing behind that thought must blaze in her eyes.

Did Christabel Wilton doubt him capable of sincere affection? Was that why she did not respond to his remark? Though habit disposed Frost to think so, the look in her eyes persuaded him otherwise. They did not betray the slightest glint of disapproval, but rather seemed to glow with a brooding warmth—as, indeed, did her whole radiant face.

Frost could not draw the slightest offence from that look. Quite the contrary, in fact. And knowing how she cherished her little son, her expressed faith in Frost's potential as a father could not be regarded as anything but the highest praise.

His aunt was waiting for them when they returned from church, excited to find the house decorated for Christmas but with no memory of having had a hand in it. She was overjoyed with his gift of a small blue parakeet in a brass cage and even more with the hobbyhorse Christabel had created for her.

'When did you get the time to make that?' asked Frost when Colly and Aunt Fanny had gone off riding their fine mounts. 'And where on earth did you find the white velvet for the head?'

'Your servants were most helpful in foraging materials for me. It was not difficult to keep my work on Miss Fanny's gift a secret in this enormous house with everyone waiting on me hand and foot. Making Colly's in our little cottage at the end of a busy day was a far greater challenge, I assure you.'

Later they all bundled up for a drive in the sleigh to pay calls on several poor families in the village with gifts of warm winter garments and game birds from the estate. The winter sun was dipping low in the sky when they returned to Candlewood for an early dinner.

A course of oysters and eels was followed by a plump and succulent roast goose. After they had all eaten rather more than their fill, the Christmas pudding was paraded in upon a silver platter alight with a blue brandy flame and crowned with a festive sprig of holly.

Frost tucked into the feast with a fine appetite. Some starved part of his heart seemed to feed on Colly's animated prattle, Aunt Fanny's bubbly laughter and Christabel's luminous smiles. By the end of the meal, he felt as well stuffed with good cheer as their goose with its sage and onions—as aglow with tipsy happiness as the pudding in its sheath of flaming brandy.

If only he could persuade Christabel to make her home at Candlewood, Frost reckoned he would taste the joy of Christmas every day of the year.

Chapter Ten

❧❧❧

The next week passed in a sweet whirl of enjoyment for Christabel. Like the Twelve Days of Christmas game, each new day brought some precious gift to warm and nourish her heart.

On St Stephen's Day, they fended for themselves while the servants dispersed to enjoy a holiday with their families. The next day a party of mummers came and put on a most comical show for the whole household.

The day after that, Mr Frost produced four pairs of ice skates and pronounced a small pond on the estate sufficiently frozen that they might take a few turns upon it. Together they engaged the better part of an afternoon on the ice with many tumbles and much laughter. More than the cold reddened Christabel's cheeks when Mr Frost slipped his arm around her waist and took her hand to support her while she acquired the proper balance.

On Sunday, Christabel and Mr Frost attended the Evensong service at the village church. In her heart, Christabel gave thanks for every small joy of the past week. On the drive home, she savoured the quiet intimacy of being alone with Frost in the carriage. It required every hard-earned morsel of self-control she could muster to keep from flinging herself on to the seat beside him and slipping her arms around his neck.

A cold wind blew on Monday keeping the party at Candlewood indoors by the fire. Even there, Christabel found the hours flew by, amusing Colly and Miss Fanny with simple card games and sketching caricatures of them. More than once she glanced up to find Frost's gaze resting upon them all, grave but unmistakably fond. In those moments she tasted the sweet, mellow wine of domestic happiness that had eluded her in her marriage.

Early in the afternoon on the last day of the year, Miss Fanny marched into the drawing room, bearing a parcel. Her waiting woman followed, toting an even larger one.

'These are from me,' she announced, her pale blue eyes twinkling like icicles melting in the bright winter sunshine. 'Christmas presents!'

She handed her parcel to Colly and nodded to Mrs Penny to give hers to Christabel.

'More presents?' Christabel caught a glimpse of Mr Frost lurking just beyond the doorway. 'Really, you should not. You have given us so much already.'

'Have I?' A look of confusion clouded Miss Fanny's eager gaze for a moment, but swiftly cleared. 'Oh, that's all right. You can never have too many Christmas presents. Come on—open them!'

She hardly needed to urge Colly, who was already tearing the paper off of his. When he saw what was inside, he let out a gasp, then a cheer. 'Look, Mama! Toy soldiers…and a spinning top…and a spy glass! Thank you, thank you, Miss Fanny!'

It was evident Miss Fanny had not known what the parcels contained, for she gave a squeal of delight and sank on to the carpet beside Colly to examine his new playthings.

Christabel settled on to the chaise-longue and unwrapped her parcel with hesitant care. She gave a faint gasp and blinked back tears as she lifted the most exquisite ballgown out of a swathe of tissue paper. A warm salmon colour with sprigs of gold, it had a diaphanous little train.

Miss Fanny turned the spy glass upon Christabel's gown. 'Oh, that is a pretty colour. It will suit you.'

Suit her? Christabel wanted to chuckle and sob at the same time. Why, this elegant garment would suit a duchess! She lifted the gauzy fabric to her cheek. Once upon a time, she'd owned pretty gowns by the dozen and scarcely noticed them except to find fault—this one was too tight in the bust, the colour of that one made her complexion look sallow. Now if she never owned another ball gown, she would treasure this one. Not only on account of its beauty and elegance, but because of who had given it to her.

She glanced towards the doorway just as Mr Frost stepped into the drawing room. 'You should not—'

He raised his forefinger to his lips. 'None of that, now. What kind of gentleman drags a lady off to a ball when she has nothing suitable to wear? If you dig a little deeper in the parcel, I believe you will find gloves and slippers and such to complete the costume.'

Christabel investigated and found a fine pair of evening gloves, a dainty pair of kid slippers and a lace bandeau for her hair that matched the colour of the gown to perfection. There was even a pair of the sheerest silk stockings Christabel had ever seen, much less owned.

That evening, when she slipped them on and felt the gossamer silk whisper over her legs, she could not help fancying Mr Frost's soft side whiskers skimming over the sensitive flesh of her thighs, followed by his lips. The scandalous notion sent a hot, sweet tingle of desire coursing through her, such as she had not felt in the longest time.

Monty had been a skilful lover when he'd chosen to. It was one of the few things Christabel truly missed about him, though it made her feel heartless and wicked to admit it, even in the privacy of her own thoughts. Now, as she dressed for Colonel MacLean's ball, she found herself unbearably curious as to what sort of lover Jonathan Frost might be.

He had strong, deft hands. That was very much in his favour. Over and over he had proven himself generous and unselfish—both excellent qualities in a lover. Christabel had once doubted the depth of his passion. Now she began to wonder if it ran very deep indeed, always under the strictest control. The thought of that passion provoked to break its bounds roused her as nothing had in a very long while.

When she had finished dressing, Christabel glanced at herself in the looking glass to discover her wanton fancies had acted on her face like the finest cosmetics. Her cheeks sported a blush no paint could match. Her eyes sparkled. Her lips looked full, ripe and eager to be kissed. She barely recognised herself from the peaked creature who had come to Candlewood.

Could it be she had something to offer Mr. Frost, after all? Something his lonely situation might have made him crave as hers had?

When Frost spied Christabel descending the staircase, a potent reminder of lush, midsummer loveliness in the dead of winter, his mouth watered with such sudden intensity that he was obliged to swallow several times in rapid succession. That proved difficult, since his cravat had somehow tightened around his throat. He prayed the carriage would be cold enough to quell the fever of desire that had taken possession of him.

He scowled in an effort to mask his feelings. Yet some renegade part of him wished the lady might guess…if she was the least inclined to condone them.

Christabel caught her lower lip between her teeth, as Frost longed to do. 'You look very severe, sir. Is there some difficulty? Does my costume not meet with your approval?'

'No…I mean…yes. That is…I approve most heartily. You look—' he plundered his vocabulary for a word half-fine enough to describe her '—well. Very well, indeed!'

'Why, thank you.' She sank into a curtsy, lofting Frost a grateful smile as if she thought his awkward stammering the prettiest compliment she had ever received. 'I feel well. Better than I have in a very long time. This holiday at Candlewood has done me a power of good.'

At that moment the butler appeared with their cloaks, giving Frost an opportunity to compose himself. 'I hope you will not mind if I exercise my advantage as your host to request at least the first two dances this evening. Once we arrive at the Assembly Hall, I fear that you will receive so many invitations that I may have few opportunities of sharing the floor with you.'

Christabel lifted the hood of her cloak to cover her hair. 'I would promise you all my dances, if you but ask me.'

Her gentle murmur spurred Frost's heartbeat to such speed and force that he wondered she could not hear it. What else might she promise him if he dared to ask?

'I could not be so selfish as to deny all the other gentlemen the pleasure of taking a turn with you. Nor would I presume to restrict your choice.' He had done that once before, resulting in great harm to both of them.

Christabel took his arm. 'At least promise you will not abandon me altogether.'

Frost chuckled at the absurdity of her suggestion. 'I can safely assure you of that, my dear.'

Perhaps their dancing the first two sets together convinced the other gentleman of Mrs Wilton's preference, for she was not deluged with eager partners as Frost had feared. Loathe to forfeit any opportunity, he was quick to step in with an invitation when no other was forthcoming. As a consequence, he passed more than half the evening most happily in her company, dancing, conversing and drinking Colonel MacLean's excellent punch.

Indeed, Frost found everything about the occasion excellent—the music, the decorations, the refreshments, the company. Especially the company. With each passing hour he became more relaxed and convivial.

At the stroke of midnight, Colonel MacLean called for everyone's attention. 'Ladies and gentlemen, as is the tradition in my country at this time of year, I propose a toast to *auld lang syne,* bygone days. Will ye join me in raising yer glasses?'

For some time, Frost had not allowed himself to think of *auld lang syne,* for such memories had brought too many bitter regrets. Now, he glimpsed his past in a whole different light. Perhaps it had taught him valuable lessons that allowed him to treasure the present and make the most of the future.

'To *auld lang syne.*' He touched glasses with Christabel, then drained his.

'To old times,' she murmured, glancing over the rim of her cup at him with a look that made Frost long to take her in his arms. 'And to old friends who grow dearer with longer acquaintance.'

Not long afterwards they bid their host farewell and drove back to Candlewood, chatting like the closest of old friends about everyone and everything at the party. Frost's butler was waiting to usher them in and take their cloaks.

'Will you be wanting anything else tonight, sir?' he asked.

'Heavens, no.' Frost waved him away. 'Off to bed with you.'

He turned to Christabel. 'Shall we warm our hands at the drawing-room hearth before we retire?'

'A capital idea.' Christabel peeled off her long gloves as she strolled into the drawing room with a graceful dance-like gait. 'Anything to prolong this enchanted night. It feels like something from out of a fairy story.'

'But midnight has come and gone.' Frost strode to the

hearth and began to chafe his hands before the fire. 'Yet you still look every inch the princess.'

'Thanks to you.' She slanted a sidelong glance at him as she warmed her hands.

That look and the residue of Colonel MacLean's punch gave Frost the provocation and the nerve to do what he did next. Turning towards Christabel, he took her hands in his, lifted them to his lips and exhaled a warm breath upon them. 'I beg to disagree, my dear. It is more than the gown makes you look so elegant…and beautiful.'

Christabel's eyes widened as she stared into his. Was it only surprise at hearing him say such things? Or dismay?

She did not try to pull her hands from his. Surely that must be a good sign.

'You have furnished me with far more than my gown, sir. All this talk of accepting gifts graciously and pretending they came from your aunt does not alter the fact that I owe you more than I can ever repay. All the same, I—'

'Please!' Frost clutched her hands tighter and leaned forward to rest his brow against hers. 'Do not speak of such things now, I beg you.'

Could Christabel not see that what she and her son had given him was infinitely more precious than any trifling material gifts that were in his power to bestow?

'What would you have me say?' she whispered. More softly still she added, 'What would you have me do?'

This was his chance to secure her. He would get no better. But was he equal to the challenge he had once failed so miserably?

Perhaps the late hour and Colonel MacLean's fine punch

had lulled his doubts to sleep. Or perhaps the pleasures of the evening and the pitch of his desire made him bold.

Slowly he drew her away from the hearth until they stood in the drawing-room doorway. He pointed up at the sprig of mistletoe that had been hung there on Christmas Eve at his aunt's insistence.

'Not as some obligation you feel you owe me,' he explained. 'But because…it is Christmas.' He stared down into her eyes and read an invitation even he could not mistake. 'And because you want to be kissed.'

'I do not want to be kissed by just anyone. Not for all the mistletoe in Derbyshire.' Her words smote Frost with a fierce stab of disappointment that healed like magic when she continued, 'But I do want to be kissed by you, Mr Frost. Very, very, mu—'

Frost did not wait to hear the rest. Before Christabel came to her senses and changed her mind, he tilted his head and leaned towards her, claiming a kiss so deep and sweet it was worth every lonely night he had waited for it.

Chapter Eleven

Because she wanted to be kissed?

The thought almost made Christabel laugh. Could Jonathan Frost not tell she wanted far more from him than that? Did he not want more from her?

The hesitant, yearning swipe of his lips over hers seared away her doubts. She sensed a powerful passion under the most tenuous curb. And she wanted nothing more than to set it free.

Tugging her hand from the clasp of his, she reached up to cradle his face. Her lips melted beneath his, and with them her heart. She would give him everything she had once denied him. If only he would take it.

In response to her eagerness, his kiss grew bolder, hungrier. He gathered her in his arms, one hand caressing her sensitive nape, gently holding her captive to the tender ravishment of his lips. For a moment, his other arm circled her waist, but as she arched her body against his in a wanton invitation, he slid his hand down to cup her bottom.

In the dark birthing hours of that new year, time slowed to a lazy, sensuous trickle. After a succession of blissful kisses, Frost's lips strayed from Christabel's to range over her chin, her cheeks, the tip of her nose, her brow…

When she gave a deep, throaty chuckle and arched her neck, he was quick to recognise and accept her invitation. With a soft, hoarse growl of desire, he drizzled kisses up and down the responsive flesh from her ear to her shoulder, setting Christabel breathless and atremble.

Mr Frost was not so far gone in passion as to neglect her well-being.

'You are cold.' He drew back with an obvious effort to master himself. 'I should not—'

'Indeed you should.' Christabel clung to him, nuzzling the warm spot between his ear and the top of his cravat. 'I am no more cold than you are.' She tangled her fingers in his hair. 'Though we might exercise a little discretion to continue somewhere more…private. If you wish to continue, that is?'

His ragged breath rasped softly in her ear. 'I cannot recall when I have wished for anything more.'

'Come, then!' She grasped him by the hand and fairly flew up the stairs.

Once in the dimly lit gallery, Frost ushered her to his bed-chamber with barely contained eagerness. No sooner had they slipped inside and closed the door behind them than he pressed her back against it and kissed her with a thrilling urgency that made her knees melt.

Then, his need slightly appeased, he hoisted her in his arms and strode to the bed, resting her upon it like some priceless treasure nestled in its most perfect setting.

'How often I would have dreamed of this,' he whispered as he struggled out of his coat and boots, hurling them to the floor, 'if only I had not feared tormenting myself.'

'My poor, dear Mr Frost.' Christabel rained kisses on his face as she loosened his cravat. 'How lonely you must have been!'

'But no longer.' He pulled the pins from her hair, releasing a cascade of curls over her shoulders. 'If this is a drunken dream, do not wake me, I pray you!'

'You have my word,' Christabel whispered as she rubbed her cheek against his and fumbled open the buttons of his waistcoat. 'As long as you promise to return the favour.'

He eased one sleeve of her gown over her shoulder, baring it for his lips. 'You may depend upon it.'

She could depend upon *him*. Even in her foolish youth Christabel had sensed it. Her great error had been to suppose a dependable, sensible man must lack passion. Could she have been more wrong?

Frost seemed bent on convincing her of quite the opposite as he dispatched her clothes with impatient haste, exploring with his hands and lips every new part of her he laid bare. When his hand grazed her thigh as he rolled down her stocking, Christabel writhed beneath his touch and gave a soft whimper of need. And when he fondled and kissed her breasts with unbridled fervour, she had never ached so with desire.

'Please!' she gasped at last, reaching for the buttons of his breeches.

When he was quite as naked as she, Christabel made bold to stroke and caress him in the way she knew would bring him pleasure. Frost threw back his head and gave a deep rolling purr, like distant thunder warning of a tempest about to break.

Christabel parted her legs and guided him into her with a shudder of delight. He filled her to perfection—not just her body, but her heart and even her soul. His quiet strength gave her the security to experience the carefree exuberance of her girlhood once again. His generosity and forbearance helped free her from the burden of guilt she had carried for too long.

Now he hovered over her, dimly backlit by the rosy glow of the banked fire. His mouth closed upon hers with a hot, deep kiss that tasted of the tart, intoxicating sweetness of the New Year's Eve punch. He moved within her in a quickening rhythm, each delicious thrust swelling the passion she could scarcely contain. Then a powerful surge of pleasure coursed through her, as a series of fierce, fevered shudders racked her lover. Together they subsided, utterly drained, yet utterly sated.

Afterwards, he held her, anointing her face with soft, tender kisses and whispering her name.

Christabel smiled to herself in the darkness. She had discovered a gift that was truly as satisfying to give as it was to receive. Already she looked forward to sharing it with her beloved again.

Frost woke with a bilious jolt that felt quite the opposite of the wild thrill he recalled with tormenting clarity from earlier on. Christabel lay in his arms, warm and limp, the fragrant tangle of her dark curls splayed over his bare chest in the pale, cool light of the winter morning. His nostrils flared to inhale the subtle musk of lovemaking that hung about them.

His body roused once again to the aching pitch of several hours earlier. It seemed greedy to want more so soon again after his craving had been so delightfully gratified. His head ached and his belly churned in an ominous fashion, his just punishment for overindulging in Colonel MacLean's potent punch. But they were nothing to the pangs of his conscience.

How could he have taken advantage of Christabel's tipsy lapse in propriety and her oft-expressed sense of obligation to lure her into his bed? There was only one honourable course open to him now. Though he would be only too happy to take it, he feared Christabel might not feel the same.

Frost took hope from the certainty that she had welcomed his physical overtures and that he had been able to bring her pleasure. Respect and fondness, spiced with a lusty attraction, were surely a fertile foundation from which love might grow. Then why did he dread the instant Christabel would open her eyes and find herself naked in his arms?

Every moment he had to wait for it, doubt gnawed at him. By the time Christabel's eyelids fluttered, he was more nauseous from apprehension than from the after-effects of the punch. For an instant she fixed him with a fuddled gaze, then her eyes widened and her mouth fell slack.

'Oh, mercy, what have I done?' She squirmed away from Frost, pulling the bedclothes up to her chin. The revulsion in her eyes was even worse than he had feared.

'Please, Mrs Wilton…Christabel!' Frost wrenched up one of the blankets to hide the straining evidence of his unquenched lust. 'I am sorry—more than you will ever know! You must believe I did not wish to compromise your virtue in such a contemptible manner. You have my word I will be honoured to make you my wife and do everything in my power to make amends for my actions.'

'W-wife?' Christabel clapped her hand over her mouth as if to hold her gorge. 'No. You must not think of it, I beg you!'

Diving out from beneath the covers, she seized her ballgown and wriggled into it before Frost could recover his wits enough to prevent her. With the garment gaping open in the back, she fled the room, leaving her stockings, slippers and undergarments behind.

Frost sat there in his bed with the morning chill creeping over him, a weight pressing down upon his heart and a stifled sob lodged in his throat. The anguish he'd felt when Christabel had jilted him was nothing compared to this.

Why had he not heeded his own good sense and kept a safe distance from the woman? Why had he allowed himself to believe time could change her feelings towards him? It had not changed his, except perhaps to intensify them. Clearly the years had done the same to Christabel's. Though he wished he could burrow back under the covers and not emerge until this cursed year was over, Frost forced himself to rise and dress.

The seductive softness of Christabel's stocking whispered over his foot as he strode towards his dressing room. Frost glanced down to see her garments strewn across the floor where he had tossed them. He could not leave them there for the servants to find. There would likely be gossip enough among them without such certain proof of his scandalous behaviour.

He gathered up the lot, pausing only to drag one of the stockings in a silken caress over the stubble of his unshaven cheek. Then his fist clenched around it and gave a fierce shake. 'No!' The words exploded out of him. 'This will *not* do!'

Thrusting Christabel's slippers and undergarments into his wardrobe, Frost pulled out whatever pieces of his own clothing that came to hand and hauled them on in an urgent rush. Once dressed in a curious assortment of attire, he stalked down the gallery and pounded on the door of Christabel's chamber.

Receiving no answer, he burst in, surprised not to find the door bolted against him. When he crossed the threshold, a bright puddle of colour drew his gaze to the floor beside the bed. There lay Christabel's discarded ballgown, but there was no sign of the lady herself. Mounting a search of the house, he soon found her getting her son ready to leave Candlewood.

When he opened his mouth to speak, she shook her head, casting a pointed gaze towards the boy. 'Not here, please.'

'Very well.' Frost schooled his voice to a temperate tone and tried to reassure Colly with a smile. 'I must and will speak my mind, however. Where will you hear me out?'

Christabel pondered the question for a moment, during which Frost noted her hastily piled hair. His fingers itched to pull the pins from it again and plunge his hand through the unruly cascade of curls. The first time she had fled from the prospect of marriage to him, he had glimpsed only dimly what he would be missing. This time he *knew* with every fibre of his flesh and heart.

She glanced up at him then, her dark eyes fairly aching with regret. 'I believe the weather has turned milder. Perhaps we might take a stroll outside…a short stroll.'

'Goody!' cried the boy. 'Can I come, too? And Miss Fanny? We can make snowballs!'

'Not today, dearest.' Christabel caught her son in a swift, convulsive embrace. 'Mr Frost and I have some things to talk about. Why don't you take…Mistletoe for a ride?'

Frost heard the catch in her voice when she spoke the word *mistletoe*. Was she recalling the sprig of innocent-looking white berries that had kindled their far-from-innocent tryst last night?

They walked down to the entry hall, then donned their wraps and hats in awkward silence. Outside the icicles hanging from the eaves seemed to weep under a melancholy grey sky.

By the time they were out of earshot of the house and the stables, Frost could not contain himself a moment longer. 'Mrs Wilton, I cannot tell you how sorry I am for what happened last night, but I beg you—do not make too hasty a decision in the heat of the moment that you may repent later. Marry me and I will furnish you with every comfort that is within my power.'

'What? And spend a lifetime imposing upon your generosity for the sake of one foolish mistake?' Christabel kept her eyes trained ahead as if she could not bear even to glance his way. 'You encouraged me not to punish myself for the errors of the past and I have come to believe you are right. I will not punish us both for one…lapse in judgement.'

'Would it be such a dreadful punishment?' demanded Frost. 'I have enjoyed the time you've spent at Candlewood and I believe you have, too.'

'We have not been married these past three weeks, Mr Frost,' she reminded him. 'Believe me, I know whereof I speak. I have endured one marriage bereft of love and I would not suffer another. Not for all the comforts your fortune could bestow and not to do a lifetime of penance for a single indiscretion. I thank you with all my heart for your generosity, but I hope you will understand why I cannot stay. Would you do me one final kindness by letting Samuel take us home in your carriage?'

Frost replied with a grim nod. What Christabel had said made a harsh kind of sense. She seemed certain she could not love him. Perhaps he had been a fool for hoping love could be learned or earned. He only wished he had not ruined his chance of finding out.

Even the fleeting bliss he had found in her arms last night could not compensate for that.

Chapter Twelve

Would Mr Frost be scandalised to know she did not regret seducing him? Christabel risked a fleeting, stolen glance at his ruggedly handsome profile as they walked back to the house in silence. What she rued was *his* regret and any mistaken belief he might harbour that she had taken advantage of his loneliness to entrap him into marriage.

She had glimpsed the suspicion of it on his face the moment she'd woken. The first words out of his mouth had confirmed it. She was resolved to prove him wrong in that at least. Perhaps the harsh lessons of experience had not cured her of her impulsiveness in matters of the heart, but she would take responsibility for her actions and not make Jonathan Frost suffer the consequences again.

She would not saddle him with a wife for whom he felt nothing more than pity and physical desire. A man capable of such passion and compassion was surely capable of love. She must leave him free to seek and find it. For her part, this sojourn at Candlewood had taught her the tantalising heartache of spending day after day near something she yearned for but could never have.

They found Colly and Miss Fanny engaged in a wild ride through the house.

'We are on a hunt!' cried her son. 'Jane is the fox and we are hot on her trail.'

'Enough blood sports for you, young man.' Christabel beckoned to him. 'We must go.'

Miss Fanny wheeled her mount around. 'Please stay! We're having such a fine time.'

Much as she wished she could oblige them both and blamed herself for bringing their merry holiday to a premature end, Christabel shook her head. 'We really must leave.'

Gathering Frost's aunt in a gentle embrace, she whispered a comforting falsehood in her ear. 'We will be back tomorrow. I promise.'

Tomorrow Miss Fanny would not remember they had ever been at Candlewood. For a passing instant Christabel almost envied her crippled memory. No memories meant no regrets— a fair exchange, was it not? But recalling the dark rapture of her midnight tryst with Frost, when he had made her feel so cherished, she knew those memories were worth the price.

She and Colly left Candlewood with far more than they had brought. As Frost's carriage pulled away from the house, Colly pressed his small nose to the window, creating a tiny patch of fog on the cold glass. With great energy he waved goodbye to Mr Frost and Miss Fanny.

Once they were out of sight, he settled back on to his seat with a sigh. 'I wish we could have stayed longer. It was such a jolly Christmas.'

Christabel only nodded, not trusting herself to speak. Bowing her head, she raised a hand to her brow to shield her misted eyes.

'Are you feeling ill again?' asked Colly. 'Perhaps we should go back to Candlewood for a few more days until you are better.'

'Your concern for my health is touching.' Christabel let out a chuckle mingled with a sob. 'I promise you, I am quite well enough to go home. Nothing could induce me to inflict myself upon poor Mr Frost again.'

Jonathan Frost had no heart for any New Year's festivities. But for Aunt Fanny's sake, he tried to counterfeit a measure of enthusiasm. Once she had gone to bed, he retired to his study with a well-aged bottle of French brandy for the single night's indulgence of self-pity he would permit himself.

He was jolted from a stuporous doze the next morning by his aunt's waiting woman, Mrs Penny. 'I'm sorry to disturb ye sir, but can ye come? Miss Fanny's all agitated. I've tried everything I can think of to calm her, but it's no good.'

Frost lurched to his feet, one hand pressed to his forehead. It felt as if his brains were in imminent danger of spilling out his ears. 'I'll come. I'll come. Only keep your voice down, I beg you.'

He hoped that, in his present condition, he could placate his aunt. Over the last year or two he had noticed she tended to regress more rapidly in the wake of a major upset.

He found her clinging to her hobbyhorse as she paced her room. Since moving back to Candlewood, he had slowly restored the chamber to a reasonable semblance of what it had looked like during her childhood.

'What's all this, then?' He pulled her into a secure embrace. 'I hear you're upset about something.'

'Something's wrong, Papa.' She clung to him like the frightened child she'd become. 'Someone's missing, but I can't think who!'

He passed his hand over her hair in a reassuring caress. 'Why, Susan, of course.' Every morning she woke looking for her long-dead nursemaid. 'Did no one tell you she's been called away because her mother is ill? She'll be back tomorrow. I promise.'

'Back tomorrow?' Aunt Fanny repeated the words in a flat, dazed voice. 'Promise. No, it isn't Susan. It's that other lady and the little boy. The ones who gave me my horse.'

'M-Mrs Wilton, you mean?' It was many months since Aunt Fanny had remembered new acquaintances from one day to the next. Why must it be the person Frost most longed to forget? 'She and Colly had to go back to their own house. They were only visiting with us for Christmas.'

'Oh. So you aren't going to marry her?'

'Marry? No!' The very thought made Frost's temples throb. 'Whatever put such a notion in your head?'

'Well, I know you must be lonesome all by yourself. I am sometimes, too. Maria Dixon says stepmothers are vile, but everybody knows Maria's a great pudding head. I shouldn't mind having a stepmother at all. Especially one who's clever at making me pretty things and good at making you laugh.'

Frost glanced at Mrs Penny and nodded towards the door, through which she swiftly retired. Then he drew his aunt over to the window seat that looked out on to the snow-covered gardens.

Reason told him he should hold his tongue. She would not likely understand what he was talking about and it might upset her more. But she seemed calmer now that she had re-membered Christabel and Colly. And he felt a desperate need to confide in someone. Especially someone who might not recall a word he had said by this time tomorrow.

'The fact is, my dear, I did ask Mrs Wilton to marry me. She refused. Told me she could not abide another loveless marriage.'

'Why?' Aunt Fanny's brow puckered and a tiny frown of concentration pursed her lips. 'Did you not tell her you love her? You do, don't you?'

'Of course…that is, of course I love her.' A brief flare of impatience over his aunt's confusion subsided into ashes of doubt. 'Mrs Wilton meant she could not wed because she does not love me.' She had, hadn't she?

'Is that what she said?'

'Yes!' Frost did not mean to snap, but it was clear he had made a mistake, trying to discuss a subject so far beyond his aunt's present comprehension. 'Though…'

He tried to remember his conversation with Christabel. Exactly what he had said and she had replied, not what he'd assumed they were saying. Because it was possible—not likely, but possible—that his assumptions had been wrong. What if she had meant…? And what if she had taken him to mean…?

Frost began to chuckle, softly at first, then more and more frenzied until it brought tears to his eyes.

'What is so funny?' demanded his aunt.

'Perhaps nothing,' Frost sputtered between volleys of laughter. 'Or perhaps everything. Listen, it is very important I go to London for a few days. Will you be all right until I get back? I promise I'll bring you a very nice present.'

She brightened. 'What kind of present?'

'A surprise.'

'Oh, good. I like surprises.'

'So do I!' Frost bounded up from the window seat, lifted his aunt off the floor and twirled her round and round until she squealed with giddy laughter. 'And you have given me a lovely surprise just now.'

'Me?'

Frost nodded and pressed a kiss on the top of her head. 'One quite as nice as any gift.'

At least he hoped it would be…for all of them.

'Mama,' called Colly Wilton on the afternoon of Twelfth Night, 'there's someone at the door!'

Christabel glanced up from sewing a button eye on to a handsome brown hobbyhorse. 'Will you let them in, please, dearest? I expect it's that nice man from the shop in Manchester.'

When Samuel had delivered her and Colly home a few days ago, he had insisted he could not leave until he'd given Christabel a purse of money from his master. At first she had been reluctant to take the gift. It felt too much like pay for her services in the bedchamber to suit her conscience. But seeing she might have Samuel as a permanent house guest if she refused, she had made up her mind to accept this final token of Mr Frost's generosity with good grace.

Besides, an idea had been brewing in the back of her mind for a way she might provide for her son. All she needed was a small amount of capital to get started. A trip to Manchester had yielded both the necessary supplies and orders from two shops for her hobbyhorses. It would take hard work and good luck to make a small income from the venture, but Christabel felt some of her old optimism returning. Besides, she needed a task to occupy her energies so she would not brood about Mr Jonathan Frost any more than she could help.

She heard Colly pull open the door, followed by the sound of a man's footsteps approaching.

'Just a moment!' she called. 'I'm almost finished this one, then you can have the lot.'

'I'm afraid I am not in the market for a hobbyhorse,' a familiar voice answered.

'Pardon me!' Christabel rose abruptly, dropping the poor beast she had been working on. 'I thought you were someone else.' Why hadn't Colly warned her it was Mr Frost?

As if he read her thoughts, Frost said, 'I sent him out to pet the horses and eat ginger biscuits with Samuel. Who were you expecting, pray?'

She explained briefly about her business venture and the order she meant to dispatch to Manchester that day.

Frost nodded his approval. 'Most enterprising of you. Aunt Fanny is quite devoted to the one you gave her from Christmas. Sleeps with it every night. Seems to remember it from one day to the next. She remembered you, too…for a little while at least.'

That thought brought a pang to Christabel's heart. 'She may forget me, but I will not soon forget her, I promise you.'

She picked up the hobbyhorse from the floor, then resumed her seat and began sewing again. Mr Frost or no Mr Frost, she had an order she'd promised to fill. 'May I ask why you've come? I thought we'd said everything there was to say before we parted on New Year's Day.'

'So did I.' Frost strode towards the hearth, then stooped to chafe his hands before the fire. 'But afterwards I began to wonder if, for all our talking, we truly understood one another. That is one of the reasons I have come. The other is…this.' He pulled a letter out of his pocket and handed it to her.

Abandoning any pretence of work, Christabel propped the hobbyhorse up beside her chair, then took the letter. 'What is this? And where did you get it?'

'It is from a solicitor employed by your late father. I met him in London. He was very pleased to hear of your where-abouts. He has been trying to find you ever since your father's death.'

'What were you doing in London at this time of year?' She opened the letter and began to read it. 'Oh, my!' she said at last. 'Oh, my word! Can this be true?'

'I assure you it is. It appears Major Wilton was right about your father after all. Not long before his death, he made a provision in his will for you and the boy, but you could not be found.'

'Do you see what this means?' Christabel fanned her face with the paper. Suddenly she felt as if her fever had returned. 'My father forgave me. He did not die angry and disappointed with me.' Almost as much as the prospect of a comfortable life for her and Colly, that knowledge elated her.

'I was tolerably certain that would be the case,' said Frost, 'which was why I sought out your father's solicitor, with the help of my own.'

She was almost too overcome to speak, but she did manage to murmur, 'How can I ever thank you?'

'By listening.' He sank to his haunches before her and reached for her hand. 'Truly listening, I mean. Not hearing what you think I must be saying. For my part, I will make myself more plain, as I should have from the beginning.'

For a man who meant to make himself plain, he was certainly talking in riddles. But if he had something to tell her, she owed it to him to listen…not that it would change anything between them. No doubt she was a fool to hope that might be the reason he'd come.

'Mrs Wilton…Christabel…my dear Christabel, for six years I have striven to put you out of my heart and carry on with my life. If it had not been for Aunt Fanny's situation, good sense might even have persuaded me to woo and wed some other lady. Or perhaps I was only using my aunt as an excuse to keep from doing something I secretly could not bear to.'

Christabel could hardly bear to listen. Jonathan Frost had *loved* her? Under different circumstances that knowledge might have brought her the greatest joy. But how could she rejoice at the thought of having broken his heart? She'd bitterly repented her treatment of him when she had believed herself guilty of nothing worse than injuring his pride.

Her feelings for him, so fresh and tender, and her heartache in believing them unreturned, gave her a harsh taste of what he must have suffered. How could she begin to forgive herself?

Frost looked a trifle daunted by the anguish he must have seen on her face, but he did not falter. 'When Fate thrust you back into my life again, I tried to keep my distance and thwart any return of those old feelings. But you rekindled them a hundred times warmer. You were a merry, kind-hearted girl when we were first acquainted, but the years and perhaps your misfortunes have refined those qualities.'

Was this how sinners felt in the face of compassionate eternal judgement? Christabel wondered. Feeling the pain of every offence and the crushing certainty that they were not worthy of forgiveness? Yet it waited, ready to wrap them in its cleansing embrace of rebirth if only they could find the faith to accept.

'I am *not* sorry I made love to you on New Year's Eve,' Frost continued with gentle defiance. 'Only that I did not first tell you of my feelings and ask once again for the honour of your hand. Then you would have had no cause to suppose I'd been compelled to propose by some other consideration.'

This provoked Christabel to master her voice. 'No! You have nothing to reproach yourself for! *I* should have confessed *my* feelings so you would not suppose I had tried to entrap you to secure a comfortable home for myself and my son.'

'Your feelings? And what are those, pray? When you refused my proposal, I thought you meant you could not countenance a marriage in which you did not love. Then Aunt Fanny said something that made me hope I might have been mistaken. And that is the other reason I went to London.'

He placed a second folded paper upon her lap. 'Now that your father's will has secured the future for you and your son, you will have no need to wed again. Unless…'

With trembling fingers, Christabel unfolded the paper. It was a special licence that would grant them leave to marry immediately rather than waiting the accustomed three weeks for banns to be read in the parish church.

There it was, represented by a single piece of paper—the kind of love that bore all things, believed all things, hoped all things, endured all things. The kind of love that was the most rare and precious gift in the world.

'Unless,' said Christabel, fighting back tears, 'I loved a man with all my heart and wanted nothing more in the world than to make a home with him.'

There was a suspicious moisture in Frost's eyes when he shrugged and chuckled. 'Yes, I suppose that would be adequate reason. Do you know of such a fortunate fellow?'

Christabel flung her arms about his neck. 'If you do not know the answer to that, Jonathan Frost, then you have taken leave of all your good sense! Will you do me the honour of accepting my hand in marriage?'

Frost cradled her face in his hands and gazed deep into her eyes. 'Here is my answer.' He pressed his lips to hers in a kiss of tender passion that set Christabel all a-tingle and eager for their wedding night.

When at last he drew back, he had one final word to add. 'I know Aunt Fanny will never get better. If you would rather wait…'

'Not another moment!' Christabel sprang from her chair and hoisted her bridegroom to his feet. 'I am certain if we stop in at Gosslyn vicarage on the way back to Candlewood, Reverend Jessup will be pleased to marry us. And his sister more than pleased to stand as a witness. I am eager to help you make a happy home for your aunt and my son…and the children I hope we will have together!'

Frost's handsome face broke into a smile of such glowing, transparent joy it quite took Christabel's breath away.

'On the twelfth day of Christmas,' he whispered, 'my true love gave to me a gift beyond compare.'

And from that moment on, not a day went by that did not bring some small gift of happiness to the Frost family. And it was said by all who knew them that every day in their home was as happy as Christmas.

* * * * *

A TWELFTH NIGHT TALE

Diane Gaston

Author Note

Christmas gives us a special time to celebrate family. Because my father was in the army and we moved frequently, in my childhood a family Christmas meant only my parents, sisters and the aunt who lived with us (the aunt in my dedication). Wherever we were, we filled our house with Christmas ornaments and figurines that now adorn my own home during the season. My father always purchased a real tree, a Scots pine, and we cut holly and other evergreens to place on the mantel, for the centrepiece of our dining-room table and around our Nativity scene.

When I wrote this Christmas story, I could so easily imagine Regency families gathering evergreen as we did, fashioning the branches into decorations, placing them on mantels, on windowsills and in vases, hanging mistletoe in doorways. I could imagine those Regency houses filled with the scent of evergreen, like the houses of my childhood. My parents and aunt live only in my memories now, but at Christmastime, the scent of evergreen brings them back to me, every time.

Happy Christmas!

This story is dedicated to the memory of my Aunt Loraine and the snowy Christmas Eve shopping trip that remains a treasured Christmas memory.

Chapter One

Yorkshire, December 1814

'I am sorry, miss. Rooms are not to be had.' The innkeeper wiped the sweat from his fleshy face with his apron. 'Other folk coom before thee.'

No room at the inn, Elizabeth Arrington thought. *Two days before Christmas. Too ironic.*

The innkeeper reached for the door to return to the taproom, but she stopped him. 'Mr Vail, you can see my companion is with child. She is exhausted as well.'

Elizabeth watched the man's expression soften as he gazed at the young woman beside her. Anna Reade was a mere girl, really, only sixteen years old and not accustomed to travelling in public coaches, stopping at strange inns, or listening to Yorkshire accents. Who could not be sympathetic to her? Anna looked like an angel with her alabaster skin, blonde wispy curls escaping her bonnet and large, forlorn blue eyes.

The innkeeper compressed his lips and shook his head.

'There's naught to be done. Thou may sit in the taproom, if there be seats.'

He opened the door, and the sound of raucous voices boomed out on a blast of hot air filled with the bitter scent of fermented hops, mutton stew, and unwashed people. The room was packed with Yorkshire workers and travellers all waiting for the roads to dry, filling themselves full of food and drink in the meantime. The roads were muddy and treacherous from the rain that had poured down for two days. In the coach that had barely managed to deliver Elizabeth and Anna to this place, the weather and the roads had been favoured topics. When their fellow travellers began telling tales of ships imperilled by gales, Elizabeth had wanted to cover Anna's ears.

Elizabeth and Anna had been travelling on the public coaches for three days, making their way from Kent on the Great North Road to Elizabeth's parents in Northumberland, the only place Elizabeth could think to go. They'd passed through York and Ripon, places where they might have found a room in which to wait out the weather, but Elizabeth had been all too conscious of the dwindling number of coins in her purse. In fact, she could ill afford to pay Mr Vail had he lodgings to give them.

Anna's eyes were wide with fright as she peered into the crowded, noisy room.

Elizabeth seized the innkeeper's arm before he disappeared through the doorway. 'A horse, then, Mr Vail. Do you have a horse for us? To reach Bolting House. I…I was once acquainted with the earl, and perhaps he would take pity on us. You could store our trunks in your stable.'

A horse might make a journey a coach could not, and Bolting House could not be more than three miles distant. The rain had slowed to a drizzle and there was still light enough to find the way there, if she could recall it. Mr Vail might not remember her from when her father had so briefly been Boltington's vicar, but the earl certainly would.

The earl had always been kind to her family the year they lived here, inviting them to dinner, including them in the parties, the Christmas festivities. Elizabeth blinked rapidly and straightened her spine. The important thing was, the earl was certain to take pity on her and Anna, and she could only hope the weather had kept his house free of other guests.

'I own a horse, if thee 'as coin to pay,' the innkeeper said.

Sucking in a breath, Elizabeth pulled out her purse and gave him the money.

He leaned into the taproom and shouted, 'Galfrid! Get thee here!'

A few minutes later Galfrid had an old nag saddled and they were on their way. Elizabeth led the horse, and Anna rode on its back.

'Are you all right, Miss Arrington?' Anna asked as they made their way on the road to Bolting House. 'I feel so guilty to be riding while you walk in the mud.'

'It is not so bad.' Elizabeth forced herself to sound cheerful. 'In fact, it feels good to be walking after being cooped up in those coaches. Besides, it is not far now.'

She lied, of course, but Anna did not need to know her half-boots were soaked through and the hem of her skirt was heavy with mud. The temperature had dropped, and the drizzle cut through her cloak like icy needles.

'Will the earl let us stay, do you think?' Anna asked, sounding like an anxious child.

It was no wonder, after all they'd been through, that Anna should worry about being made welcome. They'd been turned out of places Anna ought to have been met with open arms.

But Anna had secretly fallen in love with Jessop Nodham, the son of her father's arch-enemy, and, worse than that, she had pledged her love with her body before there could be any chance of marriage to the young man. While he sailed for the Mediterranean, Anna hid the consequences of that reckless night with the help of her equally foolish lady's maid. Anna was now seven months along.

Elizabeth did not know which made her feel guiltier: that she, as Anna's governess, had not discovered and prevented the clandestine meetings, or that she'd not noticed her charge's thickening waistline. Either justified her being summarily discharged when Baron and Baroness Reade had returned from their latest country-house party.

But the Reades had also banished their daughter, something Elizabeth could not forgive.

'Let Nodham's parents take you in,' they'd shouted at Anna. 'We won't have a Nodham bastard in this house.'

Elizabeth felt it her duty to accompany Anna to the neighbouring estate of the Baronet Nodham, but he and his wife would not even receive them. They sent a message through their footman that Anna's presence was an 'extreme cruelty.'

So nothing was left but for Elizabeth to take Anna to the only haven she knew. Her own parents, though her father could barely support her mother in the poor parish he'd accepted after leaving Boltington.

Elizabeth could hardly bear it. It was as if the wounds of her own past, such a mirror of Anna's situation, had been torn open to bleed all over again.

The horse halted, its hooves stuck in the mud. Elizabeth gritted her teeth and pulled on the reins.

Chances are *he* would not be at Bolting House, she thought. He would still be soldiering, perhaps, though the monster Napoleon had been exiled to Elba months ago and the war ended. She pulled on the reins again, and the nag lifted one hoof, then another, and they began moving.

The Earl of Bolting poured the last drop of brandy into his glass, its liquid glimmering from the glow of the library's fireplace. He held the bottle up to the light, but it was, indeed, empty. Placing it next to the other two he'd emptied, he rejoiced in this one advantage of inheriting his uncle's title: a full wine cellar. He pondered if he could make it all the way to the racks of brandy bottles without tumbling down the stone stairs and breaking his neck.

Probably not. He ought to content himself with this numbing haze rather than alcoholic oblivion.

This was not the place he fancied being at Christmas time, this of all houses, and at his least favourite time of year. He'd wanted to remain in town, but circumstances had driven him away from London's distractions.

When he'd arrived in London in the spring, he had barely finished mourning his father's death, or his brother's, or his uncle's. Two taken by a freak accident, one by illness, Captain Zachary Weston had been the only one left to inherit the title of Earl of Bolting. Fate had certainly made a cruel mistake.

Those three men had been worthy of the title, not he. He was a soldier, for God's sake. He was the one who ought to have died. In Spain, enough men had been struck down around him. Why not he?

Lady Wansford, however, had not cared which man carried the title. He'd come to London during the Season, and she and others like her saw him as a prime prospect for marrying their daughters. Lady Wansford's pursuit had been relentless. He could not attend any social event without her daughter being pushed at him. As soon as summer came, he fled to the country, touring his properties and trying to learn how a knave of a soldier could act like an earl.

Business brought him back to London in October, and, like a lioness stalking prey, Lady Wansford had been lying in wait for him. She contrived to plant her daughter in his bed. When Lady Wansford threatened to accuse him of compromising the girl, the equally conniving offspring of her devious mother, Zach had laughed at her.

But he'd also deemed it prudent to place himself out of her reach. That was how he'd found himself at Bolting House at the time of year he least wished to be in residence.

At least he'd given most of the servants a holiday, settling their Christmas gifts before Boxing Day so they might have the funds and incentive to go away. No one would decorate the house. No one would produce gifts. No one would sing.

He'd manage to pass Twelfth Night without once remembering.

Zach downed the contents of his glass and stared at it.

Perhaps a trip to the wine cellar was in order after all. Besides, if he fell and broke his neck, the wretched memories would cease.

He pushed on the arms of the chair to get to his feet, and stood a moment to be sure he had his balance before he picked up a candle to light the dark cellar stairway. The bones in his legs felt like rubber as he weaved his way to the hall, its classical statues staring at him like disapproving ghosts.

And why would they not disapprove? Zach was a debaucher, after all. When he'd been a youth he'd had grand ideas of honour and courage and chivalry, but that was before that fateful Twelfth Night.

A knock sounded at the door, so feeble that at first Zach thought he'd imagined it. It seemed to increase in volume and urgency, and he looked for Kirby to appear. Then he remembered the butler was eating dinner with Cook and the one maid left in the house. Kirby would never hear the pounding.

'Ought to have kept one footman here,' he said aloud to the statues. The heels of his boots clicked on the marble floor as he crossed the hall. He'd answer the door himself and tell whomever the devil it was to go away.

He pulled open the heavy oak door, then almost dropped his candle.

Two females stood before him, both shrouded in hooded cloaks, like spectres in the dim twilight. He rubbed his eyes, trying to determine if they were real, when a gust of wind blew open the cloak of the smaller female standing in front.

The smaller female who was obviously with child.

The wind howled and the brandy he'd consumed rebelled in his stomach. He felt his vision grow black.

'No,' Zach growled. 'Go away.'

He slammed the door.

He glanced at the statues. Had he not enough ghosts to haunt him?

'Wait!' Anna cried. 'Oh, please wait!' She turned around and flung herself into Elizabeth's arms. 'What will we do?'

Elizabeth could not utter a sound.

He had answered the door. She knew him in an instant, even from the light of a single candle. Dark, curling hair, steel-grey eyes, a worry line between two thick brows. His face was leaner—a man's face—but his lips, so perfectly bow-shaped, still drooped at the corners.

But how altered! How cruel. To close the door in their faces, ignoring their desperate need. Did he hate her? She'd never expected him to hate her.

Anna trembled in her arms, her low wail muffled against Elizabeth's breast.

'Come on,' Elizabeth said at last. 'Let us take the horse to the stable and rest ourselves. One of the stable workers will help us.'

She kept her arm around Anna as they walked back to where the horse was nibbling at grass. She'd not expected Bolting House to be so dark, so deserted. Where was everyone? Why had Zach opened the door?

The wind picked up, sending a mournful sound through the darkening sky. It blew their cloaks and made the way to the stable a struggle. Anna held the horse while Elizabeth wrestled with the door. As soon as she had it open, the old nag hurried inside. When Elizabeth closed the door behind them, all was quiet, except for the curious neighs and nickers of the earl's horses.

'Hello?' Elizabeth called, but no one answered her. She called louder and still no one came.

'There is no one here,' cried Anna. 'No one to help us!'

Elizabeth felt the same growing panic, but they could not both become hysterical. 'It is odd, indeed, but we are warm and it is dry in here. We shall be all right.'

'What do you mean?' Anna asked in a shaky voice.

'A stableman is bound to come before long. Let us find a cosy spot to rest in the meantime. I have some bread left over. We can eat while we wait.'

She found an empty stall and gathered some of the horse blankets for them to sit on. She unwrapped the bread and handed it to Anna, who ate while Elizabeth tended to the horse. She removed the saddle and their two small portmanteaux, and brushed the poor creature before finding some oats and water. While the nag hungrily supped, she returned to the pump and washed out a tin cup she'd found nearby. After quenching her own thirst, she refilled the cup with water and brought it to Anna.

'Are you warm enough?' she asked as Anna took the cup from her hand.

Anna shivered. 'I think I'll warm up shortly.'

Elizabeth found another horse blanket and wrapped it around the girl. Anna finished her bread, and Elizabeth carefully wrapped up the remaining piece, tucking it away.

'Would not a pot of tea be lovely?' The girl sighed.

Elizabeth laughed. 'Indeed it would.'

'I am so tired,' Anna said. 'It is silly, really, because I have been riding all the time.'

Elizabeth sat down on the blankets next to her. 'The coach bounced us around so, I'm surprised we are not black and blue.'

'Perhaps we are black and blue.' Anna yawned. 'I should so love a bath and the leisure to count every bruise.'

Elizabeth put an arm around her. 'When we get to my parents' house. Not long now.'

Not in time for Christmas, Elizabeth thought to herself, and she had so wanted to be in the warm bosom of her family on that day. She knew her father would be filled with joy. Her father always was joyful on Christmas day, always full of optimism for what the future year would bring. Her mother would have spent weeks baking breads and cakes to take to the poor—those poorer than themselves, that is. The house would smell of pine, and greenery would abound in every nook of the house.

She leaned her head against the stable wall. She and Zach had gathered greenery that long-ago Christmas season, enough to decorate the vicarage and his uncle's house. She remembered Zach climbing high into a tree to pluck a clump of mistletoe, rich with white berries. She'd shouted for him to be careful. When he finally swung off the lowest branch with a dramatic flourish, he'd held the mistletoe over his head and grinned. She'd run over and kissed him.

That had been her first kiss. She remembered it as clearly as if it were an hour ago. She and Zach had become friends during his winter visit to his uncle. They'd spent much time together, walking in the countryside, exploring the old ruins, just being together. Their companionship had seemed harmless enough until she kissed him. When his lips touched hers, sensation shot through her body, making her seem more alive than she could ever have imagined. It had affected Zach, too, because he flung the mistletoe aside and grabbed her with both arms, holding her so close their bodies seemed fused together.

Elizabeth felt the memory spread through her, warming her in the cold stable. She could again feel how hard his chest had pressed against her breasts. She remembered his lips parting and their tongues dancing together. His mouth had been warm and had tasted wonderful. She remembered yearning for more.

They'd heard one of the farm workers nearby and had broken apart, but from that day on, their time together had been spent in kissing rather than seeking out ruins or gathering greens.

On Twelfth Night, when Elizabeth and her parents had been among the earl's guests, she and Zach had slipped away to a secret bedchamber he'd discovered. They'd been giddy with excitement and with a few trips too many to the wassailing bowl.

No cold weather impeded their kisses that night, no fear of someone happening upon them. No sensible judgement rescued them from the thrill of the forbidden tryst.

Elizabeth opened her eyes and looked upon Anna, who was sleeping, though her face was still pinched with worry. Elizabeth tried to calm herself as every nerve in her body jangled with the memory of making love with Zach that night.

She ought not to recall the pleasure their passion created.

She ought to remember instead how afterwards they had dressed in silence, unable to meet each other's eyes, how they sneaked back to the festivities and avoided each other the rest of the night, how the next day the enormity of what she had done hit her, making her afraid to face him. She'd gone with her parents on parish calls and stayed away the whole day. Zach left for war without her saying goodbye to him.

He'd never known of the dear little baby she'd been unable to carry to term. He'd never known that she'd lost even that part of him. In spite of her resolve, tears rolled down Elizabeth's cheeks.

She stifled her sobs, closing her eyes and trying not to think of how Zach looked as he'd slammed the door on them. She tried not to feel hungry and scared and so alone.

She did not know how long she sat there, Anna restless beside her, but the stable was now plunged in darkness.

Anna suddenly sat up. 'Something's wrong, Miss Arrington. 'I—I am wet.'

Chapter Two

Zach dreamed of French drums beating the *pas de charge* and legions of French soldiers marching in column, advancing closer and closer, the pounding of the drums louder and louder, until the soldiers' faces loomed large and white as death.

He jerked awake and found himself prone on the long marble bench in the hall, stiff and cold. His mouth tasted foul, but his candle still bravely burned, although reduced to a mere nub.

The pounding resumed. Not French drums, but someone pounding on the door. He vaguely remembered a pounding at the door earlier, but that had been another dream, a nightmare of Lady Wansford and her daughter appearing as eerie spectres.

Zach groaned. Obviously drinking his way through Christmas merely brought bad dreams, an aching head and a stomach on the edge of casting up its accounts—had he eaten anything. He shivered, chilled to the bone from sleeping in the cold hall on the bench. He'd never made it to the wine cellar, but that was probably fortunate.

Forcing his joints to bend, he picked up the candle and hobbled over to the door. As he reached for the knob, a muffled cry reached his ears. 'Come quick! Come quick!'

He swung open the door. 'Thomas?'

One of the stable workers, not the brightest candle in the box, stood there, hopping from one foot to the other.

'Most call me Tom, m'lord,' the man said. 'Begging your pardon, m'lord. I've come t'front door, for I saw the light in the window and I had hopes t'summon someone.'

Zach waved a dismissive hand. 'For what purpose, man? It must be—' But Zach had no idea of the time. All he knew was that it was dark outside.

'I was up to use the necessary, pardon my plain speaking, m'lord, when I heard it,' the man said.

'Heard what?' Zach asked.

'A witch.'

Zach almost laughed. 'A witch?'

'Or could be Peg o' the Well,' Tom added pensively. 'She might have climbed out with the rain and not be able to return, now that it is icy.'

Yorkshire legend told of a female spirit living in the well. It was a story that conveniently frightened children from playing near it.

Zach shook his head. 'What precisely are you are talking about?'

'Screams from the stable, m'lord. She's trapped in there, I think.'

'Well, did you check the stable?' Zach thought it more

likely one of the horses could be in trouble. Its whinnies might sound like a woman's screams.

Tom's eyes grew huge. 'Go in the stable where the spirit is?'

But it was his job to tend to the stable, Zach thought. He gestured for the stableman to enter the hall. 'Give me a moment, and I'll come with you. I just need my coat and a lamp.'

'If we must.' The man's voice was wary.

Zach found an oil lamp, threw on his coat, and, with Tom in reluctant tow, strode towards the stable, the bracing air sobering him greatly. The temperature had dropped low enough to turn the blades of grass to ice that crunched beneath his feet. As they neared the stable, he heard the cries: shrill, pained, and primal—and very female. Definitely not a horse.

He quickened his step, unlatched the stable door, and opened it to another, very human scream.

'Who is there?' he called.

'Come help us!' a woman responded. 'Help us, please!'

He hurried towards her voice and found two women huddled in an empty stall. One woman sat on a pile of horse blankets, holding her knees and shaking.

'What…?' Zach did not understand. How was it they were there?

'The baby is coming,' the kneeling woman said, tension in her voice. She turned towards him.

Zach nearly dropped the lamp. He rubbed his eyes with his free hand, fearing he must be seeing things again.

'Elizabeth?' he whispered.

She was real enough. 'Bring the light closer,' she commanded.

Zach turned to the stableman, cowering some distance away. 'Get some help, Tom. Rouse the household. Be quick.' The household was thin of help, however. Kirby, the butler, Mrs Daire, the cook, and Penny, the maid, were the only servants to be roused.

The other female writhed and screamed again. She looked very young, as if she'd just stepped out of the schoolroom.

Zach gaped at them both. 'Elizabeth,' he repeated. 'By God—' Of all the people to turn up here at Bolting House, at this time of year.

Elizabeth.

She did not look at him again, her attention turned back on the younger woman, who had the wild-eyed look of a foaling mare. What the devil was Elizabeth doing here, with a mere girl about to give birth? Why in the stable? She could have come to him. He would have helped her.

He felt the blood drain from his face.

It had been she at the door, standing in the shadows behind her thick-bellied companion. He had not been dreaming after all, although he felt like he was in a nightmare now.

Zach cursed himself with every expletive he knew. Damn the drink, and damn him for drinking it, glass after glass of brandy. He'd wanted to purge himself of her memory. Instead he had abandoned her—again.

His hand shook, and the light flickered against the stable wall. The girl uttered a low moan that grew into a shrill keen.

Elizabeth gave him a quick glance. 'Can you find me some clean cloth?'

'Nothing is clean enough here. Let me carry her to the house.' Zach stood.

She frowned. The girl's legs parted and the rounded shape of a baby's head started to emerge. 'There is no time.'

He glanced around and spied a bag by the corner of the stall. 'Is there anything I can use in your portmanteau?'

She responded quickly, 'A clean shift. I have a clean shift in there.'

He hung the lamp on a nearby peg and rummaged through the portmanteau, pulling out a white garment. It seemed to glow in his hands as he handed it to her.

She spread it underneath the girl, whose panic was escalating. 'Push, Anna,' Elizabeth told her. 'Don't resist. Just push.'

The girl pushed, and the baby's head emerged again, out to the ears, but then she relaxed and the baby slipped back inside.

'My God,' exclaimed Zach, kneeling next to Elizabeth.

'It is too early,' she murmured, but it seemed she spoke more to herself than to him. 'It is only seven months.'

The girl cried again, the sound hitting something deep inside him. He noticed Elizabeth clasp her arms around her own belly. The baby's head reappeared—and disappeared.

'Please let the baby be alive,' he heard Elizabeth whisper.

Please don't add a baby to my conscience, Zach added silently. A stable was a dirty and cold place for a baby to be born. If he'd not closed the door on Elizabeth, this girl would be lying on clean bedlinens. Perhaps they would even have had time to summon a midwife to help her. Instead he'd left Elizabeth to cope alone.

'Push again,' Elizabeth said, but the girl looked beyond listening.

She threw her head back and then forward again, her cry

filling the stable, unsettling the horses, who neighed and blew as if in sympathy.

The baby's head emerged again, fully this time. Elizabeth cupped her hands underneath it, but Zach could not tell if the baby was alive. The girl pushed again, and the baby, a girl, dropped into Elizabeth's hands.

'Oh,' she exclaimed, quickly wiping the baby's face and swaddling it in her shift.

The baby, all blue, suddenly produced a cry, then another; loud, strong cries for such a little creature. Its tiny arms and legs trembled with the effort and its skin turned red.

He laughed in relief.

The girl extended her arms. 'My baby!'

'A girl, Anna. You have a baby girl,' Elizabeth told her, sounding as if she were close to sobbing.

She handed the baby to Anna and glanced at Zach, her face in near anguish, but still so beautiful it hurt him to gaze upon her. Her hair was the same rich brown, dark now in the dim light, but he knew it would be fired with gold in sunlight. Her brows still had their delicate arch, and her lips, God help him, still looked as if swollen with kisses.

It was almost a relief when she turned away, and the stable door opened with a blast of cold air and more light.

'Where is she?' a female voice cried.

Zach rose. 'Mrs Daire?'

The round, robust cook, dressed only in her nightdress and shawl, bustled in, followed by Kirby, holding a lamp. Tom sidled in behind them, still looking wary. Mrs Daire went directly to the girl's side.

'Aw, look at the tiny thing!' the older woman exclaimed,

squatting down. She unwrapped the baby from Elizabeth's shift and wrapped it in a clean blanket she'd had the presence of mind to carry with her. 'Put the baby to thy breast, dear.'

Zach took Elizabeth's arm and eased her out of the way, now that Mrs Daire could take over. Elizabeth leaned on him for a brief moment, before she regained her balance and pulled away.

As soon as Mrs Daire delivered the afterbirth and cut the cord, Zach sprang into action. 'Let us get them to the house, to where it is warm.'

'Penny's fixing a room,' the cook told him as she scooped up the baby.

'Kirby, fetch the bags. Tom, clean up here. Let us go,' Zach commanded.

Zach lifted Anna into his arms, and the butler fetched their portmanteaux. With the lamp in his free hand, the butler led the way. Any unsteadiness Zach had felt initially had vanished, and he moved swiftly through the cold night air. A light snow now fell, dusting the earth in white and reminding him of another winter day when he'd led Elizabeth into a white wonderland.

They entered through the front door, the same door Zach had slammed in their faces earlier. He carried Anna right up the stairs, following Mr Kirby to the nursery wing, the wing of rooms he'd taken Elizabeth through on that fateful Twelfth Night.

He headed to where candlelight shone from out of one of the doors. Penny, the maid, gestured for them to come in.

'Oh, my goodness!' she exclaimed, seeing Mrs Daire's bundle. 'The bairn born already! Come, put the lass on the bed, m'lord.'

Zach carried Anna to the bed and gently set her down, backing way, while the maid fussed with her. The butler brought the portmanteaux.

'You can leave, m'lord,' the maid said. 'And Mr Kirby, too. 'Tis no place for men.'

Mr Kirby bowed himself out quickly. Zach backed towards the door, still taking in the girl, the baby. Elizabeth.

He caught her gaze. 'If you need anything—'

Elizabeth turned her head away, and he walked out of the room.

Chapter Three

Elizabeth listened to him close the door behind her, squeezing her eyes shut. She forced herself to ignore the pain of seeing him again and turned her attention back to Anna.

'Are you all right?' she asked, walking over to the bed and grasping the bedpost to steady herself.

'I—I think so.' Anna twisted towards the buxom woman—Mrs Daire, Zach had called her. 'May I have my baby?' Anna asked.

Elizabeth remembered Mrs Daire as the Bolting cook. So far she had given no sign of remembering Elizabeth, but then she'd been occupied with the baby.

Mrs Daire smiled at Anna. 'Let us get you into some nice bedclothes and wash the little dear off a bit. Then you can hold her.'

The maid, whom Elizabeth did not know from before, laid a nightdress on the bed. 'I'll help you, ma'am.'

Anna turned so the maid could reach her buttons. 'Oh, it is miss, not ma'am. I am Miss Anna Reade.'

Elizabeth bit her lip. Anna need not be so honest about her status, even if Elizabeth had taught her not to tell falsehoods.

Anna went on with her forthright disclosure as the maid helped her out of her dress. 'My dear Jessop had to leave for sea before we could elope. He is a lieutenant, you know, on the *Saturn*. We will be properly married when he returns, but, I assure you, we have already pledged our vows.' She cast an adoring look at her baby, being sponged off by Mrs Daire. 'I wish he could see his beautiful daughter.'

The baby cried, more rasping now than before, and so small and frail. Elizabeth walked over to Mrs Daire. 'Is the baby healthy? Will she live?'

Visions of her own baby—of Zach's baby—swam in Elizabeth's mind. She'd been so frightened of delivering Anna's baby dead as well. She still trembled inside.

Mrs Daire smiled. 'She's a tiny sprog, but fair enough. Wants her ma's milk, is all.' She gently patted the baby dry with a clean linen, and cooed, 'There, there, now, dearie, now comes the nappies.'

Anna was in nightclothes with the maid tucking the covers around her when there was a knock at the door.

'Would you answer it?' Mrs Daire asked Elizabeth.

Elizabeth hesitated, fearing it would be Zach. Then she decided that was folly. He had probably been eager to escape.

She opened the door to Mr Kirby. She also remembered him from those early days. He carried a small cradle in his arms. 'For the baby,' he told her. 'And I have made a room ready for you as well, ma'am.'

The maid called to him. 'Would you show her to it, Mr Kirby? She looks a bit haggard.'

'That's right,' Mrs Daire added, handing the baby to a delighted Anna. 'Don't you fear, ma'am, we'll take care of the lass and the bairn.'

'This way, ma'am,' Mr Kirby said.

Elizabeth thought she could not walk another step, suddenly exhausted. Everything started crashing in on her. Tending to the birth, certainly, but also the torturous ride in the coach, being turned away at the inn and seeing Zach slam the door in their faces. She forced herself to pick up her portmanteau, but the butler took it from her hands and led her to another bedchamber where a warm fire burned brightly. The bed, with fresh bed linens, awaited her. As soon as the butler left, she shed her clothing, leaving it in a heap. She pulled her nightdress from the portmanteau and slipped it over her head, then crawled under the covers.

She knew nothing until the next morning, when she was roused by the maid poking at the fire.

She sat up and the maid swung around. 'Sorry to wake you, ma'am.'

'I wish to rise anyway.' Elizabeth looked around the room. Her dress was gone, but the rest of her clothes were neatly folded. She realised she had been given one of the better bedchambers, large and sunny, with painted Chinese wallpaper, and chairs upholstered in a rose-coloured brocade that matched the window dressing.

'What is your name?' she asked the maid. 'I am Miss Elizabeth Arrington.'

The maid curtsied. 'Pleased t'serve you, miss. Miss Reade told me who you were. I am Penny.' Penny went on to name

Mrs Daire and Mr Kirby and to explain that the other servants were away over Christmas. 'Shall I help you dress?' she asked.

'Thank you, no. I can manage.' Elizabeth felt they already had overburdened this poor woman. Besides, she often tended to herself.

'I'll be on my way, then, miss. There is breakfast in the breakfast parlour. Mr Kirby will be below to direct you.'

Elizabeth knew the house well enough that she'd not require direction. She dressed in a hurry, glad she had packed another gown in her portmanteau, but instead of going below stairs, she went immediately to Anna's room. Anna greeted her happily, showing off the baby, but the energetic Penny was there as well. She assured Elizabeth she would take care of mother and child, and shooed her off to seek some breakfast. Anna insisted she go.

So Elizabeth made her way to the breakfast parlour. When she walked in, Zach was there, seated at the head of the table. He stood at sight of her, his drawn, ashen face looking as stunned as it had the previous night. The worry line between his brows had deepened since his youth, and his bloodshot grey eyes seemed stark. His hair was still black as night, however, with curls a vainer man would die for.

Elizabeth took a deep breath, inhaling the scent of food that dispelled any impulse to flee. She'd eaten very little in the past few days, having needed to conserve her pennies. Her stomach now growled in anticipation of cooked eggs, cold meats, smoked herring, bread and jam. She had to walk past Zach to reach the sideboard. He seemed taller than she remembered, and thicker, as if war had hardened him. But his hand shook, she noticed, and she recalled the strong smell of liquor on him the previous night. This was not the Zach she had known ten years earlier. This was a stranger—and not a very admirable one.

Frowning, she chose only half the amount of food her appetite begged, and still filled a plate. He remained standing until she chose a chair, not near him, but not too distant as to seem rude.

'Elizabeth—' he said as she sat.

She kept her eyes on her plate. 'Am I disturbing your breakfast, Zach?'

'You are not—' He cut himself off and began again. 'How is your companion…and the baby?'

'She is well.' Elizabeth still could not believe it, but Anna did seem very well indeed, bright-eyed and flushed with excitement, the tiny baby at her breast.

Elizabeth had been feverish for days after her baby—

'And…and you?' he asked.

She glanced up at him, just fleetingly. 'I am in good health.'

They fell into silence, and he finally sat again.

Once some food was in her, Elizabeth could think again. She owed Zach an explanation of why she had come so unwanted to the door.

She set her chin. 'There was no room for us at the nearby inn, Zach, and the taproom was no place for Anna—Miss Reade, I mean. That is why we came here. I thought your uncle might house us one night or two, until the roads became passable again. That is why we knocked on the door. I had no idea the baby would come so soon.'

He looked at her, the grey of his eyes more piercing in contrast to the red. 'I did not know it was you, Elizabeth. I was...'

She noticed his hand shake. 'Indisposed?' she finished for him.

He averted his eyes. 'Yes.'

She poured herself some tea, not certain she believed he had not recognised her at the door. 'It is some comfort that you would only send strangers out into the cold, especially one about to give birth.'

He had the grace to look ashamed. 'I was not in my senses.'

The room became very quiet except for the ringing of her cutlery against the plate. He had ceased eating and had almost twisted away from her in his seat.

'Where is your uncle?' she asked, lifting a forkful of ham to her mouth.

He shot a quick glance at her. 'My uncle is dead, Elizabeth. I have inherited.'

'You?' She dropped her fork. 'But what of your father? Your brother?'

'Gone.' A muscle in his cheek twitched. 'My brother and father died in a carriage accident. My uncle died of a fever. I was called back from Spain.' He gave a derisive laugh. 'Imagine. The soldier survived, and they all died.'

Elizabeth was shocked to feel the enormity of his grief, like black clouds blocking any chance of sun. She had been so attuned to him ten years ago that she'd known his thoughts, felt his joy, ached with the same yearning. To still be that connected to his emotions was more of a surprise than the report of his losses.

'I am sorry, Zach. I did not know. I—I am not much informed of such matters.'

She used to read the newspapers, but mostly to search the lists of the battlefield dead, relieved when his name did not appear. After Napoleon abdicated, however, she avoided newspapers, thinking he would be home again, fearing she would find his name in the columns announcing *ton* marriages.

He sipped his tea, holding the cup in both hands. 'And you, Elizabeth?' His voice fell to almost a whisper. 'I know nothing of what happened to you.'

'I am a governess,' she replied. She ought to have said she was *formerly* a governess. She would never be hired as a governess again.

'And the young lady with you?' he asked.

'She is—*was*—my charge.'

She waited for more questions. Such as, where is the baby's father? Such as, how did she allow so young a girl to be so foolish? Such as, why were you travelling when the girl was so large with child?

He asked nothing. Elizabeth sipped her tea quietly.

Zach was aware that she avoided looking at him. His stomach churned as he absently pushed the food around on his plate. She probably could not stand the sight of him after his abominable behaviour.

For years he'd told himself she was probably happily married to some good man—a vicar like her father, perhaps— with a brood of children, all with her large brown eyes and rich brown hair. He had imagined some good, decent man would forgive her loss of virtue, the virtue Zach had taken from her.

Instead she'd become a governess. A more dismal fate for a girl of her spirit and liveliness, he could not imagine. And she looked so pale and thin—he could not bear it. He had no doubt that the blame for this turn in her life rested squarely on his shoulders. She'd deserved so much more.

And, God help him, he'd turned her out into the cold, her only shelter the stable, alone but for the horses and a girl about to give birth. If Elizabeth became ill from this, he would never forgive himself. He would never forgive himself for sending her away and leaving her to cope with a birth alone.

Curse the brandy he'd consumed. Curse him for thinking it safe to drink himself into oblivion just one night. To blur the memories of that Christmas season so long ago, when life had seemed so brilliant and joyful.

Because of Elizabeth.

He cast a quick glance at her. His explanation of turning her away did not earn him absolution, but that was no surprise. His transgressions had begun long before, when he'd left Bolting House without waiting to see her again and without doing what he'd been honour-bound to do. Offer for her.

He'd taken her to that hidden little bedchamber he'd discovered and deflowered her and then departed the next day to report to the 28th Regiment, rather than wait upon her return with her father and mother. At the time he'd thought he'd see her again as soon as he could arrange leave. At the time it had seemed more prudent to report to his commanding officer, then explain a need for more leave.

When his request was finally granted, however, she and

her family were gone, her father accepting the living of a parish somewhere farther north. Zach had been unable to locate them before having to sail with the regiment for Ireland.

A year later, he'd made more inquiries and discovered that the Reverend Arrington had taken a post up in Northumberland, but again Zach's brief leave did not allow him time to travel so far north. He'd composed countless letters to her then, but crumpled them and tossed them into the fire. He had no permission from her father to write to her, and no one to send a message through. He'd convinced himself a letter from a single gentleman would cause her too much difficulty.

In the end, time just passed by and he'd accepted himself as a blackguard who had not the honour to do right by her. He threw himself into soldiering. He was perfect for it, free of obligations should he be killed, a valiant fighter with nothing to lose.

Until the missive came informing him of his new life and new responsibilities as Earl of Bolting.

'We will leave as soon as Anna and the baby are able,' she said, shaking him momentarily from his reverie.

But his mind continued to whirl, the memories and regrets spinning into one thought, one idea, one chance to make amends to her, to do what was right.

Finally.

He clasped the edge of the table with tense fingers. 'Elizabeth?'

Her warm brown eyes lifted to his face, and he fancied he saw disgust there. It must not daunt him.

He swallowed. 'You must marry me.'

Chapter Four

Elizabeth felt as if her heart had stopped beating. 'What?'

'You must marry me,' he repeated.

The air around her thinned and colours blurred. 'You cannot mean this!'

His face was starkly clear. 'I am entirely serious.'

'But…why?' she managed.

He averted his gaze. 'I am certain you know why. I ought to have offered for you before. Honour demands I do so now.'

'Honour?'

'Yes.'

She wondered if he'd gone mad.

Something had changed him. He was a shell of the man he'd once been. She swallowed, remembering how love had once lit his eyes. How desire had darkened them. How they had spent days in endless conversation, confiding secret thoughts shared with no one else. His companionship had given her the most perfect Christmas she had ever had, until she'd become greedy. Because she had also coveted his body, she had lost all of him.

'You do not answer, Elizabeth.'

She glanced up and saw him staring at her.

Once she'd accepted his love without marriage, knowing an earl's nephew without a fortune of his own must look higher for a wife than an impoverished vicar's daughter. Now he offered marriage without love, for he could not possibly say he loved her. They were strangers now.

She made herself give him a direct look. 'This is ridiculous, Zach. We have scarcely engaged in conversation, and you offer for me? And you seriously expect me to answer?'

He returned her look with his red-rimmed eyes.

She rose from her chair. 'My answer is no.'

His cheek flexed. 'No?'

She marched towards him. 'Look at you, Zach. The effects of drink are still obvious—'

'I do not drink—' he began, but she would not let him continue.

'And you shut us out last night, Zach, no matter your claim not to have recognised me. That was not the behaviour of an honourable man, not at all like the man I knew, the man I fell in lo—' She clamped her mouth shut.

She tried to walk past him, but he seized her arm. His face, just inches from hers, showed some of the sincerity she remembered. 'My behaviour was reprehensible, Elizabeth. But I can only assure you that you and Miss Reade are now welcome here, as would anyone be. I have much to make up for, Elizabeth. My offer stands. I hope you will reconsider it.'

She almost wavered, in the power if his touch, the heady sense of his nearness. He did not smell of drink this morning.

He smelled of lime soap and fine wool and a scent that thrust her back a decade when he'd held her in his arms.

Mr Kirby came into the room. 'Miss, you must come. Miss Reade needs you.' His voice and manner intensified her alarm.

Had something happened to the baby? Elizabeth rose from her seat and hurried out of the room, following Mr Kirby, who set a brisk pace.

'Is it the baby?' she asked, terrified of his answer.

'Not the baby,' he replied.

Was Anna ill? But she had not time to ask. As she approached the door, Penny rushed into the hallway to meet her. Mr Kirby fell back.

'What is it, Penny? Is it Anna?' Elizabeth grabbed her arm.

The maid's eyes were red as if she'd been crying. 'It is the newspaper, miss—'

'The newspaper?'

'I…I brought her some newspapers from his lordship's desk. She wanted something to read, and I brought her old ones, so he wouldn't mind…' She paused and Elizabeth went weak with relief. 'She read one and started crying something fierce. I couldn't calm her, miss.'

Elizabeth entered the room, the maid following her. Anna lay on the bed, her face buried in the pillows, a newspaper crumpled in her hand.

Elizabeth rushed to her. 'What is it, Anna? What has distressed you?'

The girl sat up, and Elizabeth enfolded her in a comforting hug, not unlike ones she'd given Anna since her childhood.

Anna pulled away and swiped at her tears with a fist. 'I am all right. It was the shock, but I am all right now.' She handed Elizabeth the newspaper.

She scanned the page, puzzled at what could distress Anna so. She stopped on the headline 'Ship Lost at Sea.'

She read: *'HMS* Saturn, *en route for the island of Elba, realm of the exiled Emperor Napoleon, was caught in a violent gale, accompanied by a great deal of thunder and lightning, off the coast of Gibraltar. The ship broke apart, sinking into the sea's depths.'* Elizabeth's throat constricted. *'All hands were lost. HMS* Redemption, *in the convoy, sustaining damage to her masts and breaking her windlass, sailed safely to shore.'*

The *Saturn* was Lieutenant Jessop Nodham's ship. She checked the date of the paper. The account had been written weeks ago.

'Oh, Anna!' Elizabeth cried.

She reached for the girl, ready to give comfort again, but Anna held up her hand. 'No, it is quite all right, Miss Arrington. It is not true, you see. It cannot be.'

Elizabeth looked at the paper again and back at Anna. It said *all* hands were lost.

'I know what it says,' Anna went on, 'but the newspaper is wrong. My dear Jessop is alive. I would have known instantly if he were not.' Tears formed in her eyes. 'I would have felt it in my soul.'

The baby woke and started crying. Anna climbed out of the bed and picked her up. 'There, there, dear baby,' she murmured. 'You mustn't fret. Your papa will come to see you.'

She carried the infant back to the bed. 'She is hungry,' she told Elizabeth in a matter-of-fact voice.' To Penny, she said, 'We are out of nappies.'

'I will fetch some straight away, miss.' The maid curtsied and ran off.

Anna put the baby to her breast and Elizabeth found her abrupt calm more alarming than her tears.

'You know what distresses me most,' Anna finally said.

Elizabeth moved closer. 'What is that, dear one?' she murmured in the low tone she used when Anna had needed comforting.

'It will be my baby's first Christmas tomorrow and there is nothing to show for it. No Yule log. No decorations. This room is bare.'

There was nothing of Christmas in the rest of the house either, Elizabeth had noted, so unlike when last she'd been here, when she and Zach had gathered enough evergreens, ivy and holly to fill every room.

'Yes, it is bare,' she responded.

Anna glanced down at the baby. 'It is not like at home, is it, Miss Arrington? The house was always so pretty. There were gifts to think about and music and Christmas pudding. Such diversion.'

Elizabeth thought she might weep. 'You must miss it all very much.'

Baron and Baroness Reade always hosted a house party at Christmas time, all their friends in attendance, all the people who moved from house party to house party or from London to Bath to Brighton or wherever entertainment was the liveliest. Christmas was one time of year the Reades were certain to be at home. The decorations and festivities served to entertain the guests, as did their daughter, Anna, who, like a doll on display, had shown off her singing and dancing and skill on the pianoforte. It had been Anna's favourite time of year.

With Jessop's death, Anna had lost everything. Everything but her baby. And Elizabeth. Elizabeth would not leave her.

Her mind raced to think of some comfort for Anna, something she could do to ease this terrible pain. 'We could decorate this room, if you like. We could make the decorations and fill the room with lovely smells.'

Anna brightened a bit. 'Do you think the earl would mind?'

Elizabeth had no idea. She did not know him now.

She would not let that stop her, however. 'I am certain he cannot care about the nursery wing.'

Anna shook her head. 'I only thought—he must dislike us being here. He slammed the door on us.'

Elizabeth made her voice reassuring. 'He must regret not inviting us in, Anna.' She did not wish Anna to feel any worse than she did. 'He carried you all the way to the house, did he not?'

'That is so.' Anna tilted her head thoughtfully. 'I thought he would be an old man.'

'An old man?'

Anna nodded. 'Because you knew him a long time ago.'

'I see.' Elizabeth cleared her throat. 'Well, I am certain he will have no objection to holly branches and evergreens and ivy—'

Anna's eyes kindled with interest. 'And a Yule log? And a kissing bough with mistletoe?'

Elizabeth tried to smile. 'Yes. Whatever I am able to find.'

She had no doubt she could walk directly to each bush from which she and Zach had once cut branches, and each tree, including the tree Zach had climbed to gather the mistletoe, the exact place she had kissed him for the first time.

Anna looked down at the baby again. 'I am certain my baby will like it excessively.' She sighed. 'I wish Jessop could see her.'

Elizabeth put a comforting hand on her arm.

Anna blinked. 'Well, he shall see her soon enough, when he is able to return.' She seemed to force a smile. 'I wonder if Jessop would approve if I named our baby Jessica. You know, after him.'

'Of course he would approve,' Elizabeth said, fighting tears of her own.

Anna gently ran her finger over the baby's downy head. 'Jessica. Jessica. Tomorrow will be Christmas.'

Elizabeth's brow furrowed. Anna's denial of her grief was frightening. She must do something to make things better for the girl. As she had always done.

She stood and straightened her skirt. 'Shall I go and see about gathering the greenery?'

Anna nodded, still gazing at her baby. 'Would you, please?'

She kissed Anna's cheek. 'I will, then. Penny will be back in a moment, I expect.'

Anna nodded again. Elizabeth backed out of the room, watching Anna stroke her baby's head.

Once in the hallway, she leaned against the wall, pressing her forehead against its cool surface.

'Elizabeth?'

She was startled, then turned to see Zach. How long had he been there?

'I heard,' he said, answering her silent question.

'Do—do you think she is deranged?' It was Elizabeth's biggest fear.

'No.' He extended his hand as if to touch her, but withdrew it. 'Give her time.'

She wanted to believe him, wanted to believe that Anna, who had been so brave throughout her recent ordeals, had not snapped from this devastating blow. She herself had prepared for such a blow each time she'd scanned the lists of those soldiers who fell in battle, fearing Zach's name would appear.

'Come,' he said. 'Fetch your cloak and meet me in the hall. We will gather the greenery.'

He walked her to her bedchamber door, and without another word left her. She lifted her cloak from the peg where it hung. It had dried overnight and someone—Penny, most likely—had brushed the mud off. She descended the stairs to the hall and waited for him, as he had commanded.

She idly circled the hall, looking at the statues one of Zach's predecessors had brought back from some trip to Italy. As beautiful as if they'd been carved yesterday, they stood majestically, silent witnesses of the past thousand years, witness now to her own distress.

Anna had insisted Jessop Nodham would return to marry her, but Elizabeth had never believed it. The moment Anna's parents ejected her from their home, Elizabeth had known she was solely responsible for caring for the girl. Now the baby as well.

She had nothing to offer them but her devotion, and

devotion would hardly fill their bellies. This flight to her parents was a desperate one. Elizabeth had nowhere else to take them, an unwed mother and her bastard child, but her parents could not afford to feed them all.

She lowered herself on to the marble bench and clutched her cloak around her.

Zach had offered her another choice. As Earl of Bolting he was wealthy. He could afford to support them all.

She grabbed hold of the edge of the bench and bent over in pain. Another choice: the choice to marry him, now a stranger to her. To marry him for his money. For a roof over their heads, food in their bellies, the privileges wealth could bring. The baby, born on the wrong side of the blanket, would need everything wealth could give her.

Elizabeth straightened and stared at the marble image of some god of antiquity. She knew what her decision must be.

'Elizabeth?'

She had not heard Zach approach. He was dressed in a magnificent caped greatcoat and he carried a large basket, perhaps the same basket they had used years ago for the same purpose.

She stood. 'I am ready.'

He regarded her. 'But you are not dressed warmly enough.'

She felt her cheeks grow hot, realising how threadbare her cloak must look. 'This will do, I assure you.'

He stepped closer. Perhaps because her emotions were raw, her pulse quickened. He fingered the cloth of her cloak. 'Let us go then.'

They were soon outside, walking together, the tension between them so strong it seemed as if Elizabeth could reach out and touch it. Snow crunched under their heels as they headed towards the wooded area, a destination chosen without a word of discussion, the place where they had walked so many times before.

Her heart thundered in her chest. She forced herself to speak. 'About marrying, Zach.'

He halted. 'Yes?'

'I am responsible now for Anna—Miss Reade—and the baby. Now especially since Jessop—' She could not say it. She took a breath. 'I have no way to care for them, and there is no one else.'

His eyes seemed to pierce into her as he listened.

She met his gaze. 'I agree to marry you on one condition. You must accept responsibility for Anna and the baby as well.'

He glanced away, then back at her. 'You agree to marry me if I give them a home?'

'Yes,' she said. 'A home. Everything they need. The child must be given every advantage.'

He resumed walking.

His silence made her insides churn. To convince him, she forced herself to tell him everything about Anna's secret liaison with Jessop Nodham and about their banishment from her family, about her own failure to prevent these events, about her parents' poverty.

Zach frowned as he listened and as the path brought them closer to the woods. Beneath her words he heard more. Of her fear. Her loneliness.

His fault, he thought. His fault.

Now at least he had the chance to change her future. They

could never go back to that golden time of their youth, but he could marry her and give her what she asked of him.

The advantage of his money.

He glanced at her, holding herself so stiff from the cold, her nose and cheeks pink. He wished he had the right to put an arm around her, to warm her with his body, but he had lost that right ten years before.

She looked bereft as they entered the woods, whose frosted trees made it look like a snow queen's palace. Perhaps it was due to his silence, but he must quiet his emotions before he replied to her. Give up the dream of returning to what might have been, as easily as they'd returned to this wooded place. He began cutting sprigs of holly, bright with red berries, and branches of fragrant fir and pine.

They soon came upon the poplar tree he'd climbed all those years ago. Both he and Elizabeth looked up. The mistletoe still grew there in abundance, appearing as if it had waited for their return.

'Anna asked for mistletoe,' Elizabeth said, her voice heavy.

Zach placed his bundle of greenery on the ground, and shrugged out of his topcoat and hat. 'I'll climb.'

His eye caught hers, and he knew she also remembered the last time they had stood there together. He found a foothold and climbed the tree. When he glanced down, she looked as he remembered, face tilted towards him. But this time she did not smile. She did not caution him to take care. She watched him with the same expression worn by his soldiers when they watched columns of French soldiers march towards them.

He reached the mistletoe and cut it from the branch,

tossing it to the ground. To his surprise, she caught it. When he swung himself down, she still stared at it in her hands, all dark green leaves and white berries. Legend said a gentleman must pluck a berry for each kiss he was given. He wished he could pluck even one.

He still wanted her with all the desire of his youth, all the yearnings of the lonely years without her. Her eyes were wide and her full lips parted. He took the mistletoe from her hands and placed it in the basket. Then he glanced up to where the branch above them held dozens and dozens of more white berries.

He leaned down to her, closer and closer to the lips he longed to taste again. He felt her breath on his face, saw the flecks of hazel in her brown eyes.

But he forced himself to step away. She'd not asked him to rouse the passion of their youth. She had asked something else of him.

'I agree, Elizabeth,' he breathed. 'I will take care of you all.'

Her eyes searched his face, until he thought he must turn away lest he see himself, the man who left her so many years before, reflected in her eyes.

She exhaled, her breath visible in the cold. He had been prepared to lose her, deserved to lose her again, but she spoke. 'Then I will marry you, Zach.'

He wanted to press his body against hers and kiss her senseless. Beg her to forgive him. He longed to feel her arms around his neck, her hands playing in his hair. Yearned to satisfy the hunger that had gone unabated for so long.

But he turned away and picked up the pile of evergreens. She lifted the basket, now topped with mistletoe.

'Have we enough?' he asked, his voice stiff.

'She—she asked for a Yule log, but this should be enough.' She did not look at him.

'I will find a Yule log. Tom can help me bring it to the house.'

'We can go back, then,' she said.

They retraced their steps, walking out of the woods a betrothed couple, appearing more like strangers.

Chapter Five

Elizabeth felt none of the joy a woman ought to feel moments after her betrothal. Instead, she felt awash in confused emotions, engulfed in the guilt of marrying him for his money.

On that long-ago Twelfth Night, her own wanton behaviour had absolved him of any obligation towards her. If she'd wanted to, she could have trapped him into marriage then. But she'd been ashamed of herself, unable to face him. She'd gone out with her parents so he would know she would not trap him. He would leave for soldiering, and return some day to marry a girl whose name and fortune would suit him. Not an impoverished vicar's daughter.

But now she would use his misguided sense of obligation towards her for Anna's sake. Marry him for his money. Marry this stranger who never smiled or laughed, who drank too much and left helpless women on his doorstep.

Even so, something in his presence called to that dormant part of herself, her wantonness. When he came near he roused her senses, made her desire to kiss him, a desire every bit as strong as when she'd been seventeen. When they had stood under the mistletoe, she had nearly risen on her toes, twined her arms around his neck, placed her lips on his, just as she'd done ten years earlier—but he'd stepped away, and a whoosh of icy air separated them again.

She thought age had tamed her wanton spirit, but, even now, even through her worry about Anna, her concern about the baby, even now while he strode silently beside her, her senses hummed. She was aware of the powerful muscles flexing as he walked, of the cadence of his breathing, of the heat from his body. And, God help her, even now, though she could not like the man he'd become, or herself for coveting his wealth, her nerve endings jangled in anticipation of the marital bed.

They entered the house through the servant's door. He dropped the greenery—and her—in the still room.

'I will search for a Yule log,' he said, then bowed and left.

Elizabeth hung her cloak on a peg and, with shaking hands, sorted the fir and pine branches from the ivy and holly and mistletoe. The strong fragrance of the fir and pine filled her nostrils. The scent had always reminded her of him, so it was as if his presence lingered, though in a way that gave her leave to calm herself.

She rummaged for a rag, finding several folded in a drawer. She pulled one out and patted the branches dry, filling the basket again to carry up to Anna's room.

She passed by the kitchen and spied Mrs Daire busy rolling pie crust. She poked her head in. 'Good morning, Mrs Daire.'

The woman looked up. 'Good morning, miss.' She showed

no more sign of recognising her than Mr Kirby had. She had apparently been easy to forget.

'I have gathered greenery for Miss Reade's room. There is plenty to spare if you, Penny and Mr Kirby would like to decorate your rooms.'

Mrs Daire smiled at her. 'Oh, we have been decorating since St Thomas Day. We have greenery aplenty. 'Tis his lordship who would have none above stairs. A waste of time, he said it was.'

Elizabeth frowned. On that Twelfth Night so long ago, every room of this house had been filled with the greenery she and Zach had gathered. They had made many trips to the woods.

Mrs Daire went on, 'His lordship said it was a waste of time for Christmas pudding and Christmas turkey, as well, but you need not fear, miss. You shall have a Christmas dinner with all the food you could wish.' She gave Elizabeth a conspiratorial wink.

'How very kind of you,' Elizabeth said. 'Miss Reade shall be especially pleased by your efforts.'

The buxom cook clucked. 'Ah, the poor dear. Penny told us her very bad news. Tragic lass. I have a little cake baking just for her.'

Elizabeth was touched by this sympathy. After Anna so openly shared her shocking story, the servants could well have been disapproving. 'Perhaps you would like to bring it to her yourself and see how well the baby gets on.'

'I'll do't.' The cook beamed.

Elizabeth started to leave, but turned back. 'Thank you for your help last night, Mrs Daire.'

She gave an embarrassed laugh. 'T'was nothing at all, miss.'

Elizabeth gave Mrs Daire's arm a quick squeeze before proceeding to Anna's room with her basket of evergreens.

She found Anna seated on the bed, nursing the baby again. Ribbons were scattered around her.

Anna smiled when she entered. 'Penny has found all these ribbons we can use for the decorations.' She inhaled the air. 'You bring wonderful smells. I knew you were coming before I saw you.'

Tiny Jessica lost her grip on Anna's nipple, and moved her little head back and forth in search of it. Like an expert wet nurse, Anna lifted her breast so the baby could fasten on again and suckle hungrily.

She gazed at the baby for a long moment, then seemed to notice Elizabeth again. 'It is so easy to feed the baby,' Anna said, 'but it feels so strange.'

Elizabeth's breasts ached in memory of a baby who had not lived to suckle them, but she pushed that pain away with the rest created this day. She walked over to sit on the bed, placing the basket at the foot.

Picking up a fistful of red and green ribbon, she said, 'We shall have pretty decorations.'

'Yes, we shall,' Anna agreed with forced cheer. 'And it will be pleasant to make them. Like it always has.'

Elizabeth's heart broke as she spied the sadness in Anna's eyes. Since Anna had been small, they had made Christmas decorations together, filling Anna's house, much like she and Zach once filled this one. She hoped it would cheer her.

The baby finished nursing, and Anna held her against her

shoulder, patting her back. 'Penny showed me how to do this. She said she had so many brothers and sisters, there was always a baby to care for.' When the baby gave a tiny burp, Anna lay her on the bed and rewrapped her in the blanket, then she handed her to Elizabeth. 'Would you put her in the cradle for me?'

Elizabeth hesitated, but finally took little Jessica from Anna. She'd only held her once before, when the babe was born into her waiting hands. Elizabeth had not held an infant since the awful day she had given birth. Her baby's eyes had been closed like Jessica's, but Jessica's pink mouth moved as if in memory of the breast, and her skin was flushed with colour. Elizabeth's grief poured back, but she thrust it away and said a quick prayer of thanksgiving. At least this baby lived.

'Isn't she beautiful?' Anna had crossed the room to wash at the pitcher of water on the chest of drawers in the corner. She sighed. 'She looks just like Jessop.'

Elizabeth glanced at Anna, still so determined not to show her grief. Perhaps, as Zach had said, she needed time to realise Jessop Nodham would never come back to her.

Elizabeth carefully placed the baby in the crib. 'We should work on the decorations.'

Anna sat in a chair and tied branches together with ribbon, instructing Elizabeth where to place them in the room. They fashioned garlands to hang around the windows and an artful display for the mantelpiece. A vase was filled with another pretty arrangement and placed on the table in front of the window.

The last item Anna toiled over was the kissing bough. She used red ribbon to tie small sprigs of holly and ivy to the larger clump of mistletoe. 'We must hang it above the door,' she said. When she had completed it, she dropped it on to the table and yawned.

Melancholy crept into her expression. 'I wish I had a bigger room so we could make more. We have so little of Christmas here. No gifts or singing…'

Elizabeth had planned for gifts, as meagre as they might be, for she could ill afford any extravagance, but they were packed inside her trunk, left at the inn.

She picked up the needles and leaves that had fallen near Anna's chair. 'There is more greenery. If it would give you pleasure to fix them, I'm certain I can find places in the house that need some adornment.' She would tie holly and mistletoe all the day if it cheered Anna. 'But first rest a little before the baby needs you again. I fear you are taxing yourself. I want to see to our trunks. Have them brought here.'

Anna stared vacantly. 'Our trunks. That is a good idea, Miss Arrington.'

There was a knock on the door.

Penny poked her head in. 'Are you decent? His lordship is here with the Yule log.'

'Isn't that nice,' Anna said.

Zach carried in a log, thick in circumference, but not too wide for the fireplace. He set it down in the hearth where coals glowed, and stood again, glancing quickly at Elizabeth before turning to Anna.

'I hope you are feeling well, Miss Reade,' he said.

Anna gave a polite, if somewhat sad, smile. 'I am well, sir, and I thank you for troubling yourself for this Yule log. It was kind of you.'

He responded, 'I am content if it pleases you.'

'Would you like to see the baby, my lord?' Anna crossed back to the chair, not waiting for his answer. She looked at Elizabeth. 'Would you pick up Jessica and show her to Lord Bolting?'

Elizabeth wished she would have asked Penny to do it, but she could not refuse anything Anna asked. Besides, Penny was busy adding tinder to the fire and poking at the coals to try to get the log to burn. Elizabeth walked to the cradle and lifted the baby into her arms again. She carried her over to Zach.

He politely leaned in for a closer look. 'A very pretty baby, Miss Reade,' he said, his eyes flicking up to Elizabeth's for an instant.

Anna beamed with pride. 'Yes, she is a beautiful baby. Her name is Jessica, after her father.'

Elizabeth quickly returned baby Jessica to her cradle, and glanced back at Zach, who must be pining for a way to escape.

'Do you like our decorations, Lord Bolting?' Anna asked, still acting the role of hostess.

He glanced around the room. 'Very nice indeed.'

Anna lifted the kissing bough from the table next to her. 'We have only one more. Would you hang this above the door, my lord? You are tall enough. You won't need to stand on a chair.'

He took the bough of mistletoe and holly and carried it to the door. He raised his free hand to feel above the frame. 'I thought there might be a nail here. I can feel it, but I must twist it.' He looked around for somewhere to set down the mistletoe.

Elizabeth hurried over and took it from his hand. She held it while he adjusted the nail, and gave it back to him so he could hang it by its ribbon.

He looked back to Anna. 'Will this do?'

Anna's eyes had wandered, but she quickly looked back. 'Yes. It will do.' She stared at them, both standing in the doorway. 'You are standing underneath the mistletoe.' Her gaze did not waver.

She expected them to kiss, Elizabeth realised, feeling her cheeks flush. Zach must have realised it as well, because his expression had grown stony. He leaned down, and she lifted her head. He placed his lips on hers very gently, so gently she might have imagined it, had not sensation flared through her body, like fire flaring through a dry field.

Anna continued to stare at them. 'Now you must pick a white berry, Lord Bolting.'

Zach plucked a white berry from the mistletoe and placed it in Elizabeth's hand, folding her fingers over it. His expression was dark and unfathomable.

He turned to Anna again. 'I'll take my leave, Miss Reade, but you must inform Miss Arrington or Penny if there is anything you require.'

'Thank you, sir,' Anna said, her voice toneless.

Before he walked out of the door, he paused by Elizabeth. 'Is there anything you require, Elizabeth?'

Coherent thought had left her mind for the moment. She still stood under the mistletoe and all she could think was that she was wishing she could have another berry to hold. Or a dozen.

'Nothing,' she replied.

As soon as he left, Anna said vacantly, 'He called you Elizabeth.'

Penny, too, was regarding her with curiosity.

Elizabeth cleared her throat. 'Well, we knew each other years ago.'

Anna merely nodded, seeming to lose interest.

Elizabeth put on her governess voice. 'You, young lady, need to take a nap now. Let me help you to the bed.'

Penny came over and gave Anna her arm. 'I'll help her, miss.' She spoke kindly to Anna. 'But you are a strong lass, are you not? A new mum needs none of the coddling you might expect. I recall once my mum rising t'cook the dinner two hours after my sister was born.'

Anna looked at Elizabeth. 'You worry about me too much.' When Penny settled her in bed, she added, 'Come back later and we'll make more decorations.'

'I will,' responded Elizabeth.

When she hurried out of the door, she almost ran straight into Zach, again waiting in the hallway.

'She will nap now,' she said to him.

He nodded and looked down at the carpet running the length of the hallway. He raised his eyes again. 'You've had no refreshment since breakfast.'

'No, I—'

'Let us have tea.'

She could not refuse. It paled in comparison to what he would do for her and for Anna.

'I would like that.' As soon she spoke, she realised she would like to take tea with him.

He led her down to the drawing room, leaving her for a

moment to tell Mr Kirby to order the tea. She noticed a Yule log in this fireplace as well, still smelling of outside, flames licking around it as if testing its ability to burn.

He entered the room and she spun around. 'You found a second Yule log?'

He shrugged. 'I thought you might wish it.'

If she did not feel so guilty, her heart might have melted towards him. It was a good thing. She was certain she would go up in flames if it did. 'Thank you, Zach.'

He gestured for her to sit.

She chose a single chair instead of the couch. 'Perhaps you will not object, then, if Anna makes decorations for this room and the hall?'

'Why should I object?' he asked.

She did not want to say what Mrs Daire had told her. 'There is nothing of Christmas here. I thought perhaps that was by your choice.'

He shrugged again. 'I was alone here.'

That statement only made her sad.

Mrs Daire arrived with the tea tray. 'I've brought you each a little mince pie.' The pies were small enough to eat by hand.

'How very splendid.' Elizabeth smiled.

'Thank you, Mrs Daire.' Zach's voice lacked enthusiasm.

The cook winked at Elizabeth, as if they had conspired to bring this little piece of Christmas to the earl. She bustled out.

Elizabeth reached for the tea pot to pour, remembering from years ago how Zach took his tea. He watched her silently, but must have realised she had not forgotten.

They sipped in silence, Elizabeth wondering if they would always feel discomfort in each other's presence. Perhaps they would remain cool to each other, never telling all, always holding something back, never trusting, always strangers.

She gathered her courage to make another request of him. 'I am forced to ask more of you, Zach.'

He frowned. 'You have a right to ask anything of me. We are betrothed, are we not?' This last was spoken with some sarcasm, she thought.

She took a breath. 'If the roads are passable, could our trunks be fetched from the inn?'

'You have trunks at the inn?' He sounded surprised, then he put up his hand. 'No, do not say it. Of course you have trunks. I ought to have realised you would travel with more than the portmanteaux. I will ask Tom to take the wagon.' He consumed his mince pie in three bites and stood. 'I'll send him directly.' He walked to the door, but turned back to her. 'This is your house now, Elizabeth.' His voice was low. 'It is yours to decorate or not, as you see fit.'

Before she could reply, he left.

Chapter Six

For want of something better to do, Zach accompanied Tom to the inn to pick up the trunks, post a letter and return the inn's horse. The earth had frozen enough to make the road passable; though Tom could have accomplished these tasks on his own, Zach rode alongside the wagon, needing to be out of the house, free of the temptation to plague her with his presence as he had done by collecting greenery with her. That had certainly been jumping from the frying pan into the fire.

He'd only thought she should not be alone at such a time, certainly not in a shabby cloak that offered little protection against the cold.

It had been an easy matter to accompany her, and it had provided her with the opportunity to make her bargain for marriage. He had not considered, however, how it would feel to return to those memory-filled places. Fancy it. He had almost kissed her, an act that certainly would have reinforced her poor opinion of him.

Truth to tell, he'd never felt an intense physical need for any other woman but Elizabeth. He'd had other women over the years—what soldier had not?—always the sort who knew precisely what she wanted from him, and cared nothing for him.

He needed to become a man Elizabeth could admire, before he had any right to make love to her. She needed time to get accustomed to him again. Time to forgive him, if such a thing were possible.

Still, his lips burned from her kiss under the mistletoe. Still, he ached for more.

While Tom passed the time lifting a tankard of ale at the inn, Zach visited the village shops. There was not a great deal to be found in them, but enough for a bit of Christmas. The villagers he encountered were friendly, deferential and very curious. Some of the items he, the unmarried new earl, purchased could not help but raise eyebrows, but he suspected Tom would provide answers to anyone willing to buy him another pint, and that the news would spread through the village soon enough. Zach only hoped Tom's tale of a baby born in the Bolting House stable was free of witches or Peg o' the Well.

When Zach returned to the house, the scent of pine and fir greeted him as soon as he opened the door. Elizabeth had decorated the hall and for a moment it seemed as if ten years had been erased. He could almost see himself leading her up the stairway, through the nursery wing into the tiny bed-chamber so tucked away it had been forgotten.

Damned foolish he'd been, setting up a seduction that night, all the while telling himself he just wanted a few minutes alone with her before they had to say goodbye. He'd always had such skill for deceiving himself.

He was not deceiving himself now to realise he'd been given the gift of another chance, an opportunity to make up to Elizabeth for his failings. He never aspired to be Earl of Bolting, never aspired to more than soldiering, but his new wealth and position finally meant something to him, because he could indulge Elizabeth with anything she desired.

Zach carried his packages to his bedchamber, while the stableman and Kirby brought the trunks up the back stairs.

Zach was tempted to go to find Elizabeth, but he restrained himself, instead changing out of his road-spattered clothes. It was nearly dinnertime, and he ought to dress for dinner this day, in case Elizabeth decided to eat there with him.

When it came to tying his white neckcloth, Zach regretted letting that fancy new valet of his take a few days off. Since arriving at Bolting House from London, he'd not cared much about his appearance, but this night he wanted to make himself presentable to Elizabeth.

Lastly he added his uncle's ring to his finger, a ring all the Earls of Bolting had worn. He twisted it, an idea forming in his mind. He went in search of Kirby, experiencing some excitement about Christmas he'd not felt for a decade.

An hour later, he waited for her in the drawing room, now adorned with Christmas greenery. His pacing accelerated as he waited, fearing she might not appear. What a fool he was to think she would choose his company over the young lady for whom she felt so responsible.

When the door opened and she entered, he felt exactly as

he had at age nineteen. The blood raced through his veins, quickening his heart. All the colours in the room grew richer, the flame of the Yule log grew brighter, and he could hear the wood pop and hiss as loud as if it were musket fire.

'Elizabeth,' he whispered.

She had placed her hair on top of her head and adorned it with a pretty ribbon, but tendrils escaped to caress her neck and tickle her cheeks. Her dress, the same shade of green as mistletoe leaves, was plain of ruffles or trim. It was undoubtedly her *good* dress, still creased from having been packed in the trunk, and though he thought her beautiful in it, he vowed she would have London gowns enough to fill ten trunks.

Under his stare, she hesitated uncertainly at the doorway, and Zach kicked himself for making her uncomfortable.

He crossed the room to her. 'You look lovely, Elizabeth.'

She averted her face as he approached, and he reminded himself again to become what she needed him to be. He took her hand and clasped it in his. She gazed at him, and suddenly lifted her eyes upward. The mistletoe, ripe with white fruit, hung above them.

'Mistletoe,' she said breathlessly.

He nodded, giving her time to move away, but she remained as she was, looking up at him.

'Did Miss Reade ask you to place it there?' He tried to keep his tone light.

'Yes.' Her gaze faltered. 'I fear she will ask me about it.'

'Then we must oblige her.' He took a breath, hoping his choice was the correct one in her view. He lowered his lips to hers, letting them linger.

'The aim is achieved,' he murmured, as he forced himself to pull away. He turned and walked to the table. 'Would you care for some claret before dinner?'

She nodded and he poured two glasses. He handed one to her and lifted the other, a thousand toasts of gratitude for finding her again rising to his lips. 'To Christmas,' he said instead.

'To Christmas,' she repeated.

At dinner he encouraged her to talk of her life the last ten years. She answered almost dutifully, talking so much of Anna, he had to guess what life had been like for her, isolated on a country estate, the child her primary companion. The Reades sounded like so many *ton* parents, neglecting their children and their property in the pursuit of pleasure. He might have even met them during the London Season, though so many of the people he met blurred together, the ones so frivolous he could not countenance them. He vowed they would give Anna and her baby a happier home. For Elizabeth's sake.

She asked him about his soldiering, and, like her, he answered impersonally. He told her which battles he'd fought, what places he'd seen, but he neglected to detail how it felt to run a man through with his sword, or hold a dying soldier in his arms or gaze over a battlefield littered with the dead.

At one time they had not needed to be so careful with each other, but at present he must respect the distance she chose to keep between them.

After dinner they retired to the drawing room again for tea. Outside the sky had darkened, so the only light came from the flames of candles and the fireplace, giving the room a soft, intimate air. When he could tear his gaze from Elizabeth, it invariably fell on the kissing bough, and his thoughts turned as carnal as ever.

He tried to keep up the conversation. 'Did you wish to attend the midnight services? I assume the church still has them. I would escort you, if you desire it.' He remembered stealing glances at the vicar's daughter at such a service that decade ago, and hearing nothing of the sermon.

She glanced down into her tea cup. 'Do you mind very much if we do not?'

'Not at all.' He had so rarely stepped into a church in the last ten years. One of the few times had been on another Christmas Eve in a tiny papist church in the Pyrenees where he and his men had rested. God had felt so near in that modest structure of ancient stone that Zach actually dared to pray.

He changed the subject. 'I ought to tell you that I sent instructions to my man of business in town to procure a special licence.'

It seemed as if she flinched. 'Oh.'

He hurried to add, 'If you prefer to have banns read, I will not object. Whatever you desire, Elizabeth.'

She bowed her head for a moment before looking him directly in the eye. 'Are you certain of this marriage, Zach? No one else knows of it. There would be no trouble if you chose to withdraw.'

The room seemed to grow as cold, dark and desolate as it had been the previous evening. 'Do you wish me to withdraw?'

She stared at him so long he thought he would explode from waiting for her reply. 'I do not,' she stated at last.

Her words seemed to hang in the air, unnerving him with

their reluctance. It ought to be no surprise that she would hesitate to accept him, given his behaviour towards her. Ironically, just like the young ladies of the *beau monde* and their avaricious mamas, she wanted to marry him solely for his money. At least, unlike the young ladies of the *ton*, Elizabeth's desire for his wealth was not a selfish one.

He stood and walked over to the window to gaze into the darkness before going back to the side table.

'Tell me how you would like to spend Christmas Day.' He poured her another cup of tea. 'I want it to be as you wish.'

She sat stiffly in the chair. 'I have some gifts for Anna. I suspect she will wish to open them in the morning. I can think of nothing else to make it festive for her.'

He had asked her about herself, and she had replied about Anna once again. It filled him with regret.

But if pleasing Anna Reade pleased Elizabeth, he would attempt it. 'We could give Miss Reade a little breakfast party, if you think she would like it. I suspect Mrs Daire would be pleased to cook something special.'

She stared at him. 'You would take part?'

He turned away, pretending to pour more tea for himself. 'Not if my presence is unwanted.'

'Your presence would make it seem a party to her, I think,' she said pensively.

He turned around again, hoping to see that his presence would please Elizabeth as well. He could not tell. 'I shall attend to it. Leave it to me.'

They lapsed into silence again.

Finally she said, 'I need to check on Anna.'

She rose and Zach walked her to the door. As she started

to pass through the doorway, he caught her arm and she gave him a surprised look.

'The kissing bough,' he said.

Her face flushed with colour, but she nodded. He placed his fingers on her cheek and his thumb under her chin to tilt it upward. Her lips trembled beneath his, and it felt as if sunshine illuminated every part of him. He dreaded the darkness to return, but forced himself to break the kiss before he gave her more reasons to despise him.

Her eyes were wide and dark and her gaze held him. Then she crossed the threshold and hurried away.

He stood still, waiting to quiet the tumult of sensation the brief contact with her lips created inside him. It seemed as if a tiny ray of sunlight remained, as well as a glimmer of hope.

His step was a bit lighter as he went in search of Mrs Daire and Kirby to arrange a Christmas party.

Elizabeth woke the next morning, thinking of his kiss. The memory of his warm, firm lips on hers was as vivid as if she had just dreamt of it, and, to her dismay, she ached with longing. This arousal distressed her and excited her and consumed her until she realised she had quite forgotten it was Christmas Day.

Anna would be waiting for her.

She dressed hurriedly, trying to keep her thoughts on Anna, but everything she touched—the washbowl, the linen towel, the dressing table—reminded her that this would now be her home, these items would be hers. It would be she who instructed the housekeeper, sent menus to the cook. She would have a lady's maid to tend to her every need—

She spun away, squeezing her eyes shut. It was all too much to consider. When she opened her eyes again, she was facing the bed.

She thought of sharing it with Zach. Sensation shot through her again.

Ruthlessly admonishing herself, she said aloud, 'Think of Anna.' She knelt down at her trunk and pulled out the gifts packed inside. She picked up one more gift, one hurriedly made the night before, and rushed out of the door, heading towards Anna's room.

When she entered, Anna, dressed in a morning gown, was seated in a rocking chair with the baby. 'Look what Kirby found, and Lord Bolting said I might use it.'

Elizabeth placed her packages on a side table and walked over to kiss Anna's cheek. 'The chair, do you mean? You look the picture of comfort in it.'

Anna smiled. 'Jessica likes it excessively.'

Elizabeth glanced down at the babe, who was quite asleep. 'Yes, I see that she does. Happy Christmas to you both.'

'Happy Christmas to you, too, Miss Arrington. I asked Penny to help me dress, because I thought it not at all the thing to attend a party in my bedclothes.'

Elizabeth stepped back to survey her. 'You look lovely.'

'I feel so very well,' she went on. 'I feel as if I could take one of our bracing country walks, like we used to do.'

Before she had been banished from her home, Elizabeth thought. Her brow furrowed. She worried over this cheerfulness. 'Do not tax yourself, Anna. You do need time to recover.'

Anna smiled. 'Oh, I do not mean I would really walk outside, but I do feel very well. Having Jessica has been good for me.'

Never once had Elizabeth heard Anna bemoan her condition. Not when her parents sent her away. Not even in the panic and pain of her labour. Not even in wake of the news of Jessop. Anna had never expressed regret at bringing this baby into the world.

Elizabeth turned away, pretending to fuss with her sleeve. She had never regretted the life that had grown within her, either.

A table, brought into the room for the breakfast, was already set for three persons.

'Did Penny tell you when breakfast was to be served?' Elizabeth asked, thrusting her memories aside.

'She just left the room before you came in. She said everything was ready. We wait on Lord Bolting.'

Was he still abed? Elizabeth wondered, her pulse quickening at the thought of him lying sleep-tousled amid bed linens. She shook her head to rid herself of the thought.

Anna shifted the baby in her arms. 'It will be pleasant to open gifts. I have one for you and for Lord Bolting.'

'For Lord Bolting?' Elizabeth was surprised.

Anna nodded. 'It is Christmas.'

They did not have to wait for long before Zach knocked on the door.

'Would you open the door for him?' Anna asked.

Elizabeth did not see why a simple 'enter' would not do, but she crossed the room and opened the door. He stood with packages in hand, dressed in a fine coat and pantaloons. The sight of him gave Elizabeth the same giddy feeling she'd had as a girl.

'Happy Christmas,' he said, though he did not smile.

A package almost slipped from his hand.

Elizabeth caught it. 'You have gifts?'

He shrugged. 'It is Christmas.' He sounded like Anna.

They stood looking at each other, then Elizabeth stepped back to allow him entry to the room.

'Oh, wait,' Anna cried. She gave them a dreamy look. 'The kissing bough.'

Zach stared at her. He leaned down and again Elizabeth enjoyed the sweet exhilaration of his kiss.

'Happy Christmas, Elizabeth,' he murmured.

'Happy Christmas, Zach,' she responded.

Chapter Seven

'Pluck a berry!' Anna said, still watching them.

Elizabeth thought she must be thinking of Jessop, of kissing him, when she and Zach were under the mistletoe. Elizabeth took the packages from him, and he dutifully picked a white berry from the cluster, tucking it in his pocket. Elizabeth placed his gifts on the side table with the others. His mysterious packages were large, dwarfing her own and Anna's.

Penny and Mr Kirby, both smiling, appeared with trays laden with food.

Anna carefully placed the baby in the cradle, pausing to stroke the baby's head before she walked over to the breakfast table. Zach held a chair for her and for Elizabeth, too. His hand brushed hers, and the touch still tingled as the servants served baked eggs, ham, cold meats, warm bread, cakes and muffins with gaily coloured marmalade and jam.

Elizabeth looked down at her plate while Mr Kirby poured chocolate for her and Anna, coffee for Zach. She really must exert some control over herself.

She spoke little during the meal, as did Zach, but Anna filled the air with determined chatter, requiring only brief responses from each of them. Once Elizabeth caught Zach looking at her, but he quickly averted his gaze, and she did not know what to make of it.

As soon as the dishes were removed, Anna announced it was time to open the presents. 'I shall open Jessica's first because she is the youngest. We shall proceed from youngest to oldest.'

Elizabeth glanced at Zach, who did not seem inclined to counter this plan, or be offended at Anna's presumption to make it. He walked over to the mantel and leaned his elbow against it. Elizabeth chose a chair by the window near Anna. Anna gathered the gifts marked for Jessica, one from Elizabeth, two from Zach.

Opening Elizabeth's first, Anna stroked the baby dresses, caps and booties Elizabeth had sewn in secret, never thinking the baby would arrive early enough to receive them as Christmas gifts. Next Anna opened a larger package from Zach, a baby blanket as soft as down. The smaller package contained a lovely silver baby rattle.

Anna rose from the chair and crossed the room to Zach, standing on tiptoe to kiss him on the cheek. 'Thank you, Lord Bolting. Jessica will adore them.' She went next to Elizabeth, giving her a hug. 'They are lovely.'

Anna returned to the rocking chair and picked up the gifts marked for herself. She opened Elizabeth's first, a beaded reticule Elizabeth had made from a scrap of satin long before their banishment meant there would be little money to carry in it.

'Thank you, Miss Arrington!' she said.

Next came the larger package, the gift from Zach. Anna untied the string and paper and pulled out a paisley shawl, nothing so fine as Anna's mother purchased in London, but colourful and pretty all the same. She immediately wrapped it around herself. 'You are kind, Lord Bolting.'

The baby began to cry, and Anna went to the crib to fetch her. She made a quick and, to Elizabeth's mind, rather expert change of nappies, and carried the infant to the rocking chair. Anna fussed with her dress and, shrouded by her new shawl, put the baby to her breast.

Elizabeth glanced at Zach, fearing he might be offended. He merely raised his brows at her and took a breath.

Her heart pounded. It was exactly the sort of silent communication they'd engaged in when younger, able to have what seemed like complete conversations with each other in places like the church, her father preaching from the pulpit.

Zach walked over to the table and picked up two gifts. He handed them to Elizabeth. 'You are next, I believe.'

Her fingers grazed his hand as she accepted them, placing the large box on her lap, the smaller one on top of it.

She opened the small gift, Anna's, first. It was a book. '*Petrarca*,' she read.

'It is a book of sonnets,' Anna explained. 'I bought it at the bookshop in Faversham a long time ago. Do you like it?'

Elizabeth leafed through it, seeing sonnets by Shakespeare, Spenser, even Anna Robinson and Charlotte Smith. 'I shall treasure it always.'

Anna nodded. 'Now open Lord Bolting's gift.'

With trembling fingers Elizabeth undid the strings to the large box. Gingerly she opened it and gasped.

'What is it?' Anna asked with some interest.

Elizabeth's throat constricted. 'A cloak.'

She lifted it out of the box, a beautiful red wool cloak that would undoubtedly keep her warm even on the coldest days. From its folds fell a matching muff. Elizabeth placed the box on the floor and picked up the muff, sticking her hands inside. It was lined with fur.

'It was all the village could offer,' Zach explained, his voice apologetic.

It was indeed a cloak not unlike half the women in the county might wear, but she hugged it against herself, unable to speak.

'It is so much nicer than your old one,' Anna said. 'And warmer-looking, too.'

Elizabeth swallowed, more moved by his thoughtfulness than she could put into words. He had given her something she truly needed.

'Thank you, Zach,' she managed, rubbing the muff against her cheek.

'Now it is your turn, Lord Bolting,' Anna commanded.

He looked surprised. 'There are gifts for me?'

Anna pointed to the two packages left.

Elizabeth burrowed beneath her new cloak, suddenly ashamed of her gift to Zach. It showed none of the caring his gift showed her.

He picked up Anna's gift first. That Anna had even thought to give Zach a Christmas present surprised Elizabeth, and she had no idea what it could be.

He unwrapped a tiny snuffbox, made from silver and some sort of shell.

'It is made from a cowrie shell,' Anna explained.

'Very clever,' admitted Zach. 'It is quite the nicest snuffbox I have ever owned.'

Elizabeth bit her lip. Zach did not take snuff. Or, at least, he had not a decade ago.

Anna nodded. 'I bought the box for Jessop, but I have other gifts for him when he comes.'

Zach glanced at Elizabeth, and again she had that disquieting sense of communication, that Jessop would never come.

'Now open Miss Arrington's gift,' Anna said.

He gave Elizabeth a puzzled glance before untying the ribbon she'd used in an attempt to make the gift more festive. He unwrapped the two simple handkerchiefs she had sewn by candlelight, an afterthought so he would have something to open this morning.

Rubbing the small monograms with his finger, he said, 'Thank you, Elizabeth.'

It was such a small, poor gift, she thought.

He reached into the pocket of his coat and removed his old handkerchief, replacing it with Elizabeth's, acting as kind about her poor gift as he'd been about Anna's useless one.

Elizabeth stared at him in wonder.

At that moment the sounds of singing came from the hallway. Penny, Mr Kirby and Mrs Daire appeared at the door, carrying a wassail bowl. After an off-key rendition of 'Come Love We God,' they began, 'Wassail, wassail, all over the town...' pouring cups of the warm spiced ale and handing them to Zach, Elizabeth and Anna.

Elizabeth sniffed the ginger, nutmeg and cinnamon brew

and recalled when she'd last sipped it in this house. She looked up at Zach and knew he also remembered.

It seemed to Elizabeth that Mr Kirby, Mrs Daire and Penny looked at them all with special fondness. They ended with 'Joy to the World,' encouraging everyone to sing with them. Elizabeth's throat was tight, but she sang along with Zach's mellow baritone and Anna's sweet soprano.

Afterwards, as they left Anna and the baby to nap, Zach asked, 'Would you care for a walk?'

Elizabeth nodded. She was eager to don her new cloak and feel it warm her in the brisk winter air. More than that, she wanted to walk at Zach's side.

The air was cold and snow still covered the hills. She and Zach walked as far as the ruins, remnants of an old castle where they had once spun stories of knights and fair maidens. This time they did not speak much at all, but their silences had lost the tension of the previous day.

When they returned to the house, they drank tea in the drawing room and afterwards Zach offered to tour the house with her, to show her what would soon be hers. They walked through room after room, while he explained the significance of certain valuable items and the identities of the faces in the portraits.

Anna joined them for the Christmas dinner, Penny assuring Elizabeth that it would do her no harm to descend the stairs. They feasted on roasted turkey, mince pies, cakes and other delicacies provided for them. There was even a Christmas pudding that Mrs Daire had made in secret when Zach had eschewed any celebration of the day. A cheerful Mr Kirby served the meal, and Zach asked him to thank Mrs Daire for her toils.

After the dinner, Anna returned to her bedchamber, and Elizabeth and Zach retreated to the drawing room, where Zach took his brandy and poured Elizabeth some sherry.

'You have made it a lovely Christmas day, Zach,' Elizabeth told him.

'I wanted to please you,' he said. 'That was my only concern.'

She found herself believing him. She would have scoffed at such words the night before. Now she dared to hope that they might achieve at least a small portion of the happiness that had seemed in abundance in their youth.

He stared at her again, the worry line between his eyes even more creased. Her fledgling hopes wavered.

He walked over to her chair and took both her hands in his, pulling her to rise. 'I have something else for you, Elizabeth.'

He held one of her hands as he reached into his coat pocket. He dropped the item into her palm and folded her fingers over it. She glanced into his eyes before opening her fingers.

She gasped.

She held a ring. A circle of smaller diamonds around one large one, a circle of tiny sapphires separating the two.

He took the ring and placed it on her finger. It fitted as if it had been made for her.

'It was my grandmother's, I think,' he said. 'Kirby and I went through the family pieces. I…I thought a betrothal gift was in order.'

She gazed at it on her finger. The facets of the stones

caught the light of the candles and seemed to shoot with fire themselves. 'I am not used to something so fine.'

He lifted her chin with his finger. 'Become used to it, Elizabeth. It will be my pleasure to lavish my wealth on you.'

He lowered his lips to hers in another gentle kiss, a generous kiss, one that made her ache with the memory of loving him. Her arms wrapped around his neck and Elizabeth deepened the kiss, giving in to her need for more of him.

He groaned and clasped her tighter, sliding his hands down to her waist. His lips moved to caress her cheek, her neck, the tender skin of her ear. Arousal flashed through her.

It was suddenly as if ten years had not passed. She buried her fingers in his hair and moved against him, no longer aware of anything but wanting him.

'Elizabeth,' he murmured in her ear. His hand covered one breast.

She remembered. Remembered the ecstasy of his hand against the bare flesh of her breast. Remembered his hand moving lower, touching her in that most intimate place. Remembered the delicious yearning for more of him. Remembered the glory of him and giving her all. She wanted to soar to those heights again. Needed to soar to those heights again.

'Zach, do—do you want to take me to bed?'

He broke away from her, searching her eyes. 'Is that what you desire, Elizabeth?'

She could feel the blood coursing through her veins. She ought to resist, but could conjure up no reason to. She was no longer the young girl with so much to lose.

Her gaze did not waver. 'Yes,' she said, kissing him to seal her resolve.

He scooped her into his arms and carried her out of the drawing room, up the marble staircase to his bedchamber.

Chapter Eight

Zach had vowed to be careful with her, vowed to convince her he could behave in the most honourable way. That meant waiting for their wedding day to bed her, even longer if she desired it, but it had only taken one word from her to toss such resolve into the fire.

Yes, she had said.

Like ten years before, her willingness was all he needed, but, unlike ten years before, they were not young and impetuous. They were a man and a woman wanting each other, betrothed to each other. There was no reason to delay.

He carried her to his bedchamber, the room that had once been his uncle's and his grandfather's before that, and other Earls of Bolting long ago. With Elizabeth here with him, he might begin to feel even he belonged here.

He sat her upon the bed and kissed her possessively, hungrily. She pulled his coat off his shoulders, letting it drop to the floor. While he pulled hairpins from her hair, her fingers undid the buttons of his waistcoat, which landed on top of his coat as her hair tumbled down on her shoulders.

She kicked off her shoes and pulled the braces from his shoulders. While she untied his neckcloth, he loosened the laces of her dress. A moment later his shirt and her dress joined the growing pile of clothing on the floor. He gazed upon her, savouring the sight of her breasts straining against her corset as her breathing quickened. He fumbled with the laces until she smiled and untied them herself. Dressed only in her shift and stockings, she looked vulnerable, and he was reminded of the innocent girl she had been before he'd robbed her of that innocence.

Forcing himself into some modicum of control, he cupped her face in his hands and made her look at him. 'Are you sure of this, Elizabeth?'

If she wished to withdraw, he would somehow keep his hands off her, step away from her, let her go.

She brushed her fingers through his hair. 'I am very sure, Zach,' she whispered.

As if to prove it, she removed one stocking, then the other, revealing long, creamy legs. Slowly she pulled her shift over her head, exposing all her naked beauty.

Zach's gaze drank her in, the fullness of her breasts, her narrow waist, the thatch of dark hair at the apex of her legs.

When he'd been so very young, he'd not taken more than a hungry glance at her. Now he lingered over the sight of her, realising he'd almost lost this chance for ever.

She slid over in the bed, patting the mattress next to her, inviting him to her side. He made quick work of removing the remainder of his clothes, aware of her eyes upon him, knowing she enjoyed the sight of him as much as he did of her. They'd always been like that, kindred spirits, even in this frank enjoyment of each other. It made him realise how empty his life had been without her.

Climbing on to the bed, he explored her body, rubbing his hands over her breasts, feeling the hard peak of her nipples, trailing his fingers down her flesh, flattening his palm against her abdomen.

His passion had tempered, content now to burn slowly, but with the same heat. Her back arched as his hand explored farther. She threw her head back, closed her eyes, gasping as his fingers explored the most secret parts of her.

He thought of all the nights he might have spent making love to her, had he not been such a careless youth. What had possessed him to leave her? They belonged together.

She seized his shoulders and pulled herself closer to him, her hands rubbing his back, her fingernails scraping his skin. She was like a spark to tinder, a fan to flames.

He rose above her and she parted her legs for him. Giving her a kiss that became a duel of tongues, he entered her. Slick and warm, she was more than ready for him. He told himself to savour this moment, to bank the fires again and stroke her slowly. His caution worked at first, but she met him stroke for stroke, and her fingers dug into his flesh, teasing him to abandon restraint.

He stopped thinking as a more urgent, more primitive rhythm took possession of him. He was dimly aware of hearing her pant, of hearing guttural sounds come from his throat, of seeing her eyelids flutter, of seeing his passion reflected in her face. But sensation grew, and the fire engulfed him. He moved faster and faster, whipped into white-hot need.

His release came in an explosion of pleasure. He spilled his seed inside her, claiming her totally as part of himself.

Elizabeth felt him convulse inside her a moment before her own release came in a burst of pleasure that flashed through her, suspending her in its power, leaving her with limbs like liquid and no will but to stay joined to him, skin to skin, soul to soul, never to leave him again.

He slid off her to lie at her side, his arm around her shoulder so that she was nestled against his chest. 'Elizabeth,' he murmured. 'Forgive me.'

'Forgive you?' Could it be he regretted this ecstasy? She could not fathom it.

'For leaving you,' he explained, his voice filled with emotion. 'For being drunk and shutting the door when you needed me.'

Pressing her hand against his heart, she felt the strong, steady beat. 'I did not expect you to stay with me all those years ago.' She sat up and looked directly at him. 'As for shutting the door—' she paused '—I will have to think on that some more.'

A relieved smile flashed across his face, before his brow creased again. 'I will make it up to you and Anna,' he said. 'I promise you.'

His sincerity touched her like a palpable entity. She lay her head on his chest where her hand had been. He stroked her hair, taking a lock and curling it in his fingers. 'Tell me what I must do, Elizabeth. I will do it. Tell me what you want and I will give it to you.'

She did not answer him, trying to take comfort from the rise and fall of his chest, the rhythm of his heart. There was only one thing she wanted, the one thing she could never again have.

'I must tell you something, Zach.'

She felt him freeze beneath her.

She sat up again to face him, wrapping the covers around her. 'I—I cannot have children.'

He merely peered at her, as if waiting for her to go on.

'I had an…an accident, you see. An injury. I was told it rendered me unable to bear children.'

It had not been an accident, but the birth of their child that had damaged her. The pain of that loss jabbed at her again, as it had so many times since she'd learned of Anna's pregnancy. She could at least spare him the knowledge that his son had not lived. To lose a son—any child—was so much more painful than never bearing one.

He sat up and leaned towards her, his eyes so full of concern she had to glance away. 'Did someone hurt you, Elizabeth?'

'No,' she murmured. 'Nothing like that.'

He stroked her hair again, a comfort of which she felt undeserving.

'I ought to have told you when you offered marriage. You may withdraw, if you wish,' she murmured.

He enfolded her in his arms. 'I'll not withdraw.'

She felt a sob catch in her throat as he held her, rocking her like she'd rocked Anna whenever she needed consoling. She pressed her face against the warmth of his bare chest. It had been so long since anyone had comforted her.

Could she dare hope that her future with Zach would bring them both happiness? She wanted to believe it. One thing was certain—at this moment, in his arms, she no longer felt so bleakly alone.

Chapter Nine

They made love another time that night and again the next morning, afterwards talking quietly in each other's arms, a calmer joining than the tumultuous one that had them both crying out in release.

'Do you think the servants know we spent the night together?' Elizabeth asked.

'Undoubtedly,' Zach replied. 'Do you mind very much?'

She twirled her fingers in the soft, dark hair of his chest. 'A little. It is scandalous of us.'

'Not that bad, I assure you.' He squeezed her closer. 'I doubt the news would leave this house, but it might be better to explain we are betrothed.'

She shifted on to an elbow so she could face him. 'I must tell Anna first.'

He cupped the back of her head and drew her down to him, his kiss driving all other thought away.

And so again they fanned the fires of their need, and again were engulfed in pleasure.

As soon as Elizabeth returned to her room and dressed herself for the day, she went directly to Anna and, as briefly as she could, in a manner that left out significant parts of the story, explained to Anna that she was betrothed to Lord Bolting.

Anna listened with a serious expression. 'You were meant to be together,' she said when Elizabeth had finished. 'Fate dictated it.'

Elizabeth could not disagree, though she was sensitive to the fact that Anna's love had been so recently lost.

'I am, indeed, most fortunate,' Elizabeth said.

'Let me see your ring again,' Anna asked.

Elizabeth extended her hand. The diamonds sparkled from the morning sunlight pouring into the room.

Anna stared at it. 'It is beautiful. I doubt whether even my dear Jessop will be able to give me one so fine.'

Elizabeth grew cold. She withdrew her hand. Anna gave her a look that seemed to warn her not to disagree.

Elizabeth quickly changed the subject. 'But how are you feeling this morning, Anna? I do hope yesterday did not tire you.'

'I am very well,' Anna replied. 'But Jessica and I plan to rest today. I hope you will spend your day with Lord Bolting.'

Elizabeth kissed her cheek. 'I am here if you need me, dearest.'

Elizabeth left her and went to meet Zach in the breakfast room. At her entrance, he rose and gave her a long, toe-tingling kiss.

'I have informed Kirby, Penny and Mrs Daire of our betrothal,' he told her. 'I confess, they did not seem as surprised as I expected. In any event, I have asked them not to speak of it outside the house. Not until we have the special licence.'

'Thank you, Zach.' She liked that they could remain private for a little while longer in Bolting House before the rest of the world intruded. She needed time to become used to the idea of being a countess. She needed time to get to know Zach all over again and to believe that he was indeed the same man she'd fallen in love with all those years ago.

Zach sat at the desk in the library staring at the piles of estate papers, correspondence and newspapers that littered its surface. He leaned back in the chair and put his hands behind his head. Perhaps the paperwork could wait another day. Perhaps he could go in search of Elizabeth. Perhaps she would be in her bedchamber. He would be delighted to discover if the bed in that room was as comfortable as the earl's.

He was about to rise when she came in. 'Mr Kirby said you were here.'

He rose and crossed the room to her, greeting her with a kiss that she returned with such ardour that he began thinking of dragging her upstairs to any bed. Only a need to breathe caused him to move his lips from hers.

'What are you doing?' she asked.

He nibbled at the tender skin of her ear. 'I'm trying to seduce you again,' he murmured.

She laughed softly. 'I meant, what are you doing here in the library?'

He continued. 'I told you. I am trying to seduce you.'

She playfully pushed him away. 'You know what I meant.'

He inclined his head towards the desk. 'I was staring at those piles, if you must know the truth. I was hoping they would somehow sort themselves.'

She wandered over and inspected one of the papers. 'I could help you, could I not?'

He laughed. 'You will certainly make the job more pleasant.'

He pulled up another chair, so they could sit side by side. Together they sorted papers dealing with estate matters, from the correspondence, from the old newspapers.

'Do you know I have a secretary in London to take care of matters like this?' He shook his head in disbelief. 'Why the devil did I give him time off?'

The task was indeed more pleasant, and more manageable, with Elizabeth's help. After the mantel clock ticked off another hour, Zach's legs felt stiff. He rose to stretch them, walking to the window and gazing out.

The grey morning had fulfilled its threat of snow, which now fell steadily. 'I fear we are in for quite a storm,' Zach said. 'Our absent servants will have a longer holiday than they'd thought.'

Elizabeth came over and stood behind him. '*Our* servants?' She slipped her arms around him and leaned her head against his back. 'I cannot believe I shall have servants I must manage. I shall be very content to be snowbound with the few lovely ones who are here.'

Zach smiled, grasping her hands to keep her with him. Through the snow he caught sight of a carriage in the distance, coming up the drive. 'It appears we have visitors.' He released her. Who the devil would be calling upon him?

He and Elizabeth watched the carriage come closer, until it stopped at the front entrance. A footman carrying an umbrella, his face red from the cold, jumped down from beside the coachman. He opened the door and put down the steps, and assisted one woman, then another, from the carriage. A maid followed.

'Who are they?' Elizabeth asked.

Zach curled his hand into a fist. 'I am not certain.'

He hoped against hope that his eyes were playing tricks on him again. He brushed by Elizabeth and strode out of the room, reaching the hall just as Kirby admitted the callers.

Kirby saw him and announced, 'Lady Wansford and Miss Wansford, m'lord.'

The encroaching pair who had driven him out of London with their attempts to trap him into marriage.

'Lord Bolting,' Miss Wansford cried, all simpering smiles.

Her mother lifted her chin defiantly, a triumphant look in her eye. 'My dear Bolting.'

Zach pointedly ignored their greeting, speaking instead to the footman who was about to return to the carriage. 'Tell the coachman to wait. It will not be long.' He advanced on Lady Wansford. 'Explain yourself, woman, and be quick about it.'

Miss Wansford gasped, bringing her hand to her mouth. The maid hid behind her.

Lady Wansford merely lifted her nose. 'We were on the road when the coachman said the storm was becoming very bad. I remembered your house was nearby—'

'Actually, I remembered,' piped up Miss Wansford.

Her mother smiled approvingly. 'So we must beg for your hospitality.'

Zach put his fists on his hips. 'You expect me to believe you merely happened to be passing by—'

'It is the truth, sir!' Miss Wansford blinked.

Zach shot her a daggered look. 'The devil it is.' He turned to the mother. 'What tricks up your sleeve this time, ma'am? You will never convince me that this is not some calculated move on your part.'

She clutched at her heart. 'I assure you we were merely on the road—'

He laughed derisively. 'On Boxing Day?'

She gave him a wounded look before gesturing for Kirby to help remove her cloak.

Kirby stepped forward.

'Leave it, Kirby,' Zach commanded. 'The ladies are not staying.'

'Not staying?' wailed Miss Wansford, her maid still cowering behind her.

Kirby looked shocked. 'My lord, the storm—'

Zach swung to Lady Wansford. 'There is an inn in Boltington not three miles distant. You will find shelter there.'

'An inn?' cried her daughter.

'My lord, the storm worsens.' Kirby opened the door to show him. Snow blew in.

'I do not give a whit about the storm,' Zach shot back. 'Lady Wansford, take your daughter, your footman, your carriage and your own carcass and begone. You are not welcome in this house.'

The lady glared at him, and the daughter gasped.

'Zach!'

He spun around to see Elizabeth standing in the hall, a look of horror on her face.

'Do not tell me,' she said, her voice trembling, 'that you would turn these two ladies out in the cold?'

Chapter Ten

Elizabeth stared in disbelief at this man she would marry, this man who would send two ladies, their maid and coachmen out into weather that was abominable, even worse than the night he turned her away.

He had not even the excuse of inebriation this time.

She glared at him in shock, while he stood his ground, still with fists clenched at his sides. A mere day ago she'd felt overwhelmed by his kindness. Now she was appalled at his cruelty.

'Elizabeth—' He seemed to transform himself again, with beseeching eyes, into the man she'd thought she loved.

But she no longer knew who he was. 'Is it honourable to send these ladies away?'

He dipped his head and stood as if considering her question. Finally, he turned to Mr Kirby. 'Tell the coachmen they are staying.'

'Very good, m'lord.' Mr Kirby rushed out.

Elizabeth crossed the hall, unable to look at Zach as she passed him.

She walked up to the older of the two ladies—Lady Wansford, Mr Kirby had called her. 'May I take your cloak, ma'am?'

'Elizabeth!' Zach's voice behind her came sharp and angry. 'You are not a servant here.'

The older woman eyed her. 'Who are you?'

Zach strode to Elizabeth's side and spoke as if challenging some foe to a duel. 'She is the woman I will marry.'

'Mama!' Miss Wansford cried, but her mother signalled her to be quiet.

'I am Miss Elizabeth Arrington,' she told the lady.

Zach clasped Elizabeth's arm and turned her towards him. 'I will not have you serving these ladies, Elizabeth.' His eyes flashed. 'I will not have it.'

His eyes flashed with an emotion she'd not seen in him before. Elizabeth turned her gaze to where his fingers pressed hard into her skin.

He released her.

Lady Wansford seemed to force a smile. 'We are grateful to you, Miss Arrington. You are too kind.' She snapped her fingers to the maid. 'Take our cloaks, Sally, and be quick about it.'

The maid sprang into action. By the time she had both cloaks in her arms, Mr Kirby had returned and relieved her of them. Elizabeth waited for Zach to instruct the butler to alert Penny and Mrs Daire and to ready more rooms for the guests. He merely stood there. Kirby looked to her.

'We'll need rooms prepared, Mr Kirby. And tell Mrs Daire there will be more for dinner. And some tea for our guests now, if you please.' She turned to Zach. 'Shall we take your guests to the drawing room?'

He still looked as if he were a volcano about to erupt. Without a word he spun on his heel and headed towards the drawing room, his long-legged strides impossible to match.

Elizabeth waited to more properly escort Lady Wansford and her daughter into the room.

'Do sit,' she said, when Zach did not.

He held a crystal decanter, pouring himself a glass of its liquid. The ladies settled themselves on a couch, the daughter dabbing at tears, while the mother comforted her.

Elizabeth walked over to him. 'You are being rude, Zach,' she whispered. His glass smelled of brandy.

He took a sip. 'Believe me, these ladies do not deserve more.'

Disgusted, she started to walk away, but he grasped her arm again. 'Give me an opportunity to explain.'

His expression was earnest, but there was still that dangerous glint in his eyes that made her want to draw back.

She shrugged his hand away. 'If you think there is an explanation.'

Zach watched her walk back to the settee, choosing a chair near Lady Wansford and her daughter. He took a gulp of his brandy, finishing the glass. He poured another.

The presence of these two females was a bad turn of events indeed. Just happening to be driving by? He did not believe that tale for an instant. No doubt Lady Wansford was hatching some new mischief, some new device to make him marry the vacuous chit she'd spawned. It was unbelievable the lengths this woman had gone to in pursuit of this useless goal.

He regarded Lady Wansford, now speaking so cosily to Elizabeth, accepting Elizabeth's sympathetic responses as if they were deserved, exuding sincerity as if she possessed some emotion beyond avarice.

His eyes narrowed. The damned woman could be very convincing. So elegant and fine-figured. A handsome woman still, even though well into her fourth decade. He'd been deceived by her at first. He'd missed what was obvious to him now. The calculating glint in her eye. The ruthless turn of her mouth.

But would Elizabeth see?

He took another sip.

Tea was served, and Zach was well into his third brandy when Kirby finally announced that the ladies' bedchambers were ready for them. Elizabeth rose to accompany them.

He called to her, 'Let Kirby show them, Elizabeth.'

She walked on, then halted, telling them to go without her.

He listened to their footsteps fading while Elizabeth faced him.

She stood directly under the kissing bough.

What he would give to crash his glass into the fireplace and forget everything but going to her and taking her in his arms, kissing her until the mistletoe was bare of all its berries. He yearned for the ecstasy they'd achieved the night before, the happiness that seemed to be slipping from his fingers.

She glared at him, her eyes moving to the glass in his hand.

The brandy had served to dampen his rage at Lady Wansford's invasion of his happiness, but it also earned Elizabeth's disapproval.

More of her disapproval, he meant.

'You wanted me to stay, Zach.' She spoke this like an accusation, and at first he was not certain if she meant stay with him for ever or stay with him in this room.

Damn the drink.

He walked towards her, but she turned her head away as he neared.

'Lady Wansford is a viper—' He knew this beginning was done badly, but he could think of no good way to begin. 'She wants that daughter of hers to marry someone with wealth. And I, Elizabeth, am the prey she is stalking.'

She lifted her chin. 'Surely this cannot be reason enough to banish them into the cold?'

He gave a derisive huff. 'They would have reached the inn.' It would have served them right if they'd been forced to trudge through the snow on foot. 'The mistake is allowing them to stay here. You do not know these ladies. This visit to Bolting is a trick. She has some new plan…'

Her eyes widened. 'Do you expect me to believe that a lady of quality would drive out in weather like this, in order to trap you into marrying her daughter? Why, she might merely wait for you to return to town.'

'You do not believe me?' It pained him that she did not.

She blinked, and brushed past him into the room, over to the window where the snow continued to fall unabated.

When she responded to him her voice was low. 'I have no difficulty believing young ladies would want to marry you, nor that their mothers would wish them to.' She looked over her shoulder at him. 'What I find difficult to believe is your cruelty and rudeness.'

He opened his mouth, but closed it again.

How could he explain? Seeing Lady Wansford descend from that carriage was like watching a death shroud pulled over his happiness. Lady Wansford would poison Elizabeth with her venom, this he knew. She would turn Elizabeth against him. Somehow.

In fact, her poison had begun its work. Elizabeth already saw him as a villain; Lady Wansford, his pitiful victim.

He crossed the room to her, placing his hands on her arms and turning her to face him. 'You must believe me, Elizabeth. One cannot treat them politely. They take advantage. I tell you, this lady has tried repeatedly to trap me with her daughter—'

'Yes, do tell,' came a voice from the doorway. Lady Wansford entered the room, her lip trembling. 'Do tell, Lord Bolting, how many times I have caught you with my lovely daughter.' She looked to Elizabeth. 'He is clever. I am the only one who sees him, so he tells me it is his word against mine.'

Zach watched the shock on Elizabeth's face with sickening dismay. He dropped his hands and spun around to Lady Wansford. 'You have contrived those incidents, madam, as you very well know. Just as you have contrived to intrude on my privacy at this moment.'

Lady Wansford affected a wounded expression. She walked over to the couch. 'I forgot my gloves.' She held them up.

'You contrived to leave them here,' Zach growled.

Elizabeth backed away from him.

Lady Wansford did not squander the opportunity. She directed herself to Elizabeth. 'My daughter believes herself to be betrothed to Lord Bolting, my dear,' she said in a quiet tone. 'And Bolting knows precisely why—'

Zach had to grip the back of a chair to keep from striking the woman. 'I have done nothing but attempt to avoid you and your daughter, ma'am, as *you* well know.'

His words sounded feeble in his ears, however. Was he doomed to watch this woman mutilate his second chance with Elizabeth?

He might know how to command soldiers, know when to attack the enemy or retreat to fight another day, but he did not know how to convince Elizabeth that he was no longer a man who would defile young innocents, that he only aspired to be worthy of her love.

He returned his gaze to Elizabeth. 'She will try to set you against me with her subtle implications. And you will believe her, I fear, for she will be very convincing. But you will be wrong, Elizabeth.'

There was nothing to do but hope. Until the snow melted, all he could do was hope that he would not lose this chance with Elizabeth.

He doubted he could be granted another one.

Chapter Eleven

$\sim\!\!\!\infty\!\!\!\sim$

The snow was thick on the ground for two days before the sun showed promise of melting it. Elizabeth had been kept very busy during this time. Having more people in the house demanded it, but at least it enabled her to keep from dwelling on this new shift in her life.

Zach's manner towards Lady and Miss Wansford went largely unchanged. He still spoke rudely to Lady Wansford and ignored her daughter completely. That did not stop the pretty Miss Wansford from making moon eyes at him and contriving to place herself in his path at every opportunity. Elizabeth could readily understand such besotted behaviour. She had been such a girl once, but then Zach had returned her regard.

Lady Wansford was a bigger puzzle, because she seemed perfectly amiable. She did nothing to push her daughter on Zach, and she seemed genuinely wounded by Zach's ill treatment of her. Still, Elizabeth could not like the woman. There was something indefinable about Lady Wansford, something that disquieted Elizabeth, but nothing that made Zach's actions excusable. Zach had said she was subtle. If so, her subtlety was lost on Elizabeth.

The lady's treatment of Anna was another matter, however. Although Miss Wansford spent some time visiting Anna in the nursery, her mother never did. She saw Anna when she ate dinner with them in the dining room. Lady Wansford always spoke too kindly to Anna. She was always too condescending, and, to Elizabeth's mind, too false. At such moments, Elizabeth could almost cheer on Zach's open disdain of the woman.

After the snow began to melt, Lady Wansford's coachman reported damage to the felloes of two of the wheels, necessitating more delay. Soon it was New Year's Day and still they had not left. Elizabeth watched Zach's mood become blacker and blacker as the time progressed. He'd absolutely forbidden any celebration of the New Year. Had the Dark Man appeared at the door for wassail, he would have been turned away.

The improvement of the weather had brought the return of more of the servants, and Bolting House and the estate now teemed with people, making Elizabeth feel even more alien. She missed those precious few days when Bolting seemed a warm and intimate place. She missed Zach, who now kept so distant he rarely spoke. She was never alone with him, the guests taking up her time, and there was no question of sharing his bed with so many people in the house. She began to wonder if she had dreamed that one glorious night she'd spent with him.

Miss Wansford had achieved more time alone with Zach than Elizabeth had. Several times Elizabeth had seen Zach exit a room, only to see Miss Wansford follow shortly after. Elizabeth put it down to the girl's besotted pursuit of him, but it unsettled her all the same.

This morning she hoped the carriage would finally be in repair and would carry them away, although she feared things would never be the same between her and Zach as they had been on Christmas day.

And Christmas night.

She climbed the stairs after a tedious breakfast alone with Lady Wansford. She decided to look in on Anna, whom she felt she'd neglected of late. Anna still persisted in her dogged belief in Jessop's return, often speaking of it. What he would think of the baby. What they would do together. Her unabated denial greatly worried Elizabeth.

Still, she should not entirely blame Anna for wanting to avoid her grief. Elizabeth still suffered the pain of losing her baby. The dull, persistent ache had lately become sharp and immediate whenever she looked upon baby Jessica. So much so that Elizabeth avoided holding Jessica, and she feared she avoided Anna as well. Even looking at Zach sometimes brought on the memories she'd buried so long ago along with his son.

Elizabeth ruthlessly admonished herself. She had mastered her grief before and could do so now. She needed to, so that she could love Anna's baby.

Elizabeth had reached the top of the stairs when suddenly the door to Zach's bedchamber opened. Miss Wansford ran out, wearing her nightclothes, giggling when she saw Elizabeth. The girl fled down the hallway to the set of rooms she shared with her mother.

Elizabeth clutched the banister, her heart beating wildly. Zach had not been at breakfast. She squeezed her eyes shut, trying not to think of him sharing his bed with that girl, kissing her, stroking her body.

She forced herself to walk to his door. She took several breaths before she turned the knob and opened it, not knowing what she might say when she confronted him.

The room was empty.

She nearly collapsed in relief. More childish antics on Miss Wansford's part, she thought. She hoped. She tiptoed out of the bedchamber as if she risked reawakening her fears about Miss Wansford.

She started again towards the nursery, meeting Penny coming out of Anna's room.

'How are they today, Penny?' she asked. She rather missed Penny now that other maids had returned and the girl could confine her duties to meet Anna's needs.

Penny seemed to have difficulty meeting her eyes. 'Both right as rain, miss.' She paused a moment as if she would say more, then curtsied and started to walk away.

Elizabeth went after her. 'What is it, Penny? There is something you are not telling me about Anna. I beg you, what is it?'

The maid stopped and gave Elizabeth a distressed look. She nodded her head as if in decision. 'It is not about Anna, miss. It is about that Miss Wansford.'

'What about Miss Wansford?'

The maid faltered, reached for Elizabeth's arm and withdrew her hand again. 'I—I overheard the young lady telling Miss Reade something awful—'

'What?' Elizabeth feared the girl had told Anna the same tales Zach accused her mother of telling. Poor Anna had enough to worry about.

Penny gulped. 'The young lady said—she said—she

said—she was going to have a baby like Miss Reade, and—and the bairn was his lordship's.'

Elizabeth felt her legs give out. She leaned against the wall, closing her eyes and again seeing the Wansford girl run out of Zach's room, hearing her giggles.

'Miss? Miss?' Penny wailed. 'Oh, I should never have told you!'

Elizabeth took a breath and opened her eyes again. 'I'm all right, Penny,' she lied. 'You were right to tell me.'

'It could not be true, could it, miss?' said Penny, still looking upset. 'I mean, his lordship and you…'

Elizabeth made herself give a reassuring smile. 'If it is true, it is best for me to know.' She patted the maid's arm. 'Do not worry about me, I shall be all right in a moment. Go about your work.'

Penny curtsied and walked on, turning back once to check on Elizabeth.

As soon as the maid was out of sight, Elizabeth staggered to her own bedchamber, keeping one hand on the wall to keep her balance. When she reached her room she closed the door behind her and leaned against it, the emotion ripping inside her.

A baby. Zach's baby. Was that what Lady Wansford had been implying all these days?

She wrapped her arms around herself and stumbled to a chair, certain she would be ill.

A baby.

Zach entered the house from the back, passing the still room and the kitchen, which was bustling with activity now that Mrs Daire had help with the cooking.

He bounded up the servants' stairway, finally feeling a crack in his black mood. The Wansford carriage was repaired. He'd checked it himself just a few moments ago, going over it thoroughly with his own coachman so that no new damage could be claimed. The previous damage had merely been more of Lady Wansford's machinations. He would be delighted to tell that woman that she and her daughter must leave within the hour.

He charged out of the stairwell and nearly knocked Kirby over. He grabbed the poor man in time.

'I beg your pardon, sir,' said Kirby in a stiff tone.

'My fault, Kirby,' he said.

'Very good, sir.' The butler sniffed. The man glared at Zach, looking at him as if he had just pillaged a village.

'What the devil's wrong with you, man?'

Kirby brushed off his sleeves. 'Nothing that is any of my concern, *my lord*.' The words *my lord* came out like an epithet. 'Although I thought better of you. I thought your father reared you better.' The butler walked away before Zach could ask what the devil he meant. From the stairway, Zach heard him mutter, 'Poor Miss Arrington.'

Zach froze. Undoubtedly Lady Wansford had made another move. Her final move, if he had anything to say about it. He'd end this once and for all.

He crossed the hall and checked the drawing room and library, looking for Elizabeth. He stopped one of the footmen to ask if he'd seen her.

'I believe she went upstairs after breakfast,' the man said.

Zach hurried first to Anna's room, but she had not seen her.

He knocked on Elizabeth's bedchamber door.

'Who is it?' a small voice asked from inside.

He opened the door without replying.

She was seated on a chair, bent over with her arms clasped around her. She sat up when she saw him.

He crossed the room to her, crouching on one knee to bring his face level with hers. 'What is wrong, Elizabeth? Are you ill?'

She shook her head and swiped at reddened eyes.

'You've been crying, love.' He touched her cheek, but she turned away from his touch. 'What is it?'

Lady Wansford, no doubt.

She took a shuddering breath before speaking. 'A baby. She's having a baby.'

'Who, love?' he asked.

She would not look at him. 'Miss Wansford.'

He made a contemptuous sound. 'Well, that explains much.' No wonder her mother was so anxious to marry off the chit. He wondered who the father could be. A dancing master? Some penniless curate?

Her eyes wrinkled in pain. 'Your child, Zach.'

He nearly laughed. '*My* child?'

She wrapped her arms around herself again and rocked back and forth. Surely she could not believe this.

'Elizabeth, it cannot be,' he protested. 'Listen to me—'

She shook her head. 'Do not say it, Zach. I know she shares your bed. I saw her come out of your room... And Lady Wansford implied... A baby, Zach!'

He grabbed her. 'This is nonsense, Elizabeth!'

She seemed not to hear him. 'You must marry her, Zach. For the baby. Your baby. A second chance.'

He tried to make her look at him. 'You are the only second chance I want. You must believe me.'

She trembled, and her voice came out in gasps. 'I cannot let another child—not again—not all over again—not like Anna. Not—not like me.'

He went cold. 'Like you?'

She grabbed his hands and held them tight, finally looking directly into his face, although he had the notion she still did not see him.

'I had a baby, Zach,' she rasped. 'Our baby. A son. He—he was born dead. And—and I bled. That is why I cannot have children.'

Zach felt as if he'd taken a musket ball in the chest. She'd conceived a child from that brief, furtive lovemaking? Surely she would have contacted him. Her father would have contacted him.

She choked on a sob. 'I—I never told my parents it was you. But because I was—that is why we moved away from here, away from anyone who knew me. In Northumberland we pretended I was a widow, but then the baby—died.' Her eyes turned bleak. 'I became a governess and we pretended as if our child never happened.'

He felt a wave of nausea, of despair.

She pushed his hands away. 'So you must go to her. Marry her. For the child's sake. It may be the only child you can have.'

He opened his mouth, but could sound no words.

He'd spent ten years thinking himself a bounder and a cad, and he had not even known the half of it. He'd had a son—and the woman he loved had suffered the child's loss alone. He backed away on his knees. He'd had a son. A son.

She ought to hate him.

'Leave me, Zach. Please,' she cried. 'Please.'

Somehow he rose to his feet, wanting to say something to her, but what could he say? He did not deserve her forgiveness, not for this.

A son.

'Go,' she said, tears streaming down her face. 'Go to London with them. You can be married there. I'll take Anna as soon as she's able…' Her voice trailed off and she stared into space.

Zach backed out of the room.

Elizabeth heard the carriage leave the stable. She rose and wandered to one of the rooms that faced the front drive. When she looked out the carriage was pulling away. She leaned her forehead against the cool glass of the window pane and watched as it made its way down the drive, as it disappeared out of sight. She sat in a chair, still staring out of the window.

An hour passed, maybe longer before she forced herself back to her feet. She must tell Anna that they would be leaving Bolting House, after all, and that it would not be she who married Zach. They were no worse off than before, she consoled herself. Except her dream of Zach, her illusions of him, so briefly revived and gloriously relived, had been for ever lost.

At least he'd done this honourable thing.

Anna's door was ajar, and Elizabeth peeked in. Anna was singing to the baby, waltzing around the room with the baby in her arms. She stopped, lifting the baby and kissing her on the forehead.

'Oh, Jessica!' Anna cried. 'Your father will love you so! He will return to us. You must believe me.'

Elizabeth stepped back from the doorway, as Anna continued her dance. From the shadow of the hallway Elizabeth still caught glimpses of her through the crack.

You must believe me. Zack had said those same words, but Elizabeth had dismissed them.

But Anna still believed in her Jessop. She had never stopped believing, even when he had not returned to her. Even when newspapers reported his death.

'I am a fool,' Elizabeth whispered to herself, suddenly feeling as if a veil had been removed from her eyes. Suddenly realising—believing—Zach had told her the truth.

Elizabeth managed to walk to the stairway and she clutched the banister. She'd sent him into a horror. Pushed him into Lady Wansford's trap.

She must stop him.

She would chase after him. Find him in London, if not some other stop on the Great North Road. She would tell him to come home. Tell him she believed him. He had not seduced Miss Wansford. He had not shared her bed. He had not begotten a child. Not Zach.

She ran down the stairs and into the hall. 'Mr Kirby!' she shouted. 'Mr Kirby! I need a carriage!'

The front door opened.

Zach walked in.

For a second, Elizabeth thought she was seeing an apparition. Then she rushed into his arms.

'Zach!'

He clutched her to him, holding her as if she might disappear, but she would never leave him, never again send him away.

'Forgive me,' he said, his voice rough with emotion. 'Forgive me for all the suffering I've caused you—'

'I thought you had left with them. I thought I had driven you to marry her,' Elizabeth cried.

'I never touched her, Elizabeth,' he rasped.

'I believe you.' She kissed his mouth, his cheek.

Servants appeared, curious as to the commotion. Mr Kirby shooed them back to their duties.

Zach took her face in his hands, his forehead leaning against hers. 'I never bedded her, Elizabeth. Not after you. Not even before.'

She nodded. 'I know.'

He made her look at him. 'The baby is not mine.'

'What baby?' Anna's voice came from the stairway.

They both turned to her as she walked down the stairs, carrying Jessica in her arms.

'What baby?' she asked again.

Zach answered her. 'Miss Wansford accused me of getting her with child.'

'Nonsense,' Anna scoffed. 'She's not with child.'

They both gaped at her.

Anna looked at them as if surprised they would ever believe it. 'She made it up. I thought it was for my benefit. I mean, I had a baby, so she must have one, too. She was that sort.'

'How do you know she made it up?' Elizabeth asked.

Anna rolled her eyes. 'She did not know the first thing about how it feels to carry a life inside your body. And to accuse Lord Bolting was ludicrous. Lord Bolting loves you.' She sighed dreamily. 'His whole life, he has loved you. Mrs Daire and Mr Kirby remembered you, Miss Arrington. They remembered you and Lord Bolting were sweet on each other all those years ago.'

'No baby?' was all Elizabeth could say.

Zach laughed aloud, still holding Elizabeth. The joyful sound echoed against the marble and walls of the hall. Even the statues appeared to smile. He swept Anna and Jessica into his embrace as well.

'This is family enough for me,' he said, leaning down to kiss Elizabeth once more.

Chapter Twelve

The next days dawned sunny and bright, a complement to the joy in Elizabeth's heart. She and Zach spent most of their time together, enjoying the long, brisk walks to all the places where their love had first blossomed, finally telling each other what their years of separation had been like.

Their nights were spent together as well, their lovemaking more precious and intense for almost being lost to them. Each act of love bound them closer and their shared pleasure rose to heights Elizabeth could never have imagined.

Zach was impatient for the special licence to arrive, looking for a courier each day. Elizabeth already felt married to him body and soul, but she knew their union must be sanctified and she must some day be announced to the world as his countess.

Anna still managed to hold on to her happiness as well, the baby occupying her heart and time. Elizabeth discovered that, with Zach's love, she could enjoy the baby. It no longer hurt quite as much to hold the precious infant girl. Zach doted on the baby as well, and Elizabeth knew they both thought of their own lost child. Somehow sharing their grief made it more bearable.

Soon Twelfth Night arrived with all its memories, but Zach said the day marked their second chance together, so they must celebrate.

Dinner began their Twelfth Night festivities, a party including just the three of them, Elizabeth, Zach and Anna. Mrs Daire prepared a superb meal, perfectly served by the footmen. All their spirits were high. Zach found the bean in the fruit-and-spice-packed cake, and, thus, he became King of the night, teasing them with ridiculous edicts and other regal pronouncements. Elizabeth could not remember when she had laughed so unrestrainedly.

After dinner they retired to the drawing room. Even baby Jessica and her little cradle were brought there, so that Anna could stay for the whole evening. The infant slept through most of the party, even when Anna played the pianoforte and they sang the Christmas songs for the last time of the season. The decorations would be removed on the morrow. The kissing boughs would be taken down.

But Elizabeth no longer needed the kissing boughs.

In absence of a mummers play, they took turns reading Shakespeare's *Twelfth Night*. Nearing the end, Zach recited the Duke's lines to his Viola:

Here is my hand: you shall from this time be
Your master's mistress...

He looked directly at Elizabeth.

Before he could continue, however, the door opened and

the stableman, Tom, entered, twirling his hat in his hand as he walked directly to Zach.

'Beggin' thy pardon, m'lord. I know 'tis wrong to coom in. Not my place and all—' Tom's eyes were so wide they looked as if they might pop from his head.

'What is it, Tom?' Zach stood. Elizabeth quickly joined him.

Tom gulped. 'He's coomin.'

'Who is coming?' Elizabeth asked.

'T'Dark Man.' The man trembled. 'I saw him with m'own eyes. Coomin' up the walk. Carryin' a satchel, he was.'

Zach laughed. 'It cannot be the Dark Man. It is not New Year's Day.' He put a reassuring hand on Tom's shoulder. 'Besides, having the Dark Man come brings good luck.' He caught Elizabeth's eye and winked. Having a dark man be the first person to cross a threshold in the New Year was, by legend, a good omen.

Tom shook his head. 'This one's a spirit.'

Anna giggled.

Elizabeth tried not to smile. 'How do you know this?'

The stableman gave her a direct look. 'I never saw the fellow before.'

She exchanged an amused glance with Zach.

'It may be the courier,' he said, wrapping an arm around her.

Mr Kirby appeared in the doorway, wearing a smile. Perhaps the special licence had arrived. How fitting that they might be married on the morrow, the day they almost lost each other all those years before.

'A visitor, m'lord,' announced Mr Kirby, stepping aside.

A dark-haired man walked in.

Elizabeth gasped and clutched Zach's arm.

But it was Anna who was most affected. She stared as if in disbelief, then leapt out of her chair and ran into the man's arms.

'Jessop!' she cried, dissolving into the tears Elizabeth imagined she'd held in check for days. 'Jessop. I knew you would find me.'

Jessop held her tight. 'Anna, my dear one, I have been searching for you. I've asked at every inn on the Great North Road. I did not drown, Anna. I clung to the wreckage, knowing I must return to you.'

With a look of aching tenderness, Anna stroked his face. 'Come,' she said. 'Meet our baby.'

A year later, on Twelfth Night, Mr Kirby came again to the drawing room door. 'Mr and Mrs Nodham, m'lord.'

Zach left his conversation with the Reverend and Mrs Arrington and strode over to the young couple.

He embraced Anna. 'How good to see you! Elizabeth will be so pleased you have arrived!'

She embraced him back. 'How could we not come at such a happy time.'

Zach turned to Jessop. In his arms was a child, her thumb in her mouth. Zach shook his hand. 'Welcome, Nodham. Could this big girl be our Jessica?' He touched her blonde curls, and the little girl buried her face in her father's neck. Zach chuckled.

He asked about their journey, and introduced them to Elizabeth's parents, who now lived with them.

Little Jessica started whimpering, and her father said, 'I think we had better take her to the nursery. The nanny should be up there helping to prepare things.'

'Take her to Elizabeth first,' Zach said. 'She will wish to see her.'

He led them upstairs to Elizabeth, who would be eagerly awaiting them in the bedchamber she shared with him. When they came to the door, she was seated in the same rocking chair that Anna had used the year before.

Elizabeth held a baby in her arms.

'Anna!' she exclaimed.

Anna ran over to her and hugged her. 'Oh, let me see. Let me see!' She looked down at the infant.

Elizabeth smiled. 'Meet our son.'

Zach filled with pride at this miracle that was their son. It had seemed like a miracle when Elizabeth discovered she was with child. Even the baby's birth was miraculous, a year to the day Jessica was born, a year to the day Elizabeth had come back to him.

'May I hold him?' Anna asked, and Elizabeth handed him to her. 'Have you given him a name?'

'John,' replied Elizabeth.

'What other name could Zachary and Elizabeth possibly choose?' Zach laughed. 'Besides, it was my father's and my brother's name.'

Anna smiled. 'That is nice.'

Elizabeth rose to greet Jessop and Jessica, and Zach stood back and watched them all. Just a little more than a year ago he'd been alone, his life empty. Now conceive how full it was.

Penny came to the door and more hugs and greetings took place. Anna handed the baby back to Elizabeth, and Penny took them to their rooms. The chamber was quiet again.

Zach walked to Elizabeth's side. 'Let me put him in the

cradle for you.' He took his tiny son in his arms and gently placed a kiss on his downy head. 'Coom, bairn,' he said, mimicking the Yorkshire accent.

After he placed the baby in the cradle, Elizabeth grasped his arm and lay her cheek against him. 'How lucky we are,' she whispered.

Zach put his arms around her and held her close.

Yes, he was a lucky man. Lucky she had returned to him, lucky she had given him this child.

Lucky he'd been given a second chance at happiness.

'A second chance,' he murmured to her, holding her as if she were a part of himself.

On that long-ago Christmas in the Pyrenees when he and his men had sheltered in the little Spanish church, that had been his prayer—one desperate prayer for a second chance.

'Thank God,' he said, sealing that prayer with a kiss.

* * * * *